A little learning is a dangerous thing;
Drink deep, or taste not the Pierian spring:
There shallow draughts intoxicate the brain,
And drinking largely sobers us again.

—Alexander Pope
An Essay On Criticism, 1711

SEVERAL OF THE CHAPTERS IN THIS BOOK
HAD THEIR START AS ARTICLES PUBLISHED IN:

The New York Times
The Forum for Honors
The MHC Quarterly
The Scarsdale Inquirer
The Litchfield County Times
The Vassar Alumni Bulletin
The Maine Scholar

ALSO BY BETTY K. LEVINE

Hex House
Hawk High
The Great Burgerland Disaster

A
DANGEROUS
THING

*A Memoir of Learning
and Teaching*

BETTY KRASNE

BOOKSURGE
AN AMAZON.COM COMPANY

TO THE READER
This is a work of nonfiction.
All characters and events depicted in this book are real.
Further information can be found in the Sources list in the back.

Copyright © 2006 by Betty Krasne
www.bettykrasne.com

All rights reserved. No part of this book may be reproduced
in any form or by any electronic or mechanical means, including
information storage and retrieval systems, without permission
in writing from the publisher, except by a reviewer who may
quote brief passages in a review.

BookSurge LLC
An Amazon.com Company
5341 Dorchester Road, Suite 16, Charleston, S.C. 29418
Visit our Web site at www.booksurge.com

ISBN: 1-4196-3930-7
LCCN: 2006905764

Designed by Gregory Wakabayashi

Printed in the United States of America

ACKNOWLEDGMENTS

I would like to thank Mercy College for granting a sabbatical leave for the research and writing of this manuscript.

I want to thank my cousins who responded to my search for information with memories, documents, facts, and photos. Without their help, this would have been a much less interesting project.

Special thanks go to my immediate family, who devoted much time and great care to editing and proofreading the manuscript at various stages. Without their assistance, the work would be much less readable.

CONTENTS

"The Language of Ghosts"   *viii*

Introduction   *x*

Part I GETTING THERE

Chapter One : The Language of Taste   2
"Someone Comes to Dust"   15

Chapter Two : In Search of Bugopol   16
"Vignettes of a Father"   33

Chapter Three : Return to Russia   35

Chapter Four : Raphael's Way   50

Chapter Five : Philadelphia vs. New York   74
"Widow Mother"   88

Part II LEARNING ABOUT LEARNING

Chapter Six : The Education of a Dilettante   93

Chapter Seven : The Workingman's School?   111

Chapter Eight : Ethics in The Bronx   125

Chapter Nine : Sent Up the River   143

Chapter Ten : Conformity or Diversity?   155

Chapter Eleven : Nota Bene   165
"Traveling Light"   174

Chapter Twelve : Treading Water   175
    "Equinox"   190

Chapter Thirteen : Back to School   191

Part III STEALING TIME

Chapter Fourteen : *Gourmet Cookbook* Meets   207
Ideal Marriage: Its Physiology and Technique
    "The News from Fantasyland"   225

Chapter Fifteen : 1965   226
    "Missionary to the Suburbs"   242

Chapter Sixteen : The Other Side of the Desk   243
    "Wonderwoman on the Wires"   261

Chapter Seventeen : Stealing Time   263
    "The Business of Birth"   276

Chapter Eighteen : BSO   277
    "The Edges of Her Love"   287

Chapter Nineteen : What is Honors?   288
    "Their Lists"   298

Chapter Twenty : A Matter of Taste   299
    "Covering the Mirrors in the House of the Dead"   308

Sources   310

Family Trees   313

The Language of Ghosts

It took years for her to learn
the language of ghosts.
She remembered the poet who said,
"They have all gone into the world of light."
She did not speak to a world of light,
but even without the light
over the years she has struggled
to become fluent in the language of ghosts:
puzzling over the order of nouns and verbs,
the way to pose questions,
how to express complex ideas
in simple sentences.
With practice she can now put many difficult thoughts
into words:
She said, 'The glass is half full.'
She said, 'Your lilies bloomed so much
        I divided them.'
She said, 'I dialed your number,
        surprised I could recall the sequence.
        A recording told me
        "The number you have reached
        is not a working number.
        Please dial again." '

She said, 'Here is a new picture of the family.
        The balding one on the left,
        the middle one with glasses,
        the one on the right
        with an arm around a man,
        they are not the ones you knew.
She said, 'The other day there was a mirror
        at the top of the escalator.
        Rising to the top
        the person in the mirror
        took me by surprise.'
She said, 'Now I can read
        the writing on the wall.'

And it is useful,
the language of ghosts—
not for the present,
when she needs to buy stamps
and bread and wine—
but for the past,
where she gets lost,
and the future,
to which she needs directions.

INTRODUCTION

"GIVE ME A CHILD TO THE AGE OF FIVE AND THEY ARE MINE forever." The Nazis said this, the Communists followed this idea, most religions believe this. Whenever I enter an elevator with other people, I think of the saying. My elementary school had an elevator. The key to elevator decorum was that it was forbidden to speak in the elevator. For eight years (school started at pre-kindergarten) I was trained never to speak in the elevator. For years afterward I was taken by surprise when anyone spoke in an elevator and would stare at them to see who was daring enough to do something so strictly forbidden. To this day it seems natural to be silent in an elevator.

Our early upbringing is the bedrock in which our lives are carved, but by the age of five—like every child—I commuted between two entirely different environments: school and home, and these two worlds agreed on practically nothing, except perhaps that a child reading could do no harm. My family upbringing prepared me with only one capability: to spend money in good taste. That life might not provide me with either the time or the money to practice this ability never seems to have crossed my parent's

Introduction

mind. This remark is not made in a spirit of regret, much less of anger. It is merely a snapshot, as the song goes, of 'The Way We Were.'

When I set out to discover how we came to be "the way we were," I assumed this was a simple task, for which I was adequately prepared. I could read. I could write. I would send out letters to relatives, collect some family lore, read over the articles I had written over the years, and the job would be done. My firsts are not exactly heroic, but as preparation they would do: the first in the family to live beyond the Spuyten Duyvil Bridge, to earn a Ph.D. or publish a book, to teach while pregnant at a school run by nuns. In the course of these endeavors I survived forty plus years of marriage, raising three children, and instructing thousands of college students in English as a first language.

What I discovered was that Truth may be no more than a servant of Motive. The more I found out, the less I knew. Maybe, as an addict of narrative, I should have known it would take a story—plots, subplots, characters—to explain events. I can't say as I wasn't warned when I did my homework.

In the very first sentence of *When Memory Speaks: Exploring The Art of Autobiography*, Jill Ker Conway underscores the paradox: "Why is autobiography the most popular form of fiction for modern readers?" Autobiography is fiction? Sure enough, in her introduction to *Tender At The Bone, Growing Up At The Table*, Ruth Reichl adds to a reader's unease by making it perfectly clear it's the good story that counts: "Everything here is true," she states, before pulling the rug out from under the reader, "but it may not be entirely factual." True but not factual?

Gore Vidal sounds as though he is uttering the definitive statement when he announces in the introduction to *Palimpset, A Memoir* "A memoir is how one remembers one's own life, while an autobiography is history, requiring research, dates, facts double checked." Except the reader shortly discovers, in direct contradic-

xi

A DANGEROUS THING

tion, that the author has dispatched his researchers to dig up, verify, uncover, compare elements of the past all over the globe.

So much for Truth. And Motive, it turns out, is equally suspect. By the end of the twentieth century, memoirs were largely a women's game: all those women to whom no one would listen, who couldn't make themselves heard, were having their say, telling it the way they saw it. Not surprisingly, added to the usual cast of suspects (cruel and/or absent fathers, wicked stepmothers), there are a lot of objectionable straying husbands. Yet one aspect that is peculiar in a great number of memoirs is the part played by the mother. Either the mother is virtually invisible, as though the writer emerged like Athena from the forehead of Zeus, or she is the force driving the narrative because she teeters on the brink—sometimes over—of sanity, an imploding star at the center of the child's universe. Perhaps these books are proof of the theory that to create art the artist must have suffered.

It seemed, then, that I was joining an established sisterhood, for the matriarchal family vision was the forefront of my own memories of family life. But stories of childhood are like a secret garden from which we are forever locked out, and to which we must search in hidden places for the key, for it turns out my mother's model was her father, a strong and contradictory nineteenth century example who ultimately loomed like a giant shadow on the wall against which twentieth century women in the family were silhouetted. Yet when my mother married and became a New Yorker, she found a counterweight to her stern father in her new family. The man who had, in effect, become the grandfather figure in her husband's family represented an entirely different take on life from her own father. Thus began a conflict between her upbringing and her inclinations, a conflict centered on education, and it became a subtext of her new life, affecting our family life in ways I could not comprehend.

Having gained such knowledge as this, my journey into the

xii

Introduction

past, intended to clarify causes and effects, did no such thing. Rather than pinning down events, this search has produced only alternative versions of the past, thus complicating in an enticing way, rather than clarifying how circumstances turned out the way they did. What I have tracked down, like an explorer searching for the headwaters of a river, is the origins of the conflict at the center of my life. That my parents came from quite different backgrounds I sensed by the time I was in high school, but how they ever met and married, and what this meant in our daily lives was not a subject I ever thought about back then.

What occasioned my looking backward was the realization that I am the product of two traditions that have been continually at war with each other. Anyone reading over the articles I have published would conclude that the writer feels ideas and scholarship are at the heart of what is important. They would be wrong. Nothing in my upbringing was intended to make me think abstractions were significant.

Life at home exemplified how material reality, the tangible order of existence, was what mattered. The further I proceeded along the educational path, the more the two value systems diverged. The pendulum swung from one side to the other, without ever coming to rest: as I advanced in school, it was scholarship that counted; when I came back home, it was the imposition of order, practical order on the functioning of daily life that mattered. Whichever activity I devoted myself to—intellectual or material, creative or domestic—like a character in Greek myth goaded by the Furies, I was perpetually beset by the sense of being occupied with the wrong thing. Divided in this way, a life devoted to learning became, as Pope wrote, "a dangerous thing."

The materiality of daily life, the quality of which the middle class strives to improve, is antithetical to an emphasis on abstractions. Perhaps this conflict explains America's ambivalence about support for education: we don't want to buy the books, pay the

xiii

A Dangerous Thing

teachers, and push for the challenging work. From our beginning as a pioneer society we have shown that we believe the experience that counts, real knowledge, is to be found in practical matters, and practical work has always meant something different for men and for women. Women's lives were invariably more embedded in the texture of daily existence. For a Jewish girl in mid-twentieth century Manhattan, developing Taste, which meant perfecting the gracious home, was the main item on the agenda for growing up.

Home, the ordered, comfortable life my mother constructed and my father made possible, that was a given. If school too mattered, the values and causes it propounded, then what was a child to follow? Each morning, as my mother kissed me good-bye at the front door of our twelfth floor apartment with her invariable parting words, "You look very nice, dear," (an interesting refrain, with its clear emphasis on appearances) and I departed down Central Park West for the Ethical Culture School, I already sensed I was heading for an entirely different milieu. Children, as a kind of survival mechanism, develop a delicate sense of tact about what can be spoken, what left unmentioned, and by a young age I sensed already the need to keep these two lives separate.

Part I

GETTING
THERE

Chapter One

THE LANGUAGE
OF TASTE

NEW YORK CITY WAS A VERY SMALL ISLAND IN THE
1940s, not because Battery Park City hadn't been built, or
Chelsea Pier (piers were still the province of ocean liners), or the
East River Heliport. Nowadays, people think of New York City in
terms of neighborhoods, enclaves that change character every
dozen blocks: SoHo and NoHo, Tribeca and Chelsea, Carnegie
Hill and Murray Hill. That is a quaint latter day twentieth century overlay on the city grid. If neighborhoods were given nicknames
when I was little, they were all pejorative. To my sister and myself,
New York meant Manhattan, and Manhattan meant a few avenues
running north-south for several dozen blocks; there were no side
streets, no boroughs. The people we knew lived on Riverside
Drive, West End Avenue, and Central Park West. They were
Jewish.

Protestants held the east side; they lived across the park on
Fifth Avenue or Park Avenue. The west fifties was Hell's
Kitchen—Italian and Irish. Across the way, in the east fifties, there
were tenements packed with large families. Further up the East
side, in Yorkville, where apartment spires now house yuppies like

The Language of Taste

vertical fraternity and sorority houses, the walk-ups held Germans and Slavs. We had only a vague sense that people lived on avenues further east, spilled out of low buildings on side streets. Far east was where the elevated train had thundered by, shaking buildings only barely taller than the El .

North of 96th street merged into Harlem, where Negroes (the proper word then) lived, though some years earlier it had, unknown to my sister and me, been the site of family businesses. South of Central Park were the three B's: Bergdorfs, Bendels, Bonwits. The fort on this southern front was B. Altman's, way down at the frontier on 34th street. The furthest outpost of culture was The Metropolitan Opera on the west side at 39th street.

In a *New Yorker* article about the vicissitudes of apartment hunting in Manhattan, "A Hazard of No Fortune," Adam Gopnik points out "The old enclaves of the true Bourgeoisie…were on the margins of the island, and their high period was a short one." He cites as an example "My great-aunt, like everyone else's, moved into a fifteen-room apartment on Riverside Drive in the forties, and it had been broken up by the sixties, barely a generation's worth of extra closets. Each of its divided parts now costs more money than my great-uncle made in a lifetime." From the perspective of the real estate market, a generation may be nothing, but in an individual's memory bank the childhood neighborhood is the foundation forever, the second womb, entry to the world, but a place to which one can never return.

The island was small…and perfectly safe. My sister, Carol, four and a half years older, could pull me on a sled all through Central Park in the late afternoon after a fresh snow. Or the two of us alone, in our best winter coats and white gloves, could ride the subway in the evening to and from the opera.

Of course, while our little world was small and safe, it was being played out against a very different backdrop. Some social historian once declared that the generations are separated because one

A DANGEROUS THING

always remembers what it was doing when F.D.R. died, and another where it was when J.F.K. was shot, while yet a younger one thinks of what it was doing when Robert Kennedy was killed. Actually, I'm not sure we don't find our narrow niches on the time line by attaching ourselves to the dark bands called wars. Although the twentieth century had a goodly share to choose from, when someone speaks of 'the war,' for my generation it is always W.W.II. My peers may have actually participated in the Korean War, but about that war no absorbing myth has grown up.

It is the Second World War which marks the beginning of associations for my generation: dog tags and air raid drills; saving foil and making rubber band balls; victory gardens and, yes, where I was when the mellow voice on the radio announced "Franklin Delano Roosevelt has died at Warm Springs." I was in a car with a classmate riding home from Ringling Brothers Barnum and Bailey Circus and we were opposite the Museum of Natural History. My classmate's father had recently died, the only one of my acquaintances with such an exotic personal history, and I think I was mostly concerned about this news for her sake, imagining that it would open recent wounds.

Looking back, life gives the appearance of being simpler. No one had flash attachments for their cameras so all the shots in family albums show family and friends frolicking against a clear sky as though life were a series of outings on sunny days. No one pursued the possibility that F.D.R. died in the wrong arms at Warm Springs, or that war was not a good thing. Grownups never spoke of death, disease, divorce, or money in front of the children. Given the paucity of autos, it is hard to imagine what conversation did revolve around.

In an absurdly mundane way, the simplicity of that childhood world is symbolized by its whiteness. No matter what kind of sheets or towels or table linens a person wanted to buy, they were all white, like the bathrooms and the kitchens and the gloves

4

The Language of Taste

women and girls wore in summer. As late as 1965, when I first came to teach at Mercy College in Westchester County, New York, a college presently made of close to 10,000 from every class and culture, its constituency was 500 girls in white gloves. Similarly, during my childhood, cars came in all shades...of black.

As children we knew of more exotic outposts than Manhattan. There was Yankee Stadium in a place called The Bronx and the Forest Hills Tennis Club way out in Queens. But these were as unconnected to Manhattan as Alaska was to the United States at that time. Sometimes once a year we took out our directions to Forest Hills, boarded a series of trains as mysterious as the Orient Express, and were deposited in that other country called Queens. Actually, we did not think of Forest Hills as being Queens any more than people think of Riverdale as The Bronx.

The Forest Hills Lawn Tennis Association had no celebrity boxes, big business advertising, or night games. We marched up to the ticket window and bought seats for the grandstand. Most memorably, we ventured to Forest Hills in 1949 and caught one of the greatest games ever played there. We were dressed in cotton dresses, what young women wore in those days—no shorts or sweat clothes—and sat clapping through a 34 game first set that quick, small, wily Pancho Gonzalez finally lost to tall, stately Ted Schroeder. Spectators were sure the match was all over when Gonzalez lost the second set. But that was before tiebreakers made tennis less like the endless innings of baseball, the other summer game, and more like gambling. So we cheered, in the decorous Forest Hill Tennis Club way (this was before players scratched themselves, threw racquets, cursed the umpire, and audiences screamed at both players and umpires) when Gonzalez came back to take the match after 67 games.

After the matches, the practically new balls were sold on the way out, and my sister and I always collected a set. The white balls with their green grass stains made a symbolic statement when we

A DANGEROUS THING

played tennis with them. They showed we knew what was important in life: playing tennis well, and they showed we had ventured to the furthest reaches beyond our Manhattan boundaries: Queens. Even Greenwich Village, a place we discovered in high school, was an exotic destination. It took us past our known boundaries to a place of crooked streets, small Italian restaurants, the new coffee shops that sold cups brimming with frothy cappuccino, and small clubs where singers sang folk music while strumming guitars.

When I moved with husband and children from Manhattan to Westchester, I met lots of people who said they were from New York City, by which—to my surprise—they meant The Bronx. They claimed they didn't know any people who actually lived in Manhattan. One of these new friends proclaimed he never left College Avenue in The Bronx until he was 16, a generalization I could understand perfectly. Our provincialism was more than the child's eye view of home. It was, in its own way, real.

But it was not so much physical boundaries that set the tone of life; it was an insidious conflict, a war waged between family and school for our secular souls. On the one side were our educators, for whom ideas, abstract principles, creativity, and imagination constituted reality. On the other side was our home—a place in which material reality reigned. Here what mattered were the artifacts that testified to a proper standard of taste.

The grammar of the language of taste had a few simple rules. First, it could be learned. Second, it was ruled by absolutes. There was good taste and there was bad taste. There was no in between. A person with an untrained eye might look at a Mondrian or a Picasso and ask dubiously, "Is that art?" but in time come to see how the work marks an important juncture in the history of painting. So it was with the material culture surrounding us: a person might never have really paid attention to the objects surrounding him or her, taking them for granted as merely necessities of ordinary life, but with close observation that person could learn to see

The Language of Taste

differences. When I was engaged and went with my fiancé to look for furniture for our first apartment, he would sometimes regard an ordinary mirror, chair, or table and say, "That's nice." I would stop in my tracks; he had tripped the wire that set off a red alert flag of absolutes. Slowly I came to see there were smart, well-educated people whose lives were not focused on discriminating between material objects, the critical distinctions that were the underlying theme of my upbringing.

Some chroniclers of the American experience have portrayed the split between the world of home and the values of school as a peculiarity of immigrant life. This has made for touching tales by twentieth century immigrants about teachers who changed the course of their lives. But when I happened on Simone de Beauvoir's *Memoirs Of A Dutiful Daughter*, her 1959 account of growing up in France during World War II, the issues she chronicled were familiar. In this first volume of her autobiography, de Beauvoir explores in harsh detail the clash between school and home that made middle-class taste a basis for political warfare.

Emerging from a childhood de Beauvoir describes as idyllic, a time when she was cosseted and praised, education gave her another way of seeing the world; the dichotomy between the abstract values of school and the customs of home made her see the "rigid moral conventionalism" of the family as "doing violence to my soul." She depicts French middle-class life as not only anti-intellectual, but stiflingly narrow and superficial. Her family, she decided, was mired in meaningless tradition from which she felt forced to break away, a "traitor to my class," even at the cost of making herself "a kind of monster of incivility." She says of her parents, "I had sworn never to like them, I used to feel pity for them.... I moved away from commiseration to anger." Her response to the conflict between home and school was to rebel against the bourgeois values her parents embodied by totally devaluing them. She chose the academy and what it stood for, embodied in her lover Sartre, over family life.

7

A DANGEROUS THING

It took originality and intellectual brilliance to make de Beauvoir into a rebel who could renounce both the values and ceremonies of her class. When I was growing up, there seemed to be only two kinds of females: good girls and rebels. But alas, I could never summon up enthusiasm for making a spectacle of myself. My one serious act of rebellion was my refusal to eat stewed tomatoes, hardly a political statement. Our elementary school served a hot lunch every day, as though we were still settlement house children in need of a meal. Each child was allowed to bring a note listing three items that she or he could be excused from eating. My problem was that there were more than three foods I refused to eat, so I picked the most revolting (pears, for instance!) and took my chances with those that didn't make the cut (stewed tomatoes). Presented with the odious tomatoes at lunch one day, I sat with my plate long after the lunchroom had emptied out, until I was remanded to the principal's office.

The principal's office held a remote figure, Mrs. Wagner. She regarded me sadly through pale eyes in a pale face surrounded by pale hair. I felt badly for her: all that paleness had to come from the terrible problems she had to deal with, and stewed tomatoes did not measure up to the elevated sphere in which I thought principals should dwell. It was a rare confrontation with authority, from which I learned, for better or worse, that sheer stubbornness could win the day. Stubbornness, however, was not synonymous with rebellion. Conformity governed; taste reigned.

It was in the midst of the feminist revolution of the seventies, after I became familiar with *The Second Sex*, that I went in search of de Beauvoir's autobiography. I was surprised by the absolute disdain with which she treated her family, the lengths to which she would go to register her feelings when she states, "Doing wrong was the most uncompromising way of repudiating all connections with respectable people." DeBeauvoir's rebellion against home and the middle class tastes it signified in favor of school was an

8

The Language of Taste

odd choice for the author of *The Second Sex*. The struggle between home and school was not gender neutral, though this was an observation no one made until decades later, long after de Beauvoir's book.

❋ ❋ ❋

Taste was the female province. Ever since the Industrial Revolution men were assigned the role of going out to contend in the brutish business world while women were assigned the job of demonstrating family status through, as Thorstein Veblen termed it in *The Theory Of The Leisure Class*, conspicuous consumption. Despite the pejorative overtones of the word "conspicuous," it does not so much connote gaudy or inappropriately noticeable as it applies to the translating of income into visible signs, into a material language. Like any language, it was meant to communicate, and what it was intended to communicate was a family's monetary well being.

In the Elizabethan age a man could display his wealth on his chest, his back, even his legging-clad legs. Precious metals, jewels, rich fabrics and good legs with splendid garters were the making of a well-to-do gentleman. With the beginning of the Industrial Revolution, men went into a semblance of mourning: black (long pants) suits, shoes, coats, and hats. One had to look closely to distinguish signs of wealth. Meanwhile, back at home, women were ministering to household matters, exerting influence over the expenditure of capital to display wealth, defining taste. It was household appurtenances and women's accouterments that testified to a family's status.

In her authoritative compendium *World Furniture*, Helena Hayward remarks of the eighteenth century, "for a man of wealth his house and furniture presented spectacular means of exhibiting good taste." The Protestant ethic that produced an energetic mid-

9

A DANGEROUS THING

dle class made it seem as though financial success, and its translation into matters of taste, was a sign of moral righteousness.

By the nineteenth century, material standards of bourgeois comfort were so central to Victorian life that they occupy an important place in the narratives of Charles Dickens. Dickens had enough personal experience to know what made a house a home. He could have coined the phrase "Marry in haste, repent at leisure." His young and inexperienced wife was not effective in coping with the servant problem, staying on top of the bills, dealing with purveyors of the family's supplies, or managing the ever-growing number of children. Dickens imported her sister and, later in life, threw up his hands about the whole bunch, leaving wife and children in order to take up with a young actress. All his novels show two kinds of females: the good manager, who is organized, on top of the details, runs a tight ship, and the pretty little gal who can't cope. Fortunately, though the hero falls for the latter, Dickens had learned enough to condemn her to an early death and replace her with the manager.

The year we moved from Manhattan to a house in the suburbs, I retreated to our new 'study' and read my way through our complete set of Dickens, a long line of maroon volumes my in-laws had purchased at ten cents a copy through the *New York Post*. That line of books, another volume waiting each time I finished one, was my only consolation in that foreign land called suburbia. In book after book Dickens portrayed the comforts of well organized middle class home life. Poverty, and its concomitant illiteracy threatened on one side, balanced by the corrupting power of great wealth on the other side, but in the middle the warm, cozy existence of the well ordered bourgeois home was an ideal embodied in story after story. This was a place where all was comfortable without being too conspicuously grand, where hot drinks and ample meals appeared on schedule if the charming little woman was on top of her job as the organizing force. And after all, it was her job—not to actually

The Language of Taste

do any of the tasks necessary to bring about the comforts of a smoothly run household, for a key organizing skill was to see that the proper staff carried out their proper duties in the proper way— but to see that comfort and well-being reigned in a man's castle.

The Victorian division of duties between male and female and woman's role in the middle-class home was still the way of the world into which I was born in 1933. Separate was equal on Central Park West. Like a European political detente, there were his and her spheres of influence. It was a matter of money and taste: the former was my father's affair; the latter was my mother's department. Neither one would think of questioning anything about the other's domain.

Since I succeeded in catching every childhood disease, and in the first half of this century there were still a scary number to catch, I had frequent opportunities to spy on household life once the most miserable part of mumps, measles, whooping cough, chicken pox, or pneumonia was over. In our home illness was an honored state with its own regalia: there were bed jackets and bed trays and a bell to ring for assistance.

Mostly the bell was used to summon my mother to read to me. She took reading out loud to be one of the necessities of a sickroom, along with the bed jacket and bell. Already I showed all the signs of an addict. I was hooked on narrative. I would watch the door intently, desperately wishing my mother to appear and pick up the book on the bedside table. Sometimes I could tell by listening carefully to the level of sound elsewhere in the apartment whether she was coming closer or getting further away. Like any addict, when I couldn't stand it any longer, I'd reach out and grab the bell, though to my frustration, that didn't always mean she sat down next to me and read.

I was sick so much and my mother read to me so much that I saw no necessity to learn to read on my own until third grade. The concept of malingering did not exist; illness, like long summer

A Dangerous Thing

vacations, was something more to be savored than to be rushed through. To begin with, no one was allowed up and about until the thermometer demonstrated normal temperature for twenty-four hours. Going outside was another matter entirely, to be handled gingerly in stages.

During my days in sickbay, our mother, I observed, did not wash or iron, mend, clean or cook. She was a manager, in charge of seeing that the business of home was carried on efficiently. When we were young, this still meant many people came to our apartment to transact their business, so as I recuperated sufficiently to get out of bed, but not enough to go back to school, I caught glimpses of her organizing, selecting, arranging. On rare occasions when I was home ill, I would wander out from my bedroom, down the hall, through the foyer, to find bridge tables set up in the living room. Then women would appear and I would hear the clack clack of tiles. They were playing a mysterious game with ivory domino-like pieces that fit on a little wooden rack. I never understand what the pieces meant or how they knew what to do with them.

But most of the time, when I could not prevail on her to read to me, she was meeting with an odd and interesting assortment of people who came to the house, a cast of characters with whom I eventually became familiar. There was the person from whom she ordered stationery; the dapper Italian man with fabric samples for her husband's suits; the caterer; the little French dressmaker who came to take clothes up and down, in and out; and the interior decorator. Every Wednesday Alma, the laundress, an imposingly tall, thin black woman appeared to wheel our basket of laundry to the basement of our apartment house. Before dinner she resurfaced, the crisply starched and ironed shirts and dresses stretched across the top of the basket, and stood impatiently while my mother checked off her list. In residence was the cook, Edna, a southerner whose native cooking genius ran to fried chicken smothered in gravy but was constrained to cook the bland dinner menus my

The Language of Taste

mother proposed for the week.

What I did not comprehend at the time was that every decision was measured by the two reigning middle class yardsticks: good sense, good taste. There was a crucial test of every decision: did the expenditure demonstrate economic well-being without drawing attention to itself?

While home was where women exerted influence, education, for all it set out to free minds, unleash potential, and empower individuals was an invasion into a male world. We were sent to The Ethical Culture Schools, which had been founded at the turn of the century as The Workingman's School. In a spirit of coeducational fairness, we all took cooking, candle-making, or knitting, shop or printing, depending on the year and the project. But the writers whose works we read and imitated, the history we memorized, the art we learned to admire, the music we tried to play, even the theories of pedagogy that governed the institution in which we marched from class to class were the products of men's minds. From Felix Adler and John Dewey came ideas about pedagogy and society, learning and ethics.

More tangible, I could see each time I returned home and looked around, were the rewards awaiting there. A woman's triumph was that the minute people stepped through the door and over the threshold into her domain, they entered a microcosm she had created. Organization loomed large because the comforts of this good life seemed to require a rage for order. I was in my second year of college before I ever saw people throw coats and books on a bed, followed shortly by themselves. As I watched this action I was conscious of it representing a daring freedom, a revolutionary break with the conventions that governed my existence. Where I came from beds were made immediately, coats hung up pronto, and books placed in an orderly stack on a desk.

Good taste meant a place for everything and everything in its place always and forever. The authority to make everything fall

A DANGEROUS THING

into place perfectly emanated, it appeared, from marriage, which granted a woman magical power over the material world. Too late I realized that order, like sincerity, was an overrated virtue of small minds; that great art was more likely to spring from disorder. But by then I had already absorbed the knowledge that it was by order and taste I would be judged, and that was that.

Like any language, the material language manifesting taste and status was related to geography. For Simone de Beauvoir in Paris, the symbols meant upholding family honor by behaving according to traditional standards...or cultivating rebellion and shocking the family. Those who understood the language of taste with which I grew up lived on the West side of the little island that was Manhattan in the first half of the twentieth century.

Perhaps both de Beauvoir and I could have avoided conflict by absorbing her lover Sartre's statement: "Every man has his material place. It is not pride or worth that settles its height: childhood decides everything."

The Language of Taste

Someone Comes to Dust

Old friend,
when you opened the door
at my knock
I saw myself in lines
like tree rings.

As we talked of our fathers
who placed cigar bands
on our fingers
and promised we'd live
happily ever after,
I glimpse a room filled with bodies,
dolls propped on the pink spreads
of our childhood beds.

Behind the glass
in the museum
I have seen old rooms
where someone comes to dust
among the dead.
Old friend,
as we talk
fine dust settles
between us.

Chapter Two

IN SEARCH
OF BUGOPOL

MY PARENTS DIDN'T JUST SEEM TO BE TWO GENDERS; THEY seemed to be descended from two planets. My strong, silent father had no story to tell of his life, past or present. The scraps of information there were to pick up came from my mother, a woman with her own carefully crafted myths. Or perhaps it was as writers as diverse as Sigmund Freud, Bruno Bettelheim, and Joseph Campbell have pointed out: myths and folk tales represent a basic human characteristic of childhood. Whether it is a story of Cinderella in the ashes or Moses in the bulrushes, we all like to imagine our real parents are much more special than the ones with whom we are stuck. In the myth of the hero, as Campbell points out, the birth of the hero-to-be always has something odd about it and the hero is often brought up by someone other than his actual birth parent. Bettelheim has pointed out how fairy tales often repeat a key childhood fantasy: the hero—male or female—waits to be rescued, recognized, inherit his or her true and wonderful destiny.

So I took the few pieces of information I picked up from my mother about my father's background and made my own narrative. It wasn't that I conjured up illustrious antecedents; it was that in

In Search of Bugopol

my version Krasne life in the old country was picturesque, had charm. In high school, *Crime And Punishment* opened a door to Russian literature and through it came Tolstoy, Turgenev, and Chekhov. Years later along came Nabokov and Pasternak. My picture of Russian life was filtered through this literary lens. Schools did not mention writers like the Singers, I.J. or I.B., whose work would have clued me in to an understanding that Russian was one thing, Jewish another.

When I was already a parent and a teacher I discovered Isaac Bashevis Singer's "Gimpel The Fool," the story that made Singer famous in America when Saul Bellow translated it for *Partisan Review* in 1953. If a reader focused on the writing, it was possible to overlook the ignorance, the poverty of substance and spirit, and the loutishness of the characters who make a fool of the narrator. When Gimpel says at the end

> I heard a great deal, many lies and falsehoods, but the longer I lived the more I understood that there were really no lies. Whatever doesn't really happen is dreamed at night. It happens to one if it doesn't happen to another, tomorrow if not today, or a century hence if not next year. What difference can it make? Often I heard tales of which I said, "Now this is a thing that cannot happen." But before a year had elapsed I heard that it actually had come to pass somewhere....

He was taking about narrative, I told myself. The story was set in his native Poland, I told myself. But even if he had been writing about the neighboring Ukraine, the launching pad for the Krasne clan, it would never have occurred to me that he was describing the world of my father's family. This world, not only lacking charm and picturesqueness, but filled with grossness of every kind, could

17

A DANGEROUS THING

not possibly be the kind of society out of which my family came.

Because I had heard that my father's family came from 'outside of Odessa' and were grain merchants, I envisioned them living in a comfortable rambling home, somewhat along the lines of a Dutch colonial with a long front porch, as though Odessa were New York City and they were established along the banks of the Hudson in the nineteenth century instead of in an outpost of the Ukraine. I imagined the house filled with crocheted doilies, solid furniture, and a shiny brass samovar, a place of heavy-duty comfort and plenty. Grandfather Charles had been a merchant and the family, I had been told, had been saved from the pogroms by a servant. So in my picture there were maids to help with the large number of children and the household work.

The word 'merchant' had its own exotic quality. Merchants were the travelers who followed the Silk Route, who brought strange and wonderful goods from one part of the world to another—china and spaghetti, silk and Turkish carpets- along with news of foreign parts. Merchant, as opposed to peddler, had a ring of substantiality about it. In America every town had its dry goods store and every city its emporium run by a Jewish merchant, whose name frequently became synonymous with merchandising: Abraham and Straus, Gimbel, Fox, May, Orbach.

The true picture of the Krasne side of the family that emerged years later, revealed obliquely in an off-hand journal entry, was more complex. On the one hand, family origins are filled with muck...the muck of the Ukrainian thaw, of unpaved roads, of the Bug River, of a place called Bugopol. On the other hand, there was a certain degree of worldliness and wealth.

To complicate unraveling this family history, there are actually two Bug rivers in Russia. One river formed the border between Poland and the Ukraine for a good part of history. The other one, the Southern Bug River, empties into the Black Sea, Schwarzes Meer, as one map designates it, to the east of Odessa.

In Search of Bugopol

Of course, the borders we know, the names of places on the map that appear now are not the same as they were at the turn of the century. This, after all, is a part of the world where wars and empires swept away or created borders regardless of the people living in the land. In 1582, after the peace treaty of Jan Zapolski, Ukraina, Byelorussia, Lithuania appear as part of Poland, and that is only the beginning of the geographical changes, like shifting sands, that overtake and reshape the area. For the Krasnes, the geography of the world from which they came goes back to a key period of a hundred years: after the partition of Poland in 1815 altered the borders and before the Russian revolution in 1917 changed all the place names.

To uncover these lands as they were laid out at the start of the twentieth century, it was necessary to visit places like Yivo Institute and Room 117 (the Map Room) of the New York Public Library. Both of these are solemn facilities where only serious searchers are to be found. Yivo, now ensconced in an elegant new facility, ranks security up at the top of the agenda along with anything that helps document the existence of pre-World War II Jewish life in Europe. Admission only comes after checking all belongings, leaving one clutching only a pencil and sheet of paper. Then researchers with a spectrum of unusual accents help locate books and boxes of materials. For instance, they begin by looking up names in a work such as *Where Once We Walked: A Guide to the Jewish Communities Destroyed in the Holocaust*, a kind of gazetteer with an index that lists all the aliases of place names: Czarist, Yiddish, Soviet. For the mysterious Bugopol, the index explains finally that there was no Bugopol, only Bogopol (even though it is on the Bug River), and that it was subsumed into what is now a city under the name given it after the revolution: Pervomaysk

The map room of The New York Public Library is handsome, but to prevent people from being lulled by its comforts, a sign warns that it is only for those doing research, those men and

19

A DANGEROUS THING

women, young and old who generally need to stand over the long oak tables so they can pour over large maps laminated between sheets of plastic. The custodians of this special domain are not merely librarians; they are students of cartography with special tools at their command. The setting is appropriate to a study of antique maps, the large room crowned by a coffered wood ceiling, lighted by old iron chandeliers, decorated with classical ornaments carved on the wood paneling and around the marble doorway. From tall arched windows, the glare of light outside is shockingly bright, and does not blend well with the low fluorescents illuminating the tables. At the back, a high counter displays globes, under the watchful eye of a surveillance camera. Computers are discreetly located so as not to distract from the room's historic aura.

In fact, though, most people are in search of such modern information as a contemporary street map of Lima, Peru, or a geological survey of Kingston, Jamaica. They are students, planners, and business people. In every case, like the practiced researchers they are, the librarians take the questions as intellectual challenges. To locate Bogopol on a pre-revolution map, they produce maps from the Austro-Hungarian Military geographical Institute,

In one of the large, old atlases they lug out, there, at the headwaters of the Southern Bug River, 48°03/30°52 on a map of the Ukraine, is Pervomaysk, large enough to merit bold type. It is easy to see why a friend whose grandfather came from Bugopol/Bogopol/Pervomaysk was in the lumber business. The river made the city a busy port for lumber, water being more usable most of the time than roads. It may not have done much for grain merchants, for I heard vague tales of how in winter the family transported its grain in a sleigh, an improvement over other seasons when mud made the roads almost impassable for wagons. Finally, in a 1905 edition of Stieler's Hand-Atlas that the librarians lug out, Bogopol appears in place of Pervomaysk.

The exodus from Bogopol, from its river and its mud, started

20

In Search of Bugopol

early, for Yivo's records show that as far back as 1893 there were enough Jewish immigrants from Bogopol in New York City to start a fraternal organization, Bogopoler Unterstutzungs Verein (B.U.V.). In the files of this organization a letter from its President explains its purpose: "Among its major objectives was to provide for the cemetery needs of its members. This provisions an important obligation within the traditional Jewish faith. Other objectives consisted of fellowship and assistance of members in need or ill health." Another document lists its benefits as: "grave site, sick benefits, funeral discount, Endowment Benefit, Old Age Fund." Members kept meticulous records of sums contributed and distributed, meetings and social events, letters and programs. In the beginning, records were kept by hand in Cyrillic, Hebrew, Yiddish, depending on the event and the secretary, but increasingly documents are proudly and professionally typewritten, and go all the way up to the 1970's.

Although the records are yellowing and fragile, there are no minutes of meetings on file before the 1930's, long after the Krasnes were already comfortably settled and successful in their new country, so it is impossible to know whether they joined, or made use of this association set up to help immigrants. But there was one crucial event in the family's earliest American experience, an event that could have consigned the family to disaster, that might well have sent them to seek help from the B.U.V.: the sudden death of their leader.

But there is another chapter in the story of the Krasne's Ukrainian origins. A couple of members of the family went back in 1934 and 1936, approximately 30 years after they left and 18 years after the revolution. They toured cities in their journey to encounter relatives, all of who were in urban areas, and there was no mention in the journal one of them kept of that latter trip of any Russian locations other than Odessa, Moscow, Leningrad. It was in Odessa, in the heart of the city, at a hotel with a balcony overlooking the Black Sea,

21

A DANGEROUS THING

that the group spent most of its time, meeting with family, distributing goods. There was no attempt to reach an outpost once called Bogopol but re-christened Pervomaysk. There is not even any mention of Bogopol, the place listed by the Krasnes as the "last permanent residence" on the manifest of the ship that brought them to the United States.

❂ ❂ ❂

My paternal grandfather had one of those compounded Russian names that befuddle readers of Russian literature, sometimes requiring writers to add a diagram of characters at the end of their book. The S.S. Haverford, sailing from Liverpool in 1906, set it down as Krasnoschezek, the first part of which meant red and the second part which meant cheeks, in other words Redcheeks, most probably referring to a beard. He was reported to be an imposing character of six feet six inches, with black hair, a red beard, and a reputation as a bit of a gambler. But this Daniel Boone-like image sounds suspiciously like descriptions of a lot of Russian characters, literary and historical, part Rasputin, part Aleksei Vronski and Feodor Pavlovich Karamazov.

The family got on well enough, with the oldest boys able to help their father with the business and speak Russian in addition to the Yiddish in which they conversed at home. For boys, starting at the age of 4, there was Cheder, the Jewish elementary school that taught them to read in Yiddish, introduced them to the Hebrew Bible, thus giving them some Hebrew, and included simple arithmetic. If they continued past the age of 8, they would study the Talmud until they were 13. The girls in the family had to pick up what they could at home, from their parents, a tutor, or their brothers. In other words, the Jewish population was literate, but in greatly varying degrees.

Any measure of literacy was significant as a survival skill.

In Search of Bugopol

Before people can learn another language, it helps to have a concept of language as a structure, to understand how words are bricks with which one builds units of thought called sentences. One reason Jewish immigrants were able to make their way in the new world was that the majority came equipped with basic concepts that literacy conferred on them. I think of this in contrast to a friend of ours whose parents were Italian immigrants and were illiterate. In their house there were no books. It was left to him, a man of a younger generation, to make his way in the world, which he did with difficulty, climbing out of the narrow world in which his parents lived, moving beyond the apartment in Hell's kitchen where he grew up without one shelf for books.

The description of Charles, as his Americanized name transliterated, as somewhat of a gambler may have extended to his approach to business, a willingness to take risks that contributed to the family's prosperity, until pogroms at the turn of the century remade the map of the world for an entire generation. By this time Charles 'Redcheeks,' a widower with two boys from his first wife, Belle, had divorced a second wife and married a third, Anna Guberman, sister of wife number one, a widow with a daughter of her own, Clara, from her first marriage. Together, Charles and Anna had produced five additional children, bringing their combined family to eight, a not uncommon pattern at the turn of the century when a combination of mortality rates and lack of birth control produced ever-larger combined families.

Versions of the family name, Krasne as it was translated when they landed, are scattered across the map of the U.S.S.R.; from north to south, east to west there are towns and cities—Krasnyy Kohl, Krasnoslodosk, Krasnyy Yar, Krasnodar, Krasnyy Luch, Krasnyy Liman. In English, the letter 'K' is seriously underutilized. Whenever I give my name over the phone, I have to say, "K R A S N E, with a K," because Anglo-Saxon and the Latin languages have never found 'K' to be a very important letter, as a look

A Dangerous Thing

at the thinness of that section in any English dictionary reveals. To fill up the 'K' part of the dictionary there are lots of nouns. When we eventually visited Eastern Europe, I immediately noticed a surprising shift: there was not a sign, scarcely a word that got by without the letter 'K' in it somewhere. However, despite their seemingly Russian name and their business success, the family, according to one story, was only saved from a pogrom by a Ukrainian—as opposed to Jewish-servant.

As Stacy Schiff points out about the Jewish family of her subject in *Vera (Mrs. Vladimir Nabokov)*, her biography of the author's wife,

> A few rights were granted the Jews; it was understood
> that every right not expressly granted was denied....
> Furthermore, the rules were subject to change at any
> time. The Jews could be expelled from the city one
> minute, invited to stay the next.... Nor were the city's
> most privileged Jews unaffected by these restrictions.
> When the 'Railroad King' Simon Poliakov donated a
> dormitory to St. Petersburg University, Jews were
> specifically barred from living in it.

Life in Russia for Jews was a minefield.

In the winter of 1905–1906 much of Europe was on the move, in a great wave sweeping westward, preferably to the United States, typically embarking from Hamburg, Germany. Between 1881 and 1914, two million Jews arrived in the United States from Eastern Europe, with the years 1904 to 1907 alone accounting for half a million of them. Two main inspirations for an exodus that would give Jews more control over their destiny were Bundism and Zionism. Bundists sought a secular new world organized by labor. Many of them found their way to America and the union movement. Zionists dreamed of their own homeland, any place but Eastern

In Search of Bugopol

Europe for their place in the sun. Neither of these movements was the impetus for the Krasnochezeks. They sought a more secure environment in which to conduct business and a safer place to raise their brood of eight.

A pogrom in 1903 in Kishinev, a city below where the (other) Bug River fades out in the southwestern Ukraine, that killed 49 Jews and wounded more than 500 sent waves of fear radiating outward. The event, horrendous as it was, might have passed into local folklore as just one more horror in the history of indignity and danger that made up Jewish life in Eastern Europe, except for a writer named Chaim Nachman Bialik (a.k.a. Hayyim Nahman Bailik). In an epic poem entitled "In The City Of The Killing," also translated as "The City of Slaughter," he caught the emotions of a people terrified and outraged by the Russian perpetrators, but also distraught at their own impotence, at having "met pain with resignation" and having "made peace with shame.... " Bialik's verses were widely circulated in both Yiddish and Russian. In scorching words he describes his people as having "eyes that are the eyes of slaves, / Slaves flogged before their masters" and, eschewing sympathy and pity, he admonishes them:

> Away, you beggars, to the charnel-house!
> The bones of your father disinter!
> Cram them into your knapsacks, bear
> Them on your shoulders, and go forth
> To do your business with these precious wares
> At all the country fairs!
> Stop on the highway, near some populous city,
> And spread on your filthy rags
> Those martyred bones that issue from your bags,
> And sing, with raucous voice, your pauper's ditty,
> So will you conjure up the pity of the nations,
> And so their sympathy implore.

25

A DANGEROUS THING

For you are now as you have been of yore
And as you stretched your hand so you will stretch it,
And as you have been wretched so are you wretched.

But of course, for those with some means, there was a way out of deprivation and degradation, the people of whom Bialik wrote, "So let them go, then, men to sorrow born, / Mournful and slinking, crushed beneath their yoke." And go they did. The idea of America had been passed about, chewed over in every city and shtetl as word came back from the new world, from people like those 1893 founding members of the Bogopoler Unterstutzungs Verein.

The Krasnoschezeks refused to be trapped by history. The parents packed up their brood of children and early in 1906 crossed Europe all the way to Liverpool, where they set sail on March 7, 1906, for the United States, arriving after two weeks at sea. In this respect Jewish migration differed from a great part of the Irish and Italian immigration in which young men often first came alone to find work. The family also differed from the majority of the masses pouring into the country because on March 22 they entered the United States through Philadelphia where they took up life in their new country, like many immigrants, with a new name: Krasne. They were supposedly going to join a brother, listed as Morris Krasin of 532 Manlon Street.

The oldest, Abe, who was twenty and used to helping out his father, found a job to support the family by working in a sweatshop in New Jersey that made hats. By the time they arrived in Manhattan the next year, there was another child on the way. But no sooner were they settled in New York then calamity befell them, the kind of catastrophe that devastated the hopes of many immigrant families. Charles became sick and died suddenly at the old Mt. Sinai Hospital, on 67th street and Lexington Avenue, of a burst appendix. He was 48 years old.

The family was so stunned that this neighborhood hospital

In Search of Bugopol

became a place of terror; no one in the Krasne family would set foot in Mt. Sinai Hospital again for almost fifty years, even after it moved to its present Fifth Avenue site, even though it was "the Jewish hospital," a place where Jewish doctors could get privileges beyond the quotas that governed at other medical institutions. It was not until my father had a heart attack in 1953 that the family again dared enter Mt. Sinai.

Anna, who was 42 when her husband died, spoke a heavily accented English, while the children ranged from their early twenties down to the baby, and their language skills varied accordingly. There is a scene in *The Rise of David Levinsky*, Abraham Cahan's novel about the acculturation of Russian Jews to American business ways, in which David visits a family in Harlem, where the Krasnes were to set up shop. There are six children in the family David visits, and to the narrator they represent the spectrum of linguistic integration: at one end, "The oldest two sons…spoke English with a Russian accent"; at the other end, the youngest spoke only English, but understood Yiddish; while the children in the middle spoke English with Yiddish accents. The Krasnes had a similar spectrum: from Charles' first marriage there were the two eldest, Abraham and Julius. From his wife Anna's first marriage there was her daughter, Clara. Together Charles and Anna produced Israel, Benjamin, and Samuel on the male side, and Jean, Florence, and Mary, the baby born after her father's death.

The older boys were able take charge, not an easy task, considering that in 1907–1908 their new country experienced a major depression, but they had been out in the (Russian) world working with their father before they emigrated, so they were by age already men, and by trade already men of business. The younger ones went to school in America. Then there was my father, as the oldest boy from the second set of children, his life was, in a sense, the most disrupted, for he never had the time to fully grow up in either the old or the new world. Business, not education, was what life was all

27

A Dangerous Thing

about, he concluded, which put him on a collision course with the woman he would marry.

According to Jewish tradition, the first-born would carry the name of the recently dead; in this case, the first-born son would carry the name of the grandfather. So we grew up with four cousins named Charles as two of the brothers and two of the sisters married, had sons, and named them in memory of their suddenly deceased father. Since there were four of them, I was always meeting people who told me, "I know your cousin Charles."

In a calamity such as the family faced with the death of the father, a large brood of children could be the downfall or the salvation of the group. Social scientists studying urban working class families from the mid-nineteenth to the early twentieth century note "sudden death, maiming accidents, frequent and extended layoffs, sickness, and other devastating events made it essential for families to have a reserve of obligations to aid at times of such calamities." In other words, the more children you had who could be put to work, the better able a family was to survive after a calamity like the death of the father. As the largest family on the block, the Krasnes had both the disadvantage and the advantage of size: more mouths to feed, but more hands to work, especially if youngsters lied about their age and evaded school to get work. The researchers show that "families were able to operate with a margin of comfort to the degree that they could count on a steady contribution from their laboring children of both sexes." So it was that the Krasnes managed because they were able to come up with four full-time workers: a grocer (Abraham), an Order Clerk (Julius), a Dairy lady (Clara), and a laundry errand boy (Isador, who had not yet adopted Israel as a name) to support the family of ten, even though the errand boy, who gave his age as 17, was actually only fourteen years old and should have been in school.

❖ ❖ ❖

In Search of Bugopol

Selling produce was what the men were familiar with, so they followed the money, so to speak, opening stores in Harlem, which by 1910 was "the aristocratic Jewish neighborhood." The history of Harlem, still visible in wide swaths of its architecture, is inextricably linked with the history of Jewish immigrants because by the early years of the twentieth century it was home to the second largest Jewish population in New York, and these were not the Jews of the sweatshops.

Many of the first Jewish immigrants who made it big in the United States were Germans fleeing the 1848 revolutions that unsettled Europe. By the time the American Civil War was over, some of these families had amassed considerable wealth. The construction in the 1880's of an elevated railroad that went all the way to Harlem made it possible for the well to do to migrate from crowded lower Manhattan to the bucolic spaces of Harlem. Sulzberger and Bernheim, Koch and Blumstein (department stores) moved in and built their businesses and synagogues. Along with them came upstarts to cater to them, such as Schiffman, who took over and later desegregated the Apollo Theater, and Samuel Rothafel, known as "Roxy," the Harlem impresario of the first movie palace. To properly entertain the growing, prosperous population he added an orchestra in his Harlem movie house and put his phalanx of ushers in snappy uniforms like a palace guard.

Even today it is possible to trace architectural remnants of this early high Jewish tide in Harlem. Koch called upon the architect of B. Altman's to design his emporium at 125th and Lenox Avenue. He wanted the latest style, influenced by the classical revival of the Chicago Worlds Fair. The kind of work still seen today in Brunner's Spanish and Portuguese Synagogue on Central Park West first appeared in his work on Harlem's synagogues. The Mt. Morris Theater, by the architect who was to do the Ethical Culture Society, another Central Park West landmark, went up in the Beaux Arts Style that vied with the classical revival. The life that

29

A DANGEROUS THING

went on in this setting was captured by writers such as Abraham Cahan in *The Rise of David Levinsky* and Clifford Odets in "Awake and Sing." Cahan describes the women of Lenox Avenue as looking "like a meadow bursting into bloom in spring."

Lenox Avenue was a tree shaded boulevard lined with townhouses and the occasional exclusive apartment house, like the neoclassical Renaissance palazzo Graham Court, which had six to eighteen room apartments surrounding a gated courtyard with a fountain. By 1904, however, the inauguration of subway service brought a more diverse working class group of Irish, Italians, and Jews. Among the arrivals was one newly named and enterprising family called Krasne.

Abe set up first one grocery store at 129 West 135th Street, the neighborhood where they lived, and then added a second one at 1848 Second Avenue. There was nothing of the ghetto about this neighborhood. Of the 28 families surrounding the Krasnes on their block, according to the 1910 census only four families listed their place of origin as Russia, and only one of these families gave Yiddish as its language. The majority of residents hailed from English speaking countries: England, Ireland, Canada, and the United States itself. The next largest group, eight families, fans out in origin across Italy, Germany, France, Holland, and Sweden. English was the most likely language to be heard on West 135th Street.

Though stereotypically people might expect Irish families to be the largest, the Krasnes, with nine living children from their combined families, were way out in front. Most families were, in fact, not large, the runners up being the Morettas, an Italian family with five children, and the McHeavers, an Irish household, also without a father, with seven children. It is interesting to speculate what sociologists and urban anthropologists would make of family size. Does it represent some kind of survival of the fittest: the result of better access to medical care, less access to birth control, more good

In Search of Bugopol

food, better hygienic principles, or is it merely the result of the combined family that emerged from several marriages?

The neighborhood was equally mixed in terms of employment. A few boarders and older children did manual work—carpenter, bricklayer, dock worker—but there was a good representation of people who had their own businesses or professions: dentist, detective, bookkeeper, undertaker, and, of course, grocery store entrepreneur, indicating this was a neighborhood of the upwardly mobile.

And mobile they were, for before long the retail businesses became wholesale businesses, the store fronts became large operations in The Bronx, where the oldest brother, Abe, built Krasdale Foods while the other four—Julius, Israel, Benjamin, and Samuel—established Bernice Foods. It was a great rise in short order, typical of what Cahan called "the American atmosphere of breathless enterprise and breakneck speed." Their success can in part be credited to industriousness, business acumen, the experience and capital they brought to the business, but it was also opportunely spurred on by brief shortages that came with World War I, and larger ones later during World War II. It was in the spacious Central Park West apartment of "Roxy," the movie impresario from 116th Street, that Abe Krasne finally settled his growing family.

Once, when I was in middle school, a classmate asked me what my father did. When I told her he was in the grocery business, she looked at me strangely until I figured out that she thought he ran a corner grocery store, which would have been an unusual way to support children in private school in Manhattan, even back in the days when private school tuition didn't add up to the national debt of a small third world country.

In the 1990's, stalled on Bruckner Boulevard one day, I looked over and saw the old site of Bernice Foods, now another food concern, and over this scene ironically loomed a billboard for "Priceline.com…name your own price for your groceries." As I sat

31

Krasne Brothers 'new' warehouse, c. 1930.

in my car, inching along, I remembered one summer in high school before I was going away when I told my father I wanted to see what the business was all about, to work in his office. I don't know what I expected, but the place was disappointing. For those few weeks he took me with him early in the morning and I sat at a desk in a large room filled with young women adding up bills on adding machines. There were a couple of big fans that moved the stuffy air around and those who sat near them complained of the gale, while those on the other side of the room complained of the stuffiness, a running commentary that made a tune in counterpoint to the clicking of the adding machines. At the head of the room, behind a desk, like a school mistress, sat the office manager, a trim woman called Miss Morris, who spent her time commuting between my uncles' offices down the hall and trying to keep the peace in the room where the women worked.

It was a strange lark, trying to be one of the 'girls,' because we all knew that down the hall were my father and my uncles. Even after that glimpse into my father's world, though I could finally picture him at work, I still had no idea how that little pile of bills I toted up on the adding machine resulted in the life we led on Central Park West and at the Ethical Culture Schools, and the story of my father's life was almost as opaque as it had always been.

In Search of Bugopol

Vignettes of a Father

I still remember the night
I kicked the covers off
dreaming you'd died,
but I was small then
and saw our kitchen
as enormous
until that night at length,
a fallen statue,
you filled the room—
a monument assuming an instant
antique patina—
though I turned away, too late,
only moments after the crash
covering my ears
against reverberations.

Once I saw you
haunting my rosebushes.
Sir,
I can honestly say
I do not know you
in whose image I am made
though I have devoted
a dutiful share of time
to our special connection.
Now I hardly notice you
posed smiling on my desk.

A DANGEROUS THING

In all the family vignettes
you and your long shadow
smile into the sun
behind the brownie camera,
placid with expectation,
astride your horse in the mountains
or jovial under palm trees.
Summer and winter,
distant scenes faded now,
pictures coming unglued.

And the advice you gave,
"no one will ever love you
the way your mother does,"
I remember like a sampler
embroidered with pricked fingers
fumbling over the meaning
of your words.

What you did for me
was real as bread and shoes
but I would not ask
for one more word
with you.

Chapter Three

RETURN TO RUSSIA

THE KRASNES ARRIVED IN AMERICA EARLY IN THE CENTURY as part of a great wave of immigrants. Their American success story, however, has a sequel our family never mentioned. Like many of their kind, with pluck, hard work, plus some previous commercial experience, they produced successful businesses that made them well off by the time the depression struck. Their rise in this country corresponded to the years when Russia was supposedly also on its way to becoming a brave new world as a result of the Revolution. But Abe, the eldest, who was already 20 when the family left the Ukraine and remembered his Russian, stayed in touch with relatives in the U.S.S.R. and the stories that came back to him did not give a picture of a comfortable life. In fact, he filtered out the fact that existence itself was a problem.

In 1934, as a successful businessman who could afford to do everything first class, he decided to go back to the old country and see for himself what had become of the people and places he still remembered. The shock he received on that trip made him understand how much the family had achieved, but also how much more he could do for the remaining relatives trapped in the Soviet

35

A DANGEROUS THING

system. Like a one man Jewish Joint Distribution Committee, he persuaded his sister, Florence, and her husband, Archibald Shapera, a dentist, to accompany him and his wife, Mary, on a second trip in 1936. From his previous trip he knew what was needed and with four people he hoped to be able to bring in a significant quantity of supplies.

For Archie, born and raised in Holyoke, Massachusetts, working from an early age to help support his mother, then supporting his own family with a dental degree from Columbia University, the trip was a once in a life time adventure. It took him to half a dozen countries stretching away across the European continent and he paid close attention in a journal he kept, starting with the "all ashore" of the Cunard Line's Queen Mary at 3:30 P.M. on August 12, 1936, when the "half a hundred friends" who had come to see them off in their first class cabins were escorted down the gang plank. The bon voyage party was a taste of the style in which they planned to travel.

Odessa was the goal toward which they moved, sometimes with great difficulty, in an undertaking that had characteristics of a military campaign. When they disembarked from the Queen Mary at Cherbourg, they were already traveling with "twenty seven heavily laden valises" that held goods they were trying to get to Odessa. Although the greater part of this collection was destined for the U.S.S.R., first class shipboard life made its own huge demands on their wardrobe and eleven bags, several of which were large wardrobe trunks, were for their immediate needs on board and in Paris.

Aboard the Queen Mary, outfits were required for swimming before lunch, then dressing for lunch, followed for the women by the latest movie, such as "Mr. Deeds Goes To Town," with Gary Cooper and Jean Arthur. While the women socialized, the men attended to business, Archie writing and Abe dealing with cables and international calls. By late afternoon they all needed clothes for

On board R.M.S. Queen Mary, August, 1936.
Florence and Archie Shapera, Abe and Mary Krasne.

cocktails, then formal attire for dinner and dancing "in the Top Deck Grill from midnight to 3, 4, and 5 o'clock in the morning, where every body let loose; especially the so-called blue-bloods, who kept themselves distant and secluded during the day...." Naturally, the women's baggage for these five days included a supply of jewelry for each outfit and occasion. Also packed in each of the women's wardrobe trunks was a copy of the hefty newest novel, *Gone With The Wind*, but dining, drinking, dancing only left enough time for Florence to read ten pages and Mary three.

In Paris they could shop for fall wardrobes for the trip home, mid-September, at a list of special places Mary kept. But here, too, they were kept busy at nightclubs with sexy shows and touring the Russian restaurants, practicing their vodka drinking with acquaintances just back from Russia. By the time they left Paris, Archie noted, "we were still taking about 16 pieces of luggage with us, the contents of which were for relatives of [sic] Russia. For ourselves,

A DANGEROUS THING

we took only 2 outfits apiece." The rest they had left behind in Paris, awaiting their return, forever changed by this fateful trip. Considering these were serious shoppers, people used to dressing for dinner, who were going to be traveling for several weeks, only two outfits apiece sounds meager indeed, but the reader finds out later how this was part of the grand plan to save Odessa.

The trip from Paris to 'Bucuresti,' their next stop, was 40 hours long, but fortunately was made on a French train. "Ten minutes aboard this beautiful train, and we found ourselves eating a delicious dinner, cooked and served as only the French know how.... we traveled through Austria, Hungary, stopping for a few minutes in Vienna and Budapest." From here on it was downhill all the way, in terms of transportation, accommodations, and food.

They had no sense that the world they were visiting was on the brink of extinction, that they would never again see any of the people they visited. They thought only of what had happened in Russia over the previous 18 years and assumed the past was the disaster from which they wished to help people survive. They, who came back like princes scattering largesse, understood the fortuitousness of their escape from Russia, the benefits of their American citizenship, and the financial success these circumstance had enabled them to create. As Archie says six weeks later when they took their leave of the continent, "For the last time we presented the best book in all Europe to the customs officials for examination—Our American passport—The thin little book that allowed us into and more important, out of a dozen countries in Europe. Our most valuable possession, and we felt proud and privileged to own it."

In Bucharest they were entertained by relatives, upon whom, in the pattern of their journey, they showered gifts, but the journal records how "Ever mindful of his people in Russia, Abe bought 3 heavy fur coats, at $18 a piece." Shocked at the poverty they saw around them—people barefoot in the capital city, young women doing heavy labor—and how cheap the money, the Lei, was "Abe

38

Return to Russia

tried his best to spend lei, and we 'lei'ed all over the town, buying many things, especially wearing apparel for Russia. We even bought more luggage for the double purpose of packing our purchases and as gifts for our people in Russia." Just before they left Bucharest,

> We found a grocery that could compete with the best
> in N.Y. for variety and quality of foods. And how we
> bought. Abe was always the wholesaler. If he could
> only get it through, he'd have bought a carload of
> supplies, but we had to be content with 2 large valise-
> fulls of delicious food, including 4 large long 'genzine
> salamis,' of a quality and taste unequaled anywhere
> else in the world; fruits, and dozens of lemons. And
> for the next two weeks, we guarded these valises as if
> they had contained valuable jewelry, and the contents
> proved to be more valuable to us than jewelry.

It is this food that sustained them, for with each succeeding train they took, they were further removed from elements of western civilization they had come to take for granted as American citizens.

After leaving "that busy little metropolis, Bucuresti, in romantic Romania," the narrator describes the train as "fairly decent, except that the plumbing in our wash-room was bad, and the water besides being in the sink, ran all over the floor, and into our compartments. We were traveling first- class, but the train was not high class." Fortunately, they did not foresee what their future travel plans held in store for them, for soon they were in Bessarabia, "Europe's forgotten country," Archie called it, where "Early in the morning, somewhere along the road, we changed trains. This train was a sadly neglected affair—very dirty, smelly toilets, and no water anywhere." There was no eating car; the weather was getting colder and there was no heat.

It was the Russian part of the journey that had the worst in store

A DANGEROUS THING

for them. From Tiraspol, a border city on the Dnestr River, they boarded the train for Odessa "that we wouldn't use for a cattle-car in this country." The single bulb went out and they rode in darkness until the conductor brought them the stub of a candle. This conductor affected them strongly as a symbol of the new Russia:

> After eating [the food they bought in Bucuresti], I gave our conductor some of our food. Of course, he grabbed it, with a thousand thanks. He was a sad spectacle—starved, emaciated looking…. a fine representative of his country, and typical of 98% of all his countrymen. I ventured into the 3rd class cars, and found 8 and 10 people crowded into compartments for 4, and the smell of these people was so strong, that it overpowered that of the disinfectant. And these were the accommodations that served for the Soviet citizens, wherever we traveled in Russia. They have to travel third, and that third would not be allowed in any civilized country. Thus at 11 o'clock on the night of Aug. 26th this long, unsanitary, contaminated train, with its reeking cargo of unfortunate humans, came to a stop in the terminal station of ODESSA.

As far as the tired travelers were concerned, they had reached their destination. But their mission, it turned out, could not be accomplished. For days they had to do battle with the Soviet authorities over their baggage, the sixteen bags shipped ahead and the innumerable valises they had accumulated en-route, not counting the chains of watches they wore around their waists. This was not a social visit; it was a relief mission and no confrontation with authority was too major for them to try in order to import supplies.

They exited the station in August wearing fur coats over cloth coats over jackets and dresses, in several pairs of shoes, much too

Return to Russia

large, stuffed with paper. And it is a good thing, for the next day when they returned to the station in the morning to reclaim their baggage, they were forbidden to take more than two items of apparel apiece, which meant abandoning the dozens of coats, dresses, shoes, sweaters, children's clothes, plus medical and dental supplies that they had carted half way around the world. Appalled that they had struggled so hard, that the people they had come to help were in such dire need, they offered to pay a huge tax. The inflexible bureaucrats were unmoved. The lunch hour and the dinner hour came and went, the men sent the women back to the hotel, and finally, by evening, Abe got up and gave a speech, part Russian, part English, which he carried on for 35 minutes without pause, until the underlings caved in and sent for their chief, the head of the port of Odessa, with whom Abe in short order worked out a deal.

The importance of the goods was not only the immediate use for which they were intended, but as a form of hard currency. As Archie noted, "Every person to whom Abe gave one of these watches received a fortune in rubles, for a time-piece is as rare in Russia as freedom itself." In hard times everything they brought became a negotiable item, and hard times were what they saw around them. The closer they looked, the more they spoke with relatives and friends, the more they deemed the country "a poverty stricken land" and saw how it had become a "country that to us seemed to be reverting to the Middle Ages."

At the time the family had left from Odessa for Liverpool in 1906, it was the fourth largest city in the Russian Empire, ranking after St. Petersburg, Moscow, and Warsaw, and thirty percent of the population had been Jewish. Because so many families departed from Odessa, it was nicknamed "the gateway to Zion." Besides people, the biggest export had been grain, and Jewish owned companies exported eighty percent of the grain. Abe still knew a number a people there, but he was in for a shock when he met an old friend, a peer, a man of 55 who had been a successful merchant,

41

A DANGEROUS THING

who now looked 75. In the U.S.S.R., they quickly observed, the newest thing was the new "class system, more defined than in any other country we visited" because apparachiks had made the system work for themselves, while for the masses everything was worse.

Returning to their hotel late one night, in a scene that might have been out of a nightmare vision in *Crime and Punishment*, Archie wrote:

> as we four sat, two in a droshki, with the hulky,
> raggedy isvostchick in front of us, driving the weary
> skeleton-looking horse, through those dark, deserted,
> bumpy streets, we also feared—And it came to my
> mind, that fifty years ago, our grand-parents rode in
> these same rickety, antiquated two-wheel carriages,
> also always in fear—Then it was the Czar and his
> pogroms—Today, the dictator and his despotic rule—
> What curse lies upon this land, and these people?
> And what is their salvation?

When it was finally time to leave Odessa and move on to Moscow, Archie summed up their Dantesque experience: "it came to me that we were leaving a city of living dead, whose only future is the old, crowded cemetery that we had visited our second morning in Odorous Odessa."

It is in that passing mention of the visit to the cemetery that there resides the final clue to family origins. If Abe was paying a visit to the grave of his mother, Belle Krasnoschezek, and that grave was on the edge of the city, then it certainly would seem that the family came from Odessa, although the ship manifest had sited Bogopol, a place over a hundred miles north of Odessa.

Moving on to Moscow, the heart of Soviet power, they felt the political effects of the Revolution and Stalin's rule. The eradication

42

Return to Russia

of religion, the spying and betrayals that produced fear of speech had infiltrated every family with whom they spent time and made the city grimmer even than Odessa. Again, the banners and parades did not fool them. When they left, the journal noted, "we were glad to be...taken away from this place where humans were being sacrificed to satisfy the power of the Moluch of Moscow [Stalin]." In Leningrad at least they were able to do some sightseeing of the remaining monuments, between their usual routine of spreading material benefits about among their contacts.

When they were finally on their way out of the country, it was with no regrets, for the final train ride was "the piéce de resistance. Older than Methusalah, smellier than a dung-pile, it epitomized everything that is Russia." So it comes as no surprise when the scribe summed up their Soviet experience: "we were happy to be rid of all Russia. Good-bye to sorrow, misery and fear—Good-bye to poverty and filth. Good-bye to slavery and paganism. Good-bye to censored speech and censored press." What they did not, could not foresee was that it was also good-bye forever to all the people with whom they met on their journey through Eastern Europe. War, invasions, starvation would sweep away every person they knew there.

From the windows of the train that was taking them to Berlin they observed the small countries of Estonia, Latvia, Lithuania— still independent, and therefore "all poor, but orderly and clean. The trains were immaculate, the small pretty stations well kept and spotless." But this small corner of the continent too was a world that would shortly cease to exist. After the war, even with the help of a worker who knew more Russian than he did, Abe was not able to locate any of the people he had visited and helped out before the war. The family's history in Russia was finished, like a disconnected telephone line.

En route back to Paris, they visited Germany, where their initial euphoria over the superb physical conditions—"we thought we

A DANGEROUS THING

were in wonderland—never before, neither in Europe or the U.S. had we seen such modern luxury"—was unsettled from the moment they entered customs, where "Hitler dominated this room, from a full size portrait of himself that hung on the wall directly opposite the entrance." On the one hand, Archie noted, "We marveled at everything we saw, the streets, stores, parks, restaurants—Berlin was thrilling—The most beautiful city we had ever seen." They sampled the nightlife, a dim reminder of the Weimar era, but rain and closer acquaintance with people and events further undermined first impressions, and two days after they arrive the journal noted,

> the longer we remained, the lower our spirits sunk, and altho [sic] we were treated courteously and with respect, we felt that we did not 'belong— Impatiently, we awaited the hour of departure—And at 8:30 P.M. when our train pulled out, we were glad to be on it, to be taken away from the unholy acts of NEW GERMAN KULTUR.

Yet the physical well being of everything German surrounding them, particularly in contrast to their foray east, managed to mask the direness of the political situation and the extent of the catastrophe already underway. Once they left Germany for Belgium, France, and England, they naively assumed they had closed the book on the problems of the NEW GERMAN KULTUR.

In light of their German experience, there was one cultural exchange recorded in that 1936 journal at which it would have been interesting to be a fly on the wall; it is an episode on the return voyage of the Queen Mary. They had sailed from England. It was September, and in a first class lounge of the splendid ship, the journal says, 50 Jewish passengers interrupted their debates about the condition of Russia to improvise a 'Schul' and "observe the Rosh

44

Return to Russia

Hashonah." What did the other passengers make of this event? Were the 50 participants all Jews traveling First Class? By what telepathy did the 50 find each other, or was religious segregation so complete and obvious that these 50 people would all somehow know each other? Was there, someplace else on another deck, a parallel event for passengers in other classes, like the Upstairs/Downstairs social events filmed in "Titanic"? The religious observances aboard the Queen Mary, on the brink of World War II, when Germany was already launched on its way to eliminating the Jews, stands as a curious footnote to the Russian hegira.

❁ ❁ ❁

As we were growing up we never knew there had still been relatives in the old country, or that our aunts and uncles had been back to visit. In our family the past was a buried place, more obscured to me than the ruins of Troy. I had always thought my father was three years old when he came to this country, and therefore had taken it for granted that he had no story of the old country to pass on to us. Although his 1929 Certificate of Naturalization lists his age as 33, making him nine when he arrived here, old enough to remember stories about Russia, he maintained a steadfast silence about childhood. The only stories came from my mother, who had her own reasons for altering the picture, and from my father's odd practice of drinking tea in a cup with raspberry preserves as a sweetener.

In a story entitled "The Opiate of the People," by Lynne Sharon Schwartz, the daughter of an immigrant father keeps wanting to know "What it was like when you were growing up?" a question children often find themselves wondering about, usually meaning something like 'What was it like before cars or electricity?' In this case the father in the story studiously avoids the subject. He has built the good life in America and wants no part of the past. One day she

A DANGEROUS THING

goads him into saying, "We were poor.... We worked, we studied. We lived where your grandmother used to live. It was very crowded." He thinks this will satisfy her, but he has missed the mark.

What she really wants to know is what his life was like "Before you came here." His repeated answer is "I don't remember," a statement Freud tells us ranks as 'repression.' Finally, when she is fifteen, she refuses to be put off and forces him to blurt out,

> You really want to know? They came around at night
> and chased people out of their houses, then set them
> on fire. You were afraid to go to sleep. They sent you
> to the army for twenty years. They said we poisoned
> their wells and chopped up their babies. So everyone
> came here.... It stunk on the boat. People vomited all
> day long. All right?

The young woman has trouble picturing this other life, which is just fine with her father, who takes pride in having brought up the all-American girl.

The story was in a collection, *Imagining America: Stories From The Promised Land*, I was using in a freshman English course and my students, who came from many parts of the world, or whose parents did, had their own hard time with the story. Their vocabularies did not extend to such terms as 'shtetl,' 'pogrom,' 'ghetto,' 'Marx.' But more than that, they could not see why people would want to hide the past. Many of them were from Latino families and they went back and forth to their country of origin for holidays and vacations; some dreamed of eventually retiring to the old country, where life would be leisurely and American dollars would make them king and queen of the hill.

The only hint I ever caught of our Russian past occurred many years later in Paris. My husband and I were there at the same time as my Uncle Abe and Aunt Mary. Together we took a cab to din-

Return to Russia

ner one evening, and as soon as Abe climbed into the cab he struck up conversation with the cabdriver in a language I had never heard before. Somehow he immediately guessed the driver was what he described to us as "a White Russian." It was a language I had never heard my father speak, but then I had assumed he had been only three when he left Europe and it did not seem strange he had no recall of Russian. My uncle's breaking into Russian was a surprise because it was my most vivid realization that my father was a foreigner.

The Russian part of our family's story would end there, petering out like the Bug River, mud roads, and Stalin's purges, except for a latter day footnote. Before the end of the Cold War, in 1983, our oldest son—Thomas Krasne Levine—planned a trip to the U.S.S.R. He was going with an English group (people could only visit as part of a group then) but was having trouble getting his visa. No matter how many times he wrote or called Washington, nothing appeared. Finally, desperate, as the date of departure for England, where he was to meet the group, drew near, he was put in touch with a "facilitator," a man who specialized in working out problems with the Russian Embassy. Tom employed this intermediary to actually go down to Washington and see what could be done. He resolved the problem of moving papers from one desk to another, which turned out to be caused by Tom's highly suspicious Russian family middle name. They were holding on to his visa while they tried to check up on this mysterious character with a Russian name who wanted to sneak into the U.S.S.R. under cover of an English travel group.

Visa finally in hand, he met us—Mom, Dad, and sister Kate—in Scotland, where we were visiting friends in Edinburgh at the end of a trip through England to celebrate our twenty-fifth anniversary. We flew west to the United States from Heathrow while Tom met up with his group heading east to Russia, but as our planes carried us away from each other, across the world another

A DANGEROUS THING

plane diverged from course, setting off an irrevocable tragedy. Korean Airline's Flight 007 strayed over Sakhalin Island.

After we were home, our younger son, Jonathan, called. "Do you know who was on that plane? Serena."

At his words I saw his high school classmate standing in our front hall at the end of his graduation party, her straight hair hanging down her back like a splendid black mane. I saw the big smile as I wished her luck at Duke University. Horrified, I could only hope that all was over instantly and there were no sentient beings to contemplate their fate as 007 made its wide spiral to annihilation. Then there was the next piece of news: all airports around the globe had closed off access to flights from the U.S.S.R.

It was clear the city survival skills we had inculcated in our children could not help them when they were faced with violence and fear on a global scale. In the journal of his 1936 trip, Archie Shapera had described riding in a horse drawn carriage and realizing the U.S.S.R. was a land "always in fear," going from "the Czar and his pogroms" to the constipation of the communist system under "the dictator and his despotic rule." But by the latter part of the twentieth century, when Archie's grandchildren were growing up, the fear Russia could spread was worldwide. The statesman who proclaimed "We have nothing to fear but fear itself," was right, but not for the reasons he had in mind. The fear that kept us armed and arming was the same fear that, given merely one misunderstanding, at the push of a button sent weapons arching into action to cut down a civilian airliner.

It was a sunny late summer Saturday, 93 degrees in New York State. On that beautiful day I was locked indoors at an annual ritual, the convocation marking the official opening of the academic year. Back at the house, my husband was involved in other seasonal rituals: resuscitating the lawn, shoring up, cutting back, hosing down plants. But both of us were keenly aware, as we rarely were, of the disposition of our family. Neither of us could put from our

Return to Russia

minds the child at college who was attending a memorial service for his high school classmate, nor could we keep from dwelling on the other one, the one in the U.S.S.R who was trying to find a plane that could fly out and an airport that would allow it to land.

It was 2:30 when the call came through from London: the last plane from Moscow had landed. It was filled with English people, and our son. Once again a Krasne had escaped, just in time. Seventy-seven years earlier it had taken a good part of a year for the Krasnoschezeks to make their way by horse cart to Odessa, by train to Liverpool, by steamship across the Atlantic to Philadelphia, then by train to New York. In 1936 my uncles and aunts had made it back and forth across Europe and the Atlantic by train and ship in six weeks. Tom made the journey in two days, once he found a plane and an airport.

He was thin when he arrived back in New York. "The food," he explained, "was inedible. It was always a mystery food covered with sauce. What you didn't eat, they put in a drawer in the dining room for the next meal." He described the grimly colored cars, clothes, buildings of the cities and the life that went on in them, exuberantly primitive and insular, like America before the First World War. "There was nothing to buy, except this" he apologized, showing us a Russian map of the world in which the U.S.S.R. was a huge red area bleeding from the center in all directions. He told stories of the generosity of strangers. "People were wonderful. They didn't have anything, but they wouldn't let us pay for drinks or cabs." The Krasnes may have come from Russia, but it was the most foreign place Tom felt he had ever been.

We asked him about the Korean airliner. He shook his head. The U.S.S.R was a place where much was spoken but little was known, and the sound of pain that went around the world when Flight 007 disappeared into the sea was not heard by the people of the Soviet Socialist Republics. Once again, Russia had been for the family the place from which to seek escape.

Chapter Four

RAPHAEL'S WAY

DELMORE SCHWARTZ, THE POET AND SHORT STORY WRITER, has a famous story entitled "In Dreams Begin Responsibility" in which the character goes back in time and imagines the meeting of his parents. He describes the events that follow as someone watching a movie he has seen before, knowing the terrible events to follow but unable to change what is already on the film in the projection booth. He describes the characters (his parents), the streets (where they lived), and the manner in which they proceed on their date together. In an effort to avert the scenes unwinding before him, the character shouts out exclamations of warning at the screen as he describes an impending tragedy. To the extent the story is autobiographical, Schwartz obviously thought of himself as the ill gotten result of an unfortunate mismatch.

Like Delmore Schwartz, when I think that my father, Israel (né Isador) Krasne of New York City, and my mother, Hannah (né Hanchin) Goldstein of Philadelphia, ever met, fell in love, and married, it is a psychological and cultural mystery to me. But exactly opposite to Schwartz, when I try to picture the meeting of my parents, the way he does in his story, nothing at all comes to mind.

Raphael's Way

I cannot imagine their conversation, their actions, their manner together. Yet this has absolutely nothing to do with their suitability to each other. They always seemed perfectly content with each other. I never heard them raise a voice, never heard them disagree—a characteristic of family life that was to have odd repercussions since I grew up assuming married people never disagreed about anything. By the time my mother died, short of her ninety-third birthday, she had long made my father, who had died over twenty years earlier, into a heroic figure that none of her later suitors could displace.

Yet Israel Krasne was an immigrant who grew up in a rough area of New York, didn't finish high school, swam in the East River and slept on the fire escape in summer. By the time of the 1910 census he had already lied about his age, claiming he was 17 when he was actually 14, and had been out of school for a year so he could work full-time, like his step-brothers. More basically, he was never seen to read more than newspapers and *The Reader's Digest*, while Hannah Goldstein grew up in a brownstone with a library, had a subscription to the Philadelphia Orchestra, and was never without a book. The relationship was a triumph for Clara, the family matchmaker.

Of my four grandparents, only one emerges as a rounded character. Charles (Redcheeks) Krasne died when my father was only ten. My paternal grandmother I can recall seeing only once, though this can hardly be accurate. In my picture of her she is an old woman who does not speak English, at least not when she was surrounded by her children. To my childhood eyes she resembled the old crone in *Hansel and Gretel*, and was as much an object of fear. On the other hand, my maternal grandmother was a smiling, gentle, round lady who wore old fashioned dresses and spoke softly in kind tones, but died before I could register her existence as a person separate from the entire experience of traveling to Atlantic City and staying in a hotel.

A DANGEROUS THING

Which leaves Raphael Goldstein, my mother's father. To my sister and me, he was an awe-inspiring figure. His strong views, like his goatee, bristled. Perhaps we would have paid closer attention, observing his ways more carefully if we'd understood how so much of what our mother thought and did was part of her ongoing reaction to Grandpa Goldstein's program for family life. He had the odd effect of making our parents appear laissez-faire about our upbringing. We did not look forward to his visits, the tone of which was set by his first scratchy kiss.

Raphael Goldstein, my mother's father, came to America in 1890, traveling under false pretenses, having received on 6 July 1890 from the Prefect of the County of Vaslui a permit to travel in Europe for eleven months. The document, in Rumanian and French, referring to him as Rafail Goldstain and Rafail Goldschtein, respectively, lists his domicile as Vaslui, a city on the Barladul River in northwestern Moldavia, in the name of His Majesty Carol, King of Rumania. The paper describes his face as white and beardless, with brown eyes, and his age as 17.

Rumania was a Francophile country, which accounts for Raphael's documents being in Rumanian and French, a place Europeans described as a Latin island surrounded by a Slavic sea. Its history, though not for Jews, sometimes took on the character of a comic opera. After King Carol died in 1914 without heirs, the Rumanians imported a German prince with a Spanish name, Ferdinand, who didn't speak Rumanian. He married a granddaughter of Queen Victoria's; Ferdinand and Mary proceeded to produce one playboy son, Carol II, destined to be the last king of Rumania, swept away by revolution and war. Rumania also has the dubious fame of having been dubbed by Hannah Arendt "the most anti-Semitic country in prewar Europe," with good reason. The Rumanians didn't wait for Hitler to arrive; without any outside assistance, their own Iron Guard had already murdered 300,000 Jews by the summer of 1942. It couldn't have been a much kinder,

52

Raphael's Way

gentler place in the late nineteenth century when Raphael made his way out.

Raphael's travel document states he was sponsored by one Avram Gruber. Whether this sponsorship meant Gruber had to post a bond, and whether he lost that bond when Raphael took off for America, only to return several years later to collect a bride, is a mystery of the old system. In any event, by the time Raphael returned, he had the means to repay Gruber for the freedom he had bought him.

Exit papers in hand, Raphael came halfway across the world, and he came alone. A cousin found work for him in a shirt factory in New York City and, though working all day in the factory, at night he attended school and learned English. Perhaps because he came alone as a young man, without the family crises that were part of Krasne baggage, Raphael was able to nurture a broader image of success: he would be a man of business, but business would be his means to become a cultured gentleman.

It was a period when the Board of Education offered classes almost nightly in the public schools for the thousands of immigrants who desperately wanted to learn English, even after a fourteen-hour day in a shirt factory. Many who started these classes became discouraged and gave up, leaving only the most determined to struggle on, even bringing books onto the factory floor where they read during their brief lunch break. As the narrator of Cahan's novel observes, "The ghetto rang with a clamor for knowledge."

For a person in quest of self-education, New York City at the end of the nineteenth century presented endless opportunities. Every group that formed—the Workmen's Circle, the Educational Alliance, the William Morris Club, the People's Institute at Cooper Union—advertised lectures, as did every political group on the spectrum: Zionists, Socialists, Bundists. The idea of education for workers had come to England along with the Industrial

53

A DANGEROUS THING

Revolution, and then jumped across to the continent along with the factory system. Surprisingly, such education was not intended to be vocational preparation but took Western Civilization as its subject: philosophy and art, literature and history were covered, as speakers addressed political, social, and cultural topics.

If Raphael had come to America determined to earn his way and get an education, he was at the heart of a large movement. As Irving Howe points out in *World Of Our Fathers*,

> All through the late nineteenth and early twentieth century, learning came to seem an almost magical solution for the Jews, a people that had always placed an enormous faith in the sheer power of words. Learning in its own right, learning for the sake of future generations, learning for the social revolution, learning in behalf of Jewish renewal—all melted into one upsurge of self-discovery.

At the same time, Howe describes the horrendous impact the dislocation from Europe to the lower east side of America had on immigrants, the move from rural to urban setting, from agricultural to industrial society: "the sudden crowding of pauperized or proletarianized human beings into ghastly slums and their subjection to inhuman conditions of work [was a] cataclysm that leaves people broken, stunned, helpless…." These were not circumstances conducive to study at night after a fourteen-hour day in a factory, but Raphael persisted. He was a serious young man intent on making something of himself, interested in books, self-educated, always dressed impeccably for the business career he was prepared to strive toward.

He did not lose his way; rather, he caught an essential spirit of the new world as Howe describes it: "it was a social world in which no one quite knew where he stood and which even raised the sub-

54

Raphael's Way

versive possibility that where a man stood was open to his own definition." What followed on Raphael's part were a series of unusual moves, not at all typical of his fellow garment workers. For many Jewish immigrants, the dream was to be independent by owning a shop or becoming a small trader in a particular line of goods. Shopkeepers were heirs of their European peddler forbears, but more importantly, as Nathan Glazer points out, by putting himself beyond the reach of corporate bureaucracies, a worker avoided "getting into a situation where discrimination may seriously affect him…." By owning his own business, a worker put himself where "he is not dependent on the good will or personal reaction of a person who may not happen to like Jews." Becoming a shopkeeper was not for Raphael.

With his diploma in hand he went to work, first as an agent then as a manager, and finally a General Manager at the Metropolitan Life Insurance company. Working for an insurance company was an unusual job for a Jewish immigrant. As late as 1955, when I graduated from college and went to work as an "editor" for the Equitable Life Assurance Company, I never came across another Jewish person there. I made a number of good friends at that first job, but the majority were Catholics, as though the hierarchical structure of a large American company reflected the hierarchical religious structure with which employees were already familiar. Nevertheless, in half a dozen years Raphael established himself: arrived in this country, learned English, received a high school degree, found employment, and then returned to Rumania to find a wife. The woman he married and carried off to America was named Anna Donner, the kind, gentle, capable daughter of Mendel Donner. When Raphael came back to America with Anna, they set up house in Brooklyn, again an unlikely choice.

❖ ❖ ❖

55

A DANGEROUS THING

Throughout the nineteenth century Brooklyn was one of the country's largest cities, helped to a great extent by its port. To call Brooklyn the first suburb of Manhattan is a misnomer, since that was merely the name of one of the five Dutch towns that made up Kings County (Brooklyn, Bushwick, Flatbush, Flatlands, New Utrecht) along with one English town (Gravesend). These towns, and the rest of Long Island that lay beyond, were reached by ferry, which after 1814 was a steamboat service. With this service, the county saw a housing burst after the Civil War, followed by the huge development that came with the opening of the Brooklyn Bridge in 1883. The bridge included two cable roads where cars were pulled by great steam-powered cables. These cable roads were separated by a walkway. After the opening of the bridge, the population of the county rose to over 700,000. The city across the water had cobblestone streets and a thriving downtown, plus enough residential development for it to be nicknamed 'the borough of homes and churches' when it became part of the City of Greater New York in 1898.

Churches it may have had, but Jews were just beginning to migrate across the water to new communities being established in Williamsburg, and further out in Brownsville. Howe quotes a description of a turn of the century Sunday outing by a group who took "the Grand Street ferry to Williamsburg, and then the horse car to Prospect Park. It was a long ride through sparsely populated sections with views of beautiful cottages and wide lawns with flowers...." In typical fashion, Raphael arrived on the scene before other Jews and, in any event, settled in a completely non-Jewish area. On June 9, 1900 the census takers reached the Fifth Avenue building in the 8th ward of the Borough of Brooklyn where the Goldsteins lived. They recorded that the inhabitants were Raphael, age 26, his wife Anna, age 25, a daughter Jessie, age 2 years and nine months, and a daughter Hanchin (as my mother was apparently named) nine months old, and they

56

Raphael's Way

had a boarder, one Mary Mullholland, a 59 year old widow with no children.

Mary Mullholland, the mysterious boarder, could have been a family servant, though my mother always referred to the people her parents employed as "girls." Considering what the census tract reveals about the neighbors, she sounds more like their entrée to the neighborhood. Everyone on their Fifth Avenue block was a laborer from an English-speaking place, with the exception of one Scandinavian family. There are no Eastern Europeans, no people speaking strange foreign tongues, and definitely no Jews to be found on Brooklyn's Fifth Avenue. Though none of the Goldsteins ever associated him or her self with Brooklyn, that's where all the children were born, first the two girls: Jessie and Hannah, and then two boys, Morris and Raymond.

Whereas Raphael was tall, slender, elegant with a goatee and sparkling white shirts, Anna was short and plump. While he was stern and determined, she was sweet and gentle. For him, business principles and standards would always govern; for her, people came first.

In a surprising move, the Metropolitan Life Insurance Company sent Raphael and his family off to Cincinnati. Its position on the Ohio River, where barges and steamboats connected with the Mississippi river ports and eight rail lines serviced the city, made it a hub for movement of goods. The family, meaning Raphael, might have hoped for the best. Named after an ancient Roman named Cincinnatus, the city was already the sixth largest in America by the mid-nineteenth century. It had a huge Music Hall, completed in 1878, a symphony orchestra founded in 1895, and Hebrew Union College, indicating a sizable Jewish population, founded in 1875.

But nothing turned out the way this travel brochure might have made them expect. In the late nineteenth century the city had been known for pork production and its by-products, including a famous

A DANGEROUS THING

stench that Trollope, the English author, never forgot, describing it as "a stench that surpassed in offensiveness anything that my nose had ever hitherto suffered: the odor of hogs going up to the Ohio heaven." Proctor & Gamble arrived on the scene to process the waste products and hog processing was in time replaced by iron and steel manufacturing, setting the city on a path to what is now dubbed the rust belt. Industry made the city the first destination for people scrabbling out of Appalachia, just across the wide Ohio River, and attracted a vast influx of Germans, who built churches, schools, and raucous beer gardens. There were so many Germans that for a period German was the language in which school was conducted

Even Rabbi Mayer Wise, who rallied support for Hebrew Union College, would have stood out as an ambiguous figure to a man like Raphael Goldstein. The changes in religious practice Wise was willing to accept as the price of Americanization produced the Reform Jewish, or all English movement. This was not for Raphael. Hebrew, chanted in his deep baritone voice, was his language of religious ritual. Yet paradoxically, Raphael's own intense Americanizations sowed secular seeds he could not foresee.

It didn't take more than a brief stint in the interior of the country for Raphael to decide he had to get back east. It was bad enough being a Jew in an almost entirely gentile company, but to be sent into a life totally out of reach of the people and culture he thought appropriate for his family—and he was a man with firm standards—was a double blow.

❂ ❂ ❂

The next posting was Philadelphia. The city of Benjamin Franklin, the city of Quakers, the city along the Schuylkill River turned out to be a congenial place for the family. People generally think Philadelphia went to sleep after the Continental Congress put it on the world map, but it has always been up there among the top five

Raphael's Way

American cities. The brands that made their home in Philadelphia were a role call of American business history: Stetson Hats, Philco Radios, Breyer's Ice cream. Michael R. Haines reminds us in an essay for a collection on the social history of Philadelphia that "it was the second largest urban area in the United States in 1880, [and] one of the early centers of industrialization and immigration." The economy of the city was spurred on by the influx of the major groups: Germans, Irish, and Blacks. When W. E. Dubois wrote *The Philadelphia Negro*, he used the city for the first study of an American black community.

Here Raphael could purchase a brownstone at 4148 Leidy Avenue, near Fairmont Park and the river where oarsmen raced their shells. He could keep a car and chauffeur and practice his religion. Though he never learned to drive, he was never without a car and chauffeur, a four-door black Packard, with the size and solidity of a small tank, chauffeured by Mac, the Negro driver who years later Raphael sent around to take the grandchildren, my Philadelphia cousins, to the doctor when they were sick.

Philadelphia was not only the place my mother grew up, it was the place where her sister and brothers married and raised their families. In other words, Philadelphia was the place we always assumed our mother, along with our Goldstein aunts, uncles, and cousins, who all spoke with the same odd accent, came from. Since everyone else's families seemed to have sprung out of the lower east side or The Bronx, Philadelphia had an exotic ring to it, as though it were a classy suburb of New York City, a stop on the way south to Palm Beach. It came as a shock many years later, when my mother asked us to get a copy of her birth certificate, to learn that the Philadelphia clan had actually gotten its start in Brooklyn. Of course, by then we could not picture Brooklyn as the pioneer country of my grandfather.

The brownstone in which my mother grew up was situated in the Parkside neighborhood, which, according to my mother's version, was just becoming an area where Jews were beginning to live when the Goldsteins moved back east. "Sour cream?" the dairyman wanted to know, "You want to buy sour cream?" was his response to Anna's request. She could not make clear to him the nature of this exotic food. "Mrs. Goldstein, you think I sell my customers sour cream?" The dairyman was insulted. To get the sour cream Anna used in her Rumanian-Jewish style cooking (never combined with meat, of course) she had, my mother told me, to go to the part of the city where Jewish immigrants had first settled. The house that Raphael purchased had three stories and was only a block away from the grand establishments facing Fairmont Park, near where the Schuykill River takes a bend under the Girard Avenue Bridge.

This was typical of Raphael who, even though he practiced his religion, was firmly committed to a particular way the family should live. Raphael and Anna may have taken it for granted that the family kept a kosher kitchen, observed religious holidays, for which he could perform the Hebrew services in his deep voice, yet Raphael was used to moving in a wider circle that brought him in contact with more of mainstream America and he made sure life in their brownstone was a mirror image of turn of the century middle class (read WASP) existence. He was raising a family in the twentieth century, but he was the perfect model of the nineteenth century paterfamilias, the martinet described in so much writing of that period, and he set the tone. Home was more Jewish than WASP, but more Victorian than either: decorum, propriety, culture were his governing principles.

Shortly after the family moved to Philadelphia, the glamorous Leopold Stokowski arrived on the scene in 1912, took an apartment on Rittenhouse Square, and set about transforming the nascent orchestra into the soon to be famous Philadelphia Orchestra. As a sign of its cultural pretensions, the city had put up the elegant Academy of Music in 1857, a building still much in use. In the era

Raphael's Way

before radio and recordings, the orchestra was the single most significant representation of culture, and the flashy Stokowski was determined to put the orchestra, and thus the city, on the international cultural map. Among the plans Stokowski implemented were his concerts for young adults and his children's concerts…just what Raphael wanted for his family. It didn't hurt either that Stokowski's musical crusade for the city had a strong Eastern European character. Raphael's conditioning did not include learning to play an instrument, a somewhat frivolous and possibly unladylike activity, but it made my mother assume a living room had to include a Steinway grand piano.

Raphael's views on the way life should be conducted extended into unusual corners of family activity. Young women were never to walk down the street swinging their arms or sit with crossed legs; good posture was a necessity; a young woman should be dressed by the best dressmaker the family could afford, and if she was not concerned about such matters, she should be (the extra emphasis was aimed at his daughter Jessie, who did not find much to interest her in the work of dressmakers); men were never to appear in public without long sleeve shirts no matter how hot the weather was; men should go to college while women should most certainly not go to college. His words were family law. Whatever Anna might think, she was not one to oppose him on policy issues.

The result of his education dictum was that, to his bitter disappointment, both his sons chose business over college, while the one scholarly child, his daughter Jessie, was prevented from continuing her education. It is only fair to note that science was on Raphael's side. With the advent of women's colleges in the latter part of the nineteenth century—first Mount Holyoke, then Vassar, followed by their sister schools—scientists had involved themselves in the debate about how much education was healthy for women. Not too much, was their conclusion. Higher education unfitted a woman for her divinely ordained role as mother because

A DANGEROUS THING

it sent blood from the womb to the head. Higher education was not called that for no reason: it went higher. Therefore women had a choice: they could try for marriage and a family, or they could make themselves into freaks by pursuing a college degree.

The college woman was as much a stock comic character in literature and cartoons as the bloomer girl. When Amelia Bloomer, the suffragist, in the latter part of the nineteenth century advocated women wear a costume consisting of loose trousers gathered at the ankle under a short skirt so they could ride bicycles, she left herself open to ridicule on all sides. Bicycles were the latest in conveyances, and the bicycle offered women a new freedom of motion. A woman who knew how to ride a bicycle, who had access to a bicycle, had an ability to get around on her own that was unprecedented. Before the bicycle, women were dependent for transportation on those who owned the means of transportation, whether carriages or cars. Not surprisingly, this new freedom met with serious opposition, of which cartoons are a small measure, and Raphael, with his rigorous standards for proper behavior, would not have his daughters wearing bloomers or riding bicycles any more than he would allow them to attend college. They had to satisfy themselves with ice-skating, one of the acceptable ways in which young people amused themselves in coed gatherings.

College, bicycles, bloomers, ballots, these were all ways in which a woman could show herself to be eccentric. Jessie was not quite eccentric, not a rebel, but in her family a borderline case. She and Hannah differed on most counts of what mattered to each of them. Jessie was happy to spend all her time reading. While Jessie was most content in the front parlor library, with its potted palms, Hannah was always eager to go off with her father to the dressmaker, where he was the one in charge of selecting the clothing that was made for the family, and Hannah was even happier to meet her brother's friends. She understood the distinct social advantage of having a pair of brothers not averse to fun.

62

Raphael's Way

This was the tenor of Hannah's tale, as though she were a Jewish Philadelphia debutante, the princess-in-waiting for the prince, putting her time to good use perfecting her taste in wardrobe design. It was the reigning image, until a 1920 census report revealed startling facts. Jessie was 21, Hannah 20 and both were working. Jessie was a librarian at the West Philadelphia Public Library. That Jessie had found a place for herself surrounded by books was singularly appropriate, especially since she was prevented from attending college but would not marry for another thirteen years. Hannah was a telephone operator.

My mother the telephone operator? The revelation of this totally unknown part of Hannah's life made everyone in our family pause. We could not decide which was more surprising, that she worked as a telephone operator or that she had never told anyone about this part of her life. Why was this an activity she never mentioned? This line of inquiry opened a fund of possibilities: was it her father's or her utilitarian nature to seek work like that? What were her alternatives? Was her job front-line technology for women, because I know that the original operators were men, just as they were the first typists and stenographers? What kind of test did she have to take to obtain a job like that, from what age did she work, and exactly what was her job? More fundamentally, how is this employment related to the critical edge in her voice when she explains how her father would not send women to college? She always talked about Jessie being done out of a college education, but perhaps she too would have preferred college to the telephone company.

The questions piled up as I tried to envision my mother in this new role. I pictured my Grandfather having a special working-woman wardrobe made for the sisters: skirts and blouses, 'separates,' which came in with female office workers. Then I can't help running fast forward to her nineties, when Hannah is made uneasy by answering machines and vanquished by portable phones with

A DANGEROUS THING

programmable numbers. Finally, the significance of the promise Israel made to Raphael Goldstein about the future life of his daughter, "She will never have to work a day in her life," a promise my mother always mentioned as though it occupied a key position in her mythic vision of herself, took on several new meanings.

Then, too, there is that story about the sour cream, because it turns out from the census record that the Goldsteins may have been the only Rumanians on the block, but were certainly not the only Jews. The rest of the inhabitants, the adults that is, were from Russia and their language was Yiddish, like the maid in the Goldstein household, which leads one to believe they were all Jewish. Perhaps the neighborhood was undergoing change, but by 1920 it was more intensely Jewish than neighborhoods in New York City, like the Brooklyn street where the Goldsteins started out or the Harlem block where the Krasnes lived, ever were. With every small increment of research, it became increasingly difficult to unweave the threads of truth from the fabric of my mother's tales.

❋ ❋ ❋

Apparently, about each one in the family my mother built her own mythic story, like characters in a medieval morality play. There was Jessie-the-Studious, Morris-the-Cautious, and Raymond-the-Bold. In each of her portrayals there was an essence of truth. Raymond, for instance, the baby in the family, was adventurous. He ran off to enlist in World War I when he was still in his teens and learned to fly by lying about his age. In 1919, at the age of 16, he was already a pilot, a Lieutenant in what was then called the U.S. Air Corps. What could his father say, after the usual arguments, since he himself had come half way around the world on his own at the same age and fought his way up in a strange land while learning a new language. Raymond had a way of setting examples that caused constant contentions, pitting him in defiance of Raphael's governance.

Raymond Goldstein, Lieutenant. U.S. Army Air Corps. 1919.

His biggest blowup came with Raymond's announcement that he wanted to marry.

Raphael expected his sons to attend college, but Raymond had already slipped the bonds of the house on Leidy Avenue when he went off to World War I and there was no going back to his childhood life. He had found a woman, which meant he had to find a means of support. There would be no college.

The woman with whom he fell in love, Jeanne, came from a family where the mother's views on education for women were

A DANGEROUS THING

more advanced and held more weight than any views Anna Goldstein might have harbored or Raphael would tolerate, so Jeanne had started attending the University of Pennsylvania. But the ever-impetuous Raymond swept her off her feet and that was the end of higher education for the two of them. A year after my mother was married, in defiance of Raphael, Raymond set off on the adventure of marriage, the youngest in the family but the first to have children.

To support a family, Raymond went into business with his father-in-law, but years later, when he was a successful business-man with two children, Joyce and Gilbert, no one could hold back his spirit of adventure. As soon as the Japanese bombed Pearl Harbor, he applied to Washington to help build an Air Force. He told the family the war would be long and there would be great shortages, so before he left he put a new roof on the house, replaced the refrigerator, stocked up the cupboards, and then was off for the duration.

In honor of Raymond's departure for the war, members of his Green Valley Country Club sold a record $9,000,000 of war bonds. From Florida, where he was first sent, his tour of duty took him to India, Egypt, Tunisia, Malta, Sicily, England, France, and Germany. In 1943, on the occasion of his son's thirteenth birthday, he wrote Gilbert a four-page letter "from distant lands and over the majority of the Seven Seas..." pointing out the "strange paradox that as I write with so much love in my heart, I wear a gun and canteen, with a gas mask and helmet by my side." The letter, probably written from "Somewhere in Africa," was read aloud by Rabbi Simon Greenberg (later to become head of Jewish Theological Seminary in New York) in lieu of a homily at Gilbert's Bar Mitzvah, causing an emotional wave to wash over the filled synagogue as Raymond told his son "The knowledge of your love and companionship has been to me like a trumpet in the sky. I know you can hear the roaring of my heart as I hold you close." Raphael Goldstein must have been

Raphael's Way

Lt. Col. Raymond Goldstein, c. 1944.

particularly struck by the passage where his errant son wrote to his grandson, "Complete your education and graduate from a university which you, Mother and I, shall choose."

Uncle Raymond was the only person our family knew directly who was fighting in the war. My father found a pair of the first small portable radios and shipped one off, hoping it would eventually catch up to him. When his sister Jessie wrote asking about Passover in 1944, Raymond wrote back from England on April 10th:

> "For those holidays we were out hush-hush—no tents, just sleeping bags on the ground & the sky above—rain pouring down thru the night—eating K-

A DANGEROUS THING

rations, C-rations and sundry other distasteful types. But we practically observed Pesach, there wasn't any bread any way; and we only had hard biscuits. And in all the desolation and mud of the surroundings, a courier brought me a mail package, and in it was a portable R.C.A. radio set, which Hannah and Issie sent. Can you visualize and imagine the delight and cheer brought by such a gift. All I had to do was open it, and immediately it started to play."

None of us knew, of course, that when he wrote from London that "activity is accelerating in its momentum, and the atmosphere is tense. Everyone is grim, you do not hear any jokes, and individuals seem to have lost that gift of laughter," that it was the planning he was involved in for D-Day to which he was referring.

As little children we followed his exploits as he moved about the world, and finally on to the "little red school-house" in Reims, France, "where the negotiations were carried on, and the surrender papers signed....After the news had been broadcast from here to all the world, we had several military receptions with General Eisenhower...."

What our parents did not share with us were the parts of those letters, like the one written 25 April 1945, in which he described the

terrible atrocities inflicted by the Germans. Their agonizing tortures and savagery is greater than anyone can ever bear to see, let alone endure. Our armies have found thousands of bodies, still smoldering after being burned alive. And all in the grotesque positions of agonizing death. The rescued Allies, are so emaciated and gaunt that many can not be evacuated till medical treatment and nourishment. They had systematic torture & starvation inflicted upon them....

Raphael's Way

Yet at the end of every letter he sent cheerful greetings, hopes for peace, regards to the children, and his fervent wish to soon be home again.

With such an adventurous and charming brother, it was no wonder Hannah worshipped him, even though he was younger, and watched carefully how he dealt with the stern rule of their father.

❀ ❀ ❀

Exactly opposite from Raymond-the-Bold, when Morris-the-Cautious fell in love, Raphael made it clear he had to build a business to the point where it could support a family comfortably before he could marry, so instead of college he too went to work, but building his own business. Though he was the older brother, he labored on, only marrying and starting a family after a lengthy engagement, long after his younger brother already had two children. The long engagement, the children—Martin and Arnold—born decades after his younger brother's, took their toll on the family relationship. Years later Morris rarely mentioned his father. His wife, Nettie, viewed Raphael as a medieval tyrant during those long years when she was almost but not quite a member of the family. Her memory of life at the house on Leidy Avenue was summarized by the description she gave of how everyone had to be seated and silent when Raphael appeared for dinner. The scene is so quintessentially nineteenth century it could be a reenactment from the childhood memories of Elizabeth Barrett (Browning) and Virginia Stephen (Woolf).

Jessie-the-Studious was the last to leave home. In her disregard for superficial social engagements, her attraction to the intellectual life, though cut off from higher education, she showed little interest in finding a husband. After the other children were married, Raphael sold the three-story house and moved to the Pine Vista

A Dangerous Thing

Jessie Goldstein and Mortimer Cohen, c. 1933.

Apartments nearby. Eventually, when Jessie was in her mid-thirties, Raphael brought home a fellow manager from Metropolitan Life, a serious, steady, older gentleman named Mortimer Cohen. It was the only spouse Raphael had a hand in choosing for his children, and the only marriage of which he completely approved. Mortimer and Jessie were married at 4:00 P.M. on Sunday, July 2, 1933, at the Ritz-Carlton in Philadelphia, almost ten years after Hannah made off to New York. In a diary entry from her honeymoon she wrote, "We hate to see our wonderful honeymoon drawing to a close; and the finest thing we can wish each other is that our life together, in its entirety, may be as perfect as its beginning." So Jessie, too, reveled in her escape from under Raphael's roof, though, like her brothers, she settled down nearby in Philadelphia to raise her only child, Lewis. Only Hannah escaped her father's orbit, but she could never escape his influence

Hannah and her brother Raymond looked like their mother,

Raphael's Way

with her round, smiling face surrounded by curly brown hair. But when it came to family standards, all four of the children were inoculated with Raphael's high expectations. In Central Park, my mother once observed a woman hitting a child and she promptly went up to her and informed her "That is no way to take care of a child." The only day in her life she wasn't up and dressed at dawn was the day she died, as the woman who was staying with her at the end remarked in wonder. After she died, we realized that no one in the family had ever heard her complain about anything personal. If she wasn't up to par, she just didn't telephone. Old fashioned words like 'comportment' were not alien to her, as though Raphael's ideas about how a woman was to walk, to sit, and to stand had become part of her blood and bone.

Perhaps the children took after their father because Anna was always occupied with household matters, which left Jessie and Hannah to figure out on their own anything that a young woman needed to know about her body. Anna was too old fashioned to tell her daughters things that had to do with their physical development. Fortunately for Hannah, Jessie somehow managed to get her hands on information, so she could explain to her younger sister such unexpected surprises as menstruation. Hannah never figured out how Jessie came by such esoteric information, but she understood it was typical of her sister, for whom fashion and flirting were not worthwhile activities. Knowledge was Jessie's priority…and college would have been her rightful place.

My mother was an insomniac. No matter what time of night I woke up, if I wandered into the living room I could find her sitting in one of the easy chairs on either side of the fake fireplace, reading a recent novel from the local lending library. It was at times like those that she was most likely to come up with stories about her childhood. In these anecdotes her mother was a relatively minor figure. She was presented as a wonderful housekeeper who, with a maid to help her, filled the basement pantry shelves with home-

71

A Dangerous Thing

made foods: preserves and pickles, herring and eggplant salad. She came across in these stories as a kind, good-tempered woman. But my mother's tone of admiration was saved for her father. It was when she spoke of Raphael that I sensed uneasily what Hannah Goldstein Krasne valued, the things she appreciated. What I did not grasp in these stories when I was young was the extent to which her character had been formed by my grandfather, so that she was either fighting against or modeling herself after that stern figure we viewed as quite outside the smooth tenor of our lives.

Morris Goldstein, August, 1949.

Chapter Five

PHILADELPHIA
VS. NEW YORK

ALTHOUGH I KNOW FROM MY DAYS AS A SCIENCE MAJOR that evolution is a long-term affair, the drive of the Krasne clan to find spouses and reproduce has a certain Darwinian cast to it. Their lives had been interrupted by immigration and the hardships of starting over in a foreign land, but by the time they were ready to find spouses, the family was financially secure. Their choices of husbands and wives were a kind of social exogamy in which they sought out people who embodied different aspects of contemporary cultural life.

Back in eighteenth century England, when the novel had its beginnings, and essayists such as Addison and Steele were popular, the goal of much writing was to let the middle class know how they should behave, what was proper in the way of customs, attitudes, and actions. It was a literature for and about a new, rising, self-made society. A writer such as Samuel Richardson might spice up his stories, like *Pamela: or, Virtue Rewarded*, so they appeared to be tales of seduction, but he was writing for people like himself, people who had worked their way up in the business world and wanted to know how to behave now that they had more or less arrived.

74

Philadelphia vs. New York

By applying himself industriously—which included marrying the boss's daughter—Richardson became a master tradesman, respected as a leader in the printing business. At the request of his fellow printers, who knew a good market when they spotted one, he started out writing by composing a set of form letters as models for people lacking social savoir faire: "How To Think And Act Justly And Prudently In The Common Concerns Of Life." His audience was the growing middle class hungry for instruction that would give them entrée to a greater sphere of action, a group not unlike Howe's summary of culture among turn of the century Jewish immigrants in America: "Richer in morals than manners, stronger in ideas than amenities, the world of immigrant Jews could not, in any ordinary sense, be called a 'high culture.'"

Immigrants in New York who were financially successful in the first part of the twentieth century had a lot in common with that earlier rising middle class in London, as literature indicates. The eighteenth century emphasis on domestic life in fiction and essays appealed to the new moneyed merchant class in England because, above all, the newly established wanted to know what constituted good taste and to avoid being made ludicrous by being labeled vulgar. As William M. Sale Jr. points out in his introduction to *Pamela*, "Among those whose culture is not commensurate with their new-found prosperity, education of one sort or another is always in demand...." Fast-forwarding to the nineteen twenties, it is not necessary to read up on polite morals and manners. An immigrant merchant class could seek out and marry people who knew how to employ the services of experts, experts whose function it was to avoid the appearance of being nouveau riche.

Whether it was interior décor, clothes, or jewelry, there were experts who could make sure households demonstrated what was considered good taste in early twentieth century New York City. On that memorable 1936 trip to Europe that my uncle Archie Shapera chronicled, Mary Krasne, my uncle Abe's wife, showed

75

A DANGEROUS THING

she knew exactly what was called for. Archie's journal takes special note of how "Mary was the leader, and the way she could find smart little shops in out of the way streets was nothing less than miraculous, so we called her 'Eagle Eye,' and for the rest of the trip she proved worthy of that name."

Perhaps not so coincidentally it is to eighteenth century England that the American middle class turns in the 1920's for its models of taste. It was the first, some might say only, great era of English design. The preeminent eighteenth century English craftsmen, Robert Adams, Thomas Chippendale, George Hepplewhite, Thomas Sheraton, were the craftsmen whose styles of tables, chairs, and mirrors filled the houses of the Krasnes.

It was a style that had been perfected for the great houses of the English aristocracy and quickly copied for the rising middle class, those eager to hide their origins 'in trade.' Even the chinoiserie of eighteenth century decorative objects was imitated in homes of the American bourgeoisie: Chinese horses, vases, bowls, lamps, ivory figures, jade clocks decorated mantels and side tables. In pre-World War II living rooms and dining rooms of New York apartments, this English style furniture, substantial in construction and size yet delicate in carving and finishes, made a statement. It would be as hard to imagine these Central Park West apartments furnished in Louis XIV as it would to picture the Krasnes surrounded by English country chintz. The decorators employed by these latter day burghers knew what was wanted: eighteenth century English style.

In seeking out marriage partners who could bring about transformations that would transmute wealth into statements of taste, there were a number of ground rules. At the top of the list was that matches had to be made within religious groups. Protestants married Protestants, a large market in those days, but above all, Catholics married Catholics and Jews married Jews, not such large markets because the marriage market was complicated further by geography and class. Just as there were shanty Irish and lace cur-

Philadelphia vs. New York

tain Irish, Jews came in different denominations. There were Sephardim and Ashkenazim, but within this group there were subdivisions: Litvaks (from the area encompassing Lithuania) and Galitsyanos (from Galicia, an area that took in south eastern Poland and north western Ukraine).

Howe tells of a Jewish reporter trying to look into the operations of marriage brokers who was told "I have Galician, Russian and American girls." The parents of a friend of ours came from Greece, which meant they were Sephardic. When his father died, his mother married another man from Greece, another Sephardic Jew, a man who was familiar with Ladino, the language they spoke, and spanikopita and taramasalata, the foods they ate. After all, it was through their common acquaintances that she could meet a marriage prospect.

Among Jewish immigrants there were three further divisions. Those who had come here as socialists often became active in the labor movement or became academics. Those who had come as orthodox religious observers and remained untainted by the new ways they encountered in America spent their time avoiding secular ruin. And then there were the business people. One of the women with whom I taught had come from a family of socialists, free thinkers. When she was growing up dinnertime was filled with table-thumping debates about the political scene. Every discussion by her family about public events ended with the query, "But what does it mean for the Jews?"

When she told me about her family, I realized politics never made it onto our dinner table agenda. My father would dismiss the subject, and his never voting, by announcing "All politicians are crooks," a more sophisticated observation than any of us realized until Vietnam and Watergate caught up with us. The woman with whom I taught wasn't a bourgeois conformist like me; she was a fighter. While she was in college she met a man who came from a large orthodox family. He was the youngest, and the only one in the

77

A DANGEROUS THING

family who struggled free of orthodoxy to make it out to college and then on to law school. He was judicious in temperament. They married, and years later we went to their daughter's wedding, conducted by a female Rabbi who made a point of explaining that in the marriage contract the young woman and young man had signed—the ketuba—the woman and the man had equal rights to a divorce. My fighting friend's socialist side of the family murmured 'right on' while her judicious husband's orthodox side gasped at the blasphemies this faux-Rabbi was uttering. Neither of these people came from a society with which I was familiar.

Krasnes belonged to the business class: strivers, not intellectuals, socialists, or union activists. They were the synagogue twice-a-year crowd. They maintained membership in a temple so that on Rosh Hashanah and Yom Kippur they could get dressed up and make an appearance to celebrate the New Year. My father agreed to attend on the understanding that my mother reserved seats near the rear side door, which was kept open in those hot early fall days. His positioning himself for a quick getaway strongly suggested a lack of serious involvement, like the father I knew who claimed he could never attend synagogue for the High Holy Days because he was allergic to camphor, the preservative used to store winter woolens over the summer, clothes just taken out of storage in time for the Jewish holidays. The rest of the year, for the merchant class life was about business, in other words, money. Though they might, on a case by case basis, be charitable, they were not inspired by what Morris Dickstein terms "ingrained Jewish notions of social justice" or moved by "egalitarian idealism," another public spirited sense with which he credits Jews.

Contrary to ideas that may have come down to us from such tales as *Romeo and Juliet*, our ancestors, by and large, did not marry young. For one thing, since children in the labor force were a key source of additional family support, researchers have shown that young men and women "typically would enter the work force and

Philadelphia vs. New York

contribute to a family income for about seven years…" before becoming a head of household in their own right. Abe, the oldest of the Krasnes, was 30 when his wife gave birth to a daughter, Estelle. Shortly later, when she died, he promptly caused a stir by marrying an 18-year-old secretary in his office, and starting another family, but he was getting on; time was more important than money.

The matchmaker in the Krasne family was Clara, the older sister, the stepsister, the Dairylady. As one of the eldest in the Krasne family, Clara was one of the first to marry. Her husband was an insurance broker and they took up residence in Philadelphia. Clara's half-sister Florence married a dentist, Archibald Shapera, the first professional person in the family, a man interested in the arts who was disconcerted by the overwhelmingly bourgeois values of the family into which he had married, at the same time as he was intimidated by their money. In his autobiography, *The Kid Stays In The Picture*, a book that has been described as a "camp classic," my cousin Bobby Evans, the movie mogul (né Robert Shapera) wrote, "my mother's family rolled in green, but was empty on education" and claims of his uncles "The five brothers shared one thought: their beautiful sister, Florence, had married beneath her. How could she compromise, marrying a dentist—in Harlem, no less?" Bobby was more right than he knew when it came to education.

If Israel Krasne was a man of few words, it should come as no surprise to anyone able to count. He was nine when he left Russia, ten when he arrived in New York, speaking only the English he was able to pick up hanging around Liverpool while the family waited to ship out, and then what he heard on board the steamship. By 1910 he was already out of school a year, following his older stepbrothers who got to work immediately. Thus three years of American schooling and many more years of knocking about the world conditioned how Israel understood and reacted to what life brought his way. His lack of education made him hang back from becoming a naturalized citizen until 1929.

A Dangerous Thing

Julius and Essie, Anna, Mary and Abe Krasne.
Wedding photo from Abe's second marriage, January 17, 1924.

Uncle Archie, the one with artistic sensibilities and refined taste, with a degree from Columbia University, the one who felt financially challenged, had sons determined above all to be known as financial success stories. Education was less interesting to them than name recognition and making money. Cousin Bobby lost interest in becoming educated even before high school, lured away by the tantalizing promise of a career in radio and on stage. Charles carried on until after he started college, and then gave it up. The two of them changed their name to Evans and went into business with an Italian men's tailor under the name Evan Picone. From there it was on to movies and shopping centers and more movies, media being the modern version of the old British desire to get out of "trade."

Clara's stepsister Jean married a more religious man, who carried her off to the unsettled depths of New Jersey, from which she

Philadelphia vs. New York

Sam Krasne, 1940s.

seldom reappeared. She was busy giving birth to three sons while her husband was buying up and developing the county. Later, the youngest brother, Samuel, married a delicately pretty young woman whose father was a doctor.

❊ ❊ ❊

Coming from a New York family with five successful, nice looking brothers, Clara put her time to good use in Philadelphia by making it her business to check up on the eligible Jewish young women. She found several candidates, in particular two comfortably off Jewish families with eligible daughters. The families were well off in a different way from her family in New York. Because they had emigrated earlier, they had lead-time in learning language, building a comfortable life, becoming acquainted with mainstream American manners. Philadelphia had given them a larger acquaintance with non-Jews and with the cultural life of this smaller city. The young women were attractive, and therefore popular. Undaunted, Clara brought down her candidates from

A DANGEROUS THING

New York, first her stepbrother Israel and then Benjamin.

Despite the presence of eligible young men from Philadelphia, the New Yorkers made a hit. They were more worldly, having grown up in the rough and tumble of a larger city, had a touch of brash self-assurance because they were older and were running their own successful business, and they were not bad looking. At 5 foot 7, Israel was stocky, with mild light brown eyes, thin lips, a small, straight nose, his black hair already showing small signs of receding from his temples—a hint that he was several years older than Hannah.

Raphael Goldstein was not as impressed as his daughter. For one thing, he may not have gone as far as Elizabeth Barrett Browning's father, who forbade any of his children to marry, but he certainly presented obstacles in every case: Raymond, he argued, was far too young to marry; Morris was told he had to build himself a business before he could consider supporting a family; and what he saw as he got to know Israel was a mismatch. It was obvious to him that this New Yorker was not of the same breed as his own sons and their friends, who made up the circle of his daughters' acquaintance.

He saw this suitor as a man without culture, an immigrant who was not even a naturalized citizen yet. In Raphael's estimation, Israel was a grown man without the easy acquaintance with social graces that he held so important, and he warned his daughter that such a marriage would be a match between unequals. And then there was the problem that Hannah was the younger sister. Her marriage would leave behind an older, unmarried sister, a sister who did not show herself devoted to the kind of social life that led to proposals of marriage.

Hannah felt attracted to this strong, silent New Yorker, who made the smoother young men with whom she was used to ice-skating seem like light weights, like kids. But Raphael raised another consideration. Not only was this young man a stranger, he was from another state, a city with a different way of life. If she

Philadelphia vs. New York

married Israel, it would be like a Chinese marriage where the bride is carried off to become forever after part of her husband's family. She, however, did not take to her couch, as Elizabeth Barrett had done, nor rise from it secretly to run off to another country with her admirer. Instead, she remembered her brother Raymond's various run-ins with their father and how he had ways of escaping from under the parental hand: in the end, he always did what he wanted. Being carried off to New York came to seem like more of a promise than a threat, not unlike Elizabeth Barrett running off to Italy with Robert Browning to escape the family patriarch.

Israel, stung by Raphael Goldstein's reservations, thought only in terms of money and was sure Mr. Goldstein did not believe he could provide appropriately for his daughter. He set to work assuring him that his daughter would be supported in the style to which she was accustomed, would have everything she wanted, and would never have to work a day in her life. This last item became a promise with fateful repercussions in the tale my mother spun. Style, her understanding of what constituted taste, was what she would bring to the marriage, and he would support her in this. But the fabled promise takes on new meaning in the shadow of Hannah the telephone operator.

What was it my mother really wanted? Was Israel's promise directed at appeasing Raphael or wooing her? Does Hannah's absconding to New York reveal a longing to trade Philadelphia's staid provincialism for life in the big city, or is she trying to escape the drudgery of a telephone company job? Her father had made her a creature who believed there was no substitute for good taste, and perhaps she longed for scope to exercise this taste. New York, with a husband earning a comfortable living, could be such a place.

Once Israel showed it was possible to abscond with a bride from Philadelphia to New York, it was easier for his younger brother, Ben, to follow in his footsteps. Clara introduced this tallest, handsomest of the Krasne brothers to the most beautiful young

Jewish woman in Philadelphia. Wherever they went together, people stopped to stare at them as though they were a pair of movie stars. The match was another success story for Clara and it gave some comfort to Raphael and Anna to see the Philadelphia connection in New York reinforced.

After Hannah and Israel were engaged, and her hand was weighted down with a sizable diamond ring, proof of what her suitor had told her father, Israel wanted to get married as soon as possible so he could stop commuting to Philadelphia on courting trips. She said she would marry him right after her birthday, September 6th, which she had to celebrate with her family.

In a picture of the engaged couple taken July 4th, 1924, they are visiting my cousin Estelle, Israel's oldest niece, at Camp Greylock. My uncle had obviously done his homework. He knew that the children of well-to-do city parents went to camp in New England in the summer. The Jewish bourgeoisie did not own second homes on Long Island, summer 'camps' in the Adirondacks, or cottages on various coastal islands. To provide relief from city summers they founded suburban country clubs and sent their children to camp in New England, and among the oldest of these was Greylock. For Hannah, the visit was a window into her new life.

In the snapshot, Hannah is perched on the top of a rustic little bridge where a rowboat is tied up. Israel stands beside her, an arm supporting her on the railing. He is wearing a three-piece wool suit and tie, the vest buttoned. It is the urban businessman's version of summer country-weekend attire. He does not know from white flannel trousers and navy blazers, or plus-fours and tweed jackets, the gentleman's wardrobe of choice for sporting days. His face looks boyish but serious. She, on the other hand, has been to the dressmaker. I can see her specifying she needs a summer frock for a country weekend with her fiancé and his relatives, as she casually shows off her left hand with its sizable diamond engagement ring. In the black and white photo she is thin, made to appear even slimmer by the

Philadelphia vs. New York

Israel Krasne and Hannah Goldstein, Camp Greylock, Massachusetts, July 4, 1924. Engagement trip chaperoned by Mary and Abe Krasne.

white flapper dress, decorated with a long strand of beads. She bends toward him slightly, her arm resting on his shoulder. Her short, curly brown hair surrounds a face with a gay little smile.

Once Hannah took charge of her husband's wardrobe, he sat sweetly by. He was pleased to have a wife who knew when a man needed a new summer suit or when it was time to order more dress shirts. He watched proudly as she fingered the fabric swatches, approving light gray for summer slacks, gray wool herringbone suiting for fall, deciding about the cuffs for his white on white shirts. She was always the one who knew when it was time for the tailor to pay them a visit, or where to buy the best in haberdashery. They may have been his clothes, but he was happy to have her taste decide matters. That was why he had gone to Philadelphia and brought back Raphael Goldstein's daughter.

Immediately after her birthday they were married. In a foretaste of her new existence, although her whole family lived in Philadelphia, she was not married at any of the traditional Philadelphia sights, but at the Astor Hotel in New York. The Astor

A DANGEROUS THING

satisfied Raphael Goldstein's standards because it was a prominent New York hotel that, realizing the potential in New York's Jewish clientele, had installed a kosher kitchen. It was a more sophisticated environment than anything Philadelphia could offer, but not quite up there with the next official hotel photograph: the Bernice Foods annual dinner, a white-tie affair twelve years later in the Grand Ballroom of the Waldorf Astoria.

In a formal picture taken before the wedding, Raphael, in white tie and tails, stands in the back row next to Hannah's two younger brothers, handsome in their tuxedos. He grips the back of the chair in front of him, staring fiercely at the picture taker, defying the photographer to get on with it. There are no toothy grins; not one of the six of them smiles. Seated in the front, my mother has a modestly bored expression, as though she is already a part of a more sophisticated scene. On her dark hair a thin wreath circles the flapper hairstyle and a long strand of pearls wraps around her neck.

The pearls. I wonder if they are a wedding gift from her parents or my father, because the other women in the picture are noticeably naked of jewelry. Her mother, seated next to her, wears neither necklace, earrings, pin, nor bracelet. Her sister, Jessie, the librarian, seated on the other side of Anna, wears a sensible watch with a black band. Is this stark style a characteristic of Philadelphia's Quaker influenced simplicity and my mother's long rope of pearls a harbinger of New York luxury? I have a clear memory of the family jeweler, his visits to consult at home, my mother's trips to his office, but also remember that once when I asked for pearls as a birthday present, my mother informed me my father did not approve of spending money for pearls because there was no way to be sure of their value, yet Hannah always had pearls.

Much about marriage must have come as a surprise to Hannah, since her older sister, who usually had the inside track on intimate knowledge, was still an unmarried librarian. Her mother, Anna, judging by her performance during her daughters' adolescences,

86

Philadelphia vs. New York

Hannah Goldstein wedding photo. Back Row: Raymond, Morris, Raphael. Front Row: Hannah, Anne, Jessie. Astor Hotel, New York, September, 1924.

was not a likely source of information, and Raphael could not possibly speak of personal matters with his daughters. To begin with, birth control was not an issue because Hannah was, by the standards of her day, getting on in years and, as it turned out, it was fertility that would be the problem. But finally, after giving birth to two daughters, she must have acquired key information from her obstetrician; there were no more children. The idea of family planning and its importance to the life of a woman must have made a big impression on her, because as soon as I was engaged she marched me off to a gynecologist to be fitted out with a diaphragm.

In a surviving photograph of the wedding, Hannah stands on the steps of this new life wearing a pearl embroidered white silk flapper dress and a pearl embroidered tiara from which a satin edged tulle veil sweeps down, making a delicate swirl about her feet. She stands alone, composed, no husband holding her arm, no parents or matron of honor surrounding her. She has made her choice. She is moving on, ready for the big city.

A DANGEROUS THING

Widow Mother

Nobody would mistake her
for a bag lady,
itinerants in tennis shoes
sifting our lives curbside
into shopping bags.

I hurry past those
shuffling gray mutes,
content to know she is secured
by our framed bureau top gazes,
to know at least once a day
she takes out her voice
like an old leather shoe
grown stiff in the closet
and tries on its stiffness
for the grocery man, dry cleaner, mailman,
the familiar sounds erupting strangely
into the modulation of words.

Philadelphia vs. New York

This is what they come to,
the years:
a sense of place
as secure as the vault
and under the door
seeping, seeping
the lethal years.

In the end
as it was in the beginning,
you telling me stories:
"The apple never falls far from the tree,"
I remember that one.
Talking, talking,
nothing between us
but blood and your face
and your expectations.
I am the apple falling under the tree,
you were the tree
and now the worm that eats the apple.

The Goldstein family, c. 1940. *Back row:* Mortimer Cohen, Joyce Goldstein, Morris Goldstein, Carol Krasne, Raymond Goldstein. Middle Row: Jessie Cohen, Nettie Goldstein, Jean Goldstein, Hannah Krasne. *Front row:* Lewis Cohen, Gilbert Goldstein holding Martin Goldstein, Betty Krasne. *Photo on mantelpiece:* Raphael and Anna Goldstein.

Anna Krasne and her daughter Florence in matching broadtail coats, c. 1923.

Ben Krasne and his sister Florence, summer 1925.

Krasne women at the beach: Florence, Essie, Mary, Unknown, Clara Abrahms, her daughter Mildred and son Arthur, Belle Krasne, 1928.

Archie and Florence Shapera, Vanderbilt Hotel, Miami Beach, 1941.

Essie and Julius Krasne, Hawaii, 1938, visiting Dole Company plant, posed with pineapple packed for Krasne Bros. Bernice Foods.

Israel, Abe, Rita, Charles Krasne, Central Park, c. 1943.

Part II

LEARNING
ABOUT
LEARNING

Chapter Six

THE EDUCATION OF
A DILETTANTE

BECAUSE DILETTANTES ARE PEOPLE WHO DABBLE IN MANY
things, they are destined to be amateurs at everything. In my
case it was the fine balance struck between home and school that
went into the making of a dilettante.

Take school, for instance.

Fall of fourth grade we made the Acropolis out of Ivory soap.
Everyone was commissioned to come to school with sufficient
cakes to carve Doric and Ionic columns, entablatures and pedi-
ments. Mostly I remember working on columns. This was
wartime, with rationing and scarcities, and ours was not a household in which Ivory soap was to be found outside the kitchen. Since
the kitchen was not the realm of children, the household must have
wondered at these repeated requests for more cakes of Ivory soap.

For the best part of each day at school we clustered around the
paper-mâché mound that Miss Plimpton had contrived to represent the Acropolis and worked at erecting our model of an ancient
civilization. The rest of the time, but about this I am less clear, we
learned multiplication tables and tried to make our fingers form
curvaceously elegant script letters, watching out of the corners of

A DANGEROUS THING

our eyes the place to the right of the blackboard where our embodiment of the classical world was taking shape.

What could spring bring that would match such "learning by doing"? Later that year we made puppets, the kind that are worked from strings attached to movable cross-sticks. We made their heads out of more papier-mâché, their hair from wool (which we also used to knit squares that were in some mysterious way supposed to aid the war effort), their bodies and clothes. Then we wrote and presented a puppet show about the U.S.O. to raise funds for that organization, though I have no recollection of how a room full of fourth graders wrote the show or what in our young and protected lives could have provided a plot line for the script.

How can I remember anything about such activities? How could I forget. This was a progressive school and our teacher had been a student of John Dewey. No doubt these activities were supposed to be part of some major lesson plan, because Dewey specifically distanced himself from activities per se, using words that call to mind the present day child over-dosed on television. He warned educators that

> continually to appeal in childhood days even to the
> principle of interest is eternally to excite, that is
> distract the child. Continuity of activity is destroyed.
> Everything is made play, amusement. This means
> over-stimulation; it means dissipation of energy....
> the reliance is upon external attractions and amuse-
> ments. Everything is sugar coated for the child, and
> he soon learns to turn from everything which is not
> artificially surrounded with diverting circumstances.

Dewey's warning was all too accurate. Whatever the lesson embedded in our fourth grade activities was supposed to be, elementary school is a land of wonderful memories, none of them concerning

The Education of a Dilettante

a body of information that I was supposed to absorb about such basics as spelling and arithmetic.

When our own children were finishing school, after we had lived in the suburbs for over twenty years, we went to look at an apartment in the city, in a building called The Century. Though the ad said "park view," what the apartment actually looked out on was my fifth grade classroom, and what that vista immediately brought to mind was the memory of making illustrated manuscripts to show how a young man became a Knight, because we were studying Feudalism, and that was the year we translated a map of the world into a mural that went around the room by making a grid and enlarging our little map square by square. That was the sum total of geography instruction in all my Ethical Culture years. In other words, at the same time as the shape of the Parthenon was forever committed to memory, about the mysteries of spelling I acquired very little knowledge and was never able to give the sum of several figures without the aid of fingers, or tell where any country might turn up on the globe.

These may not be drawbacks of my education attributable to dear Miss Plimpton of the memorable fourth grade. Perhaps those skills were taught when I was home with the measles or the mumps. But if my mother observed these irregularities in my education, they surely must have given her pause. She was an impeccable speller and could instantly add up a long column of figures upside down while some poor counterman struggled with a chewed up pencil, back in the days when purchases were toted up on the brown paper bag in which they would be carried home. I found this upside-down addition of a long column of figures a feat so freakish that years later I would ask her to demonstrate it for her grandchildren, like a magic trick.

How did we end up in this progressive school when both our parents were the products of public school, where they had learned to count, write, read quite adequately?

95

A Dangerous Thing

We were there because when Hannah Goldstein became a Krasne and moved to New York City she was immediately informed by all the women she met, "In New York no one sends their children to public school." Public school had been good enough for Raphael Goldstein's children, who had done just fine there, so she found this piece of information surprising. She was advised that she had to go around and visit schools before she could choose. The task was less daunting than it first appeared. She immediately eliminated single sex schools. Public schools, where she had been educated, were coed, so the idea of single sex schools struck her as unnatural. Second, she eliminated all the schools that started with Saint…. Of what was left everyone understood that there were schools into which a child might be accepted under special circumstances—a descendent of an old German family, a family name that connoted a famous fortune—and then there were places known to accept Jews. These, it turned out, were generally schools involved with ideas of the Progressive Education movement: Dalton and Ethical Culture, New Lincoln, Birch Wathen, Walden, and further uptown in Riverdale, Horace Mann.

From kindergarten through college, the choice of schools was influenced by a new force in Hannah's life. Raphael, the Philadelphia patriarch, was supplanted by the patriarch of the Krasne clan: the oldest brother, Abe. Abe Krasne had a different view of education from Hannah's father. Since his first three children were girls, this meant education for women. At every stage he pursued the best schools he could find out about, so Hannah's search was simplified. Abe Krasne's example gave her the support she needed when she recommended an elementary school, high school, or college to a husband who didn't think these matters were important.

Her search was moot. There were no children, not the first year, or the second year, or the third year after her marriage. She had been quite old for her day, just turned 26, when she married;

The Education of a Dilettante

after all, her sister-in-law Mary had been 18 when she married and had already produced a child, other sisters-in-law, Florence and Essie, had already produced several children. "She's worried about her figure," they gossiped; "They're saving money," people murmured. What she was actually doing was making the rounds of doctors, being cruelly poked at, given the state of gynecology at the time, to see if anyone could find a reason for this lack of fertility. Finally, one wise man said, "Go home and forget about it. You're healthy. Just relax and enjoy your husband."

This phrase, told to me at some odd hour of the night that found me drawn like a moth to her living room light, sounded like a message in code language, something I needed to understand but could only grasp through some act of translation I was unable to make then. Several years later, she went on, after she had a child, she met the cruelest of the doctors on the steps of the hospital and confronted him. "I have a child now," she reprimanded him. "Why did you hurt me so much?" In those days doctors were not used to being questioned about their procedures. He was too startled to defend himself. As I sat opposite her in our living room in the middle of the night, it seemed miraculous to me that any conception had ever occurred between my parents. They always occupied twin beds, which Hollywood told the world was the way married couples cohabited, and I never saw any gesture between anyone in the family that required one person touch another.

While she waited for motherhood to overtake her, she wanted to work. That was totally out of the question. Israel had assured his wife's father "Your daughter will never have to work a day in her life." Yet getting her new life in hand could not have been an overwhelming job for a person raised to be thoroughly organized at all times. Coming from a substantial private home in Philadelphia she probably found the strange quirks of New York apartments particularly surprising. But it couldn't have taken her long to figure out that in New York, apartments that sounded roomy and charming

A Dangerous Thing

The senior Krasne brothers at Belle Harbor, 1934.
Charles (J), Abe, Essie, Hannah with Carol, Julius, Bernice, Estelle.

might also come with such oddities as a service elevator that opened into a living room or a second bedroom that could only be reached by going through the first bedroom.

For housekeeping, Anna had equipped her daughter with a few practical principles of management with which she could instruct the hired help. Each week she was to move the top sheet on beds to the bottom and put a fresh sheet on top (before fitted sheets, it was believed bottom sheets were more worn). Clean linens went on the top of the pile and she was to take fresh ones from the bottom. In the kitchen, she should immediately replace each item that was used.

Israel had found himself a wife who was, above all, practical. Attractive she also was, but never stunning, sexy, vivacious like her spectrum of new sisters-in-law. 'Sufficient' was the operative word,

The Education of a Dilettante

her mantra, suggesting nothing in excess, which would be vulgar, and vulgarity was to be avoided at all cost. Only late in life, at the end, did sufficient come to mean barely enough, as though the material world was a burden she sought to shake off.

With the apartment in order, there were too many long, empty days while her husband was at work from early in the morning until dinnertime. Used to the pace, pressure, companionship of life in a telephone company office, her daily isolation in a nuclear household in a strange city must have come as a form of house arrest. She was a manager in the mold of *Beeton's Book of Household Management*, the Bible of household life. The writer Margaret Atwood notes in an article called "Good Housekeeping" that Elizabeth Beeton established the idea that a wife wasn't "a delicate Angel in the House, a Beeton woman was the Generalissimo in the House, commanding an army of servants, men included. Her work was emphatically *work*, and required intelligence, tact, character, energy and dignity." That was Hannah Goldstein Krasne: the Beeton Generalissimo.

With her head for figures and her management abilities, she could have gone far in business, like her father, but her husband had to show the world that he could support her in the style to which she was accustomed. Her management was only able to shine forth in times of family crisis, when she was at her organizational peak.

After she arrived in New York she discovered a cousin who owned a wholesale lingerie business in New York, RAYMODES, a line of business where she could make use of her hours spent at dressmakers, the education her father had given her in matters of taste. That was where she wanted to work. Finally, Hannah and Israel worked out a compromise: she went to help out at the lingerie business...part time, without pay. In another year, she was pregnant.

Her father had been right about finding herself absorbed into

A DANGEROUS THING

Krasne family life. Despite the split into two competing businesses, Bernice Foods and Krasdale, the family remained close. For immigrants in the early part of the twentieth century, social life and family life were often synonymous. Families usually lived near each other; if not within walking distance, then accessible by public transportation. By the time I was born, Krasnes lived pretty much in a line extending along Central Park West, they were in the same business, and the ages of their children overlapped. When we were very little, the families rented houses at the same beaches for the summer.

One summer during World War II the Krasne clan rented summerhouses in a self-contained community near Ossining called Noah's Ark. We children could walk around the entire enclave early mornings filling a can with wild strawberries and by the time we completed the circle, we could start again because new berries had appeared. The women and children stayed for the duration, while the men commuted to work, sharing rides in one of their black Cadillacs to get around gas rationing and tire shortages.

One morning the men woke to find all the tires missing on the car nearest the woods. Desperate thieves had emerged from the woods, jacked up the car, and made off with all four tires, a calamity in time of acute shortages. The brothers pitched in and restored the vehicle to running order. The next few years, when we rented houses in Briarcliff Manor for the summer, where my father and his fellow horseback riders trotted up Sleepy Hollow Lane for brunch on weekends, I could never sleep facing the woods. I had a city girl's fear of thieves materializing out of the woods.

Families were a close support system, people from whom to learn about life in a new city, but they also meant built in competition. So many Krasne couples going into business, setting up house, having children involved a lot of looking over one's shoulder to check on who had the most or the best. Hannah must have realized

100

The Education of a Dilettante

quickly that despite her Philadelphia social life, where she compared herself to her scholarly older sister, she wasn't going to be the belle of the ball in New York City: not the most beautiful, the sexiest, or the richest Krasne wife. She wasn't going to be a party girl, like her sisters-in-law Mary and Florence who danced in the Top Deck Grill of the Queen Mary from midnight until morning, and watched beautiful girls in Paris night spots demonstrate "the 30 odd ways of making love," as her brother-in-law Archie recorded in his journal.

On the other hand, her sisters-in-law together only managed to get through a total of twelve pages of *Gone With The Wind*, the latest novel, which they had brought along on that Atlantic crossing. Hannah would have finished it off in the first couple of days. That was going to be who she was: Hannah the reader…a sensible woman with good taste.

After her first child, my sister Carol, was born, Hannah started the school tours, following in the footsteps of her New York sisters-in-law. Some of them had started their children off in public school, but all of her Krasne nieces and nephews eventually found their way to private schools. Even with advice from the family, her tours were a learning experience. At the Walden School students sat with their feet up on the desks and called their teachers by their first names. She was horrified. Her Philadelphia background, her Goldstein training had not prepared her for such a preview of the sixties. Progressive education was all right as long as theory out ran practice, at least to the uninitiated eye.

She settled for The Ethical Culture Schools, where one of the Krasne nieces was already enrolled. It looked like a school inside and out. The substantial building with a flight of steps leading up to the front door resembled a miniature version of the New York Public Library at 42nd street, not surprisingly, since the architects, John Carrère and Thomas Hastings, were working on the library at the same time. There was a large entry hall, a wood paneled

A DANGEROUS THING

library with floor-to-ceiling windows overlooking Central Park, exercise rooms top and bottom. It thus appeared to the innocent eye to make up a recognizable elementary school facility. That what went on there bore little resemblance to learning in Hannah's Philadelphia public school was something she would discover slowly, over the course of the fourteen years my sister and I each spent in the Ethical Culture school system.

I was born four and a half years after my sister Carol, a common time difference between offspring those Depression years, which meant we occupied different universes. She was in school when I was at home, in middle school way up in The Bronx when I was in elementary school in Manhattan, at college in Poughkeepsie when I was in high school in The Bronx. For a short time when we were little we had the same German governess, but when our parents realized we were speaking English with a German accent, she had to go. It's not surprising German governesses were in vogue. Our upbringing had a certain Teutonic character: punctuality, order, moderation, a formal distance between people was the order of the day. The distance people kept from each other had nothing gemutlich about it. Separateness was built into the geography of pre-war apartments: there were children's quarters; grown-up's rooms; household help's turf, as clearly divided as any feudal domain.

The German governess made a nice fit with the Victorian rigor of my mother's upbringing. Nothing exhibited this aspect of her personality more than the repeated crises over her hearing. The first of these occurred at my birth, when she was only 34, and it accounted for an immediate hearing loss, yet she went on as always. The crisis I recall most dramatically took place a few years later, when I was about 4. Though I had no idea she was suffering from an acute ear infection, our apartment became the scene of sudden drama. Doctors made house calls in those days, arriving with black bags and immediately retiring to the bathroom to wash their

The Education of a Dilettante

hands, but those were pediatricians, a familiar sight, and occasional general practitioners. The man with the black leather bag who arrived on this occasion was a distinguished looking older man I had never seen before. He was accompanied by much whispering in hallways and rushing back and forth of people with towels and boiling water. This was not a home birth but a mastoid operation on my mother performed in her bedroom.

The result of these repeated depredations on her auditory system were ever more serious hearing losses, serious enough for her to require a hearing aid. Nowadays, the idea of acquiring a hearing aid, a tiny gadget barely visible, hardly seems worth noting, but in the 1930s this entailed a large piece of equipment: an ear piece, a wire that protruded from the ear and across the chest to a heavy box that had to be worn someplace on her clothing. Once, when my mother, a woman still in her thirties, went to a school meeting using this apparatus, a woman asked her why she wore such an unattractive gadget, my mother, regarding her as some sort of idiot, said, "So I can hear." It was incomprehensible to her that vanity would come before common sense.

❀ ❀ ❀

Her hearing problems had never interfered with her reading to me, but her reading to me may have been what kept me from learning to read by myself. If this were an old fashioned novel, this part would be titled "In Which the Heroine Discovers Reading." Supposedly children learn to read in small increments. At the Ethical Culture School these must have been very small indeed because I was in third grade by the time I discovered reading. I've followed this magical process as it happened to our own children, but all I remember for myself is that one day I was home, sick in bed, and my mother was reading to me, and another day I was walking into the school library in third grade and seeing a notice

A DANGEROUS THING

that said there was a reading contest. That much I was able to make out. For the contest, students had to read a book in each of several different categories—Nature, History, Fiction, etc.—and give a report to the librarian. The contest was a revelation, not because it introduced the wonderful worlds of books, but because it triggered a latent competitive nature. When I looked around and focused on what my schoolmates were doing, it occurred to me that whatever they could do, I could do too, maybe even as well as anybody else.

There have been times in my life when this bit of reasoning has caused acute anxiety. If someone does something that requires neither particular talent nor decades of intense training—not like dancing on point or playing a Chopin sonata—I feel I too must be able to do this. But there is a fundamental problem with this approach to life: if challenge is the name of the game, then the end becomes more important than the means. Much as I admire Thoreau's advice in "On The Duty of Civil Disobedience" that we are not put here to do everything, but to do some things well, following his advice is another matter. The elements that combined to make me a dilettante were ingrained by the time I was in elementary school: the understanding that life was founded on good taste, a competitive nature, the short attention span of a spoiled daughter. By the time I came upon Pope's warning about knowledge—"A little learning is a dangerous thing"—it was far too late to retool myself into a scholar.

Competitiveness in a female, when I was growing up, was a vestigial attribute, like the appendix. A boy could channel his competitiveness into sports and, ultimately, business or professional success, but for women in the 1940s and 50s, there weren't too many constructive places to which a competitive nature could lead. Competition among girls was about the measurably material: how many sweaters or dresses she owned. But for that day in third grade when I discovered reading, it was books that mattered.

104

The Education of a Dilettante

As someone new to the reading business, I looked through the categories of books in the elementary school library and found the shortest book in each category. From what I could figure out, length was a factor those in charge had naively failed to take into consideration. The observation that adults could be careless about such details was as fascinating as the fact that I could, like a person gaining sight for the first time, make out whole books on my own, but it was scary to realize the adult world could be manipulated so simply.

After I returned the first book, the librarian asked me what I thought of it. It was a book on volcanoes from the Nature category and I informed her "It told me more than I wanted to know about volcanoes." I couldn't tell if her surprise was because she'd caught on to my short book ploy, or because she didn't expect me to be part of the contest, or if it meant disapproval of my review. I forged ahead, whizzing through categories. So this was reading.

The library became a favorite retreat. Along one side it had floor to ceiling windows overlooking the park; the rest of the large oak paneled room was filled with shelf on shelf of books, climbing to the high ceiling and reached by a rolling ladder. Its order was aesthetically satisfying, while its quiet space was insulated from demands of life outside. If I couldn't add or subtract, multiply or divide with ease, none of that mattered when I contemplated all the books waiting to be read.

The third grade-reading contest was an introduction to read-ing lists. At first, the reading list was just the spark a competitive nature needed to set off a reading binge. The lists were not lists at all but notebook size cards printed horizontally with columns. On the left was a space to fill in the title of the book, with other columns for the author and date of publication. On the right there were a couple of lines to accommodate comments about the book: what it was about, why we liked or did not like it. The system was a clever tool for teachers. At our periodic conferences, they didn't

A Dangerous Thing

Betty, Central Park, c. 1940.

have to say, "How's it going?" or "What do you think of science?" They would look over our cards and interrogate us on our reading. "Why did you pick that book?" "Do you agree with the author?" "Have you tried reading something different?" It was a form of quantity and quality control, insurance against the short book ploy or a steady diet of junk books. Like any cross-examination, we didn't look forward to it, but it had an up side: sometimes we came away with recommendations for a good read. The habit of reading lists endured, becoming, with adulthood, an aid to memory, so that when someone asks for the name of a 'good read,' I can dip into my list for prompting.

Students, particularly nowadays when so many work and have family obligations, consider themselves doing well if they plow

The Education of a Dilettante

through the better part of their assigned reading, mostly textbooks, though some students never come up with the money to even buy the texts. Thus college, to the surprise of many students, is no time for reading books—except assignments—so reading, paradoxically, has to be put on hold. Graduates of the Ethical Culture Schools were lucky, having been forced to read so much as they went along. As a consolation prize, I recommend to my college students that they keep a list at the back of their notebook of the books they want to read when school is over and their education really begins.

Eventually it was those reading cards that made me confuse vocation and avocation. As I moved from one level of school to another, reading was always the reward for completing assigned work. After deadlines were met, assignments fulfilled, that was when readers curled up with a book, the way some people might look forward to savoring a special piece of chocolate or going to a movie. I was a science major, pre-med, that was an occupation. A serious person couldn't very well make a life out of sitting around reading and talking about books. Books were purely personal.

Before I landed at college, everything I knew, what little it was, came out of books. Instead of lessons on grammar, punctuation, spelling, areas in which a school would usually instruct its students, at the Ethical Culture School we were left to absorb what we could of the rhythms of the English language from what we read. Not knowing any rules of punctuation, for instance, led to what might best be described as the 'salt and pepper technique' of punctuation, in which I would write a piece and then sprinkle punctuation over it like seasoning until it seemed to resemble pages of print I had read.

By the time I was writing my senior thesis at college, I was getting lost in sentences so convoluted that my Oxford educated advisor would shrug in disbelief and suggest the only way of extricating myself was to start over. It was not until we began teaching grammar in college, because we had students who could not compose

107

A DANGEROUS THING

sentences and paragraphs, that I discovered there were rules about punctuation and spelling. Teaching lessons about the use of the comma, I felt like a reformed alcoholic preaching the benefits of sobriety and my Handbook of Grammar was my AA manual.

My third grade conversion to reading made me, like many converts, a strong advocate: my sharpest childhood memories have to do with books. Early on there were the sumptuous centerfolds in the *Babar* books where I pored over the detailed drawings, fascinated by how things were done. Then came books with only an occasional picture, like *Dr. Doolittle* and *Heidi* that I had to wait for my mother to pick up and read to me. Roller skating and hopscotch are mixed up with reading *Wonder Woman* comics, because other girls who lived in our building were allowed to go to the newsstand and buy them, while I could only perch on the fire hydrant, my roller skate key around my neck, reading their copies, a kind of illicit material that didn't make it into our home. Some books, like Francis Hodgson Burnett's *The Little Princess*, were so mythic they had to be reread every year.

Memories of books are accompanied by a keen sense of loss. The way some people can remember where they were when key historical events occurred, the death of President Roosevelt, the assassination of President Kennedy, I can remember where I was when I finished a book, or a series of books, and the vivid sense of loss that accompanied closing the cover on the last page, raising my eyes to the present world around me, and wondering what I would do with myself tomorrow and tomorrow and tomorrow. Books for young readers often came in series. There was a series about a girl and the Royal Canadian Mounted Police and, of course, Nancy Drew. When I had found an appealing author, life opened out like a broad and endlessly beautiful road. But then there would come the day when the road suddenly ended.

Perhaps it was that I came to the end of the series, or maybe I began to see the formula the author used and knew it was time to

The Education of a Dilettante

move on. I can remember one summer day so hot there was hardly any place to be comfortable. Before air conditioning, homes in summer took on the quality of sickrooms: rugs were rolled up and stored with moth protection; cotton slipcovers were fitted over the upholstery; shades were kept partly drawn; when we were young, there were awnings that were rolled down in the afternoons. That day the only slight stirring of air was in our dining room, which faced in the direction of the Hudson River. So I sat in my father's chair with my feet on the windowsill, wearing short overalls and reading Nancy Drew. For two hours the sweltering world disappeared, but that was the end of Nancy Drew.

There was a moment several years later when I finally came to the end of Thackeray's monumental *Vanity Fair*. After dwelling for weeks in the nineteenth century, I stared at the blank page facing the end of the novel, stunned, closed the book, and looked around my bedroom. The twin maple beds with their pink chintz spreads were still there, in fact, that was all that was there. Nothing was left of the early nineteenth century England I had been living in for weeks. I felt like characters in movies about people caught in time machines who find themselves injected into the past, and just as they figure out how the game is played, they are rudely ejected back into the present.

Though my mother always had a book at hand, there were not that many books in our apartment, which made me wonder about the ones we did have. What did they signify? I poured through them, trying to find a pattern, a meaning in the odd assortment. This led to strange reading: *Emerson's Essays* might be parked next to *Kristin Lavransdatter*, but not much understanding. The books seemed to reside with us for no particular reason. My mother went through books so fast she preferred to use a lending library: the candy store around the corner, a public library, or later, into her nineties, the New York Society Library supplied her weekly cravings.

109

A DANGEROUS THING

For Hannah, family history repeated itself. Her older daughter, like her sister Jessie, had no use for fashion, eschewed dates, clothes, and parties and went her own way with books and study, defying social expectations, marrying several years later than her younger sister. Our family motto could have still been the same as it was back in my mother's Philadelphia days: A Child Reading Can Do No Harm. A neighbor who had grown up in Germany once told me that if her mother found her reading a book, she would say, "Don't you have anything to do?" It was a story I found surprising, one that my mother could not have comprehended.

The only problem was, to our father, just like our grandfather, education for daughters was regarded as a finishing school. For Raphael, education was a key to cultivation, and the kind of cultivation he had in mind for women did not require extensive education. Israel's lack of regard for education was the result of his own limited experience. He had quit school at a young age in order to earn a living, and lived comfortably ever after, which made him believe one of his favorite dinner table lines: 'Those who went to college work for those who never went to college."

If the school we attended had been less demanding, if we had been inattentive about our work, our father would not have noticed. The idea of private school, like having one's own car and a separate bedroom for each child, was a given of Central Park West existence. The particular school system came with his oldest brother's seal of approval, so it should have been fine. But the more he saw of what the school was about, the less comfortable he was with its influence. Holed up in our rooms with our books we were safely out of the way, but as Ethical Culture School social ideals came up against his ingrained prejudices, we were set to collide.

Chapter Seven

THE WORKINGMAN'S SCHOOL?

EVEN WHEN WE TOLD PEOPLE WE ATTENDED THE ETHICAL Culture School, we knew it had once been called The Workingman's School. Once in a while we glimpsed old sepia photographs of wide-eyed boys in knickers and girls in pinafores standing next to old-fashioned desks. A couple of times a year we filed into the awesome Meeting Hall of The Ethical Culture Society. It was in a mausoleum-like Art Nouveau building. Carved in the wood paneling above the stage it said, "The Place Where Men Meet To Seek The Highest Is Holy Ground," proclaiming a secularist religion.

But by the time we arrived on the scene, 'workingman' no longer meant what the founders intended. The school was founded in 1878 as a free kindergarten by a young man of 27 named Felix Adler. The free kindergarten eventually added elementary grades and, in 1890, the year Raphael Goldstein came to America, renamed itself the Ethical Culture School. With that change came a more decisive one: the school began admitting paying students. In 1904, when the building on Central Park West was dedicated and it graduated its first high school class (nine students), the school had

111

A DANGEROUS THING

400 students, of whom only 119 paid tuition, but this minority would soon become the majority. Despite Adler's speech at the dedication, bravely setting forth his egalitarian idea: "We believe that a class school is an evil for the rich as well as for the poor," the school's fate was sealed.

Adler had been born in Germany, but was brought to America at the age of six when his father, a well known Jewish scholar and rabbi, was called to the rabbinate of Temple Emanu-El in New York City. After graduating from Columbia College, Felix studied in Berlin and Heidelberg, and then returned to become a professor at Cornell University for a couple of years. But more a man of the city, he returned from Cornell to New York and in 1876, putting aside the religion of his father as superstitious tradition, he organized the Society For Ethical Culture. His secular philosophy was set forth in a series of books, starting with *Creed and Deed* in 1877. Fifteen years after founding the free kindergarten, he published *The Moral Instruction of Children*. Columbia University created a chair of social and political ethics for him, though he was still drawn back to Berlin as an exchange professor.

In another light, Felix Adler can be viewed as one of the group of German Jews who emigrated in the mid-nineteenth century and then took it upon themselves to see what they could do to bring civilization to the barbarian hordes, as they viewed the Jews pouring into the lower East Side of Manhattan from Eastern Europe at the end of the century. They founded the Educational Alliance and settlement houses, funded lectures, and tried to provide whatever service might accelerate acculturation of the masses washing ashore whose presence made them uncomfortable. Lillian Wald, for instance, went downtown as a nurse and ended up starting a visiting nurse service, which grew into the Henry Street Settlement House in 1895. Another group, with Cyrus Sulzberger of the publishing family as one of its organizers, came up with an even grander scheme. They founded the Industrial Removal Office,

The Workingman's School?

aimed at relocating Jews from the crowded inner city to other parts of the country. David Levinsky summed up the pecking order in Cahan's novel when he says, "I often convict myself of currying favor with the German Jews. But then German Americans curry favor with Portuguese-Americans, just as we all curry favor with Gentiles and as American Gentiles curry favor with the aristocracy of Europe."

Adler saw the need for an education to "promote achievement, creativity and understanding" among children "regardless of class, gender or race." A fellow faculty member at Columbia, John Dewey, was one of the influences on his theories. Dewey, a quintessential New Englander, took William James's philosophy of Pragmatism and applied it to education, coming up with a theory he called Instrumentalism. He had an opportunity to try out his new theory in an experimental school he set up in conjunction with the University of Chicago. Dewey and Adler were not that far apart in age, had both attended Harvard and studied James's ideas, were both professors of philosophy at Columbia, and both turned their attention to education, hoping to reform what they viewed as a system archaic in theory and practice.

Both men believed a new kind of education was needed to prepare people for life in a democratic society. The idea of popular self-government meant, according to Adler, that the American people "have consecrated their national life to a sublime humanitarian idea" and needed to be educated accordingly. While Dewey focused on pedagogical strategies, Adler emphasized inculcating ethical considerations, such as sensitivity to others and a sense of social responsibility. His ideas, conditioned by German national and religious experiences, became a reaction against them. For Simone de Beauvoir, who had to live in France during the war, it was necessary to despise the existing order; for Adler, transplanted to a new world, it was necessary to create a new order.

Having come from Germany, where the church predated the

A DANGEROUS THING

present form of government and the church was the founder of schools, he understood the sectarian nature of education there. He also saw that given the separation of church and state upon which the United States was founded, the government could not require all people to pay taxes for a sectarian education. As a philosopher, the question for Adler then became: What is an independent or unsectarian (the word he chose) basis for morality? In a series of talks given in 1891 at the School of Applied Ethics in, appropriately enough, Plymouth, Massachusetts, Adler attempted "to mark off a neutral moral zone, outside the domain of churches...." After some editing, these talks were published in 1893 as *The Moral Instruction Of Children*, a work with frequent echoes of such an earlier 'unsectarian' thinker as John Stuart Mill.

Adler did not take issue with the virtues he believed American public education was stressing, for instance its emphasis on discipline and the moral habits it emphasized, such as punctuality, silence, industry, accuracy, and politeness. At least, in his view, this was a more practical list to put before a class than The Ten Commandments. But he believed modern life needed to be based not on obedience to external authority, but on reasonableness, for only an appeal to reason would give rise to self-control and insight. Therefore, moral instruction needed to be part of daily school, not relegated to Sunday schools.

The curriculum he proposed went well beyond the three R's and begins to sound a lot like the Ethical Culture program: science, history, literature, manual training, music, and gymnastics. He advocated the use of fairy tales (das Märchen), fables, the Bible, and the *Odyssey* and *Iliad*, all carefully expurgated, to inculcate moral understanding through cultivation of the imagination. Imagination ranked high with Adler because he saw it as the crucial tool for conceiving of other times, other places, for inculcating empathy. School, he believed, "should be to the pupil not an intellectual drill-ground, but a second home; a place dear at the time,

The Workingman's School?

and to be gratefully remembered ever after...."

By the time Krasne children descended on the school, the student body was made up of three threads. The largest group of children was from families headed by well-to-do businessmen. These families could afford full tuition for their children, and it was traditional, particularly because the school was co-ed, for all the children in a family to go there if they could handle the work. Typically, these businessmen made their money as the founders and owners of small manufacturing industries—women's pocketbooks, cardboard boxes, bathing suits, and wholesale groceries. If you asked a friend "What does your father do?" it meant, "What does his business make?"

To this day, I can stop at a traffic light driving through Chinatown or The Bronx and look up to see an old building with the name of someone with whom I went to school still visible below the roofline. Now a Chinese department store or a Hispanic furniture warehouse, once these buildings were the source of jobs, goods, money that paid the way for families to live on Central Park West and send their children to the Ethical Culture Schools. This was the bourgeoisie, the (usually) Jewish bourgeoisie. For boys from this group, the family business hung over them like a cloud. School too, in its own way, was a factory. Just as a factory took in a cow or a chicken at one end and turned out a can of spaghetti and meatballs or soup at the other end, after a dozen or so years in The Ethical Culture School system, when the system ejected them into Oberlin, or Swathmore, or U of P, these young men were no longer part of the world of their father's.

The second thread of the student body was made up of a smaller group of students whose parents were professionals. They might be academics, doctors, or, more often, psychiatrists. Though we did not know this at the time, some of these parents constituted a famous intelligentsia World War II had sent into exile from a more sophisticated European intellectual milieu. Occasionally there was

A DANGEROUS THING

a hybrid, a parent who made something that was intellectual property, such as books or records. For boys who came from this group, life was easier. Sons of professionals didn't have the cloud of the family business hanging over them. Most of these students didn't bother to dabble in team sports, and were oblivious to the little social groups, or cliques that formed and reformed over the years. They were the precursors of nerds. Everyone, starting with our teachers, expected these boys to do something interesting with their education.

If academic life was a clearer path for boys from professional families, for girls from this kind of background life was harder. It took a strong character to withstand the materialism of the majority. A couple of years ago I emerged from a subway station in downtown Manhattan with an old high school friend whose father had been a doctor. As we came up the steps from the subway we saw the last name of one of our high school classmates written in large faded letters on the brick side of an old building that had once been the site of a family business. My friend looked at the name and said, "Do you know what I remember about her? She came up to me in school one day and told me 'That's the same dress you wore the other day.' " It was a lifetime later, but she had never forgotten the slight. In the Workingman's School it was, as Orwell concludes in Animal Farm: all pigs are equal, but some pigs are more equal than others.

I think of my friend's story whenever I read an article about school uniforms. Our school, with its progressive emphasis on individuality long before the term was used to describe 'the me generation' of American behavior, would never for a moment consider uniforms. Anything to do with the concept of uniformity was anathema. Someone once said we were a school of 100 leaders and no followers. For girls, such things as clothes were the telling sign of where they fitted in the pecking order. This was an ironic standard of distinction, given Adler's founding philosophy.

116

The Workingman's School?

The third group of students was there on scholarship. These students might be children of sociologists or scientists, or members of a minority group, which in the forties and fifties meant Negroes. Their representation among us was the one true line descended from the school's original population. There were a few basic educational principles that had gone into the founding of the school and one of them was that people were entitled to a good education regardless of race or economic situation.

What the founders meant by 'good' is key to what characterized the Ethical Culture School. Plenty of children, such as my future husband, Robert Levine, were receiving a good, basic education in the New York City public school system. But for Dewey and Adler good meant creative, although they differed on just what 'creative' meant. There was the John Dewey side of the school, which had adopted principles he developed at the University of Chicago experimental school about learning by doing. In the Ethical Culture School, Dewey's theories were extended to take into account the variety of students Adler had in mind. The curriculum, they believed, should include a spectrum of activities so that everyone could find something at which to excel. In other words, the three R's would not suffice; after all, not everyone was going to be a star at mathematics. That is why when I look back I can remember candle making, sewing, printing, and then there was the Acropolis, and the puppet show, and the medieval manuscript.

Adler's noble principles masked certain academic realities. Because of the quality of the teachers, the strong student body the school attracted, and the standards the school demanded, a student could, in fact, not get by on knitting alone, or any other non-academic ability. It might be fun to help create a harvest festival, to work on the script or the scenery, the singing and the dancing, but unless students could meet the academic demands, it was politely suggested that, for their own benefit, they would be better off in a

A DANGEROUS THING

less demanding environment. When this happened, they were exiled to what we all considered second rate schools. In our view, these other small private schools existed solely to take our rejects.

Another founding emphasis of Adler's was Ethics, which was intended to make us understand why everyone was entitled to be treated equally, regardless of race or economic status. Ethics was actually a class we were required to take every term, the way religious schools have a period for religion. Ethics was like "Leviticus" without God. We discussed how to treat other people, and in case we hadn't noticed there were other people, we were made aware of their presence or absence in our discussions. For instance, in one class we discussed why there were only white people on baseball teams at that time, and whether this was right. It is probably safe to say that no one in the class, including those who were interested in baseball, had ever paid any attention to the fact that only white men played baseball on the teams people followed. The implication of such discussions was that we were guilty of injustice by our complicity in an unjust system. The leit motif of our education was social injustice: it was a problem we were instructed first, to take seriously and second, to do something about.

❖ ❖ ❖

This concerted effort to focus our gaze outward was a direct contradiction of our bourgeois family life. My entire childhood had been directed at sheltering me from having to mix with "others." When we went someplace, we traveled in our own car, and if the trip was too long for a car, we went in a private compartment on a train. Vacations were spent in houses we rented at private beaches, or at homes in the country set well off in their own grounds. Later, our summers were spent at a camp in the Berkshires. We never visited public beaches or amusement parks.

Part of the care with which our lives were distanced from peo-

118

The Workingman's School?

ple around us had to do with the polio plagues that raged annually. One summer day I went with my mother on a boat trip up the Hudson River to Indian Point, which back then was not a nuclear power plant but a park with a public swimming pool. There was no way my mother was going to let me mix with the people in the park or enter that public pool. It seemed to me, as we sat on a bench overlooking the site, from which I watched the splashing about below with a mixture of envy and fear, we had missed the whole point of the outing. As we walked back to the boat in the afternoon, I knew it must have been fun to be part of the swimming crowd, yet at the same time I knew we were not part of that group. We were repeatedly instructed that the first thing we were to do upon entering home was to wash our hands, a simple plan to rid us of germs, but a gesture that reinforced our sense of separateness from those around us as we washed away their contamination.

Ethics took direct aim at the closed world of middle class life. To put Ethics into action, by the time we were in middle school, Community Service was added to our requirements. This was way back before the contemporary academic fad for community service. The school had a list of activities, on and off campus, for which we could sign up, but one way or another we had to put in a certain number of hours making ourselves helpful to others. Some students settled for shelving books in the library; more adventurous ones went to work at settlement houses.

As a science person, I did my time at Columbia Presbyterian Medical Center. Donning a volunteer's uniform, lending a hand in Emergency Admitting, helping out on the wards was a kind of play-acting. Knowing my way around that medical citadel made me a part of the drama there, though my community service hours didn't add anything to my meager understanding of science.

These amateur medical days were halted abruptly in the middle of a polio scare. One day when I came home to our summer beach house from my vacation job at the hospital, I was running a temper-

A DANGEROUS THING

ature. Immediately, I was hustled into quarantine. From the emergency bed set up for me, I could overhear grave murmurings. To everyone's great relief, my malaise was not THE dreaded disease, merely a summer cold. As soon as I was better, I was forbidden to return to the dangers of hospital work and left, to my family's sigh of relief, to spend my days improving my tennis game. It was, again, the triumph of family ideas of behavior over the values of school.

The families of most Ethical Culture students thought the system of society in the United States was just fine. It had made it possible for them to live in great comfort. Though most parents of Ethical students were Roosevelt supporters, they had come through the depression largely unscathed and saw nothing seriously wrong with the status quo.

A 1938 photograph of the Bernice Foods annual party in the Grand Ballroom of the Waldorf Astoria Hotel shows hundreds of people, the women sparkling in evening dress, the men elegant in white tie and tails—not like contemporary dinner jackets that make guests look like head waiters. They were ready to party. The Depression was on; Roosevelt was in his second term; Hitler was already raging across Germany. Florence and Archie are in the picture, two years after their memorable trip to Russia; my doll-like Aunt Vivian is in the picture, a few precious years before cancer, the disease no one in the family would ever name out loud, started eating away at her. My mother, of course, is in the picture, the only person in the entire ballroom not looking at the photographer, perhaps because her hearing was already severely damaged and she does not catch the photographer's cue. Compared to the sophisticated glamour of the other women at the head table, in their slinky black gowns with diamond clips, my mother looks almost out of place, her dress almost dowdy, as though she had embedded in her a chip of Philadelphia's sensible Quaker past, yet this is not the way I remember her looking. The rest of the crowd seems quite content with the part it is playing.

The Workingman's School?

In my memory of their going out on nights like this, they looked glamorous. My mother would come in, usually to my sick room, to say goodnight. She would be wearing something that shimmered in the light from the hall, a vivid green satin dress, diamonds at her throat and ears and wrist, with a white ermine jacket and long white gloves, my father standing behind her, waiting in his black tails and gleaming white shirt front.

Not surprisingly, our parents were unsympathetic to our bringing home and unloading on them guilt about inequities in the American system. One day, a week after I had given a graduation party for my entire sixth grade class, my father came up to me as our paths crossed in the foyer of our apartment and informed me it was not appropriate to invite Negroes to our home, so little did he understand the school to which he paid tuition for so many years. It must have taken a good deal of effort on his part to address one of his children directly on a personal matter of policy, for this was an area totally allocated to my mother and I can recall only one other occasion on which he addressed me about how I was to act.

A high school friend once told me that when she was grown up and her father died, she asked her brother if he had ever had a conversation with him, thinking that perhaps their father's lack of communication had to do with her gender. "Never," her brother informed her, not at all surprised by the question. If she told me this story expecting me to be surprised, no one could have been less surprised. I assumed that communication lines in families ran through mothers, who might say, "I'll speak to your father" or "I'll ask your father," but we knew that was pro forma. In the division of labor, anything having to do with children was women's business.

I felt betrayed by my father's comment, thinking that he had somehow done an end run around my mother, whom I did not think capable of so crudely sweeping aside years of education about

A DANGEROUS THING

ethics and equality, though I never thought to confront her about my father's position. Instead, I felt the first stirrings of rebellious anger, as though he had given me a cause to champion more real than anything that emerged from Ethics class. Pronouncements in Ethics classes were abstractions; the impulse to defy parental authority was a tool at hand. By setting himself up in opposition to basic Ethical Culture principles that had already been drilled into us for eight years, he was putting himself outside our comfort zone, forcing us to choose between his views and what we had been taught was ethically correct and socially desirable.

Of course, the Negroes he knew were the men who worked in his warehouse. He kept a petty cash fund to help them out when they couldn't meet the rent or needed to get out of a scrape. They were not a group with which he saw much in common. But even if he knew the classmate in question went on to become president of his class at Harvard, graduate from Yale Law School, and become a high profile figure in the United States government, he would not have changed his views. His field of vision was circumscribed by his business experience.

◊ ◊ ◊

My father was a creature of local habits; he only felt comfortable with the familiar. Early on he had made the simple discovery that all he needed to do in order to be treated royally was to always patronize the same few places: when we dined out on the cook's night off, he always chose the same few restaurants, where head waiters gave him a warm welcome. When he went away for a vacation, summer and winter, he invariably visited the same two resorts where his presence was acknowledged by the management of the resort.

While we were away at summer camp, our parents had discovered a place called the Mt. Washington Hotel, in Bretton Woods,

The Workingman's School?

deep in the heart of New Hampshire's White Mountains. Each of the American grand hotels attracted its own crowd: Christians in certain locations, Jews in others; European Jewish intelligentsia exiled to one place, Catholic Philadelphia mainline to another. During the war years, when travel abroad was not an option, people, like characters in Jane Austin novels, packed their wardrobe trunks and traveled to these hotels for extended stays. One reason the Bretton Woods International Monetary Conference at the end of the war was held at the Mt. Washington Hotel was that it accepted Jews, and several of America's top representatives were Jewish. The year I tired of camp, it never occurred to my parents to go elsewhere. They carted me along with them, a trip that was an odd blend of camp and coming out party.

We traveled by train to White River Junction, where we switched to the Maine Central, riding in a private compartment or "drawing room," although it seemed to me the train was not much occupied. Our wardrobe trunks rode in the rear baggage car, while my father's horse was transported by van. The hotel rooms were simple, in the way bedrooms were simple at Franklin Roosevelt's Hyde Park or Teddy Roosevelt's Sagamore Hill: high ceilings, iron beds, a wicker chair, space for a wardrobe trunk to stand open, bathtubs on claw feet. Since materials of all clothes were natural—linen, silk, cotton, organdy—people shared their rooms with maids who made the rounds bearing irons and ironing boards, particularly on the two evenings when formal attire was prescribed.

Guests came from all directions: there were Oppenheimers from as far away as South Africa and American families from Boston to Baltimore. The staff, on the other hand, were clean-cut American college students, blond and blue-eyed, whose separate lives I tried to sneak out and explore. One day, bored with resort activities, I tagged along with chambermaids, waitresses, and bus boys to Halfway Brook, the swimming hole where staff plummeted from steep rocks into a frosty mountain stream that came down

A DANGEROUS THING

the valley from Mt. Washington. In the White Mountains in the forties it turned out that life behind the scenes was less like scenes from "Dirty Dancing" than chapters out of "Upstairs Downstairs."

In the winter, our parents always went to the same hotel in Florida. It was the way my father wanted his life arranged: comfortable, orderly, simple, always the same few familiar things. Once he moved into the building on Central Park West, he had no intention of moving any place else. Long after World War II, as parts of the family migrated across the park to the East Side, my mother energetically hunted up an apartment so we could follow. Until, that is, her husband made it clear: she could spend whatever was needed to redecorate their apartment, but he would never move.

So it was that they stayed on, until he was carried out at the sudden end of his days, the first of the Krasne brothers to die. Early in his American experience he had formed a few elementary views on public affairs and human relationships, and they set his course in life. Unfortunately, his was a vision of life at odds with the education my mother had so carefully chosen for us at the Workingman's School.

Chapter Eight

ETHICS IN
THE BRONX

STUDENTS AT THE ETHICAL CULTURE SCHOOLS PRIDED THEM-
selves on being different, maybe because the school itself made
a point of being different. At Fieldston, the high school of the
Ethical Culture school system, we didn't have grades; we had
Forms, after the British fashion. Seventh grade became First Form.
Combined with Second Form these two grades were the middle
school. High school was Forms Three through Six.

But it wasn't only the terminology that changed. Moving from
elementary to high school, we were suddenly transported from just
down the street on Central Park West, familiar territory, to a special quadrant of The Bronx called Riverdale which, like the Holy
See in Rome, had special occupants: the Horace Mann School,
Manhattan College, Riverdale Country Day School, Fieldston
Lower, and Fieldston. The area was hilly, wooded, with the schools
tucked away between turreted Tudor stone houses and miniature
Mt. Vernons.

From a sixth grade vantage point on Central Park West, it was
difficult to imagine what school would be like in a new borough
and on a 'campus." I pestered my sister Carol every evening for

A DANGEROUS THING

details of what this new experience of high school was like. "But if I have a different teacher for every subject, how will I get to class on time when there are so many buildings?"…."You mean I have to take a shower every time I have gym?"…."Which side of that (hockey) stick do you use?"…."How do you have time to go to the library if you're always running between buildings?"

In our sixth grade graduation euphoria, we only vaguely understood the sixth grade class from Fieldston Lower would join us. Our suburban counterparts were looked down upon as country bumpkins, and we had no idea that we were to encounter sharp minded students coming in on their academic merits from such places as Hunter Elementary School and New Lincoln. The Ethical Culture crowd, which had been together for six, or even eight years, thought of itself as the height of sophistication and was perfectly ready to patronize those who were not our crowd.

Getting to Fieldston was an adventure in itself. Manhattanites could take a subway to the end of the line in upper Manhattan, and then a bus across Spuyten Duyvil and through Riverdale, or a not so nearby subway and trek up a long hill. As we progressed, we learned that the former route was easier in the morning, though the train seemed to attract more perverts and exhibitionists. The hilly walk, on the other hand, had something to recommend it in the afternoon: besides being downhill, when we got to the bottom we might meet the boys getting out of Horace Mann (then an all-boys school).

At first, the shock of Fieldston's new geography was so complete it was hard to notice what went on in the classroom, even though that was the biggest change from elementary school. Now we had history, not projects; there was literature, with everyone in the class reading, discussing, writing about the same book, often a startling work, like "Medea" or *Crime and Punishment*; there were foreign languages; science in a laboratory; and mathematics with a math teacher. For the students coming in from structured,

126

Ethics in The Bronx

demanding schools like Hunter, the work was no surprise. For the Ethical Culture people, the classes did not proceed quite the way we were used to doing schoolwork. A friend who transferred to Ethical in fifth grade summed up our elementary school experience. She had been attending a suburban public school in New Jersey, but when her family moved to Manhattan they enrolled her at the Ethical Culture School. When she saw what we were doing she said, "What a lark." She could hardly believe what fun we had, and what little work was asked of us.

When we crossed over into The Bronx, it was as though we were in an academic country so new it required a visa. In some ways we had been very well prepared: we had been encouraged to think for ourselves, ask questions, be original, read, write…not bad qualities on the way to an education. Skills were another matter. Fieldston handled these differences in our abilities with levels or tracks, the way some elementary schools have different reading groups: Pigeons, Robins, and Eagles. In math the highest group was a brainy bunch whose calculations were beyond the comprehension of most of us. My friends were in the second group.

And then there was the third group. That was where I placed, and I loved it, being no quicker at math than I had been about reading. Our teacher, Miss Rosenthal, was a compact, energetic woman with short gray hair. We learned such magic as how to use a slide rule and I could actually show others how to do their work. Unfortunately, ever the plugger, one day I found myself elevated to the second group.

No two teachers could have been more different than Miss Rosenthal and Miss Colvin. The former was short and had a firm manner that brooked no nonsense; the latter, who presided over level two, was a tall, mild mannered lady, a disciple of John Dewey. She loped around the room, always sporting a lapel pin that was a flower in a little glass holder with water, and her gray hair stood out as though she had passed too near an electric current on her

A Dangerous Thing

way out her front door. She taught mathematics by the Socratic method and spoke in phrases as enigmatic as ancient runes. The day I walked into Miss Colvin's class was the last moment in my life when I understood anything mathematical. It was a good thing my friends were in the class, because our telephone was occupied every evening with their telling me how to do the homework.

❖ ❖ ❖

There were blonde twins in our class, the Goodman girls, whose father was the timpanist with the New York Philharmonic Orchestra. If I called their house, I stood a double chance of connecting with someone who could rescue me from my mathematical haze. We became such good friends we eventually stayed over at each other's houses. They lived in Yonkers, a location as exotic to my family as a third world country. One summer day they took me to swim at Tibbett's Brook Park, the public swimming facility for the city of Yonkers. Never having been to a public swimming facility, I looked around carefully. The size of the pool and the crowd of people were a bit intimidating, while the lack of amenities was noticeable, but none of these distinguishing marks was particularly scary in the way a sheltered life had led me to believe.

Helen, it turned out, the twin with whom I became most friendly, was the only person among my acquaintances who liked horseback riding, so when she came to Manhattan we went riding together in Central Park, where I could return the experience of the exotic for her. In the center of Manhattan people rode horses around the park and I had been riding there since I was five. The family—my father and my Uncle Abe and Aunt Mary—kept horses at Aylward's Riding Academy, an old complex built at the turn of the century by a man named Durland that took up the block between 66th and 67th streets, just off Central Park West. The place was a cross between a stable and the University Club, except that horses

128

Israel Krasne jumping Blacky at Aylwards Riding Academy, 1940s.

didn't seem to make the usual club distinction between Jew and Gentile. A huge indoor riding ring had a glassed in gallery running along one side with comfortable leather lounge chairs. It opened into mysterious clubrooms that never seemed to serve any purpose. The ring was big enough to accommodate people riding and people jumping. Once, my father tried to show me how to swing a polo mallet, but I gave it up before parting company with my horse.

The place was run by a pair of Irish sisters straight out of a Broadway play about the Old Sod. They rode sidesaddle in long skirted black outfits with black hats and had everyone—everyone being their hard drinking Irish instructors, grooms, and office staff—terrorized. When Helen came to visit, it was from them we rented a horse for her to ride. Horseback riding in Central Park, to the surprise of my friend, was as much a characteristic of Manhattan life as the New York Philharmonic Orchestra.

❖ ❖ ❖

A DANGEROUS THING

The Goodman sisters rescued me in Math, but unfortunately they weren't there in French class. Since we had never learned any English grammar, the instructions in the French textbook, when it spoke of conjugations, verbs, pronouns, direct objects, past participles, were unintelligible. Our elementary school preparation had avoided study that gave the impression of memorization, and without the discipline to sit down and memorize conjugations, vocabulary, and rules of usage, learning French did not happen.

Science might require memorizing, too, but since I told everyone I planned to be a doctor, I had extra incentive. And science was intriguing because it showed how things worked: what makes water boil and how it freezes, what makes crystals form, why a particular concatenation of molecules makes water different than air. Dissection, making it possible to see how things worked inside out, was the most exciting. Some girls in our class thought their role was to giggle or gag over a cow's eye, but looking down at the eye on the science table, knowing that hidden knowledge about the workings of life was at my fingertips, filled biology with mysterious interest.

And always there were those reading cards to fill up and a library to roam through in search of books. The first year at Fieldston my homeroom teacher was a Japanese woman by the name of Ida Shimanuchi. One Monday she came in to class and recommended a book to us that she had just read, *Cry The Beloved Country*. I immediately went out and found a copy, prompting my classmates to rib me for currying favor with the teacher. They didn't grasp that people addicted to reading are like people with tapeworms: they need people to keep feeding them recommendations for books to devour. What we did not understand was how that particular book probably held special meaning for our teacher, who was Japanese and had spent the war years in this country. Despite our years of Ethics, none of us knew then about the persecution of Japanese Americans.

Ethics in The Bronx

Right after the Czechoslovakian political crisis in 1948, Fieldston acquired a history teacher from Europe. Abroad, he had probably been a well-known intellectual. He had a vivid grasp of such complex happenings as the division of Poland and defenestration as a political weapon. One day he gave us a quiz on current events and was appalled to discover we had no idea what was going on in the world, and what was worse, we didn't even know where anything was. We probably could locate England and France, but from there eastward to China was an obscure blur. Our grasp of the world was all too much like the New Yorker's map of the United States, in which Manhattan looms large, with its suburbs (Boston and Washington), and the rest of the country consists of California. That map of the world we had made in fifth grade was a typical inter-disciplinary Ethical Culture project: we measured and we drew; probably we were intended to grasp the location of countries, mountain ranges, rivers, but little firm knowledge seeped through to us.

Our Czech teacher must have been disheartened to see that in a school for the best and the brightest, in the land of liberty, nobody knew, nobody cared about politics and international affairs. To a European who ate and breathed politics, it was unfathomable. Americans had fought and died in the wars that raged across Europe, tearing countries and peoples apart, yet there we were, a bunch of comfortable, self-satisfied young people whose major concern of the week was likely to be some upcoming social event.

❖ ❖ ❖

As education delved deeper and deeper into subjects, it diverged more and more from home life. Dissecting an eye, learning about the division of Poland and Niels Bohr's quantum theory did not provide dinner table conversation. The four of us appeared for dinner every night in the dining room, even though we often ate different foods. My father presided at the head of the table, my mother at the foot, where there was a bell to ring for the cook. My sister and I sat on one side of the large table under the crystal chandelier. Ranged around the edges, various sideboards and chests were held down in place by silver candelabra, a silver tea service, Chinese bowls, testifying to the solid wherewithal of the proud possessors. We were dressed for dinner as we had been for school: tweed skirts, cashmere sweaters, while our father had donned an item called a 'smoking jacket.' Our mother valiantly attempted to keep conversation going, but hunks of silence, looming up like icebergs, testified to the distance between school and home.

We had simple meals by today's standards, so simple it seems there was only one all-purpose menu from those thousands of dinners: a salad with iceberg lettuce and tomato; broiled loin lamb chops, baked potatoes, string beans; canned fruit. If my sister complained about canned fruit, our father would quote figures on how many cans the business sold. Other than this meal with its interchange, no one in the family ever saw anyone else. My sister and I each had our own rooms at opposite ends of a hall and it was there, behind closed doors, that we retreated with our books after dinner.

One night when I was in high school this pattern of our dinner routine was abruptly shattered. As I came into the kitchen shortly before dinnertime, I saw the cook, Edna, standing in the middle of the floor, reaching for the door of the refrigerator, except where her hand was extended, there was no refrigerator. She was having a stroke. Edna's favorite kind of food, deep fried chicken baked in cream gravy, must have been even less healthy than our own steak-and-potatoes meals. My mother called an emergency number that brought police, who called for an ambulance. All of this took forever, in heart attack time. The ambulance eventually came and delivered her to Harlem Hospital, a third-world institution serving Manhattan's Negro population. She died a day later. I accompanied my mother to a church in Harlem for the funeral. As the only

Ethics in The Bronx

white people there, we felt very much the outsiders, but my mother knew we had to pay our respects. None of my ethics education could rescue Edna from poor diet and even poorer care.

Of course, Fieldston, like any American high school, was not about subject matter; it was about socializing, and socializing meant two different things. It meant being part of a clique, and it meant dates. The former was a group in one's own grade that one hung around with. Dates were another matter, since the boys we went out with were never in our grade. They could be in a higher grade at our school, or from a boy's school like Horace Mann.

Though we were adolescents, socializing was not about sex. It was about seeing and being seen. This was well before the era when kisses became meals. A young woman's life was dependent on men: to go to any social event she needed a date, and women did not call up and make dates. They sat at home and waited for the phone to ring. "Hi, this is Andrew. Would you like to go to: the dance…the play…the party…. the new movie?" These were the magic words that sprang Sleeping Beauty from being immured at home Saturday night, the worst of fates. There were party dates at people's homes, their parents discretely in the background. There were dance dates at a boy's school, like Horace Mann, because they had to import women. Or there were funky dates: a Staten Island ferryboat ride, a walk across the Brooklyn Bridge.

The young man several grades ahead of me at Fieldston who took me to my first foreign film made a great impression with his odd choice. First, we went to dinner in a French restaurant, which turned out to be pricier than he planned. We both felt embarrassed as he counted out his change to see if he would have enough, but he would never have considered asking me to dip into my pocket book and help out with one of the trusty dollars girls always carried in their bag, "just in case." Then we went to see a scratchy old print of the 1939 "Volpone," Ben Jonson's English comedy made into a French film by Maurice Tourneur with eccentric actors named

A DANGEROUS THING

Harry Baur and Louis Jouvet. It played in one of the mid-town side street theaters given over to foreign films. Like an X-rated theater, it was a small, dilapidated place. I glanced around surreptitiously, expecting to see seedy types lounging about, but could make out little in the dim light. My date, a senior, probably thought I was more sophisticated than I actually was, being tall for my age, but I was only in fourth form and wasn't at all sure a French film in a seedy theater was a proper way to spend an evening. By the time my class reached sixth form, we were all rushing off to be the first to see "Rashomon."

Dates were the one point of contact with the family. My mother could vicariously re-live her younger days in Philadelphia when her father had made sure she had the right outfits to wear for her social life. If a woman had dates, it followed she needed clothes, though my mother's stern Philadelphia lessons in good sense prevailed: you always buy the best, but you never need more than one. The ritual of shopping translated into colors: a navy dress was spring, a brown suit was fall. If there were occasional formal family events, there was a hand-me-down evening gown, bouffant and modest, and a beaver coat, all inherited from my sister.

Dates, too, followed a protocol that involved the family. In a send-up of two eras (the fifties and the nineties) entitled "The Saturday Night Date," Margaret Atwood put together a dialogue for the Special Millennium Issue of *The New York Times*. Part of The article was a diagram labeled "Saturday Night Prep Card (1 of 17)." Atwood's questioner was a late twentieth century fifteen year old who asked, "What was your social life like when you were my age?" This teenager found the mid-century customs the author recounted as exotic as "dueling and taking snuff" seem to us now.

> …"Well," I said, "first the boy would call you up
> ahead of time and ask you for a date."
>   "*Really?*" she said. (Young people her age did not

Ethics in The Bronx

go on dates by that time. They traveled in schools,
like fish, on the spur of the moment).
"Then he would ring the doorbell, wearing a
shirt and tie—*Really?*—and you would ask him in
and introduce him to your parents, who were usually
your actual biological mother and father—*No kid-
ding!....*"

The teenager wants to know what Atwood wore on a date, but
can make no sense out of such items as crinolines and cinch belts,
nylons and panty girdles. But, like an anthropologist trying to
describe a foreign tribe, Atwood forges ahead.

"Then" I continued, "the boy would escort you
to the car, open the door and assist you into it—*ohmi-
gawd!*—and he would park, and extract you from the
car, and you would go to the movie, and he would
pay—*Really?*"

The author concludes by pointing out that even such a small custom as the Saturday Night Date is like a "once-living, now-
drowned universe...."
What girls didn't know about sex could have filled a whole
corner of the Fieldston library. Of ova and spermatozoa, uteruses
and penises we knew, but scientific terminology did not translate to
any understanding of attraction, desire, and orgasm. Masturbation
was a term we vaguely associated with a stage in the early development of adolescent boys, and though recent research has revealed
that the vibrator pre-dates the sewing machine, no one had any
concept of what constituted female sexual satisfaction. It was probably just as well that our lives were conventionally chaste, because
our information moved from biological instruction at one end of
the spectrum to 'just keep your legs crossed' at the other end. From

135

movies, girls learned how to kiss, how to smoke, how to play hard-to-get, or to flirt. We assumed that by imitating dashing and adventurous gestures executed on screen we would become the height of sophistication.

If weekend social life was about dates, daily life was taken up with the maneuvering of cliques, just as in any American public high school. Amoebae-like, they formed and reformed, mercilessly ingesting and ejecting members. As middle school became high school, what I wanted was to be in with a group who seemed to have a secret language. I longed to go around speaking of people named Kafka and Don Giovanni. This group of classmates came to school knowing about art and music, and their idea of a good time was sitting around someone's living room arguing about what was the greatest opera. They appeared to be keepers of esoteric knowledge, holding themselves apart, mocking the mundane interests of our classmates. They were intimidating; they were a challenge. Admission to this group was problematic. I had not come to high school speaking the same language and I was a jock, one more sign of dilettantism

◊ ◊ ◊

Sports, especially if they were outdoors, mattered. In the fall there was field hockey, winter was basketball, spring meant tennis. Sports had come into my life with camp.

My mother had found a place in the Berkshires, although the Berkshires in the 1940s seemed as far away as Canada. The camp was called Lenore and was run by a family of Europeans who thought fresh air, exercise, and culture were what American youth needed. We were taught to perform everything beautifully, whether it was swimming or archery, modern dance or art. It may have been the only camp that employed a musical trio as full-time counselors. The founder and director, Mrs. Spectorsky, had come

Ethics in The Bronx

from Russia via Paris, where she studied music. The pianist, violinist, and cellist she hired every summer were at the heart of half the camp's activities: the Isadora Duncan style pageants where barefoot girls flitted across the lawn; afternoon concerts; and the Sunday morning dramas where stories from the Hebrew Bible were acted out in mime while Mrs. Spectorsky read from the text.

For the rest of my life I remembered those stories: Joseph and the coat of many colors, how Reuben tried to save him in a pit but was sold to the Ishmaelites for 20 pieces of silver and how his brothers "took Joseph's coat, and killed a kid of the goats, and dipped the coat in the blood.... and they brought it to their father, and said, this have we found." Every summer on the recreation hall stage counselors mimed the drama of David and Saul, while the trio played and Mrs. Spectorsky read how the women of Israel sang: "Saul hath slain his thousands, and David his tens of thousands." These unparalleled tales of sibling rivalry, jealousy, betrayal, set to music, echoed strangely because we all had uncles and cousins named Saul and David, Benjamin and Reuben.

There were team sports too; in fact, the entire camp was organized into two teams in what became known in American camp parlance as color war. Our teams were green and white, the camp colors, which showed up in our green wool bathing suits, our green shorts and white middy blouses. In a snapshot from parents visiting day, I am perched, young and skinny, on my sister's sturdy shoulders, the two of us in matching camp uniforms. Team sports at Camp Lenore are not to be confused with the sweaty competitions of current girls soccer and softball leagues. Writing a team cheer could earn points for the greens or the whites, just as well as having everyone in your canoe raise her paddle at exactly the same angle, like dancers arms in a ballet.

The emphasis on beauty of form was so perfectly at one with life at home that summer camp fitted seamlessly into the rhythm of the year. Only the abrupt shift from city noises to country quiet

A Dangerous Thing

Betty on Carol's shoulders, Camp Lenore, Massachusetts, c. 1942.

required an adjustment. Camping itself, on the other hand, hikes in the woods with homemade bedrolls for overnights, was too creepy for a city girl; instead, what we learned was to master perfect form: hitting a tennis ball, paddling a canoe, diving from a board, until we were filled with mindless exhilaration.

And camp was where we learned the saddest song: Taps. Every night, as the flag came down on the front lawn, the mournful notes of Taps sounded across the green hills of the Berkshires.

In the Ethical Culture Schools, it would seem plausible that

Ethics in The Bronx

intellectual and physical activity would be equally acceptable. After all, there was that concept of something for everyone to excel at that was part of the founding philosophy. But they were not equal. For the Kafka clique, the class intellectuals, team sports were beneath their interest. The idea that Fieldston would even have a football team was ridiculous to them. Team sports were condescendingly considered an okay activity for those with more muscle than brain, so it took a particular kind of rebel nature—not my kind—to go in for team sports.

A friend a year ahead of me who was at the top academically (through tough stuff like advanced math, physics, and German) was on the football team. But he was unusual. He came from a family whose independent ideas started with the entire social arrangement of society. Though we did not know this at the time, his father's life became so complicated during the McCarthy era that he fled to Mexico. When I went to visit my friend at Yale his freshman year, my family insisted on sending me to New Haven with a car and driver. "What," my embarrassed friend wanted to know, "is the matter with taking the train, like everyone else?" The conversation was emblematic of the Ethical Culture standoff of values: my family's view of life was firmly posited on all the exclusiveness money could buy and his was based on the economics of social justice.

No matter how much D.H. Lawrence preached against the mind-body split (we all managed to get our hands on *Lady Chatterly's Lover*), blaming Christianity for elevation of the spiritual over the physical, those of us who persisted in running around fields getting sweaty were considered to be intellectual lightweights. His senior year, my friend's football team won the league championship and he gave me his gold football with 'Fieldston '50' and his team number engraved on it. I wore it on a chain around my neck, not for social glory, like a fraternity pin, but to announce to our high school classmates: "See, athletics belongs to the intelli-

A DANGEROUS THING

gent." But a gold football wasn't a passport to the intellectual inner circle.

While students thought of school as social life with an academic flavor, the academic subtext was Ethics. It was the one subject on every year's schedule that differentiated our school from all others. The distance opened between parents and children by academic work was increased geometrically by the school's Ethics teaching. Ethics, ironically, made us see our parents as hypocrites. It was not that the actual class called Ethics sent us home with revolutionary assignments; it was that the ideas behind the Ethics curriculum insidiously undermined the status quo. From pre-kindergarten through high school, the great burden of our education was not a body of knowledge; it was the sense of being obligated to make the world a better place. Adler had said,

> the feeling of moral indignation depends on the idea
> that the injuries we receive from our fellow men are
> not important, but that it is important that the right
> be done and the wrong be abated.

If society was filled with wrongs, then the fault lay with the adults around us who, through acts of commission or omission, had failed to correct inequities and injustices. Race relations and the ills of poverty were the issues de jour. Our parents were implicated in maintaining an unjust social system and our education prompted us to reject the values that made our comfortable lives possible.

In *Memoirs Of A Dutiful Daughter* de Beauvoir tells how "bourgeois self-sufficiency" came to be "an order I despised." She describes how the unrest and dissatisfaction of young people after World War II, who felt their parent's generation had made a mess of things, led to our "turning our restlessness into a crusade...." For Fieldstonites, it was not war, but our Ethical education that opened a chasm between generations deeper than the usual adolescent

Ethics in The Bronx

rebellion. Like de Beauvoir, we had put our parents generation on trial and found it wanting. In our rejection of their middle class values, we felt we no longer had to clue our parents in to the details of our activities. We went about knowing we were in the right about social issues and represented the future, a bright, pure place from which they in their benighted ignorance were excluded.

By sixth form, when we were seniors and all the older boys around us were off in college, the Kafka crowd finally became the center of activity. We broke out of childhood boundaries and wandered down to Greenwich Village and the lower east side. We listened to jazz and folk singing, found clubs where men dressed like women, signed up for work details at settlement house country weekends, and gave coed sleepover parties. We hung out in the basement of The Museum of Modern Art watching old foreign films and went second-acting at Broadway plays, seeking out a life for ourselves of which our parents were not part, a brave new world. It was as though typical adolescent rebellion met up with political issues like those that split generations in the Vietnam era. We had no particular cause, but were sure when our turn came we would do a better job of arranging the world.

Going off to college was a final step in our rebellion. Every student graduating from Fieldston was expected to go on to college, though in our grade one young woman scandalized students and administrators alike by discovering sex and getting married, a course totally incompatible with college in 1951. In our household the American college scene was alien to both our parents, and those were not the days when parents went vagabonding about the country on college tour weekends. Since our mother had not been permitted to go to college, she had few opinions on what was best.

Our father had no serious interest in the whole project, for as far as he was concerned, it was more time at a fancy finishing school, prompting his favorite maxim: "Those who went to college work for those who never went," a nice defense mechanism for a

A DANGEROUS THING

man who dropped out of school so he could go to work. Fortunately, his older brothers, the two sons of his father's first wife, had set examples by sending their children off to places like the Wharton School of the University of Pennsylvania and, closer to home and more ready for women, Vassar College. Since there was nothing much else for a young woman to do until she married, my father accepted that college was the way to keep daughters occupied.

Everything about college was the job of the high school guidance counselor. That was the person who made recommendations and instructed us to apply to two first choice schools, Ivy League for boys and Seven Sisters for girls, and then a 'security choice.' Those who had older siblings pumped them and their friends for information and came up with a short list. There were other possibilities for people who looked further—big universities, schools known for a special field, but most of us concentrated on small New England colleges. When we had made our choice, and been accepted, and set off on this radical new endeavor, we found ourselves, to our shock, not free, as we expected, but guarded round on all sides by something we would learn were called 'parietal rules' that made us more hemmed in than we had ever been in our freewheeling New York City days.

Chapter Nine

SENT UP
THE RIVER

G ASOLINE WAS AVAILABLE AGAIN FOR FAMILY EXCURSIONS, and it was a splendid late summer day to ride up the Hudson Valley from Manhattan. In the back of the family's black Cadillac, I sat between my mother and my sister watching carefully as the driver maneuvered the sedan under the big stone arch, past the gatekeepers, and forged straight ahead for Main, which loomed fortress-like ahead of us. This was not my first day at college. It was 1946. I was 13 years old, the age at which my father left school for good, but I still had all of high school ahead of me. I do not know what I expected this thing called college to be, but the reality that was Vassar College that day became a template of higher education. Its buildings and grounds came to represent what I expected a college to be like. It formed an image I struggled with for the next half century.

What eludes me is why I can remember that September day in Poughkeepsie, down to the details of our dinner, yet have no recollection of my own first day at Mount Holyoke College five years later. Perhaps part of this great impression is due to the fact that my sister Carol was the first person I knew to disappear off into space

143

A Dangerous Thing

Betty and Carol as teenagers, c. 1946.

this way, though I understood in a vague way that in choosing Vassar she followed in the footsteps of our cousin Belle, Abe Krasne's second oldest daughter. But Belle, who blazed the original trail for Krasnes from Manhattan to that far country called Poughkeepsie, was a dim figure to me because she was even older than my sister. To our parents, Belle's experience must have been reassuring: Abe Krasne recommended the school, although he had stumbled upon it almost be accident. My father might not summon up any enthusiasm about colleges, but he respected his oldest brother's opinion, while my mother sought his views. From what they could see, Belle had ventured so far, yet returned still recognizable.

Sent Up the River

Most probably nobody asked Belle's views on her college experience, or they might have heard a different report.

As I looked around us from the car window, the girls seemed to have descended from another planet. Blond and blue-eyed, tall and slim, they wore a uniform of pleated skirts and riding jackets. Nothing about our lives in Manhattan had prepared us for this feeling of having barged into a convention of models for *Glamour* magazine's back-to-college issue. If they came from the same place we did, they occupied different avenues and attended different schools than the ones we played with our field hockey and tennis teams. We had, for the first time in our lives, invaded WASP America. How would Carol survive in this vast, strange place? Not a party animal, not a joiner, it was hard to imagine her signing up for clubs, joining activities, or just making friends.

Because it was right after the war and the GI Bill was in the process of transforming America, there were also men on campus, but they were somehow invisible. No one saw them; no one spoke of them. In short order they faded out of the picture, returning the place to its historic femaleness. It wasn't until the upheavals of the sixties caused a radical break with tradition that they appeared again, sending our family back in a coeducational future none of us could even begin to imagine in September 1946.

The day was taken up with serious academic business necessary to the gearing up of a college year…no orientation fun and games. This was not high school on a bigger scale; it was an alien place. Carol had to make her way from building to building, always amid groups of strangers, stand in lines so she could sign up for placement tests, look over complicated course registration forms, and the lists for assignment of advisors. This was not an orientation with balloons and funny hats; instead, Carol set off periodically to make her way over one of those first academic hurdles that would make up the ensuing years. It was assumed everyone was literate, but where would she place in the array of require-

A DANGEROUS THING

ments, such as French and Mathematics?

Getting settled in one of the fortresses surrounding the campus occupied only the time it took to carry up a few clothes, books, and a laundry case to the single room she was assigned, with a pleasant nod at the White Angel, the woman who guarded the desk overlooking the front door. The essential furniture was there; no one brought anything that required a lock on the door. The character of the place was a cross between a mental institute and a pajama party—bedroom doors stayed open, people wandered around halls in various stages of changing clothes, warily friendly. There were issues of class and caste to be worked out.

Big, busy, scary, foreign…it seemed to me we were doing a terrible thing, going off and leaving her in that place where she knew no one. It was late afternoon when we parted company, leaving my sister to make herself at home in that big building on that strange campus, not to be seen again until the train deposited her back in New York City for Thanksgiving.

We made our way to Poughkeepsie, where we had dinner at the Vassar Brothers restaurant before heading home in the car. From our table we were watched over by a large oil painting of two serious, sober looking nineteenth century gentlemen, their white collars emanating startlingly from black suits and a dark background. The label informed us they were the brewery brothers whose financial backing created Vassar College and Vassar Brother's Hospital.

Carol was at Vassar because her cousin Belle had gone there, but it was a good thing she did not know cousin Belle hated college, just as it was a good thing Belle probably did not know her sister Estelle, nine years older, had hated college. That was one family tradition that remained a secret. Estelle, the forerunner, had graduated from Hunter High School at 16 and gone off to Goucher College, where she had been too young, too far away from home, too quiet and bright to fit in. She solved the problem of being

146

Sent Up the River

unhappy at college, setting a pattern Belle and Carol followed: she graduated early.

The shock of transition for these women was far greater than the distance in miles from city to country. They had moved from a coed to a single sex school as well as from a Jewish to a WASP environment. From a small school where everyone—students and teachers—knew everyone, they had been transplanted to a large and impersonal environment where a progressive educational philosophy was replaced by traditional educational practices. Eastern women's colleges were also places where a quest for social justice was replaced by a society that took prejudice and discrimination as a fact of life.

For Belle, the distance she had traveled was made clear at Convocation, the official opening of the school year, when her Vassar classmates filed into the auditorium and took their seats, leaving an empty circle around the one Negro student. And then there were the rules, parietal rules that governed hours when students could go out and must be in, that decreed she could not leave campus until Thanksgiving. For a student who had been living in Manhattan, commuting to school in The Bronx, going out at night on dates in the city, these strange regulations, designed so colleges acting 'in loco parentis' could safeguard students, were infantilizing. Rules also extended to jobs, cleaning and waiting table in every dormitory; and then there were those White Angels guarding the door.

At Thanksgiving cousin Belle finally went home…and cried. The place was too terrible. "I can't go back," she declared. But of course she did go back. Unfortunately, no one had told Fieldston people that school was not supposed to be fun. It did not matter. No one asked a student in those days "Are you happy? Are you having a good time?" Those were not questions relevant to the getting of a good education. In time, Belle found some friends, put together a plan to get out in three years, after all, one year was partly over and that only meant two more.

A DANGEROUS THING

Ironically, her role at the college became a key ingredient in both family events and the development of the school, hardly something anyone would have predicted from her first semester. But by that time her role had changed; the college was a vastly different place; and she was at a decidedly different place. She had taken her Art History major and her organizational skills and parlayed them into key positions in the New York art critic's scene. It was from there that Sarah Gibson Blandings, President of Vassar, recruited her in 1961 to mastermind a major undertaking: an art exhibit to commemorate the College's centennial.

Blandings made history when she became Vassar's President in 1946, succeeding the male line going back to the founder, and preceding the other women's colleges that had forgotten they could trust a female to run the show. At Mount Holyoke, a woman had founded the school, but after the Board of Trustees selected a man to succeed the second president, Mary Woolley, she refused to ever set foot on campus again. Her strong stand had no effect; Mount Holyoke continued to be presided over by men until the sixties, as did most of the Seven Sister Schools. Yet for all her up-to-date ideas, Blandings' view of the role of a woman's college as she phrased it in 1961 sounds an old, familiar note. Vassar was "successful in preparing young women for their part in creating happy homes, forward-looking communities, stalwart states, and neighborly nations."

By the time Blandings recruited her, Belle was a professional art critic who came back to Vassar bringing her own expertise, a far cry from her first semester in the war years. Choosing her committee carefully, she was able to work with intelligent, interesting people in the arts, and leave behind as a bad dream the world of cliques, debutantes, and dilettantes that was mainstream Vassar in her college days. The team she created put together the Centennial Loan Exhibit of works from alumnae collectors, and led to the creation of an organization called Friends of the Vassar Art Gallery, a

Sent Up the River

group that, over the years, helped raise millions of dollars and attracted donations of famous work to enhance the study of art. Again in 1977 she returned to organize a show and publication so successful it resulted in the donation of over three hundred works of art to the gallery. The significance of these contributions was a measure of her triumph over the narrow, superficial standards of her World War II classmates.

Part of the problem of Seven Sister Schools in mid-twentieth century was that the idea of what a university or college was supposed to be was set early and set by men. The isolation of the university or college was part of an ancient ritual going back to the Middle Ages: the Town and Gown configuration. The gathering together of scribes, scholars, churchmen, and later a few gentlemen, may have generated its own raucous, bawdy atmosphere by the time of the Renaissance, but the place of learning was also often a refuge from the tide of civil scourges by which the rest of society was tossed about. The university was a place where men could give their full powers of cognition to how many angels could fit on the head of a pin.

Though hardly a cloister, the walled gardens and dons in academic robes still give Cambridge and Oxford the same aura of an ordered world apart that a present day visitor gets from stepping into the Cloisters Museum. At American colleges the 'quads,' as the quadrangle of buildings guarding a greensward came to be known, were an expanded version of the cloister surrounding a garden.

The trouble was that on closer inspection nothing was quite what it seemed to be, which may account for why Krasne daughters did not find what they expected at college. In Germany, for instance, universities became places for drinking and dueling, or for plotting political revolutions. In America, by the beginning of the twentieth century the ivory towers of selective institutions of higher education stood guard over the playing fields of privileged white males. They set the pattern and tone for what college was

149

expected to be. By the end of the nineteenth century that had come to mean a place that provided a gentleman with a finishing school where he could escape from the patriarchal household and sow his wild oats while achieving his gentleman's C.

As Helen Lefkowitz Horowitz chronicles in *Campus Life*, her history of the campus ethos, the dominant tone of the American college was set by young men seeking to organize a life of pleasure at odds with both administrative regulations and faculty expectations. The priorities of those attending elite schools, Horowitz says, were an "eager pursuit of the pleasures of the table and the flesh," and what resulted from this was a "high tolerance for the excesses that accompanied indulgence." This explains why Woodrow Wilson, when he was President of Princeton University and was asked how many students he had, is reported to have said, "About twenty." Similarly, Professor Alvin Kernan, in his memoir *In Plato's Cave*, describes his years at Williams College in the 1940s as a time when what mattered was "family, money, looks, athletic ability...very rarely intellect.... never virtue," making the whole enterprise sound like the movie "Animal House," that supposed send-up of college life in the 1960s.

Women's colleges, of course, considered freakish from the beginning, could not tolerate licentiousness, and countered it by making domestic duties and rules about behavior part of the regimen, as well as by keeping a tight rein on the whereabouts of students. At Vassar, the first teachers doubled as governesses, making sure rules of decorum were followed. Parietal rules were so much a part of the woman's college scene that when they were dropped at the end of the sixties, one student's parents sued Vassar.

But by mid-twentieth century, as college became the customary route connecting high school and marriage for middle class women, the intellectual milieu of men's and women's schools came to resemble each other more and more. Women flippantly claimed they majored in bridge, knitted through class, and lived for week-

Sent Up the River

ends when they escaped to men's schools for mixers called "meat markets." At Ivy League and Seven Sister schools an excellent education might be there for the taking, but it was not the priority of most students.

By the time my sister Carol was an old hand at Vassar who had, at least temporarily, made her peace with this system, she invited her little sister up for a weekend. She was living in a building called Raymond, in a place called the Quad. At breakfast that first morning we sat at a large square table in the hall's dining room. The student waitress reeled off possibilities, but uninitiated, I was always a course behind. When I told her the juice I wanted, she was on the fruit, and when I was ready to make my fruit choice, she was already on to the cereal, so I ended up with a series of items I had never before tasted: vegetable juice, apricots, shredded wheat. Thus I ended up with a meal perfectly suited to a senior citizen's residence, but at the time it only reinforced my image of the school as the height of sophistication.

This impression was sealed as we dashed off to Carol's morning class, History of Art. This was not a classroom as I knew it; it was an amphitheater in which we climbed steeply up past rows of seats. Just as Carol pointed out to me some of the students, such as the dark haired young woman several rows below named Jacqueline Bouvier, the lights went out. In the darkened room a picture was projected at the front. The teacher started speaking, pointing out details about the painting, while students hastened to write in their notebooks, illuminated at each seat by a tiny light. Watching the slides while writing furiously in the almost dark was an unexpected challenge I hadn't considered when thinking of college. So this is what it was about. I was impressed, having no perception that in the midst of that special community people could feel completely out of place.

From the breakfast food to the pictures on the screen to the students, it all seemed brilliant. It was rumored that socialites chose

A DANGEROUS THING

Vassar because its proximity to New York City meant their debuts would not have to be interrupted. As an aspiring med student, I applied elsewhere when it was my turn, to a woman's college known for its sciences. It was over 30 years before I returned to Vassar and the next time I climbed the steps of the Art History amphitheater it was for a professional symposium moderated by one of our children.

For Carol, too, like her cousin Belle, four years in Poughkeepsie was way too much. That the college was a relatively short ride from the city was meaningless. No one had a car; there were rules about when and how often a student could leave; college routine was all encompassing. She had had enough of the hermetic Vassar life and wanted out, so she accelerated to finish in three years, even though this meant returning home to Central Park West, picking up the life she had left behind. She did not feel she was leaving a student cohort to which she had any attachment, a faculty with whom she had made any particular connections, an environment in which she had ever been particularly at home.

On the other hand, she was not prepared for any of the jobs typically open to women, all of which began with a typing test. Women were supposed to graduate and move on to marriage. An engagement ring and the title of Mrs. were supposed to be the real outcome of a college education. Other than marriage, there was the publishing industry. Editing was deemed proper pink-collar employment for Seven Sisters graduates, though it was also referred to as 'the white slave trade' because of the low pay and menial tasks assigned women. Michael Korda, chronicling the mid-century history of the publishing business in his memoir *Another Life*, points out that work in publishing was considered an honor, for which an independent income was necessary, because it was impossible "to live a decent life on the kind of salary most publishers were still paying in the 1950s." For women, he remarks, "a few years as a publishing assistant after Wellesley or Radcliffe or

Sent Up the River

Smith was a kind of finishing school."

One day in the seventies I had lunch with one of my editors from Harper & Row and she tried to explain to me the nature of the contract dispute then going on between the assistant editors and the company. I found it hard to believe the pittance at the heart of the dispute. Even as a teacher whose first full-time contract as Lecturer was for $7,500, I was appalled by how little editors were paid, and that was several decades after Carol went to work. In her position as an editor of college textbooks at a large publishing house, she was asked to bring coffee, and told to keep the change. Her assignment was to see that the illustrations were right side up. It was a typical pink-collar job for college women.

She had been away from home for three years. She was 20 years old, and could say, just as de Beauvoir did after her years of education left her in exactly the same place she had always been, that the "frightful banality of my daily life" was stifling. Though unlike de Beauvoir, no one was reading Carol's mail or requiring her to announce exactly where she would be every moment, she found trying to fit back in to the conventions of family life was like trying to step into an old dress she had outgrown.

When she decided to live in an apartment of her own, no one in the family had ever heard anything so shocking; no one offered assistance; the family was embarrassed. Just as in de Beauvoir's society, daughters lived at home until they married. To add to the embarrassment, the only apartment she was able to afford on her editor's salary was a walk-up in the west twenties, someplace not even on our map of Manhattan. This was before Chelsea became cute. The tenant across the hall, it turned out, received male visitors at all hours of the day and night, visitors who often buzzed the wrong bell. The exotic quality of the neighborhood did not embarrass Carol because no one in the family considered visiting her anyway.

Her move was a revolutionary act, but she had always been the rebel in the family. Personality and early education had made home

A Dangerous Thing

Sandra, with the twins Alice and Joan and their parents, Bernice and Ben Krasne. *Life* magazine article on "The Plight of a Pretty Artist," 23 November 1953 (Photograph by Philippe Halsman).

and college equally into places where she did not see herself fitting, so there she was in Chelsea, on her own. She was leading a life for which there were no role models in our post war Central Park West society. As a photograph from *Life* magazine of our cousins closely grouped around the family piano shows, young women, however talented they might be, were stationed at home.

Seeing Carol living downtown by herself was a scary prospect, on the order of abandoning her that first day at Vassar. Not for me, that office life. I was going to be a doctor and accomplish great things, though I did not know a single woman to whom I could look as a model

Chapter Ten

CONFORMITY OR DIVERSITY?

For a city girl, South Hadley, Massachusetts, was per-petually surprising. In the fall, big black crows came cawing over the hill in back of the Mandelles, the dormitories that com-manded the far side of lower lake. On Mountain Day we rode our bikes up the crisply golden valley of the Connecticut River and pic-nicked. At sunset in winter the dark figures of skaters were out of a Currier and Ives print, and late at night on our way home from the Library, the snow gleamed white all the long winter in that enclosed, safe, carless campus.

I had not planned to go to Mount Holyoke College. For one thing, the name had a parochial ring to it, evoking nuns enveloped in flowing black garments, that was embarrassing to a Jewish fam-ily. My parents, who had come to the conclusion that my sister's years at Vassar had not been a success, would have been perfectly happy for me to go to one of the finishing schools in Manhattan that passed themselves off as junior colleges. But taking myself very seriously as a pre-med student, I focused on schools with well-known science departments. The University of Rochester headed my list, followed by Mount Holyoke and Bryn Mawr, with

155

A DANGEROUS THING

Bucknell, the one school that turned me down, as a safety choice.

Mid-winter of senior year in high school I donned boots, as though heading for an outpost of empire, and took the train to Rochester. Neither the city nor the school, which bled into each other, looked promising by the murky light of winter. Students were packed three to a room in odds and ends of post war city housing that served as a campus, giving the school no discernible shape or focus. If I was seeking the un-Vassar, this was it: a university with no interest in the quaint customs of liberal arts college life, in a city in New York State's hinterlands. That was an oxymoron: cities were places like New York, London, Paris, and Rome.

Another Friday I went down to Philadelphia on the Penn Central to visit Bryn Mawr. People arrived at the college by transferring to the miniature railroad that chugged its way, like a toy train, through the suburban towns of Philadelphia's Mainline. Picture postcard scenes flashed by: solid, symmetrical, stone houses, set amid small, carefully landscaped gardens. That was the campus too: as void of people as the vista from the train window. Wherever the guide went, people must have disappeared down rabbit holes because the college appeared empty, plague stricken. Was everyone studying in dorm rooms, library, or labs? If the University of Rochester was the un-Vassar, Bryn Mawr was the ur-Vassar, an ominously spooky stage-set for yee olde ivy covered college. Once more safely back on the train to New York, I crossed another one off the list. By process of elimination, I was going to Mount Holyoke.

Just as my family before me, cousins Estelle and Belle and my sister Carol, saw themselves as out of place in their colleges, in the images of South Hadley that come back to me I was a solitary figure. Perhaps there was a Krasne gene that gave us the temperamental bias of loners, or perhaps, like them, I was the odd woman: a city person, when most students were from small towns or suburban areas; a Democrat in emphatically Republican country; a product of a private progressive school while most others had a public education; a Jew in a Protestant community. Then, too, I was a young woman intent on pre-medical studies when the ultimate quest more often was for the engagement ring. But unlike the other women in the family who preceded me to college and found the differences unpleasant, I found them quaint, like visiting a foreign country.

There was a sense also, I realize, in which all of my classmates were outsiders too, and we were caught briefly together in a protected zone between opposing countries. On one side was the society of our families, a culture of getting and begetting; on the other side was the scholarly cloister from which our teachers—*deus ex machina*—descended to the classroom. Like characters in a fairy tale, our presence in that special land was guarded round by parietal rules and handbook instructions on how to walk in public and dress for tea.

It was hard for us to connect the professors who appeared before us with the middle class family life from which most of us came, a world where daughters subscribed to Seventeen and their mothers to *The Ladies Home Journal.* That is the world to which we were expected to return, somehow better equipped after our sojourn in the magic kingdom. A few of our teachers achieved a touch of solidity outside the classroom. Professor Holmes of the Philosophy Department and his wife served Russian tea at home Sunday evenings; Miss Lynch, of the English Department, was known to be perplexed by the surprising ways of an English war orphan she had adopted; and we knew that the Political Science Department sent its faculty out into the public arena.

However, it was difficult to imagine our professors grappling with the details of domestic existence, and connecting the faculty with life beyond South Hadley strained our imaginative faculties. They had a pale, papery look about them, as though long study in dim recesses of libraries had made them rare, like white asparagus

A DANGEROUS THING

kept out of the light. Years later, when I become an academic, I had plenty of time to think about how students view faculty.

I can see myself now as I appeared in the fifties, a solitary figure huddled in a short coat, knees visible between high socks and the Bermuda shorts that were the uniform of the day, as I made my way across campus after the library closed. It was dark and only the winter winds of Massachusetts accompanied me over the bridge at Lower Lake and up the hill to North Mandelle, where I passed the lounge filled with bridge players and smokers, the dining room where our napkin boxes held our linen napkins, and climbed to my fourth floor room. Together my roommate and I made cocoa. The quaint customs were intriguing.

At Fieldston High School there had been clubs and projects with which different groups of students became involved. They generally focused on the arts or current social causes. At Mount Holyoke, when students sought ways to belong, they took everything about the school itself as of the utmost seriousness: the rituals of Big Sisters, Little Sisters; caroling at Christmas; the class play; the class insignia; the class blazer—it reminded me of Camp Lenore with its team cheer. Watching all this school spirit from the sidelines was a spectator sport, as though I had chosen to attend college in a foreign country.

Whatever we were told to do we did: attending church seven Sundays a semester; attending chapel three times a week; signing in and out; not smoking in public; "dressing" for dinner; standing for the housemother's blessing. In retrospect, what gives me pause is our absolute docility. For those who might have raised questions, there was one answer with the power to quell doubt: *in loco parentis*. Left to ourselves—people spoke about the possibility in hushed voices—we might have run wild, but the College stood guard in place of our parents. It couldn't quite tuck us in at night, but every evening before bed it administered milk and cookies.

The problem was I did not know of anyone whose parents'

Conformity or Diversity?

demands resembled the code under which we lived, so I wrote off our acquiescence in the ways of Mount Holyoke as a big chance to partake in tradition, like an extended tour of ancient monuments. Our docility gave us a quaint innocence that connected us with the generations before us, but separates us from those of the sixties and seventies for whom the questioning of custom became a full-scale activity.

Yet oddly enough, the founding of Mount Holyoke College itself was a radical gesture, hardly an act of conformity. To have believed in the nineteenth century that higher education should be made available to women was a full scale questioning of custom. On the other hand, in her establishment of Mount Holyoke, Mary Lyon demanded social and moral conformity to her high standards—every young woman had to do housework chores, attend church, learn to serve tea—as Emily Dickinson wryly noted when she gave the place a brief try. Conformity and diversity, we were heirs to this paradox of higher education for women, though it took me a long, slow while to recognize the subtle variety that constituted diversity at a woman's college in the fifties.

The oddity of this new world was made dramatically clear to me in my very first class, Introduction to Philosophy. I can still picture the room and even remember approximately where I was sitting that mid-September day in 1951 as Professor Roger Holmes, a stocky man with a shock of straight, graying hair, came through the doorway. As Professor Holmes entered the room, a good percentage of students jump up to stand at attention next to their seats. I stared in puzzled amazement, edged forward in my seat, but could not bring myself to follow them. I felt I had stumbled onto an entirely other educational planet from the one I had been on the previous years of my life. What did this deference signify? Was I encountering another level of being than the people who had taught me before? What was to be the relationship of student to teacher in this new world? Professor Holmes may have been sur-

A Dangerous Thing

prised, but he had obviously encountered the situation before and instructed the students that in the future their gesture of homage was not called for. It was a scene and a class that come back to me years later when I was hired to teach my first class in a Catholic girl's (sic) college.

Even though I was a science major, a pre-med student, it seemed to me that what went on in Philosophy class was the essence of college. Biology, Chemistry, those were subjects we had in high school, along with Greek tragedy. But in Philosophy class we studied the ideas, the people I'd heard about and imagined college was supposed to be about: Plato and Socrates, Heroditus and Thucydides, Heraclitus and Pythagoras, they were magical names, like incantations. I felt like a child at last made privy to the conversations of adults.

If we paid attention, if we cared—and I assumed everyone was going to be intensely interested—we would discern a story that so far I had only heard as dim background sounds. At college we would find out what New Criticism was about, how chairoscuro worked, why the Greeks triumphed at Thermopolyae and the Russians at Stalingrad and, more to the point, what all of this meant for us. But college, I came to realize slowly, though it had lots of bright students, was not an intellectual place. Only in Philosophy did we seem to breathe the rarefied air of intellectual life.

Every week Professor Holmes explicated our readings, playing devil's advocate. One week we came to grips with the ideas of the Idealists, convincing ourselves of the plausibility of a worldview that held nothing material actually exists. No sooner had we seen the logic of this view, than Professor Holmes showed us how the present week's readings by the Materialists were a complete contradiction of the previous week's discussions. We were off again, arguing why this set of explanations was more logically persuasive than the previous one. Every step of the way we were forced to defend

Conformity or Diversity?

our positions on major topics with big, abstract Latin names: metaphysics, ontology, eschatology, and epistemology. Ultimately, we had to make our own peace with intellectual inconsistency.

At first, it came as a surprise that students enrolled at Mount Holyoke did not know more—more vocabulary, history, art, literature. These were matters that a New Yorker took for granted from reading *The New York Times* or had picked up from hanging out in museums. If I scored well in these areas, that was not reassuring: at Fieldston I hadn't even made the Honors English class. My own provincialism emerged on my first trip to visit my roommate's family in Plymouth County, Massachusetts. Used to walking around the corner in Manhattan for anything we needed at home, I was surprised when Ruth told me it was time to pick up the chickens for dinner and we piled into a car for a drive so long I thought we were going to end up in Canada, only to repeat this act in the opposite direction after dinner when the family sent us out for ice-cream. In New York I had not even known anyone who knew how to drive. Then there was my first confrontation with a lobster the next night when I was draped in a bib and equipped with a set of surgical tools to attack a red beast with claws and whiskers that swam into focus on a large plate in front of me.

Back at college, the students were a big blur and it was hard to make out who the smart people were. We might not have been as dispiriting to teach as the "sullen unread students" Alvin Kernan, in his memoir *In Plato's Cave*, describes encountering at Yale in the 1950s, but that was because our professors had made their peace with the fact that they were teaching young women, and had developed different expectations. What I didn't give any thought to was who taught at a woman's college and why they were there. But what I did finally comprehend was that there were different kinds of intelligence at work in our college class.

Among the courses I was signed up for freshman year was a math course suspiciously titled The Real Number System. My sus-

A DANGEROUS THING

picions were well justified as the course turned out to have absolutely no numbers in it, only letters. If I had thought I was lost amid numbers in Miss Colvin's class, I quickly realized that a course in which numbers masqueraded as letters was not going to be my salvation. Instead, I met a freshman in the room next door to mine who was set on being a Mathematics major. She nursed me through The Real Number System until one day, in the middle of a class, I saw the light.

This classmate was even more impressive to me because, when I casually asked what she did during the summer, she told me she plucked chickens in a chicken-plucking factory. Slowly I was making out signs of diversity, indications so subtle they were easy to miss on first and second glance. In Biology, my lab partner was a certifiable 16-year-old genius who had already written plays and poetry. Unfortunately, she was unable to see anything in our microscope except her own eyelashes, so, as a science major, I was called upon to help her out, just as my mathematics neighbor helped me out.

In the fifties, the academic frontier was Psychology, though I knew no one shallow or daring enough—depending on one's viewpoint then—to major in it. College curriculum has always evolved slowly. Well through the nineteenth century students studied only Greek, Latin, and Mathematics. Romance languages, novels were hardly considered academic material, and when literature finally made the grade, it was understood it was to be taught in its original language. If you wanted to study Flaubert or Dostoyevsky, you had to learn their languages. Electives, the idea of giving a student a choice, were a twentieth century innovation at Harvard.

Psychology had been working its way into academe for a while, first masquerading as part of Philosophy, finally as a department in its own right. It was not accompanied by a lab, but at Mount Holyoke students devised tests to administer as projects, and there was a model nursery school at the edge of campus with a one-way

Conformity or Diversity?

window behind which Psychology majors took up positions to do observation studies. The association between Psychology and Education did nothing to add luster to the new field because anyone with such a clear vocational goal as nursery school teaching was definitely déclassé at a Seven Sisters college. The rest of us knew we were there to find husbands so we could afford to major in Chemistry.

Psychology wasn't exactly Basket Weaving 101, but students knitted their way through class, something they did not do in other courses, although, in fairness, History of Art was held in the dark, Shakespeare around a table, and in The Real Number System students concentrated on figuring out why a course with that name used only letters. The Psychology teacher had apparently made an ambivalent peace with knitting, for at the beginning of the semester he announced "It is forbidden to interrupt class by dropping a needle."

The textbook for Psychology, students muttered, only made a pretentious business out of what was common sense. And indeed, there wasn't all that much of significance to fill the book back then: Pavlov and his dogs were there; Freud and the Id, Ego, and Superego made a prominent appearance; and Skinner, who had not so long ago made news with *Walden Two*, brought the course up to date. Most students would have agreed with William James' gloomy 1892 estimation of the discipline, had anyone presented them with it. James described the new field of Psychology as:

> a little gossip and wrangle about opinions; a little classification and generalization on the mere descriptive level, a strong prejudice that we have states of mind, and that our brain conditions them; but not a single law in the sense in which physics shows us laws, not a single proposition from which any consequence can causally be deduced.

A Dangerous Thing

Nevertheless, the Psychology major had a certain racy cachet, not so much because it held promise of dealing with people's hidden selves, but because the professor had divorced his wife and married a student. Just (the students in this women's college murmured) what one would expect in that field.

What went on in class, even for those of us who worked at being students, was only a part of life on campus. For those who didn't hang out in the smoker playing bridge, there were the dorm bull sessions. Freshman year, people stayed up way past milk and cookies discussing 'What is Religion'; sophomore year late night talk dwelt on 'The Purpose of Life'; and junior year 'Theories of Love' absorbed our talk. War, whether for rights on this continent or another, the role of race and gender, peace and politics were topics that never made it onto our agenda.

When Adlai Stevenson came to campaign at the train station in the old industrial city of Holyoke, I took the bus that ran from South Hadley into the city to hear him speak, one of only two democratic representatives from our rabidly Republican college. It was a far cry from the eighties when we went to Washington for the Abortion Rights march. Then every parking lot disgorged busloads from the old Seven Sisters Colleges and we marched with our daughter from Vassar. In the fifties it did not occur to most of us women tucked away in the middle of Massachusetts, trying to absorb the sum of human knowledge, that we could do anything about the shape of events, other than be spectators at the course of history.

Chapter Eleven

NOTA BENE

HAVING GROWN UP IN THE BIG CITY, WHERE FIFTH Avenue, Broadway, and Greenwich Village had become more than romantic names; having been introduced to theaters and opera house, restaurants and museums during my first eighteen years of life, college in the Connecticut River valley seemed charming. The idea of rusticating in a beautiful country setting devoted to learning had great attraction…for a while. Some of my relatives who went off to college found the academic community oppressive and gave up on the whole thing, while others compressed college into three years before escaping back to the city. As an aspiring med student, these were not options, so I picked my way through bridge players, people running for May Queen, those already into planning weddings, and plodded on through the science curriculum.

Organic and Inorganic Chemistry were followed by Quantitative and Qualitative Analysis. Physics I feared so greatly that I decided I had to take it in summer school. Off I went to Harvard where the whole year could be done in a summer by taking first and second semesters concurrently, which were taught, it just so happened, by a Mount Holyoke professor. Physics, the way

165

A DANGEROUS THING

it was organized then, was probably the only subject in the curriculum in which the two semesters had no logical connection, but not much about Physics was susceptible to logic. I was absolutely right to be afraid I wouldn't understand the concepts and be able to do the mathematical problems. There was nothing solid to grab onto in physics, not like Biology where a dogfish on the dissecting table was a fact, and a steady hand and eye could show how parts articulated.

The minute I was faced with the kind of question physics threw out (when someone standing at point A would hear the whistle of a train proceeding at X miles per hour when sound travels at the rate of Y), panic would set in. When a young man in the class stopped me near the steps of Widener Library one day and asked, "What's a pretty girl like you doing in Physics?" I was too flabbergasted to realize he just might have a point. Asked to calculate the force holding up a wall or the transformation of an electric current from point A to point B, panic was the answer. Fortunately, or unfortunately, Harvard offered lots of ways to forget panic, none of them helpful in getting through Physics. Somehow or other I apparently did make it through—barely—which was all I needed to do, since grades of courses taken at other schools did not transfer in as part of a student's grade point average.

The semester I took Comparative Anatomy, the lab was held Wednesday afternoons, so every Wednesday I returned to the dorm in time for dinner with hands giving off the strong odor of formaldehyde. And just about every Wednesday evening we were served creamed chipped beef for dinner, until senses of smell and taste became so intermingled that years later, served that dish once in a city far across America, it conjured up for me the entire world of my pre-med Mount Holyoke days. That luncheon brought back afternoon labs in an old science building, the cases in its halls lined with bizarre specimens; elderly female professors gliding through the room to peer over one's shoulder; a notebook full of drawings

Nota Bene

with finely sharpened pencils. And then there was the aftermath: rushing back to throw on a skirt over my Bermuda shorts for dinner; grabbing my napkin and sitting at a round table where a student waitress passed a bowl of creamed chipped beef before my formaldehyde fingers.

Programmed to keep my gaze focused on study and grades, I collected the prerequisites I needed for medical school, but couldn't ignore the fact that some courses were a lot easier than others, and none of those were science courses. History of Art, Philosophy, Classical Civilization, History of the English Novel, these were the leavening each semester; these were where ideas were a familiar language. The problem came to a head junior year after my science requirements were complete. My father had been hospitalized with a heart attack, making me wonder where I belonged. Should I be in New York, for no particular purpose I could think of, except that it seemed callous to go on about my business as though nothing had happened? I went to speak with one of the Deans who, though she wouldn't tell me what to do, made encouraging remarks about Mount Holyoke being sorry to lose me and the possibility of my doing Honors work. There was nothing like the prospect of having to suddenly depart the simple country life for making it appear newly appealing.

As the dean had hinted, second semester of junior year I was asked to do Honors work, which meant three of my courses senior year would be replaced by work on a project that I would design and execute with the assistance of an advisor. The problem was, looking around me at the other science majors, at the faculty and their laboratories, I knew I couldn't do Honors work in science. I would never have anything original to contribute; any work I did would always be derivative, pedestrian. Shape-shifting moments there were in Mount Holyoke classrooms, but they never occurred in a lab. Following Bertrand Russell's logic to its conclusion as a model for composing an argument about belief—or non belief—

A DANGEROUS THING

was an intriguing challenge; grasping the elegant, formal beauty on a domestic scale of Ludwig Mies van der Rohe's pavilion at the Barcelona International Exhibition altered in a flash my entire understanding of domestic space; unraveling point-of-view in *The Ambassadors*, these were moments of sudden enlightenment, unlike my plodding hours in the science labs.

If I wanted to do Honors work, clearly I would have to switch majors. Fortunately, I had been taking literature classes all along because they felt like the easy stuff, so the change was mostly a bookkeeping entry. I was assigned to a Miss Joyce Horner as my Honors work advisor. If students at college had to spin their own webs of meaning out of the threads the school gave them, then for me the system ultimately received its meaning from afternoons at Miss Horner's.

It was not that I picked Miss Horner, Professor of English, department specialist in creative writing, as a thesis advisor. In fact, when I was assigned to her at the beginning of my senior year, I could find hardly anyone who knew her. Even among my literary acquaintances, Miss Horner was something of an unknown, and most certainly so to me, who was neither creative nor a writer. Though I was never at home with the Organic Chemists, I was also not one of those who took Lit Crit and acquired a taste for the exotic Lapsang Souchong tea served in that esoteric seminar, nor was I one who fancied herself a writer and hung out in the offices of the literary magazine.

Miss Horner, for reasons I understood only after reading her own novels (which reside on my bookshelf now, unsigned because it was far too gauche to ask for her autograph), immediately proposed Virginia Woolf as my honors work subject. So we began. I was assigned a carrel, a kind of cell in the library padded with books of one's own choosing, and there I assembled my cache of works on Bloomsbury. The first task was to read my way through books by and about Woolf, a relatively encompassable job in the

Nota Bene

fifties. There were no articles and very few books, and of the few there were, several focused on her father or the extended family. All the books on the subject just about filled the small shelf in my carrel.

Not a bad life, I decided, spending afternoons and evenings reading novels, short stories, essays, and the few critical works the library disgorged. Except there came a day, of course, when I had to say something about this reading, had to come face to face with blank sheets of paper, fill them with plausible, intelligent ideas, and set these before my thesis advisor. While others attended classes, studied for exams, most mornings after breakfast I climbed to the top floor of our dormitory and put a plaid wool robe over my clothes. In the cold light of our north-facing windows, I communed with Virginia Woolf. Who were Leslie Stephen, Vanessa Bell, Lytton Strachey, these contemporaries of Woolf who had become new companions of mine?

❖ ❖ ❖

For me they were, all rolled into one, Joyce Horner. She was of that world of Oxbridge, pictured in the centerfolds of my reference books, where everyone was gauntly esthetic looking and—for lack of flash bulbs—it was always a summer afternoon in an English garden where thin men in rumpled suits and bony women in narrow dresses sat in deck chairs talking of literature. As the product of a traditional education, Professor Horner had come to South Hadley from a diametrically opposite route to mine. To attend Oxford meant to be firmly grounded in Latin and the classics, to be methodically read in works of preceding eras. By attending Oxford she had made that virtually irrevocable choice available to English women from the latter part of the nineteenth century on. British society allowed women to pursue a husband or an education, a fact of social life Professor Horner explored in her novel *Greyhound on*

A DANGEROUS THING

the Leash, an imaginative creation of a character's different possible paths through life.

Miss Horner was small, bony, and bent over, with a sharp-beaked face and notable buckteeth that had never had the benefit of orthodontia. Her graying hair was pulled back but frequently escaped from captivity. As I watched her obliquely when she was reading my work, I wondered who had raised her, what kind of family had produced this homely, fragile, brilliant creature who was only comfortable tucked away on a side street in South Hadley. She seemed to me like a plant on the edge of a wood that grows slant as it reaches for a few rays of sun. Her appearance, manner, intellect clearly did not fit her for the ordinary pursuits of women in English middle class society. For that matter, I could not imagine her in the distant formality of a classroom either, and when I looked for her in our college lectures by W.H. Auden, Marianne Moore, or Robert Frost, I never spotted her.

The winter I was elected to Phi Beta Kappa, my mother, who was in Florida at the time, sent me a blue lace crinoline, one of those many-layered garments that could stand up by itself, from a place called The Trousseau Shop in Miami Beach. Whether she thought it was just what was needed for college, or it was to remind me of what was really important in life, I never discovered. But Miss Horner surprised me more by a murmured acknowledgment of the Phi Beta Kappa induction because it was the only recognition I ever caught of the fact that beyond her lay an entire campus with which she was supposedly connected. I worried she would be startled if exposed to bright outdoor light and disintegrate if ever exposed to the brusque world beyond South Hadley.

What we shared was not Virginia Woolf, or an interest in ideas, for even at that place and time, often perplexing for its scant supply of scholars, there were some who were interested in ideas. What we shared was that neither of us was naturally a part of that rugged and simple New England scene. Outsiders, we lived in a

Nota Bene

world of words, but it was precisely my words that gave her pause.

When I had assembled a sheaf of typed pages I would pedal across the lake and out the gate, up the main street of South Hadley, past stone academic buildings on the right and the old white houses of the village on my left, out a bit to where the rolling country of the Connecticut River valley came into its own again. On a side street I came to the house Professor Horner shared with Miss Green, who ran the Information Service (something between a public relations and a development office). I arrived on her doorstep in my flannel Bermuda shorts, knee socks and sweater, exuding (I always felt) an air of gym, city vacations, and college weekends. In her presence I became the cartoon version of a student.

It is the pauses I remember. Miss Horner, a chapter of my thesis in hand, sat reading, now and then offering seemingly tentative comments, to which I made replies that generated silence. Maybe it was merely coincidence that the title of my thesis was "Towards the Novel of Silence: A Study of Three Novels by Virginia Woolf." For a person from a culture that had always placed a high value on verbalism, those silences were a daunting lesson. She would rise in one of those pauses, offering tea and cookies, and disappear. I never followed, but sat there glancing about, unable to grasp the idea of this intellect dealing with the pots and pans of a domestic scene, unable to imagine how she would finish her sentence.

What had seemed just hours before, as I clipped together the stack of pages fresh from the typewriter, to be profound ideas encased in fine prose, showed forth in those pauses as nothing more than imprecision, a sloppy lack of clarity. The work had, of course, to be entirely rewritten. She was lost in the chapters, the pages where my sentences tortured themselves to death. We had come to Mount Holyoke from two such different routes that it was difficult for her to imagine how an Honors student knew so little of the classics, nothing whatsoever about the English sentence and

A DANGEROUS THING

the punctuation marks pertaining thereto, and could spell only a few words with any authority. So it was that when Miss Horner wrote "n.b." in the margins of my paper, I had to master my embarrassment over my need to ask for an explanation. "*Nota bene*," she said, surprised, as though that explained everything, leaving me to run home and look up the phrase, which I should have been able to figure out meant 'Note well.' But what was it I was supposed to 'note well'?

Her critical scrutiny sounds brutal, but the process was exhilarating. To have someone whose literary knowledge and sensitivity one respected devote such attention to one's every written word was care as encompassing as love; to have known such attention was to be spoiled critically for life. The process, however, took on a life of its own, for I brought it, as best I could, to the writing of my graduate thesis, and still later to my teaching.

At some point in the silences I would grope for a sense of closure by setting forth a naively energetic plan for the ensuing days. Then I pedaled back, a little less energetically, to where the bulky shadows of campus buildings were cast across the bluish snow and the warm yellow light of the late afternoon art classes and labs, and the Tudor tracery of the library windows fell across the paths. I rode one of the nondescript bicycles which, like our standing lamps, easy chairs, braid rug, came out of a basement on campus that was the repository of generic brands: bike, lamp, chair, rug, recycled with each class in that consumerless society where no one needed a lock on dorm room door or bicycle wheel.

After graduation, when I went to Europe, one of the first errands I did in France was buy a pair of navy kid gloves as a gift for Miss Horner, though I had no idea if they would fit. Women still wore gloves all the time and the delicate kidskin, with its fragile strength, was the most superior artifact I could think of as a gift for her, though fingering them struck me once again into a state of gawky collegiate robustness.

Nota Bene

Several years later, when I was writing poetry, I sent some poems to her for comments. The frustration, the barely controlled anger of some of those early works must have come as a surprise, but she responded. Her letters, on paper as tissue thin as airmail stationary, were written with a pen that seemed to have had only a ghostly remembrance of blue ink in it; and the handwriting was akin to the markings of an English sparrow traveling across freshly fallen snow. The cards she sent were exactly what I would have expected. In one, a miniature of the flood from *The Bedford Book of Hours* in the British Museum, tiny drowning steeples and microscopic flailing feet surround a three story wood house from which an exotic assortment of creatures issues forth. The writing on the cards, so minute in its preciseness, brought to mind the bony hand that composed the message and the frail frame of which it was a part.

The last time I saw Miss Horner, in a nursing home near Northampton, she was still surrounded by the selected props of her private world—books, papers—her perceptive comments on fellow residents and their reading habits still issued as tentative suggestions from long pauses.

A DANGEROUS THING

Traveling Light

Paper and pencil,
that's all it takes,
a folder, a wallet
can hold my needs:
words
to cover my encounters.

I worry for those locked up
without benefit of paper and pencil
those without a supply
of words
whose baggage weighs them down.
They could succumb
to such a load.

It's only a change of words
morning and evening
that saves me
from exposure to the elements.

Chapter Twelve

TREADING WATER

THE CLASS OF 1955 WENT FORTH INTO THE WORLD AS UNPRE-
pared to make its own way as any group of educated women
could ever have been. We did not forge ahead into law, medicine,
academe, where women were tolerated as long as they kept their
place, which was somewhere between the supply closet and the coffee maker. The few who had majored in sciences and found jobs in
research labs soon caught on to the facts of scientific life: they
would never be more than test tube clerks. Résumés and job interviews had never intruded into our ivory tower, and if we had a job
placement office and there was anyone who found a job through it,
I never heard about it.

That was higher education for women in the fifties: an extended time out, unrelated to anything outside. The clock stopped for
four years, and then we were back outside, ejected into a society
that had been going on exactly the same all the time we were in that
enclosed world called a college campus.

It had been suggested to me, off handedly, that I apply for a
Fullbright, which I had, equally off handedly, done. Not surprisingly, when I think of the special coaching colleges now devote to

175

A DANGEROUS THING

candidates they put forward for Fullbrights, Marshalls, or Rhodes Scholarships, it had not worked out. No matter. We were biding our time, waiting for marriage to overtake us, for which we were equally but more seriously unprepared.

About research and writing I had learned a little, about English history a little more. Art and architecture had made a big impression: Gothic cathedrals, the German pavilion at the 1929 Barcelona International Exhibit, frescoes at Assisi and mosaics at Ravenna. Thus the only step for which college had prepared us was the Grand Tour. So off we went, my college classmate Nancy, my sister, and I on an eleven-week jaunt. We were going to see everything because, of course, the trip would have to last us a lifetime. Everything included Gander airport in Newfoundland and Shannon in Ireland because planes on those 12-hour flights (17 hours coming back) could not carry enough fuel to cross the Atlantic directly. That some time in the future I would get back to Europe repeatedly, live abroad for months at a time, would have been the most impossible of notions then, especially given the Europe we encountered.

The Europe we came to ten years after World War II ended was ancient, disheveled, and poor. If people now complain of encountering bland uniformity—McDonalds and The Gap on every corner from Piccadilly to Beijing, spreading like an American disease across the world—we were fortunate. The Europe we visited was the Old World. It looked old; even more memorably it smelled old. In London, bomb craters gaped and there were no buildings standing taller than St. Paul's. At our small hotel in Kensington, to our embarrassment, a mousy young woman emerged from the basement to lug our valises to the third floor. She was the same below stairs servant who came up before dawn to polish the rows of shoes left outside bedroom doors at night. She emanated a kind of servility built into the English social structure that made Americans uncomfortable.

176

Treading Water

Smell…it is our keenest sense, the one that can most sharply recall England after the war: centuries of damp stone smelling of peat, coal dust, and the farmyard. It is exuded by the countryside, green and untouched, and by the stone villages where the narrow roads came right up to the front walls of old houses.

When we bought food for a picnic at a grocery story in the Cotswolds, the woman wrapped our purchases in cabbage leaves. There was no paper, except the wax paper sheets that served as toilet paper. Cashmere sweaters, for export only (after you presented a passport and a ticket), could be bought at a special store where servile sales people bowed saying, "Yes, Madame," or "No, Madame" without seeming to move their lips or raise their eyes from our shoes. The British themselves were still on some forms of rationing, trying to raise the capital to rebuild.

We were in a time machine, a retro-theme park. There was the London of Dickens's *Bleak House*; the Devonshire of Hardy's *The Return of the Native*; the moors of the Brontes; Bath was out of Jane Austin. The lake country was Wordswoth's daffodils, except that in a heat wave we shed our clothes to swim at Grassmere, emerging to face cows, large and serious, guarding our clothes. I did not recall Wordsworth having much to say on the subject of cows up close. These were not movie sets from J. Arthur Rank films; they were scenes from books we'd been brought up on. Here was the exotic geography of our imaginative landscape finally come alive: the moors and the downs; the Broads and the Backs; the Embankment, The City, the Inns of Court. All these exotic names we'd seen in books were made real: the whole bloody march of English history from Hampton Court to Traitor's Gate was set out before us.

We could fathom what T.S. Eliot, the poet of our era, was heading for when he spoke in "The Waste Land" of "Drifting logs/Down Greenwich reach/Past the Isle of Dogs," or wrote

A DANGEROUS THING

Highbury bore me. Richmond and Kew
Undid me. By Richmond I raised my knees
Supine on the floor of a narrow canoe.

My feet are at Moorgate, and my heart
Under my feet....

We could follow his drift when he described "unhealthy souls" in "Burnt Norton"

Driven on the wind that sweeps the gloomy hills
of London,
Hampstead and Clerkenwell, Campden
and Putney,
Highgate, Primrose and Ludgate.

Geographical names that had always seemed the product of fiction or poetic license solidified before our eyes.

We had one experienced driver, Nancy, so we volunteered her and rented a car. Nan, as she was called, was lean, with short, straight, sandy color hair. A New Englander, she came from Whitinsville, Massachusetts, half way between the cities of Holyoke and Boston. She had followed her two sisters, Miff and Bark, who were already out supporting themselves, to Mount Holyoke, where she was a science major. She agreed that the Grand Tour was just what she needed as a segue to her job in New York. As a country girl, Nan had been driving since her teens...but never on the other side of the road in a car with a shift on the other side. As city girls, we were strictly back seat drivers. Carol took on the job of tour guide, researching where we should go and what we should see. I was the navigator.

We managed to drive out of London and head towards the Cotswolds without a major disaster—no ditches or collisions and

Treading Water

still speaking to each other. But on our second day we abruptly faced a problem, actually a Bobby. Driving down our selected route, we came up to a sign announcing "Deviation."

"Quick," Nan instructed me. "What do we do?"

After a hasty examination of our map, I could see no other way of getting where we were heading. "I don't know." I shook my head. "There isn't any other way."

We peered ahead. The road looked perfectly okay. "Just go ahead." That was Carol, ever the rebel. And so we did…until faced with a large, stern Bobby planted squarely in the road before us with a raised hand. Meekly Nancy rolled down the window.

He glanced at us and before we could launch into excuses about coming from another part of the world said, "Madame, we rely on your discretion. If we cannot rely on that, what can we rely on?"

Having expected New York-style police talk, we were thrown into speechlessness. Swallowing our laughter, we backed up and put our heads together over our map to find another route.

Because there were three of us, sometimes we called ahead to ask if a hotel could put a cot in a room. There was always a long pause at the other end. Finally, one day the woman at the other end asked, "How old is the child?" and we realized cot meant crib (and crib meant something else).

In odd ways we were the beneficiaries of England's poverty and isolation. Food was completely English, and surprisingly edible, with none of the ethnic additions destined to overtake the English restaurant scene. There were strawberries and clotted cream; strawberry tarts, which we wolfed down seated on the top of London's red double-decker buses; apple tarts with custard; meaty lamb chops; delicate fillet of plaice; Caerphilly and Wensleydale cheeses; flaky scones at the Tate Gallery, though even then roast beef and Yorkshire pudding at Simpson's was on the bland, soggy side. There were no lines for admission to famous sites: visitors were allowed to clamber about the ruins of

A Dangerous Thing

Stonehenge, with the only concern being threatening skies and soggy shoes, or wander in peace through empty churches and art galleries.

A critic once said people could be Anglophiles or Francophiles, but never both. Perhaps even before we set foot on English soil our adolescent reading and high school courses had, without our knowing it, made Anglophiles of us. By the time we finished our English wanderings in 1955, our cultural heritage made us devoted to the cause of that damp, green isle.

Across the channel Paris, dark and decrepit, was pockmarked from guns, and had its own distinct odor: urine from pissoires. Carol bought a Matisse drawing and when she tried to negotiate a piece of paper to wrap it in, the saleswoman threw up her hands, "Mais non." That would have required a whole separate transaction. In our Left Bank hotel, we had to find the button to push for the single bulb in the stairway, then race to the next floor and repeat the fumbling.

Yet beyond French frugality, there was a sense of stubborn adherence to tradition that could be read in the ground plan of the Luxembourg Gardens, the Palace of Versailles, and the Grand Boulevards. For France, too, was a wonderful time machine: we were walking through the setting of *The Three Musketeers*, *A Tale of Two Cities*, *The Ambassadors*.

In the evening, the tiny restaurant across from our Left Bank hotel seeped down the street until the small tables and rickety chairs ran the length of the block. At dinner there we were offered strange foods: salads from root vegetables, frogs legs, snails. No food, we saw, was too lowly for the French gourmet. Why, we wondered for the first time, was there not one restaurant in New York City where people were served food at tables on the street? It was so hot we stopped in every arrondisement for a citron pressé, the entire ritual with fresh lemons, lemon squeezer, sugar, and water giving us a time to rest our feet.

Treading Water

We took the train south to Marseilles and a local back up to Aix-en-Provence. Along the shaded main street, its trees a green arcade, we bought bread and cheese, tomatoes and peaches, and the local Rosé for a picnic on Cezanne's hillside. Food, sun, and wine took their toll; we slept off the local Rosé under a tree facing Mt. St. Victoire.

France, even at its most decrepit, had a soigné quality, captured in the Gallic shrug, accompanied by the careless gesture of the hands. Between France and England was the difference between the complex subtlety of Montaigne and the straightforwardness of Sir Francis Bacon, between frog's legs and mutton, the intricate carving of Chartres Cathedral and the stolid stone of the Tower of London. There was an elusive, tired sophistication to its charm.

Still heading south, we moved on to Italy, where we had not only the art and architecture to deal with, but the men. No American would have mistaken us for glamour girls, in our (newly patented) Brooks Brothers wash-and-wear shirts. We were recognizably American: taller, lighter, dressed in mass produced clothing, making us targets for frequent remarks and unexpected gestures. At the beaches it was the year of the bikini, and in our one-piece American swimwear we were as vastly over dressed as 1920s bathing beauties in bloomer dresses. No matter: for Italian men we were the new women from the new world, and thus fair game. We were Henry James' Isabel Archer under sail, and we could see why.

In Italy there were beautiful young girls and there were old women, with no in-between. Marriage and the culture had the effect of turning Snow White directly into the crone in the mirror. We watched the heavyset women, always in black, shopping in the markets, walking in funeral processions; the men watched us.

These scenes came back to me in the early seventies on a trip to Sicily with Robert, my husband. It was June and hot already, so we wore typical light American summer clothes: Bermuda shorts and

A DANGEROUS THING

polo shirts. By that time we had three children back home. We pulled into a garage because we had been given to understand that the oil in our rented car needed to be changed. The man who changed the oil was dressed in a long white coat, like a doctor; the room where they changed the oil was white tile, like an operating room. To make conversation while he worked, the mechanic asked us jovially, with a wink at Robert, if we were on our "Viaggio di matrimonio?"

We smiled and laughed. "Non, non. Tres bambinos," we tried to explain in our polyglot Spanish/French/Italian. But there was no way to bridge the cultural gap: in his world there was no other time a woman would be gallivanting around the country except on her honeymoon, and if I was wearing such revealing clothes, I had to be young. Sicily, twenty years after my first trip to Italy, was like Rome and Florence on our first trip. In 1955, though we stuck to big name sites, men making remarks invariably followed us.

Since there were three of us traveling together, our accommodations were sometimes odd. In Rome we had a pair of rooms on the roof, old servants quarters, so at night we could sit outside our penthouse eating lemon ice frozen in scooped out lemon shells, watching the sun set late over red tiled roofs and campaniles. At our pensione in Positano my sister sent me downstairs to check on the dinner menu. Dictionary in hand, I returned to report, "We're having melon and ham."

"Impossible," Carol told me, "You've gotten it wrong. Check it again." None of us had ever heard of eating melon and ham together. Where we came from these ingredients were two entirely different parts of a meal: ham went between slices of bread to make a thick sandwich and melon was a dessert. But melon and ham it was, though what the Italians meant by ham was nothing like what our local lunch counter in New York meant.

Our time machine had taken us back through the Renaissance to its echo of classical times. In Italy there were ever more centuries

Treading Water

of civic and religious sites to explore, from the Coliseum to The Baths of Caracalla; painting and sculpture to observe at The Uffizzi and Il Duomo; and hill towns like Assisi and Fiesole to tour. The richness of Italian craftsmanship and artistry was still around us. Everything was made by hand: embroidered silk blouses, wallets and pocket books, gloves and sandals, all of the softest leather. The products showed exquisite workmanship, in styles from the 1930s.

Venice, the city of Henry James' *The Aspern Papers* and Thomas Mann's *Death in Venice*, came to us with a faint aura of corruption. It was also the place where Carol dropped her camera, the kind that folded out like an accordion and had to be held at the waist to focus, into the Grand Canal. By 1955 it was already an artifact, having been most recently replaced by the new compact 35mm cameras, and it went to join the detritus of centuries at the bottom of the canal. Having one less camera was no great immediate loss because when we took the tram up the valley to Zermat, the sight we came to see, the top of the Matterhorn, was generally shrouded in clouds.

Nevertheless, like centuries of Englishmen, such as Virginia Woolf's father, Leslie Stephen, and his Cambridge fellows who spent their holidays walking in those mountains, we set out on a hike strangely outfitted. Our idea of hiking clothes was more suitable for the weather than their three piece wool knickers suits, wool socks, hats, and rucksacks, but a lot less practical for hiking: drip dry skirts and shirts, Capezio ballet shoes, a shopping bag with sweaters. Fitted out this way we wandered upwards, until we found ourselves with our shopping bag at the base camp for climbing the stern face of the Matterhorn. In a cabin over a stream we ate meringue glacé, before picking our way down in our not so comfortable Capezio shoes. The next day we could hardly walk.

Slowly, we were working our way toward German territory: Lake Constance, followed by Munich and Heidelberg. But the

A DANGEROUS THING

sound of the language, the signs in German were unsettling. All those 'A' words had a way of blurring together into one hazy, threatening sound: ausgang, achtung, Anschluss, Auschwitz. The sight of conductors marching through the train in uniform was unnerving. We were relieved to make it to Belgium, like characters in the movies we'd seen about refugees leapfrogging ahead of the Nazis, who were, in fact, still the majority of people all around us in Germany that summer of 1955, though we tried not to follow that line of thought too far. It seemed unfair that England, with its rationing and shortages, still had more privations than Germany ten years after the war.

At our small Amsterdam hotel, the minute the woman who served breakfast left the room, into our bags for lunch went the brown bread and cheese, the hard-boiled egg, the tomato and plum...which is one reason our eleven weeks abroad cost us each a grand total of $1,100. Holland was the perfect size for us. A day trip took us to any of the great museums, to the dikes or the beach. But we were ready to come home, to be served tuna fish salad on white bread, to see our trip on Kodak film, what there was of it.

Education might not have prepared us for employment, but for travel it did the job. We understood where to look in Norman, Romanesque, and Gothic churches; recognized the difference in technique between trecento and quatrocento schools of art; knew the historical roles played by Rome and Bruge, The Tower of London and the Palace of Versailles; could hunt up opera at the Baths of Caracalla and concerts in Aix. On the other hand, for us Europe was a museum and we went through it about the way we would walk through the Metropolitan Museum. What, if anything, did we make of current life in Europe? We noted new building, observed some of the ironies of reconstruction, but the three of us, cut off by language and each other's company from the life around us, traveled as though sealed in our own time travel capsule. We spoke with a few other tourists, but met hardly any Europeans.

Treading Water

Even the books we brought along had all been written before the Second World War.

❖ ❖ ❖

Carol, who had left our tour a couple of weeks earlier to go back to work at her editing job, was already in her New York apartment when we returned home. Nan and another college classmate of ours found an apartment to share in London Terrace, a block square building on the edge of Chelsea, the same area where Carol lived. It suggested none of the charm of the area called Chelsea we had just visited in London. The apartments in London Terrace resembled budget hotel rooms. It was the kind of place college girls lived before the high rises of the Upper East Side warehoused them.

Off Nan went to a job as a chemistry research assistant at Rockefeller Institute, where all too soon she realized no one was looking for any woman to become the next Madame Curie. At least Mount Holyoke women were fast learners: in a radical career shift she found a job at the Museum of Modern Art, for which her travels abroad were a form of preparation. I returned to Central Park West, to the family apartment and a search for employment. Medical school was an idea I had buried…at least for the time being.

"Female." It was the major heading of the Help Wanted columns in the newspaper, letting me know I was on the right page, since jobs were sorted first by gender. "Editorial Assistant…Insurance company…$84…." That was $84 a week, a not ungenerous sum in 1955. The rule of thumb was that rent should be no more than a quarter of a person's monthly salary, and a few years later, when I married and we moved into our first apartment on West End Avenue and 85th street, the rent was $103.

Fortunately, the test the Equitable life Assurance Society gave involved no typing, grammar, or spelling (though perhaps I should

185

A DANGEROUS THING

have wondered about an editing job that did not focus on these skills). It was a general information test, more like the College Bowl show I'd been selected for at Mount Holyoke. As he looked over the results of my test, the head of the department didn't know what to make of my characteristic method: slow but sure. He was stocky, wore a gray suit, and occupied one of the glass-fronted offices at the back of the floor. The floor itself was occupied mostly by women, the glassed in offices entirely by men. He shook his head. "You got them all right, which never happened before, but you didn't finish the test." He looked at me, puzzled, not able to figure out what to make of this startling turn of events.

Once I heard the results, I assured him "I'm the slow but sure type," betting that having demonstrated some kind of intelligence, the one thing they would want was a careful worker. Being interviewed by a man in an apparently superior position who was nonplused by such a small anomaly was unsettling. I couldn't help uneasily remembering my father's dictum: "Those who go to college end up working for those who never went," for though he had to have been a college graduate, he appeared programmed to think by rote.

He took me out onto the floor and passed me on to a man with a desk in the middle. He was taller, but did not wear a jacket, had sandy coloring, hair and complexion, and the freckles that often went with that color scheme, all of which were a match for his bland facial expressions and manner. He was, by my standards then, out of shape and middle age, yet younger people called him by his first name, Joe, a sign to me that he did not strike awe into his worker bees, while he yelled out to them by their first names.

My father was known as Mr. I, to differentiate him from his Krasne brothers who were Mr. B or Mr. J, and certainly none of our high school or college professors had ever been referred to by first name. Joe, I was soon to learn from my office mates, was an object of amusement to his subjects. They were all college graduates and

Treading Water

could not take seriously a man who had made a career out of work of which they made fun.

It turned out the reason we didn't need spelling or grammar was that we never actually wrote, or even corrected anything. We didn't even need pens or pencils. Every time the insurance company issued a group insurance policy, the information would appear on Joe's desk in the form of a list of numbers referring to clauses in the contract, like ingredients in a recipe. We would stop by and pick up a list, then wander over to the file cabinet as though it were the refrigerator and we were collecting the ingredients. The trip to the file cabinet was a chance to chat with fellow 'editors' about where we would eat lunch. We would dig out copies of each clause, paste them together to make up the policy, and then back it went into another basket on Joe's desk. That was Editing. If the job had been called Cutting and Pasting, would I have applied? Probably…$84 was good money for pink-collar work in 1955.

It was as though once I entered the huge old Equitable Life Assurance building that occupied a square block below Penn Station the meaning of everything I was accustomed to shifted. The world within was a parallel universe: middle class meant something different, college, New York City, and even lunch meant something different, just as Editing had its own meaning. The people I met at the file cabinet, the folks with whom I ate lunch were mostly, like myself, recent college grads. Overwhelmingly female, Catholic, and Italian, they were people who commuted in from The Bronx and Queens, where they had gone to the public colleges. True to their Italian names, their anecdotes about home life had the color of the exotic to me. There idea of a lunch sandwich was anything leftover from the previous night's dinner. They regarded the tuna fish salad, boiled chicken, or Swiss cheese sandwiches I unwrapped in the Equitable cafeteria with polite pity, while I examined their eggplant parmigiano or roasted peppers and eggs with wonder, never being able to antici-

A Dangerous Thing

pate what would emerge from their lunch bags. There was nothing I could think of taking from the family dinner table that would make an interesting lunch sandwich, except maybe caviar when we had it.

We started going out to dinner periodically after work at a small Italian restaurant called Rex, in back of the old Madison Square Garden, a neighborhood so poor nothing as colorful as streetwalkers and transvestites had discovered it yet. My associates explained to me the intricate distinctions between different pastas, none of which cost more than a couple of dollars. It was a pattern of getting together we maintained down through the decades to come, however scattered we became, whatever trials and tribulations some of the group endured.

Our parent's generation, almost all immigrants from different countries, speaking different languages, settling in different parts of the city, led lives that never intersected. But our group expanded to include each other's spouses. We all moved to the suburbs, picnicked together with our children, showed up in hospitals when there were emergencies, sent our kids off to college in New England, and eventually gathered at our children's weddings. They were a third generation, influenced even less by nationality and religion than we were, and more by the quirks of parental nature and American business.

Starting with our generation, education was the common denominator. Every stage of a career was organized horizontally. People came together across lines of class, ethnicity, race, depending only on their degrees: college graduates worked in one place, people with masters degrees in another place, while those with doctorates worked elsewhere. Each group was made up of similar degree holders, regardless of where they came from or the schools they had attended.

A year seemed par for the course at Equitable because by the end of the summer all of the recent college graduates were heading

Treading Water

to other jobs. The Equitable Group Life Insurance Editing Department was like a junction where people out of college changed trains. We all knew it was a job, not a career, certainly not our future. I made life-long friends, people I never would have met as long as I lived in New York if it weren't for answering the ad, but then it was back to school. I had saved money by living at home and could fool myself that using it for graduate school, which sounded like serious business, was a step in some direction. In fact, I had no plan for what to do with more education. I was still treading water.

Equinox

Is there a pause
or do I only wish
to make it a pause,
a day of equilibrium
when the temperature inside
and the temperature outside
are equal
and I can sit in the open doorway,
eyes soldered shut
by the sun
while on the retinas
red spots with molten edges
spin globules into yellow space
and swallow through a melted jaw
lumps of heat smoother than soup,
storing it in marrow bones
for the dark nights?

Yet through dilated blue veins
on my eyelids
I can hear the squirrel croak
in its acorn frenzy
and the cat huddled against the flue
trill stomach deep
and know there is no stasis
only momentum
and hope
and loss of momentum.

Chapter Thirteen

BACK TO SCHOOL

IT WAS THE BEST OF SCHOOLS; IT WAS THE WORST OF SCHOOLS. But it was only the best for as long as it took those of us who enrolled the fall of 1956 to figure out that Columbia University Graduate Faculty of Philosophy had absolutely no interest in its students. We were there to serve as audience for faculty star turns, and if we preferred to stay home and read their books, from which they recited, nobody cared, as long as we paid our fees, handed in our thesis, and showed up to sit for the comprehensive exam.

Not that there weren't hordes of students milling about. They came from all over the country: some had graduated from Ivy League and Seven Sister colleges; many more were from universities that no one from Fieldston had ever attended, schools like Wagner College on Staten Island and Fordham University in the Bronx.

We each had to select a period in which to specialize and, within that, a writer to whose work we would dedicate ourselves for the duration, a process we undertook entirely on our own, since the paths of faculty and students never crossed. Left to my own resources, my approach was a process of elimination, about the way

A DANGEROUS THING

I'd chosen a college. I picked a period in which I'd never taken a course, therefore about which I knew nothing: the Seventeenth Century. One lesson from my research work in college was to choose a writer whose output was easily encompassable (it was the old elementary school short book ploy), so I settled on the poet Andrew Marvell, whose poetry was anthologized in one slim volume. I was determined to finish in one year, though I had no idea what came next.

In addition to courses, students were supposed to attend occasional seminars in their area of concentration, conducted by graduate assistants, but we quickly realized these were dull affairs in which not very brilliant minds were at work on not very interesting topics. In fact, several of us soon understood that the best we could do with the place was a kind of table hopping: finding out from the catalogue what famous professor was lecturing on what subject in what room, and dropping in to hear him (it was virtually always a him) perform.

Donald Keene, for instance, a renowned Japanese scholar, had just come to Columbia and held forth in the dome of Lowe Library. Once one found one's way to this odd room, one came upon a surprisingly small man with a surprisingly large head. Having recently discovered *The Tale of Genji*, a book that conjured up an exotic society in endless detail, I wanted to know more about the man who translated this monumental first novel. One day when I popped in to hear what he was lecturing about, he had a guest. He had invited Santha Rama Rau to speak. She was an Indian author whose fifth book on the impossibility of living with or without her native country had just been reviewed. Keene and Rau carried on a lively dialogue between themselves, and occasionally with the class. It was the kind of celebrity day that happened in a Columbia classroom.

Elsewhere in the English Literature Department, William York Tindall lectured from his *Forces In Modern British Literature* and Lionel Trilling (the first Jew to be appointed to that faculty of Columbia, though I did not know this at the time, assuming being Anglo-Saxon was a prerequisite for a professorial career), could be found speaking about his work, *The Liberal Imagination*. Off in other lecture halls were the Broadway people, who students knew were called on to do translations and lyrics for shows: Maurice Valency, suave and witty in a French way that caught the delicious ironies of Voltaire's Candide; and Eric Bentley, lecturing on alienation and Expressionism in Brecht's *Mother Courage and Her Children*. In a squeaky, high voice he explained how in ancient Greek drama the choice the characters face is between two seeming goods, while in Brecht the choice is between goodness and survival. "And who in his right mind…" he put the rhetorical question to the class, "would not choose survival?" It was 1956, the year of Brecht's death in East Germany. The lectures were stellar performances, but when we'd been to a couple of each, we'd seen the show, and there was no need to go back.

Not only was the faculty all Anglo-Saxon, the professors were all males, except for Marjorie Hope Nicolson. She happened to be Chairman (there was no other word then) of the Department, most probably because none of the men could be bothered with the trivia of administration. She had already made a name for herself with work on Milton. She was a stout figure who reminded me of my deceased portly grandmother. While the men were invisible outside their lecture halls, she could sometimes be spotted sitting chatting with the department secretaries.

Our crowd of graduate school groupies hung around the basement cafeteria, met at local greasy spoons, or Margaret Rabi, daughter of I.I. Rabi, the Nobel physicist, invited us up to her family's Columbia-owned apartment on Riverside Drive. I.I. Rabi was a revered figure at Columbia, having put American physics at the forefront of the field through his work before and during World War II, so that "By the mid-1950s, American physics was leading

A DANGEROUS THING

the world." During the time I was at Columbia, he was working for the Office of Scientific Advisor to President Eisenhower, and he became known as the "statesman of science" for his international work on peaceful uses of atomic energy.

The Rabis lived in one of the big old Columbia owned buildings on Riverside Drive where every room opened into another room from front to back. One day, to the surprise of our group, Margaret's mother answered the door. She took us to the kitchen where she was making spiced pears and told a story about an American Nobel prize winner who was so gauche he picked up his dinner plate at the awards dinner in Stockholm to see where it was made and, not to show him up as an uncouth American, the King and then everyone else did the same. We were impressed by the nonchalance of the first Nobel Prize household we had wandered through.

One evening Margaret took us to an evening talk at the Episcopal Bishop's House on whether Agape, Caritas, or Eros— words with which I was not on familiar terms—was the highest form of love, confirming my suspicion that Radcliffe women were a different intellectual strain from other Seven Sister students.

Another groupie came with the fancy name Matthew Frances Keating III. His family was partly responsible for giving the city the Brooklyn Public Library. He lived with his mother in a private home in Brooklyn where the two of them dressed formally for dinner every evening. He had started college at Fordham, but had been discouraged by its provinciality after one of his professors took him aside and told him, "I might as well give you the 'A' since you're the only Catholic in the class." He could go toe to toe with Margaret when it came to abstruse medieval knowledge.

The other member of our group was Philip, who had gone to school on Staten Island. One day I ran into him at the Museum of Modern Art. I was standing in front of a painting of a pale tree on an even paler background when he came by with a tall, thin

Back to School

woman, whom he introduced as his wife, March. I pointed to the picture in front of which I was planted. "Isn't that great," I enthused. "That's my favorite painter, Milton Avery."

Whereupon March informed me "That's my father."

As I stared in awe, I realized the woman standing next to me, March Avery, was the figure in a whole range of her father's paintings. The next winter March and Philip invited me to their Christmas party. Fortunately, the man with whom I was—in my father's words—keeping company had a car because March and Philip lived in a walk-up on the lower east side. This was still a poor neighborhood in 1956. We climbed dark, rickety stairs to their apartment, near where The Tenement Museum now tells the story of the area, making it sound quite quaint.

The most striking things about March and Philip's apartment were an avocado tree and a painting. They had an avocado plant decorated for the holiday. In the fifties we all had avocado pits supported by toothpicks growing in murky water on kitchen sinks. Eventually they sprouted roots and we planted them so they could grow spindly stalks with a couple of large leaves, and then, when we moved, we threw them out as failures and started again, hoping for more leaves. It was part of the graduate scene, like butterfly chairs and bookshelves made out of bricks and boards. March and Philip's tree was a big success: lots of glossy leaves and small lights.

There, in the midst of their holiday gathering, were Milton Avery and his wife, Sally. She was an illustrator who had supported the family because Milton was one of the few American artists who devoted himself entirely to painting: no teaching, illustrating, lecturing. He was a tall, gray haired man, slightly stooped, who spoke softly, as though painting himself in the muted palette for which he had a special gift, while his wife emerged sharply in the foreground, like her own clear-cut line drawings that appeared periodically in the Book Section of *The New York Times*.

On the wall there was a painting of Milton's: a pink background with what appeared to be a white platter that had something black on it. The black turned out to represent caviar, which they had been served at the home of someone we knew in common: Roy Neuberger, investment banker, art collector, and father of my high school tennis team partner, Ann Neuberger.

At the Christmas party, when I admired the painting on March and Philip's wall, it became clear the Averys had ambivalent feelings about collectors like Neuberger. They couldn't help being grateful for purchases that acknowledged Milton's talent and the money that helped them keep going, but at the same time there was a certain sense of resentment at being dependent on bourgeois largesse. This was the ironic subtext in the painting of black caviar against a pink background.

My involvement with the Neubergers made me see their role differently. Ann had been in the class behind me at Fieldston, so I was already ensconced at Mount Holyoke when the Neubergers made an appearance on a college tour. They were curious, knowledgeable, and gracious. I persuaded Ann that the school was a good place for her and her parents sent me a large care-package in thanks for hosting their tour. They might not have been so gracious if they could have foreseen the chain of events that were to follow.

When she left college before graduation, I lost track of Ann and only pieced together the story the year after Philip and March's party when I discovered our far less than six degrees of separation. After we were married that spring, Robert arranged one weekend for us to drive up to Rockland County to have dinner with his cousin Paul, from Boston, whom I had never met. We walked into a small living room and there was Ann Neuberger, my old tennis partner, presiding over a crowded suburban ranch house filled with little children, not a painting on the wall. Ann, it turned out after our amazement had settled down, had roomed at Mt. Holyoke with Robert's cousin Patsy, who had introduced Ann to her brother Paul, and Ann had given up Mt. Holyoke to follow him.

Back to School

The scene before us in the little house was a shock. Here was Cinderella in reverse, as though a wand had been waved over my old tennis partner and she had turned into a house frau, held captive not by wicked stepsisters, cinders, and a straw broom, but the demands of children, a husband, and a suburban ranch house.

Just married, still living in Manhattan, it had never occurred to me that this was what life had in store for us. This was well before Betty Friedan drew women a map of where they were and explained how we got there…the problem with no name, as it came to be called. It was a sobering drive home along the Palisade Parkway as the picture of being immured in a suburban ranch house with little children replayed itself. The aftermath was even less happy. Before we could become one extended, happy family again, Ann and Paul decamped to California, had their third child, and her husband, Robert's errant cousin, took off, leaving Ann to raise their three children. It was years before our paths crossed again.

But the future as a married woman still lay ahead, that spring of 1957 as our small band of graduate students prepared to flee Columbia. We were leaving the city, like rats abandoning a rotten ship, which Manhattan on hot, sticky summer days tended to feel like. One summer evening before we all left, a bunch of us were invited for dinner at a penthouse a couple of graduate students were subletting for the summer. They lit the oven and large roaches flew out in all directions, as though a cave of bats had been invaded. No one seemed much surprised. Graduate students were accustomed to the basics of city life. It was the last time our group saw each other.

Before abandoning the city, I handed in the thesis I had been writing instead of attending classes. This time I had proceeded through the research, writing, rewriting on my own, with only the ghost of Professor Horner looking over my shoulder as I struggled through paragraph after paragraph, chapter after chapter. There

A DANGEROUS THING

was nobody to care if it was readable, to oversee it section by section, so I took what I knew about writing a thesis, packaged it in the prescribed Columbia format, and handed it in, the entire work all at once. In my research on the seventeenth century I had picked up on ideas I had dealt with in the previous thesis, making this a kind of prequel to the Mount Holyoke project.

❖ ❖ ❖

For those with a taste for literary theory, my ideas went something like this. In doing my research for the Woolf thesis, I had discovered that people's ideas about time changed throughout history. The Ancient Greeks had their ideas, replaced in the Middle Ages by a different set of ideas, which were altered in turn by the Protestant Reformation. The nineteenth century viewed time one way, but the twentieth century introduced a different concept. Time itself, I realized, could be a subject for research.

After reading all of Woolf, I saw major shifts in her technique from early work to later writing. One way to account for the changes was that during the period in which she lived people absorbed the ideas of Freud, Henri Bergson, and Einstein's special theory of relativity. These theories emphasized the importance of our subjective sense of time, and showed how people operated with two kinds of time: subjective, or duration, and objective, or clock time. Writers such as Henry James, James Joyce, T.S. Eliot, and Virginia Woolf were struggling to develop the literary techniques that could render these new ideas about time.

As examples of the movement from external to internal time, I had examined Woolf's three seascaped novels, *The Voyage Out*, an early work; *To The Lighthouse*, her most famous book; and *The Waves*, a late work. These novels show Woolf's development of techniques by which she could move from a largely objective, external context in the first novel, to a predominantly interior world in the second work, and then to a book so completely a set of

198

Back to School

interior riffs that this late work hardly seems to be a novel.

The fifties was an era when literary technique was considered the most proper matter of study, as a kind of pseudo-scientific approach. That Woolf was a female who had various family troubles, including a particularly difficult Victorian father and a stepbrother who sexually assaulted her, were not matters with which critics concerned themselves, certainly not students of literature. It was left to Kate Millett a decade later to do battle with the assembled forces of Columbia University over what constituted appropriate dissertation material. In her preface to the work that became *Sexual Politics*, she wrote in 1970:

> This essay, composed of equal parts of literary and
> cultural criticism, is something of an anomaly, a
> hybrid, possibly a new mutation altogether. I have
> operated on the premise that there is room for a
> criticism which takes into account the larger cultural
> context in which literature is conceived and produced.
> Criticism which originates from literary history is too
> limited in scope to do this; criticism which originates
> in aesthetic considerations, "New Criticism," never
> wished to do so.

New Criticism was the way my generation had been trained, though in trying to break out of that limited perspective on literature some of us included a bit of cultural history in our work. The idea that gender would be a valid lens through which to examine literature would never have occurred to us in the fifties, nor did it go over well at Columbia when Millett tried to get the department to accept her work in the late 1960s.

When it came to ideas about time, I discovered through my reading that the seventeenth century saw time in a different framework than I was used to. It was firmly understood in Marvell's era

199

A DANGEROUS THING

that the world was going to end at a specific date not very far off. Poetry throbbed with urgency…"Gather ye rosebuds/While ye may." So "'Time's Winged Chariot' In the Lyrics of Andrew Marvell" (my thesis title) was devoted to a study of the implications of this finite worldview of time in Marvell's writing.

Preachers of doom were plentiful in the Seventeenth Century. Mankind had sinned, Christianity proclaimed, letting evil into the world and one had only to look around to see that God would shortly be calling an end to a bad business. Sir Thomas Browne set the gloomy tone for the times when he wrote, "time that grows old in itself bids us hope no long duration…." Marvell picked up on that theme by setting a number of his poems in gardens, which allowed him to play on such words as "shade" and "grass," using the figure of the mower to remind his readers of the general decay, the brevity and abruptness of life. But Marvell was on the cusp of another change in the concept of time. Just as seventeenth century poets were instructing people to hurry up because the end was near, the Puritan work ethic remade time into a commodity that could be ransomed by making it profitable.

All of this mooning about in library stacks, reading one's way through piles of books with feet up on the desk was fun: no responsibility, no boss to report to or time-clock to watch. It was the aimless lure of graduate school for the perpetual student. Even better, now that the thesis was handed in and had been applauded, I packed my books to study for the exam and took off for Maine, where I had rented a house for the summer with two high school friends who were also graduate school groupies.

❖ ❖ ❖

Just before flying up to Maine, I met a newly minted young lawyer, tall, thin, and smart in a way that was knew to me. I told him I was taking off for the summer to go study in Maine, a story that must

Back to School

have sounded only a bit less implausible than if I'd told him I was going to live in Paris (which, as it turned out, is what I did tell him 28 years later on my second sabbatical leave), but that I would be coming down to take my comprehensive exam. He offered to drive me back to Maine after my test. This offer sounded like an awful lot of togetherness for such a short acquaintance, but I suggested we stay in touch.

Our paths had crossed by what was considered the acceptable route in the fifties. There weren't too many New Yorkers at Mount Holyoke, and of those only a token number were Jewish (did we know there were quotas? Probably. Did it register as something unacceptable? Apparently not). A few doors down from my college room senior year there was a junior from New York. When she mentioned the Krasne name at home, her parents took notice, although they lived in Brooklyn and I had no idea how they had heard the name. She had a brother who had gone to Yale and was finishing up at Harvard Law School, and she asked if he could give me a call when we both were back in the city after graduation.

The brother and I went to dinner at the Yale Club, enduring one of those evenings when it is excruciatingly difficult to make conversation. In all fairness, it is hard to imagine now what young people did talk about: movies were not a big part of life, young people did not flock to the theater, sports were, at best, a small part of anyone's interests—maybe a man followed baseball and a woman some tennis—politics was not an American preoccupation, even cars—which city dwellers did not bother with—came in so few varieties that they were not worthy of discussion.

Realizing that this acquaintance was going no place, the young man traded names with a Harvard classmate of his when they met on the steps of the Brooklyn courthouse. This roundabout means by which I happened to be speaking on the phone to someone by the name of Robert P. Levine was not exactly a terrific recommendation, but when we did meet, we never ran out of things to talk about.

A DANGEROUS THING

Maine, more particularly the area around Mt. Desert Island, was a place I'd been going to with the same two friends almost every year since 1952. The attraction, in addition to such natural wonders as mountains, lakes, seacoast, and the only fjord on the Eastern seaboard, was that the island had two laboratories where science students worked during the summer and one of our group was a regular at the Jackson Laboratory. The summer of 1957 her line of research, and her triumph, involved breeding a strain of mice that could be used for cancer research, research having to do with the effects of smoking. The connection between smoking and cancer was something the scientists at Jackson were so sure would never be proved that they all smoked up a storm. Since they were science labs, they attracted many more males than females, even though the three of us renting the house had all been science majors.

Three young women in a rented house and two laboratories full of recent college grads added up to what the neighbors must have felt was an attractive nuisance. There was no dining room, so brazenly we redecorated our rental, moving the kitchen table out to the front porch to make a dining room. On weekends, after sailing, hiking, and tennis, we gathered a group to cook up lobsters and crabs. The house was in a blue-collar neighborhood and the locals peered at our comings and goings from behind their curtains, like the narrators in Faulkner's story "A Rose For Emily." Speculation about what was really going on at our innocent late night dinner parties enlivened the block. Our actual dissipations tended toward lobster races on the kitchen floor, beer, and moonlight walks along the shore as the three resident females juggled a changing cast of budding scientists.

By August it was time to pack up the books and fly home for a week to sit for Columbia's Comprehensive Examination, as it was ominously called. I had kept to a schedule, working my way through the texts I thought needed to be reviewed. The only paper I had not considered carefully was the one explaining about the

Back to School

exam itself. I arrived at Columbia early in the morning, naturally assuming such a momentous event would take place first thing in the day, only to find out that the test was actually given in the afternoon, as though it were some sort of academic afterthought. Fearful if I bumped into anything, everything so precariously stored in my head would spill out and be lost forever, I carefully found myself a seat in the library and gingerly picked up a book lying on the table.

It was entitled *Mimesis*, by Eric Auerbach. This was not a work unknown to me, but also not as well known as it should have been, since almost every teacher in every class had mentioned the book, and the title appeared in my notes more than any other single work, though somehow I had never found the time to read it. By the time of the test I had skimmed the entire contents, had decided that what I wanted to do with my life was write a book that did for the changing concept of Time what Auerbach did for the changing concept of Reality. More crucially, everything in my head had been wiped away and replaced by what Auerbach had to say. It was in this state that I found my way to the exam.

At first glance, and at second and third, the test was impossible. I had nothing to say on any of the questions…except what I had just read in Mr. Auerbach, which therefore became the substance of my first essay, and a good part of my second, until by the time I was on to Milton and his blindness I could manage on my own, with a little help from Marjorie Hope Nicolson's lectures. Mr. Auerbach might have been surprised by the uses to which he was put, but I have always hoped he would have appreciated the ingenuity involved.

Several days later, with much trepidation, I made my way to the English Office to find out if I had passed, and there was the Chairman herself, seated with the secretaries. This presented a delicate problem: I was not sure to whom I should address my inquiry, not wanting to treat her as a mere functionary, but she sorted

A DANGEROUS THING

through the papers on the desk and came up with a list. Running her finger down the names, she announced, to my surprise, "You passed," and then there was a pause as she ran her finger across the line, sat up, and focused her attention on me. "In fact, with honors." I thanked her for the news and beat a quick retreat before she asked about suspiciously familiar ideas I'd spouted stolen from *Mimesis*, or launched into the talk my section teacher had already given me after reading my thesis, about how I really must continue for the Ph.D.

Columbia was in New York, instead of remote South Hadley; it was a university rather than a college; it was filled with famous faculty, but it was still as detached from my middle class life as a factory would have been in its own way. I could no more see myself buried for decades in its library stacks than I could see myself on the Ford assembly line. A thesis was an intellectual game, a game at which one could become adept, like a professional tennis player, but a tennis player could get pleasure out of playing as an amateur or pro, while there was nothing to do with this skill I'd perfected once I stepped out of academe.

Columbia did have a placement office, though, and it did actually come up with a few suggestions, which were an education about education. I could get a fellowship at a mid-western university, which meant decamping for the hinterlands, teaching some undergraduate sections, and studying for the Ph.D. But if my four years in Massachusetts had taught me anything, it was that being in a college town was being buried alive, while my year at Columbia had taught me that scholarship at a big university was a state of suspended animation. The next proposal from the Placement Office took me driving up to the Riverdale Country Day School, where I was offered a job teaching several classes with three different preparations at a salary that would just about cover my commuting costs over the Spuyten Duyvil Bridge. Teaching was not where I was going to be headed.

204

Back to School

Instead, I climbed into the front seat of Robert's used blue Chevy, and we headed for Maine. The car burned more oil than gas and had windshield wipers that worked off the gas pedal. I was fascinated that this lawyer knew how to deal with these mechanical peculiarities. There was no way we could know it in August of 1957, but it was a trip we would make repeatedly over the next forty plus years. Fortunately, when we drove north to Maine again, just the two of us, or with children, and eventually to visit our children, we never again needed so much oil to keep the wheels turning.

Part III

STEALING
TIME

Chapter Fourteen

GOURMET COOK MEETS IDEAL MARRIAGE: ITS PHYSIOLOGY AND TECHNIQUES

To be married in the fifties, women only needed four things: an engagement ring; *The Gourmet Cookbook* (volumes I and II); a diaphragm; and a copy of *Ideal Marriage: Its Physiology and Techniques* by Theodor Hendrik Van de Velde, MD.

Fall, when I came back to the city from Maine, I saw my newly minted lawyer friend increasingly, which in the fifties meant we went out on more dates with each other than with anyone else, and eventually with no one else. One night in January after a date (even when two people were considered 'a couple,' what they did was go out on 'dates' together), as I was brushing my teeth and looked up into the mirror, a picture unfolded: like the Hall of Mirrors at Versailles endlessly reflecting itself, I saw myself married to Robert Levine and living happily into infinity. I put away the toothbrush and picked up the phone, though it was midnight and Robert lived at home in his parent's red brick house in Queens. He did not sound surprised.

At 24 and 26 we considered ourselves old, and therefore mature, but this was still the fifties and society marched to only one drummer. Once we announced we wanted to get married, life

A DANGEROUS THING

around us had a momentum of its own. We became objects to be moved through the system. No matter how casual or original a couple might want to be, they had a hard time escaping The Program because The Program ignored them.

Example. A quick survey showed that none of the adult women around us wore engagement rings. They had been retired to some special place where engagement rings go after several years of marriage. So "Engagement rings are silly," Robert and I concurred, which was just as well, since neither of us was making what could, even in those days, be termed a good salary. "Diamonds aren't interesting and an engagement ring is a big waste of money," we announced. But by no means was this allowed to stand as the last word.

My prospective mother-in-law was mortified. "What will people think of us, of you?" she protested to her son. She insisted I take her diamond engagement ring that, naturally, she never wore. Not to be outdone, my mother pitched in and had a diamond wedding band made from old Krasne jewelry that, naturally, she never wore, to go with it. No one noticed that we spent our time designing gold wedding bands with a jeweler in Greenwich Village.

Example. No matter what problem you consulted your gynecologist about—birth control, cystitis (the honeymooner's disease)—the doctor would devote serious attention to moving the letter opener and calendar around on the desk and point out sternly that you had to read your Van de Velde. For our children's generation, the mysteries of birth control were explored and revealed early, but the exotica of wedding rituals was a subject to be studied at great length and later age. For us, wedding procedure was a given, but the facts of birth control came as a surprise. For one thing, the options were limited in 1958. Then there was the unpleasant fact that devices, whether they went over or in, whether they were disposable or reusable, whether they went pop in the night or developed pinholes, required preparation, something fic-

Gourmet Cookbook *Meets* Ideal Marriage

tion and film had neglected to show me about love in its many forms.

But my mother informed me I had to be fitted for a diaphragm, so off we went to a doctor who came with the awesome double title: Obstetrician and Gynecologist. His probings and pokings were an immediate unpleasant introduction to the facts of future female medical history. Down that road lay an entire medieval line of torture not even to be imagined: childbirth, epesiotomies, cauterization, mammograms, not to mention various diseases no one spoke of.

Margaret Sanger, in her efforts to make birth control respectable in the 1920s, had seen to it that only physicians and clinics could supply diaphragms. Since fitting for the device required this awkward introduction to a new medical specialty, it's not surprising that diaphragms were the least popular form of birth control, used only by a quarter of middle class women. Everyone else made do with what could be found hidden away between mouthwash and band-aids at drugstore counters.

Example. Once we told our parents of our desire to get married, everything happened without effort or input on our part: announcement in newspaper, selection of dates for engagement party and wedding, printing of invitations, engagement of caterer, Rabbi, wedding cake. About none of this did we have any say. When I think of our own children and their friends marrying at later ages, agonizing over every detail—visual, auditory, gustatory—of their weddings, I realize how little an idea we had of what was going on around us. We only knew we were to be married Sunday, May 4 at 4:00 P.M. (a date chosen because it slipped in between numerous religious holidays no one in the family had ever heard of). The event was to take place in the chapel of our synagogue and the reception for 87 relatives and close friends was to be at my parent's home.

It would never have occurred to us to question what the Rabbi would have to say, the menu for the supper, or the contents of the

A DANGEROUS THING

wedding cake. We did hear unsettling rumors: the baker died upon completing the cake, the organist failed to show up at the chapel, a piano playing husband of a friend had to be conscripted into trying his hand at playing an organ for the first time so the show could go on. But since we were like invited guests, we merely did what we were told.

Our memories are glimpses from odd angles, as though we were the hired help peering through doorways and around guests, noticing people standing around with plates of food. Were there flowers, was there music, who among our friends was there? We have no idea, and the handful of snapshots that survive give an equally haphazard glimpse of the event. Did we have a good time? The question was no more relevant than asking if someone was happy at college.

It was May 4, 1958, and originality was not what people were seeking, unlike some weddings of the next two decades that come to mind. There was the daughter of a friend who staged her wedding on top of a mountain in Vermont, without a tent. It poured; the bride donned hiking boots; the guests took off their drenched clothes and went skinny-dipping in the lake below. There was the cousin who invited us to his second wedding one Thanksgiving, held at Alcatraz Island State Park where guests were asked to bring their own Thanksgiving turkey. Such improvisation was unimaginable in 1958.

The honeymoon was going to be a drive to the Adirondacks, not a brilliant choice for the first week in May. We were saved from a week in the cold and wet by my father, who arranged a trip to Bermuda. This was round one in the generational battle and the pattern for years to come: our idea of independence up against my parents' idea of practicality. Before flying off to Bermuda, we spent a night in our apartment on West End Avenue.

Manhattan was going through one of those periods when people could only find apartments if they knew someone. Fortunately,

210

Gourmet Cookbook *Meets* Ideal Marriage

an aunt and uncle were able to get three rooms for us in a building where enormous old apartments had been chopped up. As Adam Gopnik pointed out about the big old West Side apartments, "their high period was a short one." Our apartment had been lopped off from a grand eleven room home to form a bedroom, with a closet big enough to be considered a room in 1990s buildings, a bathroom only accessible through the bedroom; a narrow kitchen, and a living-dining room. It had undoubtedly been the rear end of the apartment because the entire place faced west over a courtyard. When we came home after work in the summer, the western sun pouring in was hot enough to cook food without an oven. As gifts we received a television and an air conditioner, both of which we installed in the bedroom, where we camped out.

That first night the apartment contained little more than our bed and a box with two Danish pastry my father, sure no husband could provide properly, had sent along for our breakfast before we departed for the airport. In an ominous gesture that my brand new husband was never to live down, he woke up hungry in the middle of the night—we had never quite gotten around to eating at the wedding—found his way into the kitchen, and proceeded to consume both pastries, his and hers. In the morning when I woke up hungry, I discovered the treachery of my spouse of thirteen hours.

❁ ❁ ❁

What did newlyweds learn from Van de Velde? Recently I went in search of a refresher course in sexual physiology, but despite the millions of copies that made the rounds, *Ideal Marriage* (the book, that is) was a hard item to come by at the end of the twentieth century. The man at the desk at the New York Public Library read the name on my slip of paper and shook his head, darkly pessimistic, predicting that "Books like that disappear quickly."

I felt like a suspicious character and glanced over my shoulder

A DANGEROUS THING

to see if scholars engrossed in serious intellectual pursuits were leering at me. In the reading room, I waited so long for the book to emerge from the depths of 42nd street that I believed his gloomy prediction had come true. Finally, I went up to the counter and asked the man distributing books what had happened to my number. "What book are you waiting for?" he asked. When I mentioned, *Ideal Marriage*, he looked up at me surprised and asked, "Ideal marriage, is there such a thing?" which seemed to do the trick because the book appeared as we spoke.

Van de Velde, Theodor Hendrik, M.D., formerly Director of the Gynecological Clinic at Haarlem, the Netherlands, author of over 80 books and papers, wrote *Ideal Marriage* in 1926. He feared "unpleasant results," even thought of writing under a pseudonym because he was expecting harassment and hate mail; what he got instead was a best seller. It is easy to see why: every young woman with whom I grew up had her very own copy before she was married. The book was first translated into German, where it went through 42 printings in 8 years, until it earned the distinction of being banned by Hitler. Heinemann brought out the English edition in 1930 and Covici Friede published an American edition in 1933. It immediately went through seven printings.

In an introduction, J. Johnston Abraham, CBE, DSO, MA, MD, a Harley Street physician, called the book a godsend for doctors. What he meant was that it took them off the hook when it came to explaining anything to do with sexuality, making it unnecessary to move around those paperweights and letter openers. All the doctors had to say, sternly or gently, was "Read Van de Velde." The first and only book of its kind—in those days publishing's copy-cat instinct was a lot slower—it had sold over a million copies by the time Random House brought out its 1945 edition, a success the author could not entirely enjoy for he died in 1937 at the age of 64.

"Marriage is a science," a quote from Balzac, is inscribed on the title page, setting the tone for a book in which lengthy footnotes are

Gourmet Cookbook *Meets* Ideal Marriage

balanced by poetry quotations and aphorisms from Goethe, Virgil, Nietzsche, Stendhal, Luther, the Bible, to drop just a few names. From the beginning the doctor makes it clear he is addressing himself "to married men" and the wife whom he describes as an "unlessoned girl." In other words, the text is heavily homocentric in its biology with the man expected to do the heavy lifting in a delicate relationship. For instance, to educate these poor mystified chaps there is an appendix with charts and diagrams...of the female, though a modern reader wonders if men in 1926 weren't likely to be more familiar with the female body than women were with the male body, and the author himself notes "the beginning of married life is a school and an apprenticeship for her."

To ward off thrill seekers, voyeurs, and heavy breathers, Van de Velde outlines a formidable table of contents: Part I, General Physiology of Sex; Part II, Specific Anatomy and Physiology of Sex; Part III, Sexual Intercourse, Its Physiology and Technique; Part IV, Hygiene of Ideal Marriage, which breaks down into no less than 6 chapters, with its own supplement on Psychic, Emotional and Mental Hygiene, followed by the Appendix. This comes to 323 "punctilious and passionless" pages not likely to be thumbed through by anyone in search of excitement. In fact, at the same time as I kept the title of my reading out of sight, I couldn't help envying the young men seated around me in the Main Reading Room of the New York Public Library studying for their banking, brokerage, and real estate exams.

Van de Velde was heavy going, though a contemporary reader can derive some amusement from the way the doctor's drift takes sudden and unexpected turns. For instance, he starts out, as though lecturing to a Physiology class, to define the sexual impulse, and ends up in another department entirely:

> *It is an urge or impulse to sexual activity (or manifestation or expression) which has its seat, i.e., its initial ori-*

A DANGEROUS THING

gin, and its irradiation not only in the genitals, but in the whole body and the whole psychic personality. Hence its power is almost supreme, almost divine, and extends far beyond its specific province. Let us only consider one example of that power: the incalculable influence of the sexual impulse on Art in all its forms.

Or there is the startling off hand comment, in a section on the difference in smell by race, that "The semen of the healthy youth of Western European races has a fresh, exhilarating smell."

Finally, despite all the references to "mating" as "communion," there is the bottom line:

> What both man and woman, driven by obscure primitive urges, wish to feel in the sexual act, is the essential force of *maleness*, which expresses itself in a sort of violent and absolute *possession* of the woman. And so both of them can and do exult in a certain degree of male aggression and dominance...."

Not much of this material sounded familiar, and I wondered if I had also been put to sleep by it in the fifties, though I certainly owned a copy and had looked through it. But it wasn't intended for us girls anyway, as the good doctor finally concludes:

> Here I have tried to put them [a book of rules] before him; but let him remember that I have not written the preceding pages to be skimmed through—and still less, to be read as "spicy stuff"—honour and conscience forbid!—but for his earnest and reverent study."

Marriage, of course, turned out to be about a lot of other things besides those on Doctor Van de Velde's mind, such as how two peo-

Gourmet Cookbook *Meets* Ideal Marriage

ple squeeze a tube of tooth paste or where they drop their shoes or eat snacks, or how many children they want.

Zero, was my first thought when it came to babies. Growing up I knew no one with a baby, so I was convinced babies did nothing but choke and throw up, and that nothing I knew or could do would make them grow into people we might want to know. Robert, with the wisdom of Solomon, managed to accept both my "no children" dictum and not believe a word of it at the same time, which turned out to be the best move. Children were certainly not on our mind when we married.

Ever since graduate school I had been working in the Publicity Department at Gimbels department store, writing news releases, but there had been a reshuffling of departments, which put me into Advertising, where writing and editing amounted to putting together the weekly flyer handed out at the door announcing three pairs of stockings for the price of two, bedding (seconds) at half price, and whatever other exciting news eager department buyers rushed into my office with. The job was about a half a step up from cutting and pasting at The Equitable Life Assurance Society. I should have recognized this dead-end job for what it was: a prelude to motherhood, but women weren't so quick to recognize the pattern back then.

Robert, at the time we were married, left the firm he was working for and launched himself in partnership with an old friend. A year later he settled a serious case and just at that time we received a notice that the Village Independent Democrats were offering a special group fare to northern Europe in the fall. I left my job and mid-September off we went for a month; travel, like everything else in life, was more leisurely in the fifties. Our excuse was that Robert had never been to Europe and we were sure this was our one and only shot at a trip abroad.

We traveled light, one of those practical decisions we lived to regret. Robert borrowed a reversible topcoat from a friend (one

Betty and Robert Levine, joint passport photo, 1959.

side rain, one side tweed) and I packed four outfits. It was only three years since the supposedly one-and-only trip and showing Robert around threw a new light on London. In Paris we were fêted by my Uncle Abe and Aunt Mary, who introduced us to the better things in life, such as champagne on their terrace at the Maurice overlooking the Tuilleries and lunch at the Ritz. In return, they gamely climbed into the back seat of our rented Volkswagen bug for Parisian touring.

Our goal was Norway, where my college roommate, Ruth, had married an architect, but we made a big loop to take in as much as time would allow. From France we headed to Switzerland and then turned north through Germany, the weather getting ever colder, which eventually necessitated wearing all four outfits at once. This meant that when Robert stopped short on the Autobahn while I was drinking chocolate milk, all four were stained. In

Gourmet Cookbook *Meets* Ideal Marriage

Denmark we spent our wedding gift money on silver at Georg Jensen, a financial investment so good we can never afford to use the precious pieces any more for fear of losing them. We came out of the store to see the King ride his bicycle down the main street. In snapshots of the trip we are eating outdoors wearing coats over our several outfits, and gloves.

Finally, from the balcony of our decoratively carved old wooden hotel in Holmenkollen, Norway, Robert surveyed Oslo Fjord, fogged in. The balcony had a sign on the railing that we assumed was trying to tell us not to lean over too far…which is how we learned our first Norwegian: Robert returned to our room with a stripe painted across his trousers. By evening, in our excitement over meeting with Ruth and Eric, he managed to forget and repeat the trick of creating horizontal stripes with his only other pair of trousers. The hotel recommended a cleaner, who assured us "Yes, yes, I will do what I can with white spirits." We looked at each other doubtfully: was he going to dip Robert's only two pairs of pants in a vast vat of turpentine? We left one pair and he wore the other (striped) ones.

Ruth and Eric were camped out in medieval splendor at Eric's parent's house while they worked on their apartment in Oslo. Eric came from a large family. His father, before World War II, had been an international banker and art collector with medals from the British government for his service to the Empire. The Sejersted Bödtker house, a big yellow square with an art gallery wing attached, sat imposingly on a hill overlooking the city. During the war the paintings were hidden and the house commandeered by the Nazis. Mr. Sejersted Bödtker barely escaped deportation to a concentration camp. Instead, through the influence of powerful friends, and perhaps because the Nazis thought he might be useful, he was put under house arrest in Oslo. The living room, where we were greeted, had an enormous fireplace (no screen); the dining room, where we ate at a baronial dining table surrounded by high

A DANGEROUS THING

backed chairs upholstered in painted leather, had a chandelier that still used candles.

The meal was classic Norwegian. For a starter, large pieces of herring—I could see as I cautiously looked around—were to be washed down with a small glass of Aquavit and a large beer chaser. I glanced in nervous fascination at Robert: he never ate herring but I knew he would be too embarrassed to make a scene before strangers in this imposing setting. He swallowed the fish whole, hastily washing it down with the alcohol, the way a snake would ingest a mouse. With relief I saw the next course was some kind of roast game with potatoes and cabbage, followed by cloudberries. Food in northern Europe in 1958 was still what could be grown, preserved, caught, or shot locally, no exotic imports confused menu readers.

Sunday morning we took a trolley up to the edge of the woods where the cross-country ski trails ran north toward the Arctic Circle. There we joined Ruth, Eric and everyone else in Oslo out for a stroll in the woods in their hiking knickers. Every crossroads of the trails was as busy as the main street of Oslo on a weekday.

Finally, we had to make our way back to Amsterdam to meet up with the Village Independent Democrats for their charter flight home. At a pub in Amsterdam a young woman chatted with us. "That is so American, so stylish," she said of my navy blue tweed suit. Even though it was a sensible piece of my trousseau, I would have taken it off and given it to her, I was so tired of it after having worn it every day for a month. But fall weather had followed us north and now south, and we still had to wear all our gear to get home.

Home. Unemployment, job hunting, pregnancy. It was a familiar pattern for women. Couldn't find the right job? Well, it was really time to get on with having a baby. Pregnancy meant moving, fixing up a bigger place, in other words, plenty of things with which to keep from thinking about a job. It was the beginning of the pattern I assumed would be life, all of it, forever. Did it make

Gourmet Cookbook *Meets* Ideal Marriage

sense that a young lawyer just starting a practice of his own would have a pregnant wife with no plans to work? Of course not, but it was the life for which we had been brought up: decorating, keeping house, giving little dinner parties, taking care of children were what young middle-class women did, even if they had college degrees, even if they had graduate degrees.

John Updike wrote a story summing up this era in its title, "When Everyone Was Pregnant." He describes it as a time of strange freedom: "Jobs, houses, spouses of our own. Permission to drink and change diapers and operate power mowers and stay up past midnight." For instance, he describes how at his wife's college it was not permitted to smoke in dorm rooms, so "she made herself do it in our home. Like a sexual practice personally distasteful but recommended by Van de Velde. Dreadful freedom. Phrase fashionable then." It was a given that Updike's readers would know who Van de Velde was.

There was a certain challenge involved in keeping house, since we went from our parent's homes to our own with no idea how to market, cook, clean, or do laundry, not that there weren't plenty of old ladies in New York City ready to tell the young married woman what she was doing wrong. It was only necessary to go down to the laundry room and put brown socks and white handkerchiefs in the same machine to be given a lecture on doing laundry, or take a walk with a baby and be told how the infant should be dressed.

Surely, we playground backbenchers told ourselves, we're smart, we're educated, we have all these degrees, we must be able to figure out how to run a household, manage to get a dinner on the table every night of the week. Our husbands were struggling to make their way in the world; we had to hold up our end by producing bright children and tasty meals. Restaurants were for anniversary dinners and take out food meant what you bought in the market to cook up in your kitchen. What we did was what we'd been taught in all our schooling: we got a book.

A Dangerous Thing

❋ ❋ ❋

A writer about food once noted that each generation has its own cookbook, that one book which is considered the culinary Bible of the age. Our Bible was *The Gourmet Cookbook*. After a couple became engaged, subtle negotiations would go on as to exactly which friend would give *The Gourmet Cookbook* to which other friend. When it arrived, it was unwrapped and handled with the reverence and care due a Bible. Actually, the gift consisted of two hefty volumes in darkly serious maroon bindings with the weightiness of legal tomes, and in those days we who were home with young children studied them with the high seriousness the men of our era devoted to the insides of their professional tomes.

The volumes were filled with intimidating recipes for which no degree of higher education was preparation: catch a hare and marinate in a crock for three days (what was a hare, what was a crock?). We learned to pick our way carefully. To this day I can flick through the pages of the two volumes and see smudges and speckled spots where recipes were much used, followed by pristine areas where I never had the occasion or the courage to venture. The quality of the paper, the illustrations, the way the recipes were written in paragraphs bring back a flood of memories not only about food, but also about an era in our lives.

Cooking, more specifically the small dinner party, was a competitive sport. Recently, several women have written entire memoirs to explain the central role food played in their lives. Ruth Reichl (*Tender At The Bone*) explains her psychological and social development in terms of food, while Betty Fussell (*My Kitchen Wars*) uses cooking as a metaphor for marriage. She talks about refusing to wear an apron, "the badge of a household drudge," and explains

> The solution to the drudge problem was to make
> cooking an art, or at the very least a craft, like...all

those genteel accomplishments that distinguished the ladies who chatted in the parlors of Jane Austen from their servants. A lady could become extremely accomplished…as long as no one took her work seriously…."

So we studied our book and strove assiduously to produce the perfect little dinner party that would be our work of art.

One of my strongest recollections of these volumes is the quantity of recipes that started out with the command "Separate a dozen eggs." Maybe I recall this particular instruction because of an incident that occurred in our kitchen one morning. I was standing in front of two bowls of twelve separated eggs while answering the telephone when I spied a mouse traveling north to south across the kitchen floor. The yell I let out must have terrified my mother, at the other end of the wire, who imagined her grandchild falling out a window. But more drastically either the mouse or my scream had caused my son to tip the bowl of yolks into the bowl of whites. Or maybe these recipes come to mind because since those days of 'separate a dozen eggs,' medical researchers have told us 1) eggs are forbidden food, 2) eggs can be eaten occasionally, 3) eggs are good for us.

There is a certain sense of sadness connected with recipes acting as our life in review. Were there actually days when we ate roast beef and Yorkshire pudding (can that be concocted from egg whites and tofu in some combination, like so much of the present post-middle-age diet?), cheese soufflés, filet mignon with sauce Béarnaise, shrimp in cream sauce? The sense of loss is like the point in life when we realize for the first time that there are some things we can never be: it is too late to become the ballet dancer, the flutist, travel around the globe in search of the perfect wave for surfing. So it is we will never enjoy these foods again, unless the health professions decree next year that cream and roast beef and egg yolks are good for what ails us.

A DANGEROUS THING

But it is not only a matter of 'where are the meals of yesteryear,' a cookbook also serves as a history of the circles of friends and family, expanding and contracting over the years with our waistlines. Like redoing the family address book, where I am confronted by the MIA's, the divorced, the deceased, the cookbook brings back memories of people and parties gone and nearly forgotten except for smudges and splatters on recipes.

For our thirtieth anniversary my mother gave my husband, who had joined the ranks of cooks, the new one volume *Best of Gourmet*. It was a thin book, and despite its glossy paper and scrumptiously colored illustrations, the recipes were set forth in a business-like way with lists of ingredients, followed by directions. True to the *Gourmet* spirit, there were no tofu look-alikes, but there were many dishes just light enough to make us feel virtuous. But 1988, as the food writer pronounced, was a new era that needed a new Bible.

By 1960, the year our first child was born, life had become a simulacrum of what it was supposed to be, and for the next five years we settled into what we thought was its intended form. We lived on West 93rd street, around the corner from my parents. True, the building wasn't on Central Park West, wasn't, to put it mildly, fancy. But we had a six room, two bath apartment for $168 a month. True, it wasn't exactly six rooms because the dining room had been divided to make a third bedroom, which meant the remaining piece left for dining was more like a hallway to the kitchen.

For my father, whose response to having two daughters was limited to complaining about the white polish from their summer shoes coming off on the black upholstery of his car, the birth of his first grandchild, a boy, was the best thing since arriving in the promised land, since meeting Hannah. He took him everywhere with him. That child, Tom, was enrolled in the Ethical Culture School. True, without family help, which we considered ourselves

Gourmet Cookbook *Meets* Ideal Marriage

Thomas Krasne Levine, 123 West 93rd Street, New York City, 1963.
Jonathan Krasne Levine, sailboat pond, Central Park, 1966.

too independent to take, the tuition was a struggle. And then there was the food, which arrived in our kitchen the way it had always arrived in my mother's kitchen: my father had it delivered.

With the arrival of our second child, Jonathan, we were more than ever tied to Central Park and the park benches and the sandbox. The institution of the playground took a bad rap when books with titles like *Up The Sandbox* came out later in the sixties. The park bench next to the sandbox had women with enough degrees to staff a college. It was the high point of the day when women escaped from their apartments to sit down and talk with peers; it was where we found out the latest in birth control research, what to make for dinner, and how to spot Roseola.

At some point between our first and second child I thought again about medical school, studied for the exam and took it. The minute I started answering questions, I knew I was in the wrong place, that I shouldn't be sitting there trying to think about valences and electromagnetic currents and the formulation of ethanol, because I was incredibly bored, and in a self-defeating gesture

A Dangerous Thing

Edwin Sheldon and Carol Krasne, wedding photograph with Betty and Robert, 350 Central Park West, 1963.

applied to only one medical school. It was with relief I returned to the park bench and the cooperative playgroup five women in our apartment building had set up.

When my sister Carol married in 1963, she too moved to 93rd street, completing a triangle in which we all lived within a block of each other. She and her husband, Edwin, proceeded to have two children, Marjorie and Michael, one right after the other (after all, she was 34 when she married, considered ancient in childbearing terms then) providing our sons, Tom and Jon, with cousins close by.

Could life have gone along like this forever? Probably not. In the years that followed, one woman from the park bench came down with multiple sclerosis, another one was divorced, while the rest of us disbursed to what, on its surface, appeared to be a far far better world.

Gourmet Cookbook *Meets* Ideal Marriage

The News from Fantasyland

Never in my wildest
childish dreams
would I have imagined this
as fantasyland:
secure under the adipose tissue,
between packed dresser drawers.
Never would I have dreamed
after the anniversaries—
tin and glass—
to know you
is not to know myself.

Numbed by warmth
I have shed all
but my mammalian status,
like a flaccid cat
curled against warm brick,
sucking viscous yellow sun
through fur, skin, veins
to anesthetize the centers of the brain.

The news from fantasyland
is frighteningly adequate.
Waking alone all the mornings
before or after
my veins could not hold such warmth.
I would have to be again
the lost cat
recurled against the sunless air.

Chapter Fifteen

1965

THERE ARE TURNING POINTS IN LIFE WHEN EVENTS HAPPEN SO unexpectedly, when life takes such a sharp turn there is no way a person could ever have envisioned the new direction the road takes. Looking back, the familiar path is suddenly out of sight, beyond the bend. Faced with a new, unfamiliar landscape, a person has to move tentatively, as though feeling the way in the dark. That was 1965.

❀ ❀ ❀

October 1964.

Every morning on his way to work, my husband, Robert, and son, Tommy, walked hand in hand from our 93rd street apartment building to Central Park West, where they boarded a city bus, leaving me at home with our second son, Jonathan. But there was one morning that was different. It was Father's Day at the Ethical Culture School. Robert Levine, tall, thin, with short hair and horn rimmed glasses, dressed for work in a suit and tie, found himself on the school roof looking out at Central Park instead of on the way

1965

to his office. Across the way he could see the tops of buildings on Fifth Avenue, to his right, buildings on Central Park South marked the other park border. He was supposed to be watching the pre-kindergartners doings, showing their stuff on the rooftop play equipment.

What he was actually doing was listening to the other fathers discussing the probability of their sons being admitted to Yale (Yale was purely a boy thing then). He was wondering what he was doing there. He was a public school man through and through, elementary to BC, as he once heard a pretentious acquaintance call Brooklyn College. A joke in the family was that the first time Robert left Brooklyn was to attend Harvard Law School and it was a trip from which he never recovered. Like most jokes, buried in the hyperbole is a telling kernel of truth. He was brilliant, and perhaps provincial, like a character in a novel by Stendhal who struggles to make it to Paris from the Provinces, except when Robert sent off postcards to the top law schools, all of them accepted him.

Despite his teenage and college forays into Manhattan, the insouciance of Harvard students, who were all—for the first time in his life—as smart as he was, threw him off balance. He was taken aback to hear students with Southern drawls who sounded like redneck know-nothings raise their hands to answer abstruse questions. He was surprised when students from Catholic colleges stood out as the best and the brightest. And subtle, politely masked anti-Semitism discomforted him. Unlike many of his new peers, he did not spend his summers traveling abroad or improving his backhand. He worked as a busboy in Catskill mountain resorts to earn his tuition. Standing on the Ethical Culture School roof he was reminded of those feelings of being out of place that he carried with him from his Cambridge days.

But when it came time to send our first child to school, I opted for the familiar: the Ethical Culture School. Among friends and family, opinions were divided. The dissonance between what the

A DANGEROUS THING

school preached and actual practice was too great for some who had gone there. As one cousin said dismissively of her time there in the fifties, "The school preached democracy, but what it really had was a bunch of well to do middle class Jewish students and a few brilliant Black scholarship students." She sent her sons elsewhere. When it was our turn to choose, my memories of puppet shows and pageants, of afternoons taking printing and shop, of filling out reading cards still made me argue "It's a place children want to go to every day. It's what education should be like."

Standing on the roof that October, Robert was not so sure. He did not feel he was part of the group gathered for Father's Day.

February 2, 1965.

In a golfing resort on the West Coast of Florida, my Aunt Jean, on vacation from Philadelphia, woke up and told her husband, Raymond, my mother's youngest brother, "Today we must go see your father. We've been here for weeks and we haven't been to see him yet." Raymond objected. He had a golf game scheduled. "You have a golf game every day," his wife pointed out. "You'll have to change it. We'll drive across, have dinner with your dad, stay over, and come home tomorrow."

Ever since his retirement from the Metropolitan Life Insurance Company at 65, Raphael Goldstein had been spending winters in Florida. In the family albums he stands under the palm trees in light colored trousers and a long sleeve shirt; next to him Anna, rotund and smiling, wears a simple crepe dress almost down to her ankles. After Anna died in 1955, he appears in the pictures with visiting sons and daughters. The rest of the time he resided at a kosher hotel on the Boardwalk in Atlantic City. Either place, he began every day with an energetic three mile walk.

Reluctantly, Raymond acceded. He called off his golf game, alerted his father, and made a hotel reservation in Miami Beach. They met Raphael in the lobby of his hotel, where he proudly

228

1965

Goldstein family party, Philadelphia, June 12, 1966. *From lower left:* Gilbert, Joyce and Leonard Goldberg, Betty and Robert Levine, Hannah Krasne, Edwin and Carol Sheldon, Raymond and Jean Goldstein.

introduced his son and daughter-in-law to his buddies, before leading them to the dining room. He had instructed the headwaiter to reserve a special table for him and his guests. No sooner had they been seated, and the waiter served the soup, than Raphael Goldstein, age 94, took his last breath.

His body was flown back to the Goldstein family plot in Roosevelt Memorial Park Cemetery, outside Philadelphia. Hannah and Israel Krasne, their daughters and their husbands, drove down from New York to join the Philadelphia clan for the funeral. It was winter, but the grass was green on the neat hillside where the white tent was set up. The cemetery had a well-kept air that came from open space and careful manicuring.

A rabbi from Uncle Raymond's temple intoned the ceremony. He spoke of a long life well lived. Glancing around at Raphael's prosperous sons and daughters, their spouses, children, and grandchildren, anyone would have had to agree that his American life had played itself out just as he must have dreamed it could.

He had risked much and worked hard for his vision of the good life. It was a complex vision. Its material side encompassed a town house, a chauffeured car, and designer clothes. Then there were Raphael's strict rules for proper behavior, which had shaped two daughters and two sons into four strong individuals. Like a continuo playing along with these themes there were books and music. But there was no place in his vision of the good life for higher education for women. Over lunch after the funeral service, Raphael's children celebrated his long life, some with affection, some with respect, some with more mixed emotions.

For the Krasne contingent from New York, the dream of the good life was destined to take a different turn. None of us on our way home in the black Cadillac could have dreamed of the next funeral we would attend. No one sitting under the tent that February morning in Philadelphia could have imagined that all too soon we would sit together again, listening to a rabbi chant the prayer for the dead.

April 1965.
Robert departed for Washington, D.C., where he joined a group heading for a retreat in Virginia. They were there for a week of training by The Lawyer's Committee For Civil Rights Under Law, a group of establishment-type Ivy League attorneys set up by President Kennedy, then sponsored by President Johnson. They were being prepared to go to Mississippi in the summer to work for integration through law.

Life at home went on. Tommy was at school. Jon's play group met five days a week, with one mother taking care of four children for the morning, giving the rest of us four mornings to catch up. None of us worked. In contemporary jargon, we were childcare providers. Of the five families in the group, for some tragically

1965

unfathomable reason, we will be the only pair of parents who both live to see our children grown up.

May 17, 1965.
It was dinnertime. My father called to find out what we were having to eat for dinner. He called every day, once in the morning to see what we needed, and in the evening to see how everyone was. In between, he sometimes dropped in at the playground on his way home from work to check on the children. "Veal roast," I informed him.

"How are the children?" he wanted to know. "Do they need anything?" As he left for work in the morning he was always instructing my mother to buy the children socks or jackets. On weekends he took Tommy to his barbershop to introduce him around, or bought him a tricycle or boots.

"No," I assured him, "they are fine. We're putting them to bed."

The 'we' was a fiction. At this stage Robert was mostly a spectator when it came to parenting, and that evening he was busy preparing for a trial. After the children were safely in bed, we sat down to eat, a meal that was never to be touched, a menu never repeated. Before we could pick up knife and fork, the phone rang.

"Something has happened to your father," my mother's tense voice announced.

"We'll be right there," I told her, and called our neighbors upstairs to watch the children. We walked the one block east and one north to the building where I grew up. My father was stretched out on the kitchen floor, stiff already, his color turning gray-green. He was the first dead person I had seen up close. His body seemed to fill the large old kitchen. He was 69; my mother was 66. She had known from the moment she heard the crash, as he stood up from the table and fell to the floor, that he was dead, but she had not said the word on the phone. We were all quite collected; we were all in shock.

231

A DANGEROUS THING

The Krasne family arrived. My father's heart specialist arrived. "If I'd known he was going to die so soon, I wouldn't have pestered him so much about his diet," he told my mother.

The family lawyer arrived. "He'd just made a new will, but he hadn't signed it," he explained to us.

Only the presence of a four year old and a two year old running underfoot kept us all firmly planted in the here and now as we made funeral arrangements. It was a large gathering: workers came from the business; family came from Philadelphia.

People did not have wardrobes of black clothing in the sixties, so we had to hunt around for appropriate clothes. The only piece in my closet that was even close was a sleeveless deep blue linen sheath I'd worn for my sister's wedding two years earlier.

The ceremony had the eerie quality of being a mirror image of our wedding: everyone assembled in the special room, the rabbi ready to make pronouncements, the family marching in last and taking its place up front. Just as our wedding had been scripted out of a fifties formbook, so too the funeral was the work of others. No one in the audience thought of taking the rabbi's place and speaking; no one had any words for what had happened.

Washington Cemetery in Brooklyn bore no relationship to that green and calm place we had buried Raphael Goldstein. It was one of the oldest burying grounds in New York, and wound its way between houses in the shadow of the elevated subway. The large family contingent trying to find its way to the Krasne plot wended its way between fallen stones whose inscriptions were almost obliterated. Some sections we wandered through had rusted iron fences with gates that stated the area was the site of a burying society with a foreign name. Other sections had rows of small stones, fallen at haphazard angles, for children who must have succumbed to an epidemic in a previous century.

At the Krasne site there was one large stone and lined up in front of it the footstones of my father's parents. On one side was the

232

grave of Aunt Vivienne, my Uncle Sam's petite wife who had died of cancer. Then there was the empty hole for my father's coffin. He was the first Krasne of his generation to occupy the plot. The shrubs over the graves had been given a hasty trim, but around us there were family places that had gone wild; whether the family had died off or moved on, the overgrown plots gave the place a despairing air. The family recited the prayer for the dead, and went back to the apartment on Central Park West for a luncheon.

For several days afterwards we took turns staying with my mother, until she was no longer haunted by the sound of the crash in the kitchen. The first night it rained, I could not bear to think of my father alone out there in the ground in Brooklyn. A month later, waiting for the crosstown bus at 96th street and Fifth Avenue, I thought I saw him in his black Cadillac waiting at the light.

July 1965.
With the children in tow, I went to the East Side heliport to watch Robert leave in a helicopter for Kennedy Airport. He was catching a plane to Mississippi. A week later, when Jon saw a helicopter flying by, he asked, "Is that where Daddy is?"

"No," I tried to explain. "Daddy is far away in a place called Mississippi."

His letters were about the heat, the cast of characters in his group, and others he met, people who changed the course of his law practice. He told us about the day a black man dove into the pool at the motel and the white people jumped out, like an old film run backwards. He wrote about the day he went to Philadelphia, Mississippi, and had to pass between Sheriff Rainey and Deputy Price, two enormous figures trying to block his way in the court-house. "If I hadn't just used the bathroom," he told us, "I would have peed in my pants." They were scary guys, even though it was just before the government was able to pin the murder of Cheney, Goodman, and Schwerner on them.

A DANGEROUS THING

Central Park was deserted. Heat and soot reigned. One hot, humid afternoon when we came in from the park I stuck my head in the sink and let the boys pour cold water over Mommy's head. They thought it was the most fun game of the summer. One weekend I decided to take the children to the beach, but the hose in the car broke and the nearest garage on the highway to the beach had nothing with which to fix it. Two small, restless children packed in the car was a big incentive to Yankee ingenuity; I jerry rigged the hose with a piece of string.

One family in our playgroup gave up on the city and bought a house in Westchester. We went to visit them in this strange, far away place. They had moved into a contemporary: lots of glass and wood overlooking grass and trees. For the first time the idea of a house had something to recommend it. Comfort and style, I saw, came easier outside Manhattan. A limited income bought a lot more home. I consulted their real estate broker, who showed us a Frank Lloyd Wright-style house, twelve rooms of cypress and glass, every room a corner room, nestled among rocks and trees. It had a certain fascination that 93rd street in August couldn't match.

When Robert returned, I sprung the idea on him. Having lived in a house outside the city, he saw nothing odd in the idea of leaving Manhattan. When we drove up to see it, there was no electricity because the house had been on the market for a year (a fact to which we paid no attention), so we viewed it by flashlight. "It's like a tree house," I pointed out. "What do you think?" It was, we decided, as good a use as we could think of for the insurance policy my father had left us.

October 1965.
My mother was packing up the large apartment on Central Park West, moving across the Park to Fifth Avenue, an apartment with a terrace overlooking the sailboat pond. It was the kind of place she had tried to convince my father to move to for years, but none of us

234

1965

could imagine him in these four rooms, however bright and comfortable she made them. But it was her place… the place where she would die in her own bed twenty-seven years later.

Suddenly we noticed my mother had gotten rid of her Space Shoes, those tanker-size custom-made footwear she had been sporting for the last several years. Now she appeared again in leather pumps; she got rid of the old family photos; she called in the decorator, upholsterer, and painter. She was in charge, launching herself on a new stage of her life, independent, with no one to answer to about anything she wanted to do. The effort of packing and unpacking left her bedridden with a major case of sciatica, but when she got up from her sick bed, she went off on the Queen Elizabeth to England and France; she entertained her grandchildren on her terrace.

On Tommy's fifth birthday, October 9th, we had a birthday party with children perched in a circle on packed boxes. Two days later we left the city. We would return… in thirty years.

❂ ❂ ❂

"We looked at this house…."

"We saw this house…."

However they said it, the first years we lived in Westchester County that line seemed to be virtually the ticket of entry to our home. The house had been on the market for more than a year and touring it seemed to have been a local obligation, somewhere in the order of importance with attending the parade opening Little League season and the caroling accompanying the lighting of the village Christmas tree. A nation of voyeurs, we apparently feel the next best thing to seeing how people live in strange houses is seeing the strange houses themselves.

It was always at that moment in the introductions that our guests would suddenly realize that we, after all, <u>had</u> bought the

A Dangerous Thing

place, and would hastily attempt to cover the awkward inference about the oddity of our taste or lack of sense or both by some such remark as "But it didn't have a two-car garage."

In fact, it didn't have a one-car garage; in fact, not even a carport. And it was at that point that we would have to acknowledge, at least to ourselves, that when we bought it we never noticed this apparent omission. We were city people, adept in the ways of shifting a car from side to side in perpetual sport with the city's sanitation engineers.

When I think about my routine in the city (holed up with two small children who, taken collectively, were sick all year, moving a car back and forth across a street filled with broken bottles, fire engines, neighborhood quarrels, bicyclers), I feel the awe reserved for singular events. There are events, like painting the house, writing a thesis, upon which one looks back in disbelief, wondering how one ever did that. That is the way city life came to seem after years in the suburbs. But in the beginning, when we first moved to Westchester, it was quite the opposite.

I was the first person in the family to leave Manhattan. As far as my mother was concerned, North of Spuyten Duyvil was Alaska. My going away present from her was a fur-lined coat. The children had to learn a new language: "This is my property," one of them was soon overheard proclaiming from the top of the rock behind which our house crouched, and on which all the neighborhood children congregated. There was the strange sensation of their venturing out, and in and out, unattended, unlike the days when we marched to the playground sandbox: tricycles, children, dump trucks, pails leashed to me like Marley and his chains in *A Christmas Carol*.

They were out and I was in, in our big beautiful house, ministering to its insatiable needs: a dozen rooms, three bathrooms, and a garden. There were no more afternoons seated on the park bench, exchanging stories with other mothers. Every room had a mini-

1965

mum of 100 square feet of glass. Because the house was built on a hill, the main floor had our living quarters and down a circular staircase the ground floor belonged to the children. The basement included a rock. All the walls, ceilings, beams inside and out were cypress. Some visitors thought it looked as though it belonged in California, but others mentioned Usonia, the Frank Lloyd Wright development in Westchester.

"Very comfortable, dear," my mother pronounced when she came up from Manhattan for her inspection tour. One of our neighbors, occupying a house by the same architect, told us that her mother had said, "Very nice dear, but I hope someday you'll have a real house."

The second week in October, when we moved in, the leaves were off the trees and on the ground. From the windows of this tree house there were now other houses to be seen, but also miles of New Jersey visible, the tip of the Empire State Building, and yards of sunshine in every room. And the leaves below, knee deep, it came to me with the slow horror of inevitability as I focused on them, were each and every one waiting for me. Was it possible that in the city I had actually gone out and bought a bunch of leaves to celebrate fall?

One break from house beautiful was a tour of the local elementary school. It was a perfectly orderly, perfectly silent place. This second week in October the bulletin boards lining the halls were filled with four word poems describing the ups and downs of leaves, inscribed on brown and yellow paper.

One class had the school banner decorating the door. "That's the best class," my guide pronounced in a hushed tone. I swelled, instantly picturing my children behind that banner. "They march in the hall without touching or making a sound," she explained. Ethical Culture it was not, and I had a queasy feeling we had not quite thought through the implications of this move. I thought consolingly of the comment Robert had brought home from his first

A DANGEROUS THING

week on the commuter train: "Ardsley? Isn't that where people live until they decide where they're going to live?"

When the snows came that first winter, we shoveled ourselves further in. By some reflective trick of our infinite glass, we watched the fire in our fireplace as it flickered over the snow in which we were perpetually embedded. We watched cars chugging up our steep hill while we had to leave ours at the bottom, innocent of such inventions as snow tires.

Spring surprised us with slopes of crocuses, pink and white dogwood, cherry blossoms, purple and white rhododendrons, azaleas with bell-like flowers in flecked shades, tree peonies with overblown pale papery petals. Apparently the doctor for whom the house had been designed had been an amateur horticulturist, but before we learned to appreciate what we'd inherited, we city folks managed to kill off a good bit. Then summer cast its umbrella of shade, turning everything green, and we had lived through our first year. Living in the suburbs was insidious. In time we came to think life should be beautiful; we were entitled. It sapped tolerance for the eccentric, the heterogeneous, the dynamic, like a body too long on antibiotics.

For children as they got older, it was an era when the suburbs gave a kind of freedom. They could go everyplace on their own. With their bicycles or on foot they could get to the village, the schools; to their friends; to tennis and swimming. This was a kind of independence for children that the city had already lost by the seventies.

And the suburbs gave the illusion of democracy in action. Like the friends I had made at the Equitable Life Assurance Society, our neighbors in Ardsley had migrated from all the boroughs of New York City. They had all landed on our street in Westchester, but they worked anywhere from Wall Street to White Plains. We found people who liked hiking and formed The Ardsley Outdoor Club, a group of families who organized trail walks, mountain

1965

climbing, and canoeing expeditions on weekends. Robert helped found a Fair Housing Committee, to try and monitor prospects for integration, but bringing blacks to the community was a lot harder than organizing a climb up Breakneck Ridge. Good schools, we learned, took hard work on campaigns to elect sensible people to the school board. These activities were alternatives the suburbs offered to Little League, Brownies, and Boy Scout troops. They brought us together not only with people across the street, but also with people across the village who were willing to work for better education and a more diverse community.

The house came with membership in the local swim and tennis club, not to be confused at all with a country club. It was the perfect compromise between upbringing and education: it was private, but anyone could buy a membership when a bond became available. Families with picnic baskets camped out for the afternoon while children learned to swim and play tennis. Weekdays, there were tennis courts available for as many hours as a person wanted, because for several years there were hardly any other women who played. Neighbors who grew up in the Bronx hadn't spent summers cultivating a graceful forehand at camp in the Berkshires. They discovered tennis after they migrated to Westchester, so they had some catching up to do. Weekend mornings the courts were reserved for men. When Labor Day came and the club closed with a grand finale, the summer crowd evaporated; women disappeared into their houses, not to reappear until Memorial Day.

Robert eventually became head of the Zoning Board, quickly learning this was the shortest way to make the most enemies. Later, he was Assistant Town Judge, but when we eventually moved back to the city he said with puzzlement, "How could I have lived some place for thirty years, been so happy there the whole time, and I haven't thought about it for thirty seconds since we moved?" It was a smooth life and its best legacy was wonderful friends.

A DANGEROUS THING

But we would never have known these facts of life from that first year. Parent, businessperson, cook, laundry and cleaning person, with these jobs we had a vague familiarity; but handyman, electrician, plumber, gardener, roofer, blacktopper, to these enterprises we were foreign. At first, we simply were not strong enough: raking, shoveling, digging, planting, racing up and down stairs, attending to vast wood floors and glass walls produced sore backs, callused hands, dispositions in advanced states of decay. People would joke that it wasn't less expensive living in the suburbs, just less fun. Living in the city, they spent all their money and a little more; living in the suburbs, they spent all their money and a little more...at the hardware store.

Yet the physical ordeal was the least of the adaptation. For the men, who went off to work by train, each day took them back into the world. Robert bought a 'station car,' so old a neighbor thought it must belong to our maid, but there was no maid, and though I too had a car, there was no place to go with two small children and a limited income. When I proposed a cooperative playgroup, it was a hard sell. Though none of the other women worked (several had never finished college, leaving to help a husband get on in his career), they could not see why they should bother when they could just send children out to play. So there we were, each of us stuck in her own house all day every day. It was the problem with no name, until Betty Friedan discovered us.

There was one exception. A family who lived in back of us had four children, three of them older than our eldest. Frieda, their mother, a psychologist at a residential treatment center for children in need of supervision, warned me: "If you don't get something to do, go to work, you'll lose your mind."

If she could do it with four children, surely I could swing it. After all, I only had two. Instead of sitting at home, working my way through our set of Dickens, I would go forth and preach the one gospel I knew: reading fiction. There was no teaching experi-

1965

ence to put on a résumé, but I sent it around to the Adult Education Program of our school district and every college in Westchester, along with a cover letter suggesting courses I would like to teach. Hard as it is to believe in an era when college teaching jobs in the liberal arts are hard to come by, in 1965 almost every college was interested. I picked the closest one, Mercy College in Dobbs Ferry, and started teaching part time.

To make my escape possible, we hired Mrs. Bowen, from Barbados. She arrived to live in, even though my pittance of a lecturer's salary was less than we paid her. A kind, skinny, elderly lady, she went about softly, like a ghost in the house, drank tea from a saucer, and told people who called for Robert "The master is not at home." He waited for lawyers with whom he was setting up the Westchester Legal Services program to remark on that form of address.

Born again, that's what I felt like.

A DANGEROUS THING

Missionary to the Suburbs

It is not just policemen, firemen
who move past me
with the urgency of accomplishment
like toy trains accelerated
on a figure eight track.
Without sirens you too
travel on serious missions,
your briefcase specially designed
to carry the closely kept word.

My shoulder bag
crammed with scraps
(children's extra hands, legs)
I move in slow motion
insulated better
than in a down sleeping bag
by the hot air you provide,
awaiting your advents
like the native trader
whose arrivals leave us
vaguely satisfied
with our store of trinkets.

Chapter Sixteen

THE OTHER SIDE
OF THE DESK

"How do you like our new habits?" The nun rose from behind her desk so I could see her outfit.

Speechless, I could only stare at her. I had rehearsed information about the course I proposed teaching, the research I had done, but never having actually spoken with nuns before, I had no idea what kind of remark was called for at that moment. It was 1966, and what I could not know from where I sat in the Dean's Office at Mercy College was that I had just been swept into the revolution that would go down in history as Vatican II.

Who was I, granddaughter of the Goldsteins and the Krasnoschezeks, to understand that the previous year the Sisters of Mercy wore wimples (head-dresses that showed no hair), making them indistinguishable from each other, and flowing black dresses that covered their sensible black shoes. Now, daringly, there was hair emerging from short veils, ankles showing below dark blue gowns, and dark blue shoes with low heels. But I had no frame of reference for the Dean's remarks, nor did I understand how, with degrees from Mount Holyoke and Columbia, I fit nicely into her master plan.

A DANGEROUS THING

The Sisters of Mercy, an Irish teaching and nursing Order, had started a Junior College in 1950 to educate young women entering the Order. They established it on land adjacent to Rockefeller property in Westchester. Fortunately, Rockefeller coveted their space, so he found them a splendid site overlooking the Hudson River in Dobbs Ferry, where they erected a convent, chapel, and college building. After they moved, the Sisters extended the College to four years in 1961, opening it to paying students. By the time I arrived, there were 500 girls and some young nuns, all of who appeared in white gloves for every occasion. The plan was to seek accreditation and then become coed. Since the existing faculty of nuns, as well as the few lay teachers, had almost exclusively been educated in Catholic colleges and graduate schools, my credentials had great appeal. The Dean understood that the accrediting agency would look askance at a faculty whose education was entirely parochial. She coveted my credentials.

Having taken the idea of a college for granted, I failed to grasp how this band of women had only recently, like magicians, created this college *ex nihilo*, out of nothing. In an era when my own woman's college, in its day an historic first, still had a man as President, as did most women's colleges in the sixties, the Sisters of Mercy had built a college from the ground up: campus, library, student body, into a four year institution of higher learning. In time it would become a secular college of 10,000 students.

As a teacher, I was a blank slate, so I asked the head of the Department of English Literature if I could sit in on one of her classes. This was supposed to give me a sense of how they went about things at Mercy College. On the appointed day I dug deep in my closet to find a dark blue suit left over from my Manhattan days, tied my hair back, and set off to take a seat in the room to which she had directed me. Sister Joannes Christie, R.S.M., Ph.D., a small, thin, alert woman entered the room and the young women leaped to their feet in unison, reminding me of my first day in

The Other Side of the Desk

Philosophy class at Mount Holyoke. Except here they broke into a rapid chant, reciting something at such speed that I could make out none of the words. They were, I guessed, reciting a prayer.

Before class was quite over, the loudspeaker came on, an incongruous voice from outer space that jolted me, but that everyone else took in stride. Students must have been used to high schools where the word from on high was promulgated this way, but it wasn't quite what I expected in a college. Worried that my teaching career could be derailed before it got started because prayer had been given short shrift in my education, after class I asked Sister Joannes, "Is it required to start the class with a prayer?"

She paused, puzzled. "Well, my dear, how else would you get everyone's attention?"

Answering this seemed obvious to me, so obvious I was afraid of being considered impertinent. Searching around in my memory bank of classes I had attended, I suggested "Couldn't I just shut the door?"

Tactfully, she agreed to let me handle the situation my own way.

Out came the books. References piled up around me in our study as I moved back into a semblance of my academic days, a time when only books and ideas mattered, not the dinner menu and the children's transportation to after school activities. Except now there was a husband, two children, and a twelve-room house to orchestrate. It was the beginning of a war, a battle between the domestic and the scholar, wife/teacher, mother/writer. I was heir to a tradition that taught me home, children, entertaining, and above all appearances were of paramount importance.

It was the twentieth century, but this was the same lesson Jane Austen had to deal with as she tried to scribble her novels in the living room of her father's house and tend to his parishioners; that George Eliot had to cope with as she put up the preserves and the pickles. From here on every moment devoted to reading and writ-

A DANGEROUS THING

ing was a moment stolen from something to be done on the other front, making it impossible to take either direction as totally serious. The battle was wearing, so wearing that down the road I packed up periodically and ran away.

A friend who was a college teacher told me a story of preparing for a course carefully, but running out of material during his first lecture. Haunted by his story, note cards piled up around me as I assembled enough material to get me through weeks of classes. Nervous but prepared, I went to meet my first class. All went well, as I drew the students—a room full of young Irish and Italian women—into the excitement of reading fiction. Exhilarated by the lecture, I stopped at the market on the way home. In front of the pasta section, my hand extended to grab a box of thin spaghetti, I realized I had to go back and do this again...and again. I felt ill, grabbed the pasta and hurried home. Though with time and practice I became used to the rhythm of classes, each new semester, as I stared out at the sea of strange faces, the scary feeling was there again: what could I impart to these students, all turned expectantly toward me, that would make a difference?

After I handed out the first writing assignment to students in that first course, there was silence in the classroom, and then a hand went up. "How are we going to write this paper? You haven't told us what to say," one bold student asked.

There was a pause as I contemplated the distance between my Ethical Culture education and my students' catechism training. In the Ethical Culture schools, where there were all leaders and no followers, characteristics of independent thinking—creativity, originality—were the prized and rewarded qualities. Thus the idea that a teacher's job was to recite and a student's to repeat after her precisely what had been said was not even a concept that came under the heading 'Education' in my mind.

But on the spot it fell to me to move this room full of young women from where they were to where I wanted them to be in

The Other Side of the Desk

terms of discovering analytical powers and their own voices. Could I accomplish this in the face of their training, and was I allowed to lead them down this road? Gently I tried to explain how they could proceed. At least, I thought, there was something I could learn from them: I would get to know about the Christian Bible, a neglected part of my education.

Though not my favorite Thomas Hardy work, I had chosen *Jude the Obscure* as one of our texts. The previous summer I had been introduced to a man from India who asked what I taught, and when I informed him it was English Literature he said, "Ah, *Jude the Obscure*" as though in that one book was encompassed all English Literature, so Jude it was. But when we got to *Jude* and I asked the class why the author chose that name for his protagonist, no one was able to tell me about St. Jude, the patron saint of lost causes. It was a good thing I had done my homework.

The road to becoming a teacher had other bumps in store for me. When we were scheduled to read Henry James' *Portrait Of A Lady*, there were some students who gave up, an approach I had never encountered before in education. They were willing to fail two assignments rather than cope with James' subtle convolutions. On the other hand, by the end of the semester most students had found their own voices, had caught on to speaking up about their own ideas. But then on the last day of class, a pale, shy girl wearing the short dark blue veil and ankle length dress of a Sister of Mercy stopped by my desk. "I'm leaving the Order," she told me.

Horrified at the thought it was my teaching that had somehow turned her into a rebel, I worried that I would lose my job. From where I stood I could not grasp how the Order was changing because the church was changing. By the following year the "new habits" were gone, replaced by no habits. Soon nuns were moving out of the convent into apartments of their own, some to make a home with another woman, some out of the Order altogether to marry ex-priests and Monsignors. Their vocation being ministering to other people, most of these ex-religious gravitated to social science fields: psychology, social work, sociology; or they became counselors, therapists, and advisors. It was hard to understand how a church could recover from such a brain drain, from the loss of so many caring professionals.

Teaching one course filled every nook and cranny of time I could find. It is the story of women and part-time work. They take part-time jobs because that fits in with family life. But they end up putting in full-time work for a part-time salary. So I agreed to work full-time, trading in my status as Adjunct Lecturer (two courses) for the title of Instructor (four courses), salary $7,500, no benefits, but I was finally making more than we were paying our housekeeper.

Our latest housekeeper was a stalwart, determined woman from Jamaica who attended school on her day off to become a practical nurse. She was saving to bring her children to the United States, and when she managed to do that, her eldest attended Mount Holyoke College. When it came to children, she sported a no nonsense attitude that was the result of raising three children in a British colonial environment.

As a kind of signing bonus at the College, Sister Joannes asked if I would teach an upper level course, traditionally entitled Modern British Literature. It was, however, as I looked at course outlines, neither very modern nor very British. In preparation, I struck a bargain with Robert: the summer of 1967 we would take a his/hers trip. Our first stop: Ireland, so I could hunt up literary sites. Then we'd move on to countries with histories in which he was interested, Spain and Portugal—still ruled by Franco and Salazar.

Leaving the children at home in the care of our housekeeper, with Robert's parents to check up on the ménage, we went off to Europe. In the West of Ireland we found our way to Lissadell, the decaying mansion of the Gore-Booths, one of the families and

Carol and Edwin Sheldon, Robert and Betty Levine,
Hotel La Pérouse, Paris, June, 1967.

places William Butler Yeats wrote about. Like something out of Tennesee Williams, it was an inhabited ruin where, for a couple of shillings, Lady Gore-Booth herself showed us around, pointing out the pictures of family killed in two world wars fighting for England.

We found Lough Gill, where Yeats had written "The Lake Isle of Innisfree." It was surrounded by cow droppings, which made it not quite as poetic as it sounded when I'd read, "I will arise and go now/ and go to Innisfree." At Thoor Ballylee, the home Yeats built for himself, we saw his words inscribed:

> A winding stair, a chamber arched with stone,
> A grey stone fireplace, with an open hearth,
> A candle and a written page...;

A DANGEROUS THING

Finally, we found our way to Yeats' grave in Drumcliff church-yard, with the epitaph he composed:

Cast a cold eye
On life, on death.
Horseman, pass by!
W.B.Yeats
June 13th, 1865
January 28th, 1939

Afterward, we wandered through Dublin in search of Joyce sites. Finding them was difficult because in 1967 Joyce was still forbidden fruit for Irish students. While we were in Ireland, the Six Day War in the Middle East broke out, and we were able to pick up two minutes of news about it at night because Ireland had troops involved.

That fall, when I entered the classroom for Modern British Literature, every seat was taken. I stared out in panic, especially as my first bit of news for the class was that the material was neither modern nor British. Then I hastily launched into a quick survey of Irish history, as background for a study of Yeats, Joyce, Shaw, and Beckett. After the week of Irish history, one of the nuns came up to the lectern and told me "My father says this is the first worthwhile thing I've learned since I've been at college." She was one of the last nuns to pass through our classes, replaced by an odd assortment of males infiltrating student ranks in our newly coed college. The pace of change was accelerating.

Those of us caught up in the political and pedagogical turmoil of Mercy College thought we were unique, but in fact the Ivory Tower period of American educational history was undergoing a general breakup. Federal funding for veterans and policemen, and an increase in the number of women returning to school resulted in a rise in the average age of undergraduates to 28. Funding to

The Other Side of the Desk

encourage minority enrollment in colleges was contributing to further diversification in the student body. Adding to these seismic shifts in the college scene were the expansion of community colleges and the growth of public universities.

To all appearances, Mercy college's first jolt was when the college became coed, but the much more significant development was the institution of evening and weekend courses in 1968, to meet the needs of Cuban immigrants. This one small step was actually the beginning of a revolution. From here on education was offered wherever and whenever a given population needed it—Russians in Brooklyn, Koreans in Westchester, Dominicans in upper Manhattan; corporate workers in White Plains, housewives in Yorktown Heights. The corollary of this expansion was a geometric increase in the diversity of the student population, for ultimately students from these varied sites had to come together at one of the satellite campuses to complete their work. Day or night, weekday or weekend, winter or summer, like AAA emergency road service, Mercy education was always available.

❋ ❋ ❋

One evening during this time of rapid change, Robert and I attended a double-bill in New York of two dramas, the most memorable entitled "An Actor's Nightmare." The main character found himself either wearing the right costume but walking into the wrong play, or wearing the wrong costume but cast in the right play. He entered stage left, garbed for a part in "Hamlet,"—doublet, tights, sword—only to find the scenery, dialogue, and leading lady proceeding with a Noel Coward style drawing room comedy—flapper dresses, Art Deco decor. From there on it was perspiration and improvisation all the way, or so it was made to seem. The audience loved it.

Afterward, it occurred to me that every profession or stage of

A DANGEROUS THING

life has its own nightmare. That's why I can hear lawyers 20 years after law school recounting their law school nightmare: "I was sitting in seat 82 of Torts when Professor Bartlett called on me and said, 'Mr. Smith, would you....'" And mothers of young children exchanging their nightmares: "I was in the supermarket and suddenly I realized I'd lost...." As Mercy acquired students of every age group and background, my teaching nightmare gained specific focus. Typically it took the following form.

I saw myself in front of a class. It was far enough into the semester to know already that the grandmother sitting near the door was never going to take off her coat; either it was her security blanket against youth or she had been traumatized by fire drills. I could see that the two guys passing notes in the back should give it up because one of them probably wouldn't pass; and that the nurse in the front row had already underlined the entire text. It was the second month of the semester and, according to the Course Outline, we should have already heard Ibsen's Nora slam the door and we should have arrived at the twentieth century, having successfully navigated our way through the first unit, the one on drama. But we were still discussing "Hamlet," Act II.

In this nightmare, each day I announced, in a small, hopeful voice, "Tomorrow we will finish 'Hamlet.'" And each day, as I sensed increased movement in the group and glanced over my shoulder at the clock, which had mysteriously sped ahead to the end of the period, I still could not see that farther shore which was the end of "Hamlet": "Let four captains/ Bear Hamlet like a soldier to the stage...."

The chairman of the department, who suddenly appeared in my dream scene to observe the class, increased my anxiety in the nightmare. She regarded the outline and saw that we should be studying the sonnet form of poetry. But as soon as she was settled in her seat, pencil and pad ready to note down my performance, a student who was absent last time raised a hand and wanted to

The Other Side of the Desk

know why Hamlet didn't kill Claudius after the performance of the "Mousetrap"; and another one, a foreign student, wanted to know—again—what was with Hamlet and Ophelia; and the young man with the splendid tattoos pointed out that Hamlet was too smart to be good; and the mature woman in front interrupted to say he was too wishy washy to survive.

Caught in this nightmare, I stood in front, like the referee at a tennis match. It was perfectly clear to the chairperson of the department that we were nowhere near where we were supposed to be: the middle of the second unit, the one on poetry, nor the beginning of it, nor the end of the drama unit. We were still stuck in "Hamlet," albeit Act III.

In my nightmare I began to sweat, convinced I would never get out of "Hamlet." All life might end up encompassed by "Hamlet." Did this happen elsewhere? Was the chemistry teacher upstairs unable to get from the atom to the molecule, or the math teacher to advance from the point to the line, or the history professor from World War I to World War II? As I stood in front of the class, taking root in the Elizabethan Age, I was sure everyone else was marching to the right beat.

The department chairperson frowned in this nightmare, scribbling on her pad, recording my desperate performance as I pushed on, metaphor by metaphor, pun by pun, scene by scene. I polished off Ophelia, while the others, male and female, high and low, clever and obtuse, waited in the wings to be annihilated. Their fates became excruciating burdens I longed to put down. Any month now I hoped to wake up and it would be the twentieth century and W.H. Auden would be saying, "About suffering they were never wrong,/ The Old Masters…," and, temporarily, the teacher's nightmare would be over.

It was the kind of nightmare where the dreamer is treading water and knows, as a subtext, that the alternative is drowning, and when she can't tread water any longer, she wakes in a sweat. The

A DANGEROUS THING

classroom nightmare was the result of radical changes in higher education, and Mercy was on the front lines of these changes.

The alternative to the classroom nightmare, I discovered after several years of teaching, was something called academic administration. Administration, I thought, could be the way to channel change in positive directions. Fortunately, when I eventually became an administrator I did not know there were a lot of jokes circulating in academe about administrators, such as: An Assistant Dean is a mouse in training to be a rat. Administration was the job awaiting me, though I had never thought of a teaching job as meaning anything except standing up in front of a class.

❖ ❖ ❖

As a student seated in a classroom, gazing up at a professor for enlightenment, I had assumed that was the whole picture: there was us and them, students and faculty. I did not give any thought to the fact that behind the scenes, like The Wizard of Oz, there was a power called The Administration. When I moved around to the other side of the desk I learned that faculty were actually caught in the middle between students and administration. And I learned that though we thought in the fifties our professors were descended from another planet, in the vastly altered college scene of the late twentieth century, the disparity between the expectations of faculty and the experience of students was even greater, just as my nightmare showed.

It was, I came to the conclusion, the humanoid problem. A humanoid is an artificial construct made out of biological materials. It bears a resemblance to, but is not human. In the classroom there is a strong tendency for faculty and students to regard each other as humanoids, for differing reasons. To some students, faculty are somewhat like other people they know—parents and grandparents, aunts and uncles, ministers and doctors—but to most

The Other Side of the Desk

students faculty are not really like anyone else they know. They are strange beings who actually concern themselves with things like subject-verb agreement, dangling participles, and sentence fragments. Similarly, to faculty students are somewhat like people they know: themselves at a vaguely recollected earlier age, their own or their friends children, but many Mercy students were not much like any of these. From the teacher's side of the desk, trying to convey to students how writing and reading mattered sometimes seemed like administering a form of torture.

After a while, faculty responses to students risked fitting the description by Nabokov in *Pnin*. He says of the professor, "Like so many aging college people, Pnin had long ceased to notice the existence of students on the campus, in the corridors, in the library—anywhere, in brief, save in functional classroom concentrations." In other words, student and teacher were destined to remain just as foreign to each other in the real classroom as they were in my nightmare. Paradoxically, the ultimate end of the process that removes students from the outside world is to return them to it better able to make their own way in the world at large.

The more time I spent in front of the classroom, the more I saw how the alienating effect of the academic scene came from several sources. I remembered the Columbia professors quoting themselves and realized when faculty and students met in the classroom, they were not on neutral ground. This was academic turf and the vast majority of students were not destined to be academics, with the exception of future elementary school teachers. Though the teacher was on home ground, the language, methodology, values, and goals of academe were a foreign tongue for the student.

Teachers were there for the long haul, while year after year admissions offices delivered class after class of new students. This meant that to a great extent education followed a factory model, just like my experience in the Columbia Masters program: students were the raw material in a production line. It was the task of facul-

A Dangerous Thing

ty repeatedly to convert this raw material into a finished product. Along the way the semi-finished product was periodically inspected and tested to see if it met standards. Just as on a production line, each faculty member was assigned a task that dealt only with a specific, small aspect of the product. Hence, none of us had responsibility for the end product. In my classroom I was in charge, but only of the three or six credits the student needed out of the 120 total. For the rest? We threw up our hands and shrugged our shoulders.

Ultimately, success is measured for the institution, just as for a business, by whether or not the product commands a high price in the market place. Education thus has the same alienating effect as nineteenth century English social observers noted about the factory system during the Industrial Revolution. Workers, observers noted, had become less than human: they were merely 'hands'; nowadays, students are merely social security numbers or, even less, TCRs (total course registrations).

During the first part of the twentieth century the image of college was a cloistered quad where students lived in ivy covered buildings. By the time I was involved in educational issues, the average age of the undergraduate had risen ten years and a large number of students made the transition between the microcosm and the macrocosm, academe and the larger community, on a daily basis. The image of college may still be an ivy league campus with students right out of high school, but statistically Mercy is more typical than exceptional: most of our students work, most have families of their own, and they may also have parents with whose well being they are involved.

While the student body had changed drastically from my Mount Holyoke and Columbia days, inside academe the educational configuration had not changed much. What I found myself doing in the classroom wasn't much different than the way Vassar, Mount Holyoke, or Columbia faculty had proffered knowledge

The Other Side of the Desk

when I attended their classes.

Students were expected to store as much of this information deposited by us teachers as possible, like a bank, and then give an accounting when called upon. If I had thought the faculty at Mount Holyoke was descended from another planet, it was pretty likely my Mercy students also looked at me as unlike people in the environment from which they came and the business/professional scene into which they hoped to emerge. The big difference was, now I was experiencing the scene from the other side of the desk.

From that vantage point, it was clear that students were more than ever alienated from the academic environment. For Mercy students, education was viewed as a means: to earn a better living, to get a promotion, to kick off a new career. For us academics, the assumption was education was an end in itself, a concept previous generations of college students accepted, without taking it very seriously. We went to college to acquire knowledge about culture, to be able to carry on informed dinner conversation.

Just as the music our students listened to, the celebrities they admired, the magazines they read were of a different kind than those faculty gravitated toward, the written and spoken language was different. The kind of language heard on streets and escalators had infiltrated classes where "That sucks" passed for literary criticism. Then there was the mundane fact that the flickering images of television's soundbites and teen movies were in contrast to both the form and content of the linear presentation of 'great books.' In other words, students expected to be entertained.

Perhaps in the end the result in my classes was not so different from my days at Columbia. Just as I learned how to turn out theses and, later, articles for publication, our students learned how to work the system. But for them, knowledge unrelated to their next job was seen as merely academic, whereas we had assumed that academic knowledge was a beautiful patina, like a polish applied to us.

From the other side of the desk I could see a further chasm

257

growing between faculty and students. The alienation between faculty and students was increased as students generally held education at arms length, as though it were a disease they feared catching, while faculty could only make their way in the academic world by being absorbed into their field. This meant we had to busy ourselves with research, conferences, and papers on abstruse topics that we could hardly expect our students to appreciate. From the other side of the desk I could now see how remote we must have been from our own teacher's concerns.

The embarrassing reminder of the distance between professors and the rest of the human race came up whenever someone asked me, "Got any good books to read?" or "What should I read on my trip?" As an English professor they were sure I could name some good reads, but I was forced to admit, "I don't read books." This tended to give the teaching profession a bad name, even if I hurried to explain that what I meant was "I don't get to read the kind of books with which it might be nice to curl up at bedtime or take on a trip." I would try to make clear how I was compelled to read essays on indigestible topics like semiotics, post-structuralism, and narratology.

After a number of years in academe, I noticed, all life appeared to professors through the lens of their discipline. At faculty meetings the philosophy faculty saw things philosophically, the social scientists viewed matters culturally, and the math department crunched numbers. My own narrowing focus was brought home to me one morning when I awoke with a sore finger.

It was painfully swollen, but it was also full of literary resonance. The diagnosis seemed clear: it was infected. The prognosis was another matter because all I could think of was Hemingway and my many classroom sessions leading students through "The Snows of Kiliminjaro." As I lay in bed watching the sun rise through bedroom curtains I expected to see vultures circling; if I didn't get that infection removed fast, the plane would be coming

The Other Side of the Desk

for me and it would be a far, far better place I would be going to than I had ever been before.

As I struggled into clothes and regarded the finger, now the size of a rolling pin, I knew it was no accident. Teaching literature had taught me that disease was an inescapable sign of moral frivolity. Tolstoy had shown me that in class after class. I could hear those excruciating sounds issuing forth in "The Death of Ivan Ilyich" and see the light at the end of the tunnel being snuffed out if I didn't get moving.

The trouble was, I didn't have a doctor, but I called the office of a friend and made clear how terribly serious my situation was, so they fitted me in. Fortunately, the waiting room, which I looked around carefully, was not too crowded because I had recently spent a week with my freshman class in the memorable waiting room of Flannery O'Connor's "Revelation" and that was more than enough time in the grip of moral/medical treatment.

"Penicillin," was the doctor's sage verdict.

That was it? For that one word I had brushed the snow off the car and driven to White Plains, the medical capital of the county? Where was all the drama I'd seen watching *The Citadel*, where Ben Cross operated every Sunday at 9:00 P.M. on Channel 13 in his "Surgery." It was understandable the doctor didn't rush in and whip off a dripping trench coat and hat because the sun was shining. Nor did I expect him to reach into a black bag to find a nail file instead of a saw to remove the rotten finger, for after all we were in his suite of offices. Nor did I expect him to rip off his shirt to use for a tourniquet…but still. The doctor relented. The call went out for nurse and needle, antiseptic and gauze.

Driving home, the formidable finger extended in its wrapping, I reflected on literature and science, students and teachers. In much of the fiction I taught it was tea, chicken soup, steam, hot soaks, in other words varieties of hot water that characters had on their side in the battle against the decline and fall of the body. No wonder the

259

A Dangerous Thing

contest had such dramatic literary potential. As I paid the neighborhood druggist for the penicillin, I didn't personally regret having lost the drama of mortality that made for memorable plots, but I felt I had an emotional line of credit unavailable to previous generations. In the fiction I taught, characters could pray or soak and authors could easily get rid of unwanted characters. In my actual life, for every ailment there was a pill that erased its life threatening quality.

It occurred to me then that the security with which I could pronounce "penicillin" and snap shut the file on intimate disaster was part of what enabled us to absorb the worldwide disasters that came to us live on the evening news. It was a perfect example of poetic justice: the first generation to be armed with miracle medicines was also the first to live with everyone else's floods, fires, plagues, famines, genocide in the intimate recesses of our homes every evening at 6 and 11 P.M. That was how we expended our emotional line of credit.

Yet given the disconnect between faculty and student, how could teachers ever move students to see connections between literature and daily life? I thought of Wilson's comment when asked how many students he had at Princeton and he replied "About 20." Twenty good students: maybe that was all a teacher could ask for, which was a good thing, because creating an academic community that would nourish a core of eager and able learners became my administrative assignment. There had to be a way to make students excited about college and I was going to have to find it, or make it by piecing together a crazy quilt from the best material Ethical Culture, Mount Holyoke, and Columbia had given me.

The Other Side of the Desk

Wonderwoman on the Wires

Struts tucked into flaps,
tail secured
as an agile keel,
she plays it out,
her Wonderwoman kite.

From the shore
the breeze puffs it up
over the gray bay,
over the willow trees,
into thick blue,
her whimsical fortieth birthday present.
Flaunting its petrochemically
impervious skin
to the sun's bold gaze
it strains at her arms,
her gravity,
until the breeze catches its breath
and Wonderwoman
surprised
makes a half-hearted curtsy
before tripping over
the high voltage wires.

A DANGEROUS THING

She hangs there,
her tremors the foreground
for all things free flying:
the white wake rippling to shore,
the seagull
in its wide ellipse,
the plane
clearing the willows,
while she watches her gift
immobilized,
Wonderwoman
hung up
on the power lines.

Chapter Seventeen

STEALING TIME

"THERE'S NO FREE LUNCH," ANNOUNCED THE NEW PRESIDENT of Mercy College in 1972 when he called a meeting inviting the faculty to lunch. He came brandishing a carrot and a stick. The stick was that faculty without doctoral degrees would have to get them if they wanted to advance. The carrot was that the College would pay half the cost of tuition. As it turned out, they did better than that, but I put aside the idea, as though it could not possibly apply to me, even as the implications of the president's policy crept closer and closer, a flood seeping under the door. The Columbia experience had left a bad taste: graduate school was at best impersonal, but perhaps also irrelevant to teaching.

Besides, teaching was only a job; my real work was elsewhere, at a place called home. To take up the president's challenge would mean shifting the balance, moving research, writing, and publishing to the top of the agenda, a radical change that threatened the family status quo. But maintaining the status quo in 1970s America turned out to be a large order, well beyond the control of any individual.

Although in my nightmare of teaching at Mercy College, Sister

A Dangerous Thing

Joannes Christie, Chairperson of the Department of Literature, was watching me, what she was actually doing was observing the changes sweeping over Mercy and deciding she did not want to preside over the kind of department needed to implement them: hiring and supervising evening and weekend faculty, devising new curriculum for a changing student body, planning and implementing new programs. Well before the new president and his regime arrived on the scene, Sister Joannes announced her retirement from the chairmanship. All politics may be Byzantine in its intricacies, but none more so than the operation of religious orders. However, when the votes were counted, Betty Levine—or Sister Betty Levine, as someone wrote to me—was the new head of department. Being head of the Department was a totally new kind of challenge, with a black cloud lining: there was no doctoral degree hanging on the wall.

The main problem was back at home and, at the time the new president arrived, she was two years old. Inspired by neighbors who had two boys older than ours and then suddenly announced they were having a third child, who turned out to be a girl, we had started looking at the empty bedroom in our house in a new light. At 36, I was considered very old for the baby business, as though there were something rather disgusting about being pregnant at that age. Also, having a third child wasn't the smartest move for a woman trying to make a career in academe. It indicated a lack of intellectual focus; it indicated teaching was a job, not a career. But when I went in to tell the Dean that I was pregnant, expecting her to part with me, hoping she would do it reluctantly and only for the duration, she had a different view of the situation. She sat bolt upright. "I hope you're not planning on leaving us." This was not spoken as a question.

Once again taken by surprise in the Dean's Office, I managed to say, "Not if it isn't a problem for you.

"No," she assured me. "We are happy to have you stay."

Stealing Time

Kate on top of Mt. Everett fire tower,
Appalachian Trail, Massachusetts, Friday, July 25, 1974.

It was spoken like an order. Fall of 1969 this was still a college owned and run by nuns and I had visions of my age and pregnant state causing traumas as I maneuvered the halls of Mercy. The pregnancy was another first for the college, but those Mount Holyoke and Columbia degrees trumped tradition. Fortunately, the Dean was amused that winter when the Italian mother of a student who received a 'D' in one of my fall courses came to plead for him on the basis that he was distracted by having a pregnant teacher.

Since all of our children were born at least a week or two late, it makes one think obstetricians did not know how to count well in

A DANGEROUS THING

the sixties. But like some kind of new fortune telling scheme, the way in which each of our children finally emerged into the world was emblematic of his or her future character. Thomas, our first son, later referred to by his sister as 'the prince,' was a little late and took a reasonable and measured time in presenting himself. His brother Jonathan was even later, but true to his decisive nature when he made up his mind, he took only minutes to emerge. Kate, occasionally referred to as 'the princess,' in keeping with her disinclination for change, had one false start, changed her mind, hung around longer, then finally joined the family after a 2 A.M. trip to the hospital.

Robert was one of two boys, his brother had three boys, we had two sons, and so we had never allowed ourselves to dwell on the possibility of producing the other gender. When the hospital staff announced, "It's a girl," I paid no attention, not truly believing a woman could give birth to both kinds. It took us a long time to come up with the name Kate, which we thought was quite original, except when she was in her teens and taking a school bus there were three Kates on board.

This third child managed to be born at the beginning of spring vacation, so that by the time school resumed after the two-week break, I was back on the job. The phrase "maternity leave" was not part of vernacular speech in 1970. Pregnancy was acceptable, as long as working women acted as though nothing special was going on. So this time around we had a Mexican housekeeper who spoke no English but was a great Mexican chef. Along with her cooking we acquired a bilingual daughter who learned how to stand on a kitchen chair and fashion Masa Harina into tortillas.

At college, the new regime forged ahead with its carrot and stick policy. Without a Ph.D., I was forced to relinquish the chairmanship, released—though I did not at first think of it that way—into new freedom. Summers were my own again. It was 1973; Kate was three and our housekeepers gone. We hired a college girl to

266

Stealing Time

Hannah's grandchildren on the terrace of 923 Fifth Avenue, September, 1973. Marjorie Sheldon, Jonathan, Thomas and Kate Levine, Michael Sheldon.

help take care of Kate and every afternoon when they went off to the swim club, I retired to the garden to write. In order to get to this state of blissful organization, each winter and spring there were desperate weeks when we hunted around for something to keep our pair of teenage boys occupied. But finally there came the time when they were deposited or shipped off to tennis camp, or survival camp, on a bicycle or academic trip, whatever we could cobble together for each of them. Only then could I sit down with a yellow legal pad and focus on the project germinating in my head.

A series of novels for young readers grew out of those summers hiding out in the back garden. *Hex House*, the first, was inspired by the actions of a boy we mentored from The Graham School, a home for children without parents. The story was set on the Croton Aqueduct, in a house modeled on the actual Octagon House. *Hawk High*, the second novel, was an adventure story that came out of our experience hiking the Litchfield County hills, after we built a small house in the foothills of the Berkshires. *The Great Burgerland*

A DANGEROUS THING

Disaster, set in Westchester, combined different episodes in the lives of our sons and their friends. In each work, a sense of place was the essential building block for adventure.

Every writer expects her first published work to change her life. And there were reviews, followed by requests from school librarians for talks, and appearances at book fairs. But life went on, teaching and academic administration fighting it out for face time with husband and children. Meanwhile, all of these activities were inexorably moving toward a bigger project, one that would bring about changes: a doctoral degree program.

It was the seventies: anti-war protests, women's Lib, exploding labs, burning bras. *Up The Sandbox*, *Fear of Flying*, and *Sexual Politics*. At our house, every time the phone rang and someone asked for Robert, disguising his or her voice, it was always to ask him, "Do you know a good divorce lawyer?"

At Mercy, to keep up with the changing times, a group of teachers started a reading group, The Forum For Women, to digest the flood of new books coming out. Each department selected an important new book and teachers, students, administrators gathered to discuss it. The Psychology Department recommended *Women and Madness*, while the biology faculty gave us *Our Bodies, Ourselves*. Some of the books presented information from a new perspective; some were just angry.

We could not guess it from this modest beginning, but this group had legs. An ad hoc assortment of faculty and administrators, it was typical of female organizations in that it operated with neither budget nor hierarchy. Periodically we met for coffee and out of these gatherings came events large and small: for college students, high school students, faculty, and local residents, with audiences ranging from 50 to 500. Every semester for the next twenty year the Forum helped people explore changes in attitudes about gender and society. It was one way the women of Mercy were keeping up with the times and meeting a community need.

Stealing Time

Between what went on in these extra-curricular activities, and in my classes, and at home, there was always a struggle to find enough time. Then there came the day when the college president confronted me with the prospect of graduate school. On the path between our buildings, he stopped to say, "I've heard about a program that might interest you," and gave me the name of people to speak with. With my Columbia experience as a template, my response was wary. What he had come up with, however, was another kind of education: an external degree program for adults with Masters degrees who were already working in their field. The more I looked into it, the more I recognized echoes of Ethical Culture.

The Union Graduate School in Ohio had three requirements: proposals for study had to involve social change, be interdisciplinary, and unable to be carried out in a traditional doctoral degree program. The one problem was that the school was not used to literature students because it wasn't quite sure what constituted social change in that field. Most students were working in the social sciences, where it was easier to come up with a project directly addressing social change. It took a couple of interviews for me to explain my proposal, and even when it was accepted, that was probably because the school felt it should at least have some representation from the literary side. With admission secured, I arranged for my first 'residency,' a two-week conference in the Boston area.

If teaching was the first great escape from domestic demands, graduate school for a doctoral degree was the second. In the seventies it seemed as though women and men were taking off in all directions, and I was excited to join the trend. But when I started attending conferences, I felt that I was only playing at being grown up and away from home, and was sure everyone could tell I was really just an escaped mom. There was no turning back, though, and after the summer meeting in Boston, there was a winter one in

Chicago. As I started writing, there were conferences in different parts of New York State where I presented chapters of my work, and finally a summer stint at the Aspen Writer's Conference, where Robert joined me at the end for hiking and rafting.

At each escape into the grown up world, I was, Cinderella-like, transformed into another person. Children's birthday parties, orthodontia appointments, mending and marketing, the impediments of daily household life fell away, and there emerged a person whose thoughts become part of the currency of contemporary ideas.

A decade later, on the third great escape, seven months spent in France during a second sabbatical, I was further shorn of family. When husband or children showed up in Paris, they were there to visit Madame Krasne, ecrivain. I was there to write, to try my hand at a new genre: short stories for adults, the material inspired by our town in the northwest corner of Connecticut. Members of the family flew over eight times to see what was going on across the Atlantic, putting the family finances in serious jeopardy, and each time they arrived I showed them around my new turf where life was wonderfully simple. That sabbatical became one of those defining events where family history is measured as coming before or after Paris, 1985.

In 1978 travel for graduate study was followed by my first sabbatical. Although technically sabbaticals were not granted to finish graduate work, the Department of Literature and the administration both understood that was my plan: to finish the dissertation. To keep me from wandering too far on that sabbatical, the family bought a puppy that needed constant attention. They were keeping both of us on a short leash, for the days narrowed down to a well-worn path between my desk and the street where I walked the dog. That is, until I had to add the allergist to my routine because dog hair, added to cat dander, put my breathing system on constant alert. In the process of getting weekly shots, I met anoth-

Stealing Time

er woman who had developed allergies to the family dog. "We got rid of the dog," she told me. I stared at her in awe. That was a more radical suggestion than anyone in the Levine family was about to entertain.

Going back to school in the seventies meant gender issues were on the table. Undergraduate and graduate students were able to spend their days reading feminist history, psychology, anthropology, and literary theory. From these readings it emerged that it was popular to blame mothers for their role in a patriarchal society. They stood accused as the ones who inculcated children into a patriarchal system with all its inequities. These were intriguing theories on the printed page, but didn't quite fit living people, such as my mother, Hannah Goldstein Krasne. It was hard to place my mother's managerial skills in the popular spectrum of oppression. Yet now there is the question of how to explain her complete omission of any mention of her days as a telephone operator and her emphasis on how her father did not believe women should attend college. Perhaps, although she had never appeared as a victim to me, this was a way she saw herself.

The Union Graduate School required students to have a dissertation advisor and, in addition, to put together a committee for consultation and evaluation. Rounding up a group of academics willing to devote time to my work wasn't easy, but eventually I put together an advisor in New Haven, and committee members from various places in the northeast, such as the University of Massachusetts at Amherst and the New York State University at Oswego.

Suggestions from these academics helped me craft a doctoral dissertation entitled "Beware of Death By Water: A Study of Myth and Literature." This work was a hybrid, part exploration of myth, part history, and part literary criticism from a feminist perspective. A much larger undertaking than either my undergraduate or graduate theses, it was also more interesting to work on because of the

A DANGEROUS THING

interesting mix of reading involved. In addition to literary texts, I had to study up on anthropology, sociology, psychology, and art.

Getting the committee together for their final evaluation meeting was like the old Excedrin commercials with their surefire headache-producing scenarios. The meeting was at our house, which caused instant schizophrenia: housewife and scholar fighting it out as I made both lunch and the academic agenda. But Robert, as all through the doctoral process, was always there when weekends came around to help hold the pieces together.

In addition to the dissertation, there were two other parts to this doctoral project. From the Aspen Writer's Conference experience came "Playing the Part," a collection of poems about stages in women's lives. While the dissertation dealt with theory, the poems were an artistic embodiment of analogous material. The final piece to emerge from the graduate school experience was experiential: a plan for an interdisciplinary Women's Studies program.

As a step toward implementing the program, I was given an opportunity to work with another professor (male) to design and teach two courses: Women, Myth and Reality and Myths of Masculinity. For the most part we used traditional materials, everything from Greek drama, the Bible, and folk tales, to twentieth century novels. But for the former course, we also found a book hot off the press. It was a 1975 anthology of short stories entitled *Bitches and Sad Ladies*, edited by Pat Rotter, who had been on the staff at *Esquire* and *Harper's* magazines. The stories were all by current women writers. In her introduction Rotter described her collection as "power fantasies."

It probably should not have come as a surprise that in a collection of stories designated as "power fantasies" food played a central role. After all, from the get-go in the western world ("Genesis") food signifies an exchange of power: Eve gives Adam an apple and, lo and behold, the raw material is transmuted into dangerously powerful knowledge. But we were surprised.

Stealing Time

For one thing, in previous work by American women writers that I had taught, food was at another pole from the stories in *Bitches and Sad Ladies*. It was a sign of women's powerlessness. For the women in such works as Chopin's *The Awakening*, Olsen's "Tell Me A Riddle," Toni Morrison's "The Bluest Eye," and Arnow's *The Dollmaker*, supplying food is shown as a woman's job, a job for which she is not given the tools, but for which she is blamed nevertheless. The need to provide, and the inability to do so signals the weakness of women's position

In the Rotter anthology, the weapon of choice in the gender wars was food. Stories had titles such as "Still Life With Fruits," "Food," "The Good Humor Man." Even when a story had an innocent title like "Interstices," it turned out to be a lethal food fantasy: a wife in a picture-perfect suburban home allows the family freezer to go into serious melt-down and plans to serve a "sumptuous last supper" with the spoiled food. From the point of view of the women in these angry tales from the seventies, preparation of food was a mindless trick they had learned in an attempt to be accepted and pleasing to the opposite sex, only to find, in one way or another, that they were rejected and abandoned anyway. The stories were bitter stuff.

At first, our students don't recognize anything in their own experience that corresponded to the way-out fantasies of the authors in *Bitches and Sad Ladies*. But as we prodded them to think about domestic life, the stories become a bunch of hand grenades lobbed into our classes. Students argued about the kitchen as turf and food money as a power weapon. Their debate made me wonder: was I, Associate Professor of Literature, the mother of three children (who were in their turn possessors of a cat and a dog), trying to run two houses and complete a Ph.D., giving away my power base if I shared the kitchen with my spouse? Was food a weapon I should, or should not be wielding? I looked back to my mother and her household for guidance. Not much help there. The

A DANGEROUS THING

revolutions of the sixties and seventies created a gulf between past and present generations as vast as the one between my college days, when we did everything we were told to do, and the contemporary students who made it a point of honor to challenge authority.

The Gender Studies courses finished. The degree was finished. When the graduate school office asked how I wanted the name on the degree to read, I remembered that back in high school and college I had wanted to be a doctor. I decided I would follow the women I'd met on my travels who had never changed their names: I'd use my own name. I'd be Dr. Krasne, or Dr. K, as the students took to calling me. Resuming my old name had unexpected consequences. People who had known the Krasnes recognized the name. People whom I had known in my previous incarnation were able to find me again: someone from my Camp Lenore days, someone I had met on a trip when I was in high school recognized the name when I took back this part of my identity.

If I was a Krasne, then our children were also part Krasne, so I asked them to take that as a middle name. They were willing to go along with my new identity, but the result were mixed. Out oldest son had already been named Thomas Krasne Levine at birth, so for him this was not an issue. But his brother had been given the other part of Robert's family as a middle name: Newman, so he just added the Krasne in and became Jonathan Newman Krasne Levine, in the style of South America where names are piled on to make a family tree. Our daughter's middle name was Israel, after both our fathers; she replaced it with Krasne, but then changed her name when she married, giving her, too, a string of names.

Along with my new name, there was a promotion and a new undertaking. I was asked to coordinate the College's honors courses. One issue had been settled: I did not have a job; I had a career, with all the shifting priorities that entailed. At work I was Dr. Krasne; when I stepped through the looking glass, I was Mrs. Levine.

Stealing Time

The seventies were finally over and we had survived. The freedom that came with graduate work made up for the stress and labor involved. Family responsibilities rearranged themselves and the distance I sometimes had to put between the family and myself had a way of increasing the bonds between us. By 1980 we had all moved along. Our oldest child was off at college while the next in line was already thinking about where he wanted to go.

While I was working on the dissertation people would ask me, "What are you going to do afterward?" as though a doctoral program comprised all of life; as though I did not have husband, children, friends, houses, pets, cars...all the usual paraphernalia of daily life. Finally, I came up with a response: "I'm going to learn to make blintzes," I told those who asked. As soon as graduate school signed off on my work, I took the car out to Bayside, Queens, and sat myself down at my mother-in-law's kitchen table to see how Esther Levine made blintzes.

ESTHER'S BLINTZES

Filling
Mash 3/4 lb. Farmer cheese with 4 oz. cream cheese.
Add 1 tsp. vanilla and 1 egg. Add 1 tbsp. sour cream if
too stiff.

Batter
Blend until smooth: 2 eggs, 1 cup flour, 1 tsp. salt,
1 cup milk, 1 tbsp. melted butter. Pour into and out of
hot frying pan to coat. Cook on one side. Keep soft in
a towel. Mound filling in center of each cooked side
of a crepe. Fold over like an envelope. Fry when
ready to eat. (Makes 10–12).

A DANGEROUS THING

The Business of Birth

In the moment
you were drawn out female
we were closer
than couples can ever be.
Only you will know
this swelling into strangeness,
not an old wive's tale
but a rite impressed on you
like the salmon working upstream,
the mosquito sucking
its blood full.
You too will be drawn to this spot,
this sterilized steel and white cell
where we have each been
in the business of birth.
We who have been to that room
pushing against life
know you already.

Chapter Eighteen

BSO

THE NEXT TIME I RETURNED TO VASSAR COLLEGE, AFTER THAT
visit to my sister in the 1940s, I was sitting beside my husband,
who was driving our large Chevy station wagon, a kind of gold suburban hearse packed with clothes, crates of records, hi-fi equipment,
typewriter, lamps, a rug. Our sons loaded anything that hadn't been
too firmly anchored at home into the car. It was 1978 and our son
Tom was starting college. When we drove under the archway, bevies
of young men and women in shorts and straw hats, creating a carni-
val atmosphere, ran alongside the car asking us where we were
going and how they could help: it was the Before School Orientation.

The atmosphere was about as different from my sister's first
day at Vassar in 1946 and mine at Mount Holyoke as a visit to the
dentist is compared to a trip to the circus. It was as though the
Before School Orientation staff was constantly checking everyone's
pulse to see if they were having fun yet. At Mercy College, I was
reminded, though much planning also went into orientation, we
were lucky to get a handful of students who could or would give up
a day's work to spend several hours meeting peers and learning the
lay of the land.

A DANGEROUS THING

The guidance department at the Westchester high school our sons attended hadn't ever thought of recommending Vassar for its students, but in addition to my cousin and my sister, I knew that over the years children of three of my cousins had gone there. There had been several years when Vassar itself wasn't sure where it was going. Aftershocks from the earthquakes that rumbled through American education in the sixties had affected Vassar's students and faculty, propelling the college toward coeducation. By the sixties a majority of students were coming from public rather than private, coed rather than single sex preparatory schools, and the faculty, previously a nun-like gathering, had also shifted so that many were married. Coeducation had come to seem like no big deal for the majority on campus by the end of the sixties. After considering a merger with Yale, the schools had each decided to go coed on their own.

In those years of adjustment, each school tended to favor the opposite sex in admissions—girls had an edge at Yale, boys at Vassar—while they tried to balance the ship. Having been through this at Mercy, I knew how it went, so I suggested Tom include Vassar on his list. It wasn't his first choice, but he took a car and his brother and drove up to look around. The Guidance Department at his high school picked up on the idea and had half a dozen other students, mostly male, apply. Almost all were admitted, starting a trend. Every year after that Ardsley High School sent a good size contingent to Vassar.

We had a neighbor who had done the college tour circuit the year before with his son. He decided to drive his son around because he himself was a graduate of City College night school and was curious about what was out there on the academic horizon. At one of the old northeastern colleges the tour guide showed them through the music building where each room had a piano, and over each piano there was a skylight "So there won't be any shadows on the music" the guide explained. "How," our friend wanted to know

278

about his son when he returned home, "could he ever adjust to the real world after that?"

Tom did the college tours on his own, so it wasn't until the first day of his Vassar College experience that we surveyed the quad from the steps of Lathrop. It looked surprisingly like my memory of the campus from that first day in 1946. It was another two years before we were introduced to new arrangements, garden apartments tucked away well beyond ye olde quad, as though the college had not quite decided in which century it dwelt.

On that first day in 1978, a woman walked up the steps carrying a laundry case and I challenged the family to identify this historic artifact. Before anyone could figure out what it had been used for, students toting forbidden televisions and refrigerators followed her. At the desk, a 'White Angel' still presided. 'White Angels' were the elderly ladies stationed facing the front door who acted like benign French concierges. But the students, their mien, attire, and racial background were a study in exotic contrast to her sphinx-like presence. Tom's peers were also a marked contrast to those regulation blondes I remembered from the forties who seemed to have stepped out from the back-to-school issues of fashion magazines.

The rooms were definitely the same, I realized as I caught a glimpse of the faces family made staring at the battle scarred beds, desks, chairs that marched forlornly along the walls. We set to work. While Tom went off to take care of business, brother Jon wired the room for sound, Robert put things together, and I tucked things in, transforming the place as best we could into a semblance of home.

As I worked, I thought of opening day at Mercy. For most of its history and the vast majority of its students, Mercy was a commuter college. As I stood back and admired the transformation in Tom's room, I was reminded that home for my students was the place where parents and siblings, or husband and children demanded part of their time. College was a place anywhere from

A DANGEROUS THING

one to three hours away, often by an awkward mismatch of public transportation.

That day in 1978 at Vassar, there was only one important chore: to get on The Line. When the new students had wound their way to the head of the line, they were face to face with…the telephone company representative. And when they had made up their mind whether it was to be Mickey Mouse, a duck, plain black, or a colorful number, they could rest easy because they had taken care of the important business of getting settled. Heaven forbid that such basic academic elements as placement tests that had kept my sister, Carol, busy on her first day intrude on the fun and games. Placement tests, to a certain extent, are predicated on core requirements, and in the sixties revolution much of that structure had been swept away from America's colleges as not 'relevant.'

There were five in all, besides Tom, from his high school class who had come to Vassar that year. Jangling his keys, he could not wait to lock up his possessions, get us out from underfoot, and make the rounds to see how the others were fitting in; after all, there was no phone yet. Our quick exit was of little import because a week later he and a friend drove home to collect anything they might have left behind that wasn't nailed down. The art course, that survey with the lights out that had so impressed me when my sister took me to a lecture, was as good as it had been reported to be, he told us.

The following year, when we drove him up to college, he brought us over to see a friend and neighbor who was a freshman housed in Raymond. He had been assigned a small room done in white tile at the back of the main floor which seemed, at first, quite odd, until I realized it was the pantry from which my shredded wheat had issued forth when I went to visit my sister. As part of the major makeover when it went coed, the college had done away with individual dining halls and built the All College Dining Center, in common parlance ACDC, which freed up an unusual set

280

BSO

of ground floor rooms at the back of every dorm because the administration hadn't taken any trouble to disguise their history. I didn't get to see what use they found for meat lockers and freezers, but I was pretty sure they were part of some students storage unit.

Over the years, our contacts with the college were mostly in the form of bills and books, both of which kept coming in ever increasing amounts. At the end of every academic year we had to add a dozen feet of new bookshelves. Dense, new, esoteric material came back to us from that strange outpost in Poughkeepsie: deconstruction, the aesthetics of film, Marxist interpretations of the Civil War, linguistics. As the boxes of books came home at the end of each year, I couldn't help thinking of our own students who sometimes didn't have the money for textbooks, or wouldn't write in them because they planned on reselling them, or shared a book with a friend— none of these being the best of all approaches to an education.

But in spite of being at the top of the higher academic food chain, Tom and his friends did not see themselves as "students," not in the sense Woodrow Wilson meant. They saw themselves as second stringers, those who hadn't made it to Yale, for instance, where they assumed the serious and brilliant were quarantined. They, on the other hand, felt they were assigned a different part; they were at college to live life to its fullest: drugs, sex, alcohol, whatever it took, they were going to do it all. It was the end of the seventies and experimentation was the name of the game: ballet and wine tasting courses appeared on schedules along with History, Biology, and Art. They were being served at a large buffet, but they were more interested in tasting than eating.

Few Mercy students, I reflected, had time for fun and games. Life outside of college—family, jobs, commuting—preempted their schedules. For them education was the crux of the matter, the one thing that could change the course of their lives from all the generations of their family that had preceded them, but education had to compete with daily practical life. Unfortunately, all too often for Mercy students this kept their college experience teetering on the brink of disruption by family and personal crises. Disease, death, court appearances, broken down cars, and financial woes were always just around the corner, not to speak of the inordinate number of grandmothers who had a way of dying mid-semester.

The summer before his junior year Tom went off to Europe, supposedly to attend the London School of Economics for the year, but at the end of the summer he came back, declaring "I can go to Europe any time, but I have only four years at Vassar." By senior year he was echoing my sister Carol and cousin Belle, wondering "Who needs four years in Poughkeepsie?" So he spent a good part of his time in New York City, when he wasn't working on his thesis for History and Art, tracing "The Rise And Fall Of The Neu Zachlicheit," an art movement in Germany between the wars. For our students at Mercy, New York City was a foreign country for which they might as well have needed a passport. To get them to venture there for theater and museum trips took much persuasion. They were sure once they crossed a bridge to the island of Manhattan their lives were at risk.

When Tom graduated, his circle of Vassar friends showed up wherever he went: New York, California, Connecticut, even on my sabbatical in France two of them came to spend the winter holiday with our family. College was an ongoing web of relationships. I thought of my commuter students at Mercy who made it through whole semesters without knowing anyone in their class from whom they could get an assignment if they missed a class; the minute class was over, they were back in their cars, heading for work.

Tom's classmates who had hung on to the goal of graduate school made their way into professional programs, but for many of these children of the seventies it took a while to put their lives together. Drugs and alcohol took their toll, and they drifted about like characters Hemingway and Gertrude Stein wrote about in Paris after World War I, the Lost Generation. In my parallel uni-

BSO

verse at Mercy, students were lucky to hang in at college long enough to graduate because their need to work full time was so pressing. Whenever the job market was poor, we could hold onto them, but in a good job market, they spent more and more hours on the job. Often our best students would start out in low-level jobs and find themselves promoted to managerial positions where employment hours and responsibilities governed their schedules. Getting students to graduate school was a tough task, not because they didn't have the smarts, but because they could not postpone supporting themselves and their families.

At our home, life seemed to present almost too many options. While Tom had considered only small liberal arts colleges, his brother, Jon, was only interested in large urban universities. He moved into Columbia University fall of 1981 to set up a home away from home with even more paraphernalia than his brother had taken. As we lugged lamps and books and rugs into the elevator, we watched over our shoulder as some of the Asian students carried in a small bundle and a typewriter.

The reputation of Columbia's graduate schools attracted pre-professional types to the undergraduate college, but even engineering students knew they would start out in the famous Columbia humanities core curriculum, a combination of Western Civilization and Great Books. Like many of his peers in this new decade, Jon came to college knowing what he wanted to do with his life: he was headed for law school. At Columbia that career goal didn't keep him from majoring in English and minoring in Architecture. That was what students did at liberal arts colleges: they got themselves a first rate general education.

The down side at a college like Columbia was the fierce competition among pre-professionals. In one of his architecture courses his meticulously drawn assignment was stolen. Nevertheless, though Jon had enough credits to graduate early, he couldn't bear to leave Columbia, so he became a Resident Advisor, in charge of one of the

A DANGEROUS THING

new dorm buildings. One day a student was discovered throwing a piece of furniture out a window and it was Jon's duty to report him and have him expelled. Columbia had recently been sued for several million dollars when a piece of cornice from one of its apartment buildings fell and killed a young woman on Broadway and if there was one 'crime' for which there was zero tolerance, it was causing an object to fall from a great height. This strict atmosphere was poles apart from Vassar's laissez faire style, but as different as Columbia University was from Vassar College, when compared to a place like Mercy College, both were sheltered environments where students had the luxury of academic excellence.

August 23, 1988, just after Jon had finished law school, we found ourselves again driving through the entrance gate to Vassar College. In the interim my sister Carol's son, Michael, had graduated from Vassar. This time we were bringing our daughter, Kate, for Before School Orientation. Once again, the family station wagon, this time a Subaru, was filled to the roof, the excitement as high as though we were crossing a brand new frontier.

Though the weather threatened rain, the cheerleaders were in evidence again. Among the cheering throng was one handsome philosophy major who would turn out to be husband material. This time it was computers that were being lugged up the stairs. There was no line for phones because students had already filled out forms checking off who their long-distance carrier was to be, and buried in Kate's baggage was an answering machine for the suite.

"Suite" conjures up images of a gracious life. Once, Kate's accommodations must have been a comfortable retreat for a pair of young ladies. How long ago was that? Was it comfortable 42 years ago on that day a year after the end of World War II when our family first drove under the arch? My memory was of very basic accommodations back then, several steps down from a cheap motel.

The suite Kate moved into consisted of a main room, off of which were two cell-like rooms. There were four young women

284

Jonathan, Kate, and Thomas Levine, Vassar College, April 1998 for a panel on "The New Hollywood," moderated by Thomas Levine, '82, Senior Vice President, Paramount Pictures.

sharing these quarters. The present slum-like conditions were one of those odd by-products of coeducation, like the white tile kitchens that had become bedrooms, and the unofficial unisex bathrooms that startled parents. The two people in the small rooms could only get in and out by walking through the main room, a plan that defied the facts of how college dorm life actually worked. In one of the small rooms there was barely space for the hefty books Kate brought along for the art course. Bookcases, no doubt, had once been in the living room, where two beds were already made up. If there was anything else the four of them needed, or could squeeze in, it wasn't going to be a problem because several of her classmates arrived driving their own cars. Instead of a wait for a telephone, the wait this time was to get into beginning Japanese.

The last time we were at Vassar, April 18, 1998, we were seated in Taylor Auditorium, the same Art History lecture hall where my sister had pointed out Jacqueline Bouvier just before the lights went out. The family had assembled from various points in the country to hear a program on "The New Hollywood," moderated by our son Tom, a Senior Vice President at Paramount Pictures, who had put

A DANGEROUS THING

together a panel of alumni in the industry. His sister, Kate, who also worked in film, was in the audience. When she had changed her major Sophomore year from Art History to Film, Tom had told her "Film is something you see, not something you major in," but by 1998 Film had split off from the English/Drama Department and was the most popular major on campus, so the auditorium event attracted a good representation of undergraduates.

Proud as I was of the assembled family, there was always that double exposure, the picture of my own students that I kept seeing. They chose their majors so they were prepared to work at something specific the moment we sent them forth: Accountant, Physical Therapist, Guidance Counselor, or Paralegal. One bright young man had come to me once to explain that he wanted to major in Literature, where he did his best work, but his father was aghast at such impracticality and insisted he major in Business Administration, one of those pre-professional subjects that did not even appear in the catalogues of major liberal arts colleges.

It took half a lifetime to turn me from a dilettante to a professional, with some unfortunate consequences. One result was that the distance between Mercy College and Vassar or Columbia became almost unbridgeable. Ultimately, it was easier for me to empathize with the exigencies of my students' situations than to understand our children's options. Too often it seemed to me, when I compared my children and their friends to my students, that those emerging from a life of relative privilege were spoiled.

Another consequence was guilt. Not only was I guilty of greater empathy for my students than for our children, I was also guilty of stealing time from work for family, but more often from home for work, and from both for writing. Perhaps I should have followed Simone de Beauvoir's example and totally rebelled against upbringing in favor of education, but I could never bring myself to disavow where I had come from: my early education in good taste that required every aspect of domestic life be conducted impeccably.

The Edges of Her Love

Of all the games they play
this is the worst:
every afternoon
disguised in castoffs,
one always the mother,
one the child.

She shuts the door
against the raucous tones
of their masquerade,
but their childhood rites
seep between the pages
of her book.
In their daily soap opera
the wily child
insistently demands;
the cruel mother
continually berates.

Between the lines
she reads their parody
of togetherness,
their sly instincts
filtering out the course family sound
like sand onto sandpaper.
She hears it grating,
grating
as they expose the edges of her love.

Chapter Nineteen

WHAT IS HONORS?

HIGHER EDUCATION BECAME A FAMILY MOTIF. OUR CHILDREN followed college with graduate school, if not immediately, then eventually. Yet the most remarkable aspect of the family investment in education was that the two strains of education, our children's experience and mine, were parallel lines that never met.

During the years our children were growing up in a comfortable suburb (someone once joked about a neighboring village that an integrated area was a block where both doctors <u>and</u> lawyers lived), I was working at an educational institution with a totally different student base. My student assistant for many years was one of twelve children, almost all of whom had put themselves through college and several had gone on through graduate school. One time, when her father lost his job for a while, the family collected free surplus food and American cheese was plentiful in the office. All my student workers were scholarship students with noteworthy academic records and formidable leadership qualities. Some of them worked two jobs.

It was hard for me to figure out what the level of expectation should be. Should I expect my students to know more about cul-

What is Honors?

ture: the difference between Frank Lloyd Wright and the Bauhaus, the Renaissance and the Reformation, Marx and Freud? Should I expect our own children to be self-starters who dug into their work without prompting and held down jobs too? Ideally, I wanted everyone to have everything: the students at Mercy to be exposed to the richest cultural experience possible while our own children became responsible, hard workers.

The result was pressure on both fronts: excursions for my students, jobs for our children. There was the land of the privileged, over which I had limited control, and there was every place else. This divide drove me to try to create programs and events for Mercy students so that they too could have a taste of the riches available in a larger vision of education. In this crusade to democratize education the question was: How much could the circumstances of my students and my children be altered?

The vehicle for this dream of a richer college experience at Mercy became the Honors Program. In fact, I had never taught in these honors courses, having looked on the students and faculty as an elitist club. So I had no idea what it was I had been selected to do. But the job was a challenge. I had had plenty of opportunity to study the problems of education at Mercy and when I was asked to coordinate the two existing honors courses, I was given the opportunity to do something about them. I was easily seduced into thinking I could make a difference.

Fortunately, our department had a small amount of grant money left over from an interdisciplinary project, which enabled me to bring in a consultant. It was clear my academic role had changed when this professor spent a lot of time wining and dining me, as the surest way to his hotel room. Meanwhile, staying on message, I learned that there was a national organization of Honors Programs, with regional branches, and that our region had some of the most noteworthy experts a short drive away. They would be able to answer my questions about what a college honors

A DANGEROUS THING

program did, what it meant for students and for the institution.

In the interim, I had learned that the two courses I had been asked to coordinate had been instituted years before as a way to lure students who had been given academic scholarships, which originally meant able young women from local parochial schools. But diversity had become our norm: more than 50 percent of our enrollment was minority, African-American and Latino, and these students came from public schools. Then there was the increasing age of our student body. By the 1980s what we were expanding was our remedial program for people who did not meet previous standards for admission to college. Every department, but particularly the English Department, had added courses to deal with the changing population.

By the time I came into the Honors picture, Mercy was no longer giving many academic scholarships and no longer attracting much of the parochial school crowd. A new approach was needed. It was possible, I argued to higher ups in the administrative chain, to view an Honors Program as ballast that would keep the good ship Mercy afloat; it would keep the stern end, filled with the ever-growing weight of remedial students, from pulling down the ship.

Figuring out what I should be doing to create a community of motivated learners seemed like a pleasant enough challenge for a couple of years. Then I expected to get back to writing. It was a chance to draw on the best of Ethical Culture, Mount Holyoke, and Union Graduate School. Fifteen years later, when I gave up administration, I ruefully remembered how blithely I had assumed the job.

There was a big learning curve. The first stops were at other colleges to see what they were up to. Honors directors, happy to spread the word, gave me a quick tutorial in the elements of an honors program, and insisted that I hit the road for the regional and national meetings. At my first National Collegiate Honors Council meeting, in Omaha, I tagged along for dinner with a couple of mid-westerners who seemed to know where to go. I felt like

What is Honors?

a fifth wheel, especially when I was the only one who regarded a meal of steak and coffee, served together, as odd. Jetting about alone, it turned out, was not as exciting as magazines about the new businesswoman made it seem. Before long, though, some of the smart and capable Honors Program directors, many of them in our northeast region, took me under their wing and introduced me to people with creative ideas.

The job, it turned out, took everything: time, perseverance, and imagination. It was one thing to find out what was needed, but figuring out how to implement what was needed was another matter. From the front of a classroom, faculty didn't concern themselves with such practical matters as office space, staff, budgets. Where did I go to negotiate space for the program? With whom did I work out released time to do the work? How did I get a budget for activities? What was the most tactful way to recruit faculty? Regional and national honors meetings helped answer these questions. Then I had to go home and put the ideas into operation.

Being an Honors Program director was a giant black hole into which the gravitational pull was enormous, obscuring life at home with cosmic dust because the challenges put my competitive nature in overdrive. What any other school could do, we could do as well, maybe even better because by tailoring our honors program to fit Mercy's distinctive situation, we were breaking new ground, showing the way for other programs. The more I found out about the workings of other programs, the richer our program became, until eventually I became one of the people dispensing information at regional and national meetings.

On the academic side, Honors went from being two courses to a full two-year program of classes. First, it was necessary to put together an honors faculty board so there were people with whom to brainstorm. The board then helped institute a basic humanities core, right out of my freshman year at Mount Holyoke: philosophy, art, literature. Next, we put in place a second year. To recruit new

A DANGEROUS THING

students, we used the students we had, so they could tell about the small classes, personal attention, interesting courses, and special activities in the program.

We had students, faculty, a curriculum. What we needed was real estate. I had learned in my travels that an honors student center was an essential element of a successful program. On the other hand, an essential fact of life at Mercy was that a person could always find money for a project, but a request for space brought on major turf wars. Getting our hands on the right rooms, fixing them up, fostering activities there, brought out the bourgeois wife and Jewish mother in me. There had to be a window seat with cushions, facing out over the Hudson River, a couch, coffee table, and comfortable chairs; refrigerator, coffee maker, and microwave, everything to make students and faculty want to hang out. And each week, each month, each semester there had to be events planned—invariably involving lunch—to make students in our commuter school feel they belonged to an academic community.

But often the biggest challenge was not designing interesting courses, or seducing the most exciting faculty to take on extra work, or even finding space and money. It was prompting students to be proactive. Mercy didn't usually enroll the kind of students who had been editors of their school newspaper, presidents of the student council, or stars of the debating team. More generally, Mercy students, in pointed contrast to our own children, did not approach life as though they had a divine right to all its goodies.

Education's role in creating leadership was a legacy from Ethical Culture. Once, I suggested to a group of students at our Bronx campus, that they could get money for activities if they formed a club, made up a budget, and submitted it to the Student Activities Coordinator. They sat down, drew up a budget, and took it to her office. "She wasn't there," they told me, as though that concluded the matter.

"So what are you going to do now?" I asked them. They had-

292

What is Honors?

n't, it appeared, planned a next move. With some prodding they put a copy of the budget in the coordinator's mailbox. When they didn't hear from her, I asked them what their next move should be. Finally, they cornered her, which gave them an opportunity to explain the budget. They got their money, but then they had to learn to organize the activities, administer and account for the funds. As much as possible, the goal was to have students in the honors program take responsibility for their own education.

Fifteen years later, when I resigned as director of the Honors Program and moved on to something else, I left behind a college within the college. The program was a model of what could be done to attract and hold on to talented students, and it was a structure that developed leadership potential. By the time I retired from the Program, I left behind friends across the country who had helped me put Mercy College on the National Collegiate Honors Council map of the United States. At the beginning there was no budget: I was a kept woman, living out of the pocket of the Dean, to whom I went begging whenever a project sounded crucial. By the time I left, we had a five-figure budget; there was an honors student center, a funded grant for travel, a string of publications, and a number of firsts to our credit.

The job was woven together out of all the pieces of my previous life. In addition to Professor and Administrator, I played Jewish Mother, team leader, hostess, decorator, policy maker, manager. It is the way women often find the most satisfaction in work: they build their own job from the ground up. But it was not only the job I was able to construct. Women, studies point out, are associated with transient parts of life. We clean, cook, wash…and then do these jobs all over again because our tasks are not durable. Men, on the other hand, create structures that endure: spectacular stone ones, like the Parthenon; artistic ones, like the Sistine Chapel and its ceiling; conceptual ones, like the Bill of Rights. Their currency is policies, ideas, enterprises that are recorded for posterity.

A DANGEROUS THING

Of course, these are exceptional structures created by exceptional men, one could argue, but towards the end of *My Kitchen Wars*, her memoir about a struggle for a room of her own, Betty Fussell sums up the problem in more mundane terms:

> I yearned to create something permanent, something concrete, to have something to show at the end of a few decades' hard work. Instead of making a loaf of bread that might keep for a week,
> I wanted to make a book that would last for years. I wanted longer shelf life.

When I read Fussell's words, I understood her feelings perfectly. The Honors Program I left behind had shelf life.

Someone asked an old friend, who was an excellent public school elementary teacher in The Bronx, what she thought was the most important thing she had done with her life. Without a moments hesitation she said, "My two children." The way she saw it, raising her own children was her greatest contribution to the world. Yet as a first rate teacher she had impacted the lives of class after class of students. When the questioner turned to me, I could not answer so fast. The elements that make up the Mercy College Honors Program endure, making a difference for class after class of students. Students who made presentations at conferences, who went on special semesters to other parts of the world, who participated in symposiums at Mercy were transformed by these experiences. The nature of the courses, the events to which the students are exposed, the goals the program sets change the college experience for year after year of participants. That change is a geometric improvement, and often proved to be a model for the rest of the college.

Being director of the Honors Program was an important and rewarding job, but there came a season when I knew I had to ran-

What is Honors?

som time. I had to give up administration so that when my courses were done, the rest of the time could be for writing. This was the way it worked, but only briefly, for there was another administrative challenge waiting.

Mercy had entered a new era with another new President. This man came with his own carrot and stick. He decreed that the College, which was almost entirely tuition driven, was going to become a significant recipient of grants. The college relied on federal and state aid to students for most of its budget. The new president was determined to change this. He informed the faculty that departments would get a cut of any money that a faculty member brought in through winning a grant. Spurred on by his vision, Honors Program faculty worked on various humanities grants for NEH, but after a couple of disappointments the faculty decided that, given the odds, the process was too labor intensive.

However, after I was comfortably enjoying the administration-free life after Honors, a group working on a McNair Scholars Program grant asked for my input. In short order I was at the center of drafting a proposal for the Department of Education. To everyone's complete astonishment, we were awarded three quarters of a million dollars for four years to set up a program, and to my surprise I was asked to create the program.

Ronald McNair was the first black astronaut and the program named for him was aimed at identifying promising students and preparing them to go on to graduate school. McNair students were supposed to be financially needy first generation college students, and Mercy College had plenty of students who fit this bill. In addition, the majority of McNair students were supposed to come from groups underrepresented in graduate school: African-Americans and Native Americans.

From the beginning, it was a tough assignment that threw into high relief the enormous burdens our students shouldered in getting even a basic education. Yet the McNair Program asked them

A DANGEROUS THING

to take on an extra measure of work. The program required them to take tough courses, like Statistics; learn to do in-depth research; practice and take GRE's; and postpone employment in favor of years of graduate school.

Once again, I was constantly being reminded of the great gap in our society between the academic life experienced by our own children and the lives of those I taught. There was a support network, but the simplest steps required constant rethinking. We ordered laptop computers and cases, only to have our students tell us it was too dangerous to walk around their neighborhoods carrying something like that, so we had to find computer cases disguised as backpacks. The orientation for each group began with a three-day mini-research project, carried out at an off-campus location. This experience was designed to introduce the concept of primary source material and build *esprit de corps*. But for our students to free themselves from jobs and family obligations for three days was a major hurdle.

We recruited our first and second groups, but attrition became our slow, sure companion. We were constantly battling family problems, academic problems, transportation problems, health problems, and employment. Having chosen good students, the closer they come to graduation, the more in demand they were in the market place. Not only were they offered jobs, but jobs that came with perks such as health insurance. How could they say 'No' to offers that sounded like salvation?

Dealing with the Department of Education was a civics lesson in itself, and almost enough to turn any good Democrat into a Republican. Fortunately, the year I was appointed to head up the McNair program was the last year the Education Department found money in its budget to hold a workshop for leaders. The meeting was an education in politics. At honors gatherings the atmosphere was created by people who wanted to build up Honors

296

What is Honors?

Programs, and they saw the best way to increase and multiply was by helping each other. In a government grant situation, everyone could be viewed as competition. People at the meeting gave the impression of looking over their shoulder to see who might be gaining on them. The one unifying element was that it was us against the Department of Education. There were nuggets of info to be picked up, but as a Caucasian I was definitely the outsider, and suspect by other participants as taking up too much space.

As it turned out, despite the problems our program encountered in holding on to students, after four years the program was refunded, but not on my watch. After setting the program in motion with the first and second groups, I found the new administration too intrusive and the stick much mightier than the carrot. Time, I decided, mattered more than serving at the whim of Mercy presidents.

Free, I was free at last from every kind of problem outside the classroom. It was on to great escape number four: summers staying in Connecticut, my private writer's retreat. There I could write all day, dive into the pond late in the afternoon, and work in the garden before the sun set late on summer afternoons over St. John's Ledges, across the Housatonic River.

A DANGEROUS THING

Their Lists

In her dream
she lies in the snow
making a snow angel
but feels neither
wet nor cold.
Lying back in the snow
she no longer remembers
the inside of her house
the children,
iron filings without a magnet
sift into corners like fine dust,
each in a room composes a list.
Waking she recalls the Eskimos
have more than twenty words
for the temptation
of white forgetfulness.

Lists tacked to doors—
chores, supplies, errands—
bar her way
like Luther's 95 theses,
the particulars of their demands
are love letters
pumping numbed remembrance
back to reluctant toes,
making fingertips throb.

Chapter Twenty

A MATTER OF TASTE

IN A TRICK OF FATE, THREE PERIODS OF AMERICA'S SOCIAL
history came together in my mother's last big public appearance.
She was over 91 that winter when the family gathered at the
Harvard Club dining room for lunch, before we dispersed for the
Christmas holiday. The club was festively decorated—the way it
would be seven years later when our daughter Kate was married
there in December to Greg, her philosopher from BSO. The dining room was unusually lively.

Robert had reserved a long table and reminded our children of
the club dress code. So our offspring, and their partners or guests,
were spiffed up for the occasion, like little children brightly
scrubbed and decked out for a holiday dinner. Their rough
attempts to appear orderly and grown up took me back to those
years when we would try to assemble them for their annual fall
appearance in New York City at Temple B'nai Jeshurun for the
Jewish New Year. There were always frantic moments hunting
around in the back of their closet for last years clothes that might
still fit them, digging under tennis racquets to find real shoes, not
sneakers or hiking boots, hoping the final affect would not give the

299

A Dangerous Thing

impression they were prepared for a costume party.

What they were actually doing at that moment in the Harvard Club dining room was wolfing down popovers as fast as the white-jacketed waiter could fill the basket, in an inevitable sibling competition to see who could consume the most. Yet their very frivolity was made possible by the self-assurance their education had given them and to which the setting testified. Male and female, they knew they would take their degrees and have careers that would somehow make a difference in their world, though none of them could have said quite what it was they would do down the road.

My mother presided serenely. At 91 she had lived through a century of incredible changes, yet the demanding training of Raphael Goldstein never left her with doubts about the right course of behavior. As I watched her presiding at the head of the table, I was reminded of an afternoon in her living room a couple of years earlier. She was holding the morning's copy of *The New York Times* and regarding an ad for a blouse, an elegant, pricey garment. She raised her head and asked me, "Do you think I should buy that?"

She must have been 89 at the time, sitting in a straight back Chippendale-style armchair, her thinning hair a dark gray. I came over to look over her shoulder at the picture and said the only sensible thing I could think of, "I think you should buy whatever you want," not adding the implied "at your age."

She turned the page and looked over at me as though I had failed a test. "There is always something better to do with your money," she announced. It was the 'rule of one,' that blend of her Philadelphia upbringing and her New York experience: you only need one, but it should always be the best.

When Robert Levine first showed up at Central Park West he looked around and said, "Marjorie Morningstar."

Herman Wouk's novel by that name had come out two years before and was still a best seller. The name Marjorie Morningstar had become short hand for a type: female, middle class, Jewish, liv-

A Matter of Taste

ing on Central Park West. In Wouk's novel this added up to vulgar, nouveau riche people.

Best sellers were not on my radar in the 50s, so it wasn't until I started seriously reconstructing the past that my eye was caught by an old paperback copy of Wouk's novel. The book was not what I expected. Blurbs talked about "the social constraints of her old-fashioned New York Jewish family," which sounded familiar, but nothing in the novel was recognizable. It was a sure thing my mother read the book when it was published and just as sure that she found the Morgenstern/Morningstar clan vulgar and nouveau riche. If the Morgensterns were "old-fashioned," then my mother's family occupied a different dimension of history.

When I pointed out that there wasn't any resemblance between my family and the characters in *Marjorie Morningstar*, Robert said "But your family was nouveau riche."

"It's a good thing you never said that to your mother-in-law," I told him. Two generations of the Raphael Goldstein family had gone into making sure nothing could ever be construed as vulgar or nouveau riche.

If there was any room in Manhattan that represented the antithesis of the vulgar and nouveau riche, it was the dining room of the Harvard Club. That day at lunch, my mother looked around the room, taking in the portraits of Harvard's eminent, grave academicians punctuating the wood paneled walls. Above the paintings, trophy animal heads with their annual holiday wreaths around their necks surveyed the white tables, around which clustered prosperous alumni. And then she gazed the length of the Levine table.

I could see from the wry expression on her face how she appreciated the irony of her position: she, Hannah Goldstein, who had not been allowed to go to college, wife of Israel Krasne, né Krasnoschezek, wholesale grocer, mother-in-law of Robert Levine, whose family had resided in a small brick house in Queens, was seated comfortably with her entire family in what had previously been an inner sanctum of the WASP establishment: the dining room of the Harvard Club. Around her, children and grandchildren took it all for granted.

Education as a kind of exterior decoration for women is a view with a substantial history and long pedigree. The feeling that education was not something women needed to concern themselves with to any great extent has often modified the old canard that education is the focus of the immigrant dream. Raphael Goldstein and Israel Krasne were in good company when they believed any system would teach their daughters to read, write, count, and beyond that was home. They were confident the system would process their children appropriately, which meant if we were girls we would then go on to marry and—somehow—understand how to manage a household properly (meaning elegantly but efficiently); if we were boys, manage to make a living that would support a family (elegantly and sufficiently).

Neither my grandparents nor my parents were familiar with the hierarchies and complexities of institutions of higher learning. More importantly, they weren't convinced they possessed magical qualities of transformation. Practical experience carried a lot of weight, though paradoxically it was in extremely short supply in our upbringing, which was one reason Robert fascinated me when I met him. Here was a person who knew what to look for under the hood of a car, how to use an electric drill, how to find his way around Brooklyn or Queens, knowledge that could, under certain circumstances, actually be useful for the conduct of daily life.

For my grandparents and parents, the business of life was business because it was the most direct and accessible way to achieve security and comfort, to be insulated against the vicissitudes they had lived through. They had experienced major geographical moves, the Depression, and anti-Semitism. Securing the material comforts of bourgeois life was not dependent, from our parents'

A Matter of Taste

perspective, on degrees in higher education. For our children's generation the formula was different. Material comfort was taken for granted; success was connected to credentials and institutions. We were the bridge connecting these generations.

Some of the changes that occurred in society for our generation became clearer to us when we moved back to the city after Hannah's death, thirty years after we had left for the suburbs. Back in the fifties, when we were married, our life flowed in the pattern set at the end of World War II: domesticity, decorum, decor. Men went to work wearing suits, ties, and hats. Women went to the playground. In a photo taken at Ellsworth, Maine, the airport for Bar Harbor in the fifties, I am stepping out of a little plane in the middle of a field wearing a suit, pumps, and gloves. We learned to muddle through housework and cooking because the only alternative was to employ a cook, not a likely move for young married couples. Most of us took public transportation, a few had cars, and then there were the people who employed chauffeurs. For a Fieldston graduate, college meant the Ivy League, the Seven Sisters, and a couple of major universities. The parameters of life were simple and defined.

By the time we moved back to Manhattan we found ourselves in another time zone. Working women left in the morning...via car services, in express buses, in vans, or pouring into subways. People went out to buy their morning coffee, while prepared food arrived around the clock seven days a week. Dress was so casual that if women didn't wear black, we couldn't tell they were going to work, except that when people weren't working, the uniform was exercise clothing. Playgrounds filled with nannies suggested there were whole islands in the West Indies with no women left. Mothers occupying benches behind the sandbox were rare birds, and if spotted, might be pecking at a computer. Now we lived on the east side, way east where only walkups had existed in our previous Manhattan life.

A DANGEROUS THING

My insider experience of changes in higher education should have alerted me to these social shifts. My career at Mercy spanned the period of the greatest change in the shortest time in American educational history, but from suburbia the world beyond academe had been a blur. From my Mercy experience I knew the average age of the American undergraduate had crept up to just below 30. I knew that for people of every age and background there was a school, two year or four year, public or private. If a housewife wanted to finish an interrupted degree, a policeman prepare for law school, a nursery school teacher become a physical therapist, there was a college where they could go. This always appeared most striking when we traveled abroad and people in other countries asked about my work at Mercy College. When I explained that our students could be anyone from 16 to 90, they were bewildered by our system, or non-system.

None of this retooling, I also knew all too well, came without a price. In spite of expanded funding from state and federal loans and grants, as well as greater scholarship assistance, for many people the price of higher education was still out of reach, the debts too heavy to manage. And above and beyond the education cost, there was always the personal price. Remaking oneself meant stealing time.

Changes in higher education were driven in part by the employment scene. Areas of specialization and expertise first appeared in want ads and then made it into college catalogues. Fields that were once administered through traditional departments—Mathematics, Biology, English—divided and multiplied into specializations. Students going into the sciences might be heading toward scientific writing or illustration, or trying to become nurse practitioners or physician assistants, options not on the menu when I thought it was medical school or nothing. The study of film at Vassar started as a course in the English Department, became a specialized sub-set of drama, and then a major in its own right. Just as people's clothing told little about

304

A Matter of Taste

them, the name of their college might also tell little. Their first job could be a matter of contacts, but after that, people were making it on what they showed they could do in biotechnology, computer graphics, or gerontology.

In our own family this trend had already begun. When Tom went to college he majored in History, a traditional liberal arts field. But his career was in the movie business in the time before film was in college catalogues. His brother, Jon, majored in English, minored in architecture, and thought he would work on intellectual property matters, but spends his time commuting to states across the country on class action law suits. By the time their sister, Kate, arrived at college, she ended up majoring in film, before moving on to a Masters Degree in Marriage and Family Therapy.

Education had changed, the city had changed, and my role had changed. Books had been a resource and refuge on my mother's side of the family for a couple of generations, but making a career out of reading and writing was another matter. A career meant always rushing and being late…for nursery school pickup, children's performances, games, music lessons, even doctor's appointments. It led to a need to escape the perpetual conflict between home and work. My father did not live long enough to see this transformation, but my mother lived through it, cultivating the role of grandmother, dispensing decorum and good taste to another generation

It was only later, when the children were grown, that she managed to sneak in comments about my role. If we went out to lunch and I stopped to try on a blouse in a store, I'd overhear her saying to the saleswoman, with an undercurrent of pride, "She's a professor. She can't wear something that sheer." Or if I was eyeing a suit, I'd catch her observing to the salesperson, "She's a professor. She needs something like that for meetings." Pride and approval, however, were not the same thing. She herself had once been a working woman, but that was a secret she kept hidden throughout the

A DANGEROUS THING

remaining stripped down years of her life. She admired strong, successful women, but Raphael Goldstein had taught her there was no substitute for good taste, and assuring it was supposed to be the focus of a woman's life.

All adults are immigrants from the country of childhood. The cocoon of comfort and security in which I was raised spoiled me forever. With four and a half years separating me from my sister, I was like an only child, expecting life to move around me like planets around a sun, expecting life to always continue comfortable and secure, tasteful and orderly, with no idea of how to make this happen. Making it happen turned out to be hard work. Marriage with its constant negotiations and compromises was nothing like the picture presented by parents who were never seen to disagree. Raising three children (with cat and dog, to which I was allergic), refereeing dinner conversation, mediating sibling disputes, running two houses (with three cars), becoming a professional in an office, were not in the model we had been set because it wasn't the life my parents had envisioned for their daughter.

Even before I was working at Mercy, if I could get away from the children for an hour, I'd play tennis, and my father would say, "Why don't you just take it easy?" It was his view that I always did things the hard way, and perhaps he was right. After all, who needs three children, two houses, three cars, and that cat and dog? But life was a constant test.

It was as though someone had seated me in a doctor's office with piles of magazines on the table in front of me in order to check my reflexes: What would I reach for? Would my hand go out to grab *Better Homes And Gardens* or would I settle on *The American Scholar*? Because if I chose the former, I knew any self-respecting academic would have picked the latter, and if I picked up the latter, I knew I would prefer to be reading the former. If the doctor's secretary summoned Dr. Krasne, I knew that was just a persona and behind it a dilettante was hiding.

A Matter of Taste

And so I sit here in my book-lined study, dressed in hand-me-up clothes from our children, waiting for a new teaching semester to begin after the family assembles for Labor Day weekend. I can sit here fashioning words into sentences and paragraphs because downstairs the pink coneflowers and white phlox are already arranged in a vase, the gazpacho is in the refrigerator, and the blueberry lemon tart is on the kitchen counter. Everything is in its place.

Outside, rain falls on the windows of the house we have built in the Litchfield hills, and the garden that I have rescued from the wilderness, where goldfinches fight for a perch on the feeder, deer nuzzle for apples in the old orchard, and wild turkeys compete with rabbits to eat the white lilies growing below the tossing white heads of dripping hydrangeas.

Families and individuals, like cultures, have their myths and they are built up in the same way: simplification, exaggeration, and the passage of time. Time smooths out family history like water running over rocks in the bed of a river until its original hard-edged form is no longer recognizable. My father said little about his life, while my mother's stories seemed full of life, yet neither version, as it turned out, was the way it was. Their values and decisions, shaped by history I never knew, were the rocks in the riverbed over which my life has sometimes slid and sometimes tumbled onwards.

A DANGEROUS THING

Covering the Mirrors in the House of the Dead

The Hall
    The mirrors are covered,
    the last of them here by the door
    where only last week
    you turned to tie your scarf,
    a wrinkled cameo
    framed in gilded curlicues,
    hidden now,
    not erased
    by these white sheets.

The Children's Room
    You glided towards me,
    the hall light
    barely showing
    your silk gown,
    green on white.
    In my maple dresser mirror
    I feel the fragrance
    of your kiss.
    You were younger then
    than I am now.

A Matter of Taste

The Parent's Room
    Goldilocks home alone
    while the bears vacation,
    I modeled your dressing gown,
    your satin high heels.
    I will do better someday,
    I thought
    of the reflection
    on your closet door.

The Widows Room
    With difficulty
    you sought in the mirror
    to adjust your sweater.
    The cast on your arm
    kept fingers from warming,
    kept even toes blue.
    It is your color now.
    Coming into the room
    I did not recognize you.

SOURCES

Adler, Felix. *The Moral Instruction of Children*. New York: Appleton, 1893.

Arendt, Hannah. *Eichman in Jerusalem*. New York: Viking, 1963.

Atwood, Margaret. "Good Housekeeping." *The New York Times Magazine*. 16 May 1999. p. 164.

_____. "The Saturday Night Date." Special Millenium Issue *The New York Times*. 5 December 1999. p. 148.

Bailil, Hayyim Nahman Bailik. "The City of Slaughter." *The Penguin Book of Socialist Verse*. Ed. Alan Bold. Harmondsworth: Penguin Books Ltd., 1970.

Belenky, Mary Field et al. *Women's Ways of Knowing*. New York: Basic Books, 1986.

Brodkin, Karen. *How Jews Became White Folks: And What That Says About Race in American*. New Brunswick: Rutgers, 1998.

Cahan, Abraham. *The Rise of David Levinsky*. New York: Harper & Row, 1948.

Calta, Marialisa. "Grand Survivor of Another Age." *The New York Times*. 4 May 1997. XX 8.

Daniels, Elizabeth and Clyde Griffen. *Full Steam Ahead in Poughkeepsie: The Story of Coeducation at Vassar, 1966–1974*. Poughkeepsie: Vassar College, 2000.

de Beauvoir, Simone. *Memoirs of a Dutiful Daughter*. Trans. James Kirkup. Cleveland: World Publishing, 1959.

Dedman, Bill. "What's Doing in Cincinnati." *The New York Times*. 20 June 1999. TR 10.

Devons, Samuel. "I.I. Rabi: Physics and Science at Columbia, In America, and Worldwide." *Columbia*, Summer 2001. pp. 36–49.

Dunlop. David W. "Vestiges of Harlem's Jewish Past." *The New York Times*. 7 June 2002. E42.

Evans, Robert. *The Kid Stays in The Picture*. New York: Hyperion, 1994.

Fussell, Betty, *My Kitchen Wars*, A Memoir. New York: Farrar, Straus & Giroux, 1999.

Good, Harry G. and James D. Teller. *A History of American Education*. New York: Macmillan, 1973.

Gopnick, Adam. "A Hazard of No Fortune." *The New Yorker*. 21, 28 Feb. 2000. pp. 183–194.

Gray, Christopher. "Streetscapes/Meeting House of the Society for Ethical Culture." *The New York Times*. 5 Aug. 2001. RE 7.

_____. "From a Ring For Horses to a Studio For Anchors." *The New York Times*. 28 March 1999. RE 7.

Hayward, Helena, ed. *World Furniture: An Illustrated History*. New York: Crescent Books, 1965.

Hershberg, Theodore, ed. *Philadelphia: Work, Space, Family and Group Experience in the Nineteenth Century*. Oxford: Oxford University Press, 1981.

Horowitz, Helen Lefkowitz. *Campus Life*. New York: Alfred A. Knopf, 1987.

Horowitz, Joseph. "The Maestro Who Made Philadelphians Fabulous." *The New York Times*. 24 Jan. 1999. AR 29,39.

Howe, Irving. *World of Our Father's*. New York: Harcourt Brace Jovanovich, 1976.

James, William. *Principles of Psychology*. New York: Henry Holt, 1890.

Kaplan, Alice. "Endangered By All His Friends." *The New York Times Book Review*. 5 Nov. 2000. p.12

Kernan, Alvin. *In Plato's Cave*. New Haven: Yale Univ. Press, 1999.

Korda, Michael. *Another Life: A Memoir of Other People*. New York: Random House, 1999.

Leman, Nicholas. " Letter From Philadelphia: No Man's Town." *The New Yorker*. 5 June 2000. pp. 42–48.

Millett, Kate. *Sexual Politics*. New York: Doubleday & Co., 1970.

Mokotoff, Gary and Sallyann Amdur Sack. *Where Once We Walked: A Guide To The Jewish Communities Destroyed in the Holocaust*. Teaneck: Avotaynu, 1991.

Nabokov, Vladimir. *Pnin*. New York: Avon, 1957.

Resnick, Lauren B. *Education and Learning to Think*. Washington: National Academy Press, 1987.

Rotter, Pat. *Bitches and Sad Ladies*. New York: Harper & Row, 1975.

Sartre, Jean Paul. *The Words*. New York: George Braziller, 1964.

Schiff, Stacy. *Véra (Mrs. Vladimir Nabokov)*. New York: Modern Library, 1999.

Schwartz, Lynne Sharon. "The Opiate Of The People." *Imagining America*. Ed. Wesley Brown and Amy Ling. New York: Persea Books, 1991.

Shapera, Archie. *My Trip Abroad*. Unpublished manuscript, 1936.

Tone, Andrea. *Devices and Desires: A History of Contracptives in America*. New York: Hill and Wang, 2001.

Trilling, Diana. 'The Girls of Camp Lenore." *The New Yorker*. 12 Aug. 1996. pp. 57–68.

Updike, John. "When Everyone Was Pregnant." *Museums And Women And Other Stories*. New York: Alfred A. Knopf, 1971.

Van de Velde, Theodoor Hendrik. *Ideal Marriage, Its Physiology and Technique*. London: Heinemann, 1930.

Vital, David. *A People Apart: The Jews In Europe, 1789–1939*. New York: Oxford University, 1999.

Wouk, Herman. *Marjorie Morningstar*. New York: Little Brown, 1955.

FAMILY TREES

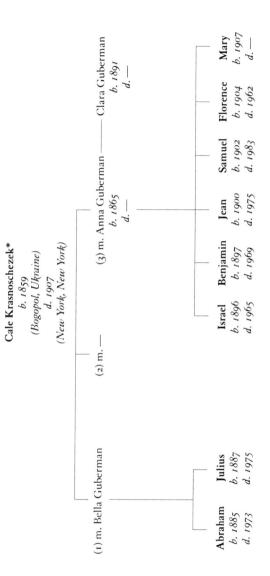

*Spelling according to ship manifest, S.S. Haverford, 22 March, 1906, Philadelphia, PA.

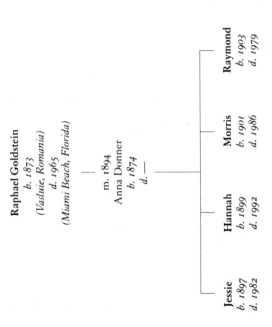

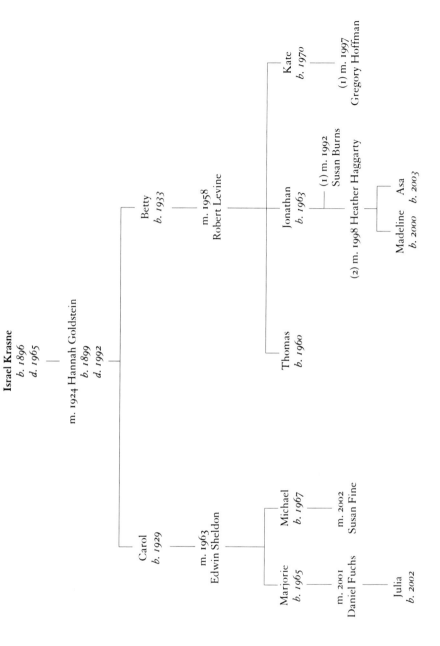

BETTY KRASNE is a writer and a professor of Literature at Mercy College. She is the author of short stories, poems, articles, and, under the name Betty K. Levine, novels for young readers. She was born in New York City, raised her family in Westchester County, and lives in Connecticut, all places that have worked their way into her writing.

For more information about the author and her work go to
www.bettykrasne.com